DEFINITELY, MAYBE IN LOVE

Irene,
Cranberry Kisses
to you! :)
Best,
Ophelia
London

Also by Ophelia London

ABBY ROAD

The Perfect Kisses series:

PLAYING AT LOVE
SPEAKING OF LOVE

DEFINITELY, MAYBE IN LOVE

OPHELIA LONDON

Entangled Publishing, LLC
2614 South Timberline Road
Suite 109
Fort Collins, CO 80525
Visit our website at www.entangledpublishing.com.

Edited by Erica M. Chapman and Stacy Abrams
Cover design by Jessica Cantor

Permission pending for epigraphs from *To Kill a Mockingbird* and *Bridget Jones's Diary*

Manufactured in the United States of America

First Edition October 2013

To Jane Austen. Without you paving the way, this chick writer would not be here.

Part I

Fall

Chapter 1

"Spring Honeycutt, nice of you to finally join us."

All eyes, including Professor Masen's, were glued on me as my attempt to stealthily enter the classroom fifteen minutes late failed.

"Sorry," I said, hovering just inside the door. "I was… held up."

With his gaze still boring into me, Masen tilted his head but didn't speak, as if waiting for me to further explain.

"Um." I gripped my backpack. "On my way to campus, I found a cat in the bushes."

A few guys at the back of the room snickered.

"It was injured. I called the SPCA and waited. There wasn't any blood, but it couldn't walk, so…" I wondered why Masen was allowing me to take up lecture time. Weren't we discussing Thoreau and *Walden* today? "It, uh, was a gray tabby with a collar but no tags."

Masen leaned against his desk and did his chin rub thing.

It always gave me the impression he was annoyed.

"I don't even like cats," I added for some reason, "but, I mean, I couldn't just leave it." I felt a lump in my throat, remembering how its sad, glassy eyes had looked at me and how, when I'd gently stroked its back, it tried to purr. "There was a group of people by the time Animal Control arrived, so I left then. Anyway, yeah, that's why I'm late."

As breezily as possible, I walked down the third row and slid into an empty desk, wondering how red my cheeks were.

Masen nodded, his expression kind of baffled, then he pointed at the whiteboard, continuing with his lecture.

I barely had time to round my mouth and exhale before a sneery female voice hissed in my direction. "Classic entrance, Spring. So very *thorough*."

I didn't have to look to see who had just hissed at me. When we were freshman two years ago, Lilah Charleston had forgotten to leave her "mean girl" mentality back in high school where it belonged. It sucked enough that her sorority house was only two blocks away from my digs, but we also both chose Environmental Earth Science as a major. So I was forced to share a classroom with her at least twice a semester.

Usually I just ignored her, but wouldn't that be setting bad precedents for the rest of our junior year? Not that stooping to her level got her off my back. Ever since I'd beaten her out for a freshman-year internship, her goal had been to make my life a living hell. I eyed her outfit. In a perfect world, Lilah decked out in head-to-toe leather while sitting in our Sustainable Earth class would have been grounds for automatic failure.

"Thanks," I whispered to her when Masen's back was

"Yeah," I confirmed, eyeing the screen.

He arched his bushy eyebrows. "Pretty ambitious."

I shrugged.

"So that means you're ahead of schedule, credit-wise."

Oh, please don't ask me to be your aid. I'd rather take on another shift waiting tables at the country club than correct freshman papers.

"Have you ever considered picking up an econ minor? A few of your core classes cross over. It looks like you're halfway there."

This was a surprise. "I took the two required business classes," I said, "but other than that, I don't know much about economics."

Masen toggled back to my proposal. "I know," he said deliberately. "That's my point."

"Oh." I swallowed, visions of seeing my name in a periodical vanishing like the Amazon rainforest. "How do you think an econ minor will help?"

"Did you do debate in high school?" he asked, which seemed out of left field.

"No," I admitted.

"But you understand the concept?"

"You argue either side of an issue," I began, hoping it sounded like I knew what I was talking about. "You have to know enough about the opposition to fight for both sides."

"Exactly." He pointed at my proposal on his screen. "That's precisely what this needs. The opposition."

Under my braids, the back of my neck tingled in alarm. The sensation spread up my throat and across my cheeks. A year ago, fearing that I wasn't getting noticed in my classes or community, I'd made some pretty big changes. It wasn't just the heavier work load or Green Peace marches, it was the braids, the vegetarian diet, the purposeful lack of a social life…all in the name of being taken seriously. Finally, I felt the part and *looked* the part. Everything should be falling into place by now. But if Masen, my advisor, still didn't get how resolute I was, what more could I do?

I was starting to get that drowning feeling again.

"Professor Masen," I began, "for the last two years, Environmental Science has been my life. Sustainable living, promoting free and healthy land, supporting the local EPA. I chose Stanford because of its liberal programs, and you're saying you think I should—"

He lifted a hand to stop me. "I don't mean for you to drive a Hummer or drill for oil. Sustainability is a critical issue, and I think you've got a handle on it. A clear understanding of the economic side will round out your research, give it some meat." He pointed at the screen again. "Judging by your proposal, you're too close to the subject. I need you to step back and get a new perspective."

"Perspective," I repeated, my head feeling heavy.

"In any arena, to truly best your opponents, you must understand them, inside and out. You have the heart, Spring, but you don't have the business mind. Not yet." Masen did his chin rub thing again. "You mentioned the EPA. What if you went the other way and studied up on the human impact, the *benefits* of land development?"

Before I followed my natural instinct to blurt out that there *was* no such thing, I forced myself to stop and think. Perhaps I couldn't see Masen's vision yet, but I trusted him. I kind of had to. The man held my academic future in the palm of his hand.

"The *benefits* of land development?" I paused, waiting for my brain to wrap around the concept.

"Talk to a few econ students," he suggested, "or better yet, someone who knows the finer points of land development—that's key. Delve into your research. Maybe then your proposal will flesh out and we can talk publication."

That word again. *Publication.* It was intoxicating. Whether he was using it to guide me or manipulate me didn't matter. It worked. "Whatever you say," I replied, picking up my bag. "I'll start on it right away."

Masen slid on his glasses. "I look forward to hearing about your progress very soon. Let's set up another meeting."

After he gave me a few more instructions, I felt like clicking my heels together and giving a salute, but refrained and headed down the hall, dodging other overachievers as they rushed to class. Once the initial adrenaline was gone, though, panic set in. And by the time I was halfway home, I was in a pretty deep haze, my backpack feeling heavier with every step.

When would I have time to start a brand-new research project and maybe add a minor? Where, exactly, was I going to find a land tycoon at Stanford University? And more importantly: how much of my soul would I be willing to sell to learn from such a creature?

My focus was pulled to a U-Haul truck parked in front of the house across the street from mine. Three moving guys were unloading boxes. So I guessed the wannabe *Big Bang Theory* physics students had moved out. Too bad, I would miss their weekly explosions.

As I got closer to the house, about to cross the street, a guy came wandering out the front door. Because of his height and long legs, *striding* was probably a better term. After running a hand through his dark curly hair, he slid on a pair of black sunglasses and stood in the middle of the newly sodded lawn, signing a clipboard one of the movers handed him.

He turned his head. Even from a distance, I noticed the cut of his jaw. It was a nice cut. As he handed off the clipboard, he lifted his sunglasses for just a second, revealing the rest of his face.

Hmm, not bad. Not bad at all. In fact—

"Hey," the guy said, kind of barking at one of the other movers. "Do *not* touch the Viper." He pointed at a long and sleek black sports car parked crooked in his driveway. "It's worth more than your life."

Sheesh. What the hell?

I was halfway across the street, still gaping at the guy, when my roommate Julia called from our front door.

"Spring!"

The guy's head snapped in my direction. When my eyes locked straight onto his sunglasses, I felt my face go red.

Totally hated getting caught staring, but it wasn't like I was snooping around. I was crossing a public street in front of my own house in the middle of the day. Not exactly a felony. Still, I knew the guy was watching me as I headed toward my house.

"If you want me to do your nails before tonight," Julia added, "we need to start now. Hurry up."

I cinched the strap on my bag, feeling his eyes on my back. *Great. Nice first impression, Spring. I'll be known as the woman who not only cares about manicures, but can't do one herself.*

"Yeah, coming," I said, hustling up the path and inside my house. "You didn't have to yell that." I dropped my bag by the door and followed Julia's red hair up the stairs.

"Yell what?"

I shook my head and laughed under my breath. "Never mind."

Ten minutes later, I was sitting on the floor in a corner of our oversized bathroom, my legs stretched out in front of me. Julia bent forward to apply a second coat of Russian Navy to my toenails. Anabel, our other roommate, drifted in and out of the bathroom with a group of her friends, their banter skipping from lipstick and the new frat house to Adam Levine and stilettos. Before I was tempted to bust in and direct the conversation to an item I'd read in the news, I grabbed a magazine off the floor and concentrated on fanning my toenails.

"Do you have plans for dinner?" I asked Julia.

"I thought I was meeting up with Tommy," she replied, "but I haven't heard from him."

"Tommy called the house phone this morning right after you left for class," I said. "Anabel talked to him."

Julia's bright green eyes grew wide in alarm, but then she smiled and rolled them to heaven. "Oh, really."

I patted her arm. "I'm afraid you lost your date to our demonstrative roommate, bunny."

She rolled her eyes again. "It would seem so."

"Anabel knows no shame when it comes to nabbing a man. What possessed you to give a male of any species our home number instead of your cell?"

Julia bit her lip. By far, she was the prettiest co-ed in a five-mile radius. Tommy, or any guy, was hers for the taking.

But she didn't compete for dates.

"It's your own fault," I continued. "You should learn to play dirty. Next time the house phone rings, use your elbows. That's why God created them."

"I'll remember that," Julia said. "Now sit here and don't move your feet." She drifted to the mirror, continuing with her own primping routine. "Do you ever miss this?" she asked as she pulled a brush through her hair.

"Never," I said. "My way is low maintenance."

"I just wondered, 'cause when it's not braided, your hair looks like a movie star's."

I tugged at one braid. "Which movie star?"

"No, I mean, you've got that whole blue-eyed, all-American, long, blond *Gossip Girl* hair thing happening."

"Who's Gossip Girl?" I asked. "Was she on *Grey's Anatomy*?"

Julia tossed a hand towel at me. "Never mind. I forgot you *claim* to only watch CNN."

I bent forward to blow on my toes. My fingernails were the same dark shade. I usually wouldn't take such pains as to match the color on my fingers and toes, but I promised my friends I would join them tonight at the first big party of the school year. I also promised that I would check my cynical attitude at the door.

There was a slight chance one of those things might happen.

I really shouldn't have been going out at all. Professor Masen was expecting an update on my new project Monday morning, and so far, I didn't have even a glimmer of a plan.

"As I recall," I said, going back to a less traumatic subject, "you didn't even like Tommy. Wasn't he the one who made you go Dutch when he took you to dinner?"

"That's him." Julia *tsk*ed. "A gentleman should treat a lady like a lady. That's what my grandmother always says."

Julia was as old-fashioned as they came. In that respect, she and I were about as opposite as you could get. Even so, I loved her—from her perfectly blown-out hair to the delicate Celtic knot pinkie ring she wore every day.

"Hello? Anybody home? Springer?"

"Up here!" I called out to my best friend, Melanie, as she slammed the front door below.

She'd texted an hour ago. Already pissed off at her dorm-mate for parking in her spot, Mel was walking over to tonight's street party with us. By the time she made it up the stairs, she was wheezing, face flushed, brown eyes wild. I thought she might be sick, but she was all smiles. Her curlicues of coffee-colored hair were bouncier than usual.

"So, tell me everything." Mel beamed, catching her breath. She was dressed in a black lacy top, black low-rise pants, and black sling-back open-toed heels, Stanford crimson red splashed across her nails. While hanging on to the door jam with one hand, she bent back like a contortionist and reached behind her to adjust the strap of one shoe.

"About what?" I asked, hobbling to my feet, careful not to smudge my shiny polish.

Mel's smile practically split her face. "About the new guys across the street."

Oh. I said nothing, but continued to gaze at her blankly. She didn't need to know I'd already been caught semi-spying on one of them.

"New guys?" Julia froze, her eyeliner hovering in front of her face. She was going for the whole nonchalance thing,

even though she knew—as we all did—that Mel was the
eyes, ears, nose, and throat of "Cardinal Society" at Stanford.
She'd worked in the admin's office freshman year and still
had major internal connections. Nothing went on at our
university that she didn't catch wind of first.

A grin of satisfaction spread across Mel's face. "They're
moving in as we speak. Today. Right now." She paused, taking
in my blank expression. "Seriously, where have you been?"

"I've got a research project I'm trying to wrap my brain
around, so I've been…" I trailed off, noticing that Mel
was gazing at me while pointing in the direction of Julia's
bedroom window across the hall, the one facing the street.

Following the point, Julia made her way to the window,
Mel right behind her. I stayed put in the bathroom.

"Know anything about them?" I heard Julia say.

As if she had to ask.

"Well, the blond one's name is Dart," Mel said. "Transferred
from Duke. He's a grad student in Kinesiology. He's had three
serious girlfriends and his father won a Nobel Prize."

Melanie was a fountain of information.

I bit my lip and pushed off the wall, caving to curiosity,
keeping up with current events, so to speak. I *should* know
about my new neighbors, right? More than the fact that one
of them drives a Viper, has the face of a movie star but is
kind of a jackass.

Mel grinned when I entered the room.

"Not a word," I warned her as I came up beside Julia,
who was staring out the window. While Mel talked on about
Dart, I lifted up on the balls of my feet and peered through
the window. From what I could make out, there were two
guys milling about their front yard. I spotted the dark-haired

one first. The light-haired one I didn't find nearly as eye-catching.

When Julia unleashed a wistful sigh, I glanced at her. One side of her mouth curled up.

"Dart." She said the name, then repeated it twice. Methodically, her long fingers tucked a wisp of hair behind an ear. "That's an interesting name, don't you think? I wonder what it means. Sounds familiar, right? Like it's short for something." She moved her lips, muttering the name over and over like a tick.

"So, Mel," I said. "What—"

"D'Artagnan!" Julia exclaimed, making me jump. "I'll bet anything his real name is D'Artagnan. It's from *The Three Musketeers*. He's a royal knight."

Her use of the present tense did not escape me. She pressed her fingertips against the glass and leaned in. "Dart. He's very handsome, isn't he? Almost *dashing*."

"Oh," Mel interjected in a cautionary tone. "He's Lilah's brother."

Julia whipped around, mouth gaping open, frozen in silent horror.

"Lilah?" I said the word like it was the name of a poison I'd just swallowed, and then half expected to hear the "dun-dun-dun" music that accompanies a tragic twist in a movie plot. I gazed through the glass at our neighbors, a sickly familiar feeling sweeping over me. "Fantastic." I moaned. "The alpha she-snob of this university has a brother. If this Dart dude is anything like Lilah, we'll be lucky if he ignores us completely."

Mel offered me one somber nod in agreement.

Dart knelt in the driveway, digging through an open box.

I'll give Julia credit, he was pretty cute, but not my type.

Our dark-haired neighbor faced us, sunglasses hanging from the collar of his shirt. He made a deliberate one-eighty turn, stared toward his front door and planted his hands on his hips. His butt—I mean his *back*—was to us.

Oh, my.

Directly on the heels of fascination, my pride flicked at the back of my neck, reminding me that I was not someone who reduced herself to slobbering over a man, at least not publicly. Therefore, I let exactly five seconds lapse before my questions began.

"So, um, the other one?" I rubbed my nose, forcing my voice to sound blasé. "What's his story?"

When Mel turned to me, she displayed a toothy grin, like she'd been waiting for me to ask. "Yeah, Springer. I *thought* you might like him. Yummy, no?"

I rolled my eyes, not willing to join in on the drool fest just yet. "I take it the poor guy is *your* target of prey for the upcoming year?"

"Oh, no. I've decided to save *that* little morsel"—she tilted her head toward the window—"for you, babe. And you'll never believe it when I tell you about him. Go ahead, guess who he is. Ask me his name."

Mel was not about to make this easy for me. She knew how I was about guys. If I showed the slightest interest, she wanted it to be written on the side of the Goodyear Blimp.

I turned my attention to my nails, picking at a spot of polish on a cuticle. If she wanted to share her gossip about the secret identity of our dark-haired neighbor, I wasn't about to beg for it. Nice butt or no nice butt, the thrill was gone.

"He's *Henry Knightly*!" she exclaimed, perching herself on the windowsill.

I turned to Julia for a clue, but she was staring down at their garage where Dart had disappeared a minute earlier.

"You know." Mel twisted an earring. "*Knightly*?"

Still no clue.

"Knightly *Hall*? The new building behind Stone Plaza?" Her mouth twitched, giving me a smirky grin. "That building you and your little environmentalist group protested against being built last year. I helped you paint all those stupid picket signs. Totally wrecked my French manicure."

Hmm. That did ring a bell, but the demonstrations I'd attended were starting to blend together.

"Did he build Knightly Hall?" I asked.

Mel laughed. "No, Einstein. His father donated three million to the university, and they named a building after him."

My stomach tanked. Oh. *That* Knightly.

I'd researched the family last year. They owned a bunch of land all over the western United States. If they weren't chopping down forests, they were damming up rivers, leasing their land to strip miners who bulldozed *everything*, or selling out to drillers for the latest earth-killing craze: fracking.

"Oh, frack," I muttered.

My gaze left Mel and moved out the window again. Henry Knightly was buffing the side of that shiny black car with an elbow.

It's worth more than your life... His words echoed in my ears, causing earlier thoughts of his hotness to melt like the polar ice caps.

"Precisely what this university does *not* need," I said. "Another rich kid zooming around in his gas-guzzling sports car, and probably going to school tuition free because his father was a legacy."

"What?"

"Nothing," I said, shaking my head. "It's just...Stanford isn't cheap, Mel. My three jobs are barely keeping me afloat, and my parents have never paid a dime of my school costs. My mom can't afford it, and I haven't spoken to my father in years." I pointed toward the window. "Here comes this guy, probably studying to be a high-flying business mogul while riding Daddy's coattails. Kind of unfair, don't you think?"

"He's in law school, Springer. And no financial aid."

"Oh," I said, frowning.

"What's *that* look for?" Mel took my chin in her hand. "Are you disappointed that you don't already have a justifiable reason to hate Henry Knightly?"

My mouth opened, ready to deny this. But as always, Mel was pretty dead-on. I didn't know this guy, and the loathing in the pit of my stomach wasn't exactly hard evidence against him. Even though his connection to Lilah Charleston was pretty damning on its own.

"He went to Duke too," Mel said, fluffing the back of her hair. "That's where he met Dart when they were freshmen. They were roommates, played ball together. They've been best friends for years."

Julia suddenly unthawed. I'd almost forgotten she was there, as still as Venus de Milo. "Mel," she said, "how the hell do you know all this?"

I snickered, always loving it when Lady Julia swore.

"I will never reveal my sources," Mel said.

Dart reappeared in the front yard. He walked over to Henry Knightly, who was on his cell. It was evident that Dart wanted to talk to him, but his roommate held up an index finger in a curt "silence, I am already speaking" fashion.

"Is it going to absolutely kill you?" Mel asked, picking at a nail. "Living across the street from him?"

"Nope," I answered, my eyes fixed on my dark-haired neighbor as he turned around, pressing buttons on his phone. He slid his sunglasses to the top of his head, giving me another very clear view. I couldn't help moving a couple inches toward the glass. "His presence isn't going to affect me in the least—"

My head jerked back when Knightly suddenly looked up at the window, zeroing in on me. When he took a step forward, I drew away from the glass and spun around.

"I…" I cleared my throat. "I'll probably never speak to him."

"Not even tonight at the party?" Mel asked, catching the tail end of my reaction, then peering outside. I hoped the guy wasn't still staring up.

"Especially not tonight," I said firmly, toying with a handful of braids.

Mel glanced from the window to me, then snickered under her breath. "You keep telling yourself that."

I didn't like the way she was grinning.

Chapter 2

"I don't see him." Julia clutched my arm so tightly that I was losing feeling from the elbow down.

Mel flanked my other side. "How's my breath?" she asked, then exhaled in my face like only a best friend could.

"Like ponies and rainbows," I reported.

As we approached the street known as Party Cul-de-sac, I could hear it was packed, simply by the shrieks from flirty girls. Just for tonight, I didn't mind joining the crowd of two hundred other students ready to celebrate a fresh beginning.

Chinese lanterns lit the perimeter of the street while blinking white fairy lights wrapped around all trees, telephone poles, and street signs. Friends, classmates, and colleagues we hadn't seen since June greeted us as our threesome, arms linked, made our way through the crowd.

Despite the chilliness in the air after the sun went down, Julia wore a lemon-yellow spaghetti-strap sundress. Then there was the modish dark-haired, dark-eyed, black-clad

Melanie on my other side. They probably would have made a more impressive entrance had I not been between them.

The white cotton peasant top I sported came from my favorite consignment shop in San Francisco. My jeans were faded to a sky-blue; their threadbare hems and holes further endeared to me. For tonight, I also chose to wear my one pair of silver dangly earrings.

It was a rarity, but my festive mood swelled, something about the start of a school year. I knocked my hip against Mel's, and we shared an animated smile.

"Spring," said Julia, "I still don't see him anywhere."

"Who?"

"Dart!"

Ahhh, right.

"He might not be coming," I said as we passed by the DJ corner. The guy behind the barricade held a single earphone up to one ear. His other hand moved between a laptop and an equalizer, body rocking to the beat. "He looked pretty conventional, Jules. This party might be too bohemian."

Julia's grip on my arm went slack, my opinion apparently making her depressed. I wished I could have offered a kinder excuse, but instead sealed my lips. Better she was disappointed about Dart Charleston now than crushed later. Any acquaintance of Lilah was bad news for us.

My lab partner from last semester called out from a few feet away. I waved back. She held a red Solo cup over her head. I waved it off. No drinking for me, thanks.

"Oh, I *love* this song!" Mel exclaimed. Not two seconds later, she was swept away by a tall stranger in a Kappa Alpha T-shirt. I laughed, watching her disappear into the sea of people.

Then I spotted Lilah.

Dressed in the latest fashionable finery, she blew Hollywood kisses to people she passed. Her shoulder-length bleached hair was straight as a razor, perfectly framing the conspicuous year-round tan on her angular face, light eyes behind dark and heavy eye makeup, and the reddest lips this side of Taylor Swift. Surprisingly, no leather.

Dart was beside her, smiling ear-to-ear, nodding to strangers like he was actually enjoying himself. Huh. So maybe I was wrong about that. He was much cuter up close. His light hair was tousled yet tidy, and his pale eyes were radiant, mirroring another similar set of eyes right next to me.

I peeked at Julia, who had also spotted him. Beautiful, blushing color swept across her face as she zeroed in on him.

Oh, boy. Heaven help poor D'Artagnan Charleston.

She whispered to me in second-year French, her words tumbling from her mouth too quickly for her twisted American tongue. The only coherent message I could make out was that I must promise not to leave her side.

"*Calme toi!*" I replied, patting her arm. "I'm not going anywhere, bunny. Stay cool."

The dark shadow a few steps behind the siblings, I guessed, was Henry Knightly. None of them was turned our way, but the next thing I knew, Lilah made a hard left and stood directly before us. She looked me dead in the eyes without the slightest hint of recognition, then set her gaze on Julia, giving her the crustiest up-down dismissive glare before turning to talk to whomever stood beside us.

Being this close to Lilah outside of class—in the wild!— made a ball of heat churn in my stomach.

After an appropriate amount of time passed, she looked our way again. "Oh. Hey, Spring," she said in that low, sultry voice she'd been honing. "Didn't see you there."

I boldly held my stance, even though I wanted nothing more than to walk away from the scene.

"I never would have recognized you," she continued.

"Nice to see you, Lilah," I lied. "How has your first week been?"

"Oh, you know, I'm chairing *this* club and I'm president of *that* union…"

As she droned on, I stole a glance at Julia. She'd lowered her chin, probably not knowing where to look and not wanting to say anything, fearing Lilah would twist it in some malicious way. For that, I wanted to clock Lilah squarely across her collagen-injected mouth. It was fine for her to have it in for me, but she had no excuse to hate Julia. My sweet, guileless roommate didn't understand girls like Lilah, girls who were mean for no reason.

I attempted a smile, hoping it would stifle my desire to thump Lilah's skull, then I glanced at Dart. He seemed, well, *pleasant*—not at all like Lilah. After a subtle clearing of his throat, he elbowed his sister.

"Oh, pardon me," Lilah purred. "This is my brother." She waved one bony hand at me by way of introduction.

Dart extended his hand. "It's so nice to meet you." His voice was happy and spirited. "Spring? That's a cool name."

"Thanks," I said. "I've always liked it." I wondered if I should tell him the rest of it, but rattling off Spring Elizabeth Honeycutt McNamara Shakespeare-Barnes always earned me the most peculiar looks. I kept meaning to scold my mother for changing our name to something so ridiculous.

Dart's gaze held on me for only a second before it rolled naturally to Julia, who was pinching my arm so hard I was probably bleeding under my shirt.

"Ouch!" I winced. Julia elbowed me, and I'm sure Dart caught the gesture. "Uh, this is my roommate Julia," I said, wondering if she'd cracked a rib.

Dart's hand was now held out to my roommate. Her free hand slid into Dart's as Lilah muttered some kind of apology about not noticing Julia standing right there next to me. Dart was smiling, Julia was glowing. They weren't speaking, but their eyes were locked. Even *I* felt the sparks.

Lilah shifted her weight to one side impatiently, then pursed her lips. "Dart," she said, "let's mingle. You asked me to introduce you to the *pretty* girls on campus." She narrowed her eyes at Julia.

Dart didn't seem to hear his sister's sneery remark. And with Julia's hand still in his, she slowly began to pull away from me. Then Julia's vice-grip hold on my arm was gone as the two of them broke free from the group.

"I like your hat," Dart said to her, as they were swallowed up in the sea of other couples. When I turned back, I allowed my eyes to linger on Lilah, feeling one corner of my mouth lift. She was furious, causing the other side of my mouth to lift in response. I took one step backward, then turned on my heel. My job here was done.

"Oh, Spring, wait." Lilah's voice was nails on a chalkboard. I squinted in preparation before turning back. "You haven't met *my* date." Without moving her eyes from me, she reached one arm back and dragged forward the person standing behind her.

"Henry," she said, "this is one of the girls who live across the street from you."

A vague look of recollection crossed the guy's face, making me wonder what catty tales Lilah had told him, and further wondering if he recognized me as the girl who'd caught him chewing out his moving man earlier today.

It did kind of stun me, though, how good-looking he was up close. He had the whole tall, dark, and handsome vibe going on. Too bad it seemed his personality was just as brooding.

Lilah grinned sardonically at Henry Knightly's confusion. "We all call their place the *Brown House*," she explained. "It's the only house on your street not painted a decent color. Quite the eyesore, if you ask me. The city should have it condemned."

"Be sure to write your city councilman," I said.

"Always have to be so *clever*, don't you?" she accused with another sneer. "Save any more cats lately?"

Knightly's eyes suddenly moved to mine, but he didn't speak.

Lilah waved in my direction. "This is Spring," she garbled to her date. "You know…"

He looked at me for another moment then nodded. "Hello."

I replied out of convention, mirroring his nonverbal gesture and disyllabic greeting. His eyes didn't remain on me for long after the introduction. When they slid off my face, I took the opportunity for a more detailed physical appraisal.

I *am* only human.

Sure, the bone structure of his face was what *may be* referred to as chiseled. There was definitely a defined chest there, nice shoulders, and long legs. If I had a yen for dark, curly hair, he might have been extremely appealing. Up close, however, his brown eyes were flat, and their glazed-over expression informed that he didn't give a flying frack about meeting me or about being at a party.

He wore a blue, gray, and black-diamond argyle sweater under an open charcoal jacket. It was a Friday night, the end of summer, and the guy was dressed in business casual.

At the same instant that I moved my gaze to his face, Knightly looked at me again. An expression of confusion paired with disapproval creased his brow. Oh, yeah, Lilah had definitely been talking crap. Why else would a complete stranger be staring at me like I was his worst enemy?

"Henry!" Lilah stood right next to him, but her shrill voice was loud enough to be heard from fifty feet. "I promised you the first dance, remember?"

Knightly's eyes remained on me, but he nodded in Lilah's direction.

"See you later, Spring," Lilah said, linking her skeletal arm through his. I snickered under my breath as I watched them walk away.

It startled me when Henry Knightly turned and looked at me over his shoulder, locking our gazes once more. Not until he was out of sight did I realize I hadn't been breathing.

Chapter 3

I waved to Julia as I strolled by, but she didn't notice. She appeared natural in the arms of Dart, and dancing to what was sure to be her new favorite song. Mel's entire left arm waved to me, flailing over some frat guy's head like a castaway signaling to a rescue plane. I wiggled my fingers at her as I passed, continuing my solo meander around the perimeter of the party.

A tall, red Hawaiian shirt stepped into my path, practically walking right over me. "Dude," I growled. "If I bruise, you're so dead."

"Sorry."

"*Alex?*"

Hawaiian Shirt spun around, looked down, and blinked, trying to place me. But I would've known those lazy blue eyes with pink-hooded lids and that lanky frame anywhere. "Spring?" he said at last, his face brightening. "Hey. Wow." He actually did a double-take. "You look amazing."

"Oh, well, thanks." I gestured at him. "You, too. I didn't know you were back at Stanford."

Freshman year, Alex Parks and I had had a class together. There'd been a mild flirtation, but nothing much. Couldn't remember why. As I looked up at his smiling, carefree face, his sun-streaked hair falling across his forehead, I kind of regretted not going out on at least one date with him.

"Took a couple semesters off," he said, sliding his hands into the pockets of his khaki shorts. "But it's good to be back." His eyes kind of slid up and down my body, not a very subtle check-out. "And it's *great* to see you. Really. That hair is crazy cool."

I toyed with the end of one braid. "Thanks."

He ran a hand through his surfer-boy hair. "So, what's — "

His words were cut off by a thunderous clash of cymbals and a drum roll. When tropical music blared through the speakers, cheers broke out. From the ripple effect of the crowd, I knew something was happening to the left of the dance floor.

"They're starting a limbo contest."

"Is that where you're headed?" I asked, trying not to sound disappointed.

"I was." He pulled back a slow smile. "Not anymore." Seeing all those teeth made me wonder what his breath smelled like. If it was anything like his aftershave, I was already wanting to be a little closer. He grabbed a drink and chugged half the cup. "Want one?" he asked.

"Not right now," I said.

"Yeah, I'm done, too." He handed his cup to some guy who was walking by.

"So, you took time off?" I asked. "Where'd you go?"

Our heads naturally drew together as we moved off to the side, away from the center of revelry.

Alex was two years ahead of me in school and should have graduated last year, but he explained that he'd decided to defer his senior year to travel. As information poured out, I decided that such a decision—to just take off like that—was a pretty gutsy move. It made him intriguing, probably because I didn't have that kind of freedom in me.

"Hi, Spring," Julia said, appearing from behind us. Dart was at her side, their shoulders touching.

"Having fun?" I asked her.

"Yes, we are," Dart answered for the both of them.

Oh, brother.

Alex's muscular arm reached out as he and Dart shook hands while I briefly introduced them. Neither Dart nor Julia seemed to hear a word I was saying after that, so the four of us settled into two comfortable yet separate conversations.

But it didn't last, as something hard and sharp jabbed me between the shoulder blades, knocking me forward, right into Alex's chest. It wasn't completely unfortunate, and we both laughed as he steadied me.

"Didn't see you standing there, *dear*," Lilah's acidy voice apologized. One of her thin arms was looped through Knightly's as she perched herself at her brother's side. She combed her fingers through her ashy hair and prattled on about some band she'd seen over the summer.

Knightly stood silent, his dark eyes staring down at his cell. For ignoring Lilah, I gave him two points. With no one willing to add anything to Lilah's line of conversation, she flung herself toward my guy, asking him about ten questions in a row.

"Yep, LA's my home," Alex answered, after she'd asked where he was from. "The sun, the beach, the babes. Home sweet home."

"Well, isn't this so cozy," Lilah said over the music, applying another layer of red lipstick. "We should hang out together like this all night."

No one replied.

"Right?" She turned her chin over her shoulder. "Henry?"

From the slight jerk in his jaw, I could tell her date heard but didn't reply, his eyes still stuck on his phone. I mentally gave him another two points.

"Henry?" Jeez. Lilah would not give up.

Upon hearing his name repeated, he lowered his phone and took a step in our direction, then he froze. "Parks," he muttered, although his parted lips had barely moved.

I looked from him to Alex, who was mid-way through asking Lilah to dance. They were gone before I had the chance to take another breath.

Knightly remained frozen right where he was, watching them leave. Behind him, Julia and Dart had missed the subtle yet tense exchange between he and Alex.

When I shifted my weight, Knightly's eyes shot in my direction. A mixture of shock and indignity stared back at me, like he'd caught me listening in on a private conversation. The way his deep brown eyes weighed me down made my knees feel like they might buckle.

A moment later, his eyes snapped shut, and a little notch of stress appeared between them. When they opened again, they were right on me, as steady as before. He took a step toward me, his mouth opening.

"We're going out again," Dart called in our direction,

cutting off whatever Knightly was about to say.

I turned to see Julia and Dart heading toward the other dancers. Alex and Lilah were along the outskirts. I could even make out the back of Mel's head, her brown curls bobbing as she boogied. By the time I turned back, I was alone.

Chapter 4

"I'll be…" I pointed off to the far side of the street.

After getting the A-Okay overhead wave from Mel, I headed through the crowd toward the curb. I weaved around a row of portable tables set off to the side where various card games and chess matches were going on under large lamps. Despite the dozen or so people gathered around those tables, it was the only semi-quiet corner of the street party. I slid between two tables, sat on the curb, and pulled out my cell to check messages.

There were two emails and one voicemail. I checked the emails first. They were both from econ majors blowing me off. Crap. Before playing the voicemail, I braced myself for more bad news. A couple hours ago, I'd emailed Professor Masen a few pages of notes, figuring that would tide him over while I kept searching for a source. I took in a deep breath, then pressed my hand over my free ear, listening to the voicemail. It was some guy from Statistics wanting to form a study group. I saved the message and exhaled in relief.

Not ready to return to the center of the action, I stayed where I was, practically hidden under the last card table where three guys were playing poker. Between their heads, I could make out the top halves of party-goers as they walked by. This view was temporarily obscured when a couple stopped directly over me to make out.

"Hello!" I yelped when the guy stepped on my foot.

Without bothering to remove his tongue from his partner's throat, he leered at me in acknowledgement, then they stumbled away.

Maybe my location was a little too secluded. If there was a mass evacuation, would I be trampled and left for dead under a table surrounded by chess pieces? Just as I was about to stand up and find Mel, a glimpse of some tousled light hair came into view.

"You can take off, but I'm not ready."

Through the poker players, I watched Dart Charleston reach into a red tub and pull out an icy can. I could see him pretty well. I could hear him perfectly.

"That's obvious."

The guy dealing cards blocked my view of who Dart was with. Whoever it was waved off the drink Dart offered.

"She's amazing, man." Dart's back was to me now, his words less audible. "We're hanging out tomorrow."

"She's clearly into you." Henry Knightly's head came into view. He leaned against the card table. I looked to my right where two girls suddenly appeared, watching something on an iPad. To my left was a line of five or six guys wearing nothing but towels around their waists. I was pretty much trapped in place for the time being. Eavesdropping by default.

"Convenient that she lives across the street," Knightly continued.

I grinned when I realized they were talking about Julia. It wasn't surprising, but it made me happy that Dart was already smitten.

"What about you?" Dart said. "You've met a dozen women tonight and you're ready to bolt."

Knightly shook his head. "No one I care to see again."

Guy-talk was so uninteresting. At least I could report back to Julia that she had a fan in Dart.

Curving myself into a crouched position, I balanced on the balls of my feet, hands gripping my knees, ready to hobble away.

"No one?" Dart said, sounding surprised. "What about Julia's roommate?"

I froze, staring down at the sidewalk.

"What about her?"

Still concealed behind the card table, I turned to peek in their direction. The sliver of Dart's face that I could see was grinning. "I don't have to tell you this, but dude, she's hot."

I couldn't help smiling. Despite my mindset of brains over beauty, it was nice to be thought of as hot. I approved of this Dart guy more and more.

"I don't remember meeting anyone hot," Knightly said.

I rolled my eyes, trying not to be insulted.

Dart chuckled good-naturedly. "Whatever, man."

"If you're talking about the blond," Knightly said, crossing his arms, "she's not my type."

Lucky me. My legs wobbled, straining from holding a

tight crouch.

"The gorgeous type?" Dart asked. "She seems fun and damn smart. You're saying that's not your type?"

"Someone like her is not anyone's type." Knightly pulled out his phone. "Obviously."

My mouth fell open.

"I think she's studying biology," Dart said. "You'd like—"

"She's a tree-hugging feminist."

Wow. How very *un*original. The comment barely fazed me. Over the past year, I'd been called much worse than the antiquated "tree-hugger." Coming from someone like Henry Knightly, the slur was practically a compliment. Sure, it was a little weird squatting there, listening to a stranger pick me apart, but nothing he said should matter.

"Your sister gave me an earful the other night," Knightly said. He stared down at his phone, so I couldn't hear very clearly, but I swore I heard the words "liberal" and "attention," maybe even "phony."

I ground my teeth. What had Lilah been saying to him? And what poison was this guy passing around?

Dart shrugged and took a drink. "Her hair is wicked cool. Those braids."

Knightly muttered something about ridiculous and dirt, ending with "snakes."

Oh, no, he didn't. Say what you will about my politics, but leave my hair out of it.

"Hopeless," Dart said. As he turned in the direction of the crowd, his expression brightened. "Here comes Julia. I gotta go. Sure you won't stay?"

"I'm leaving now. See you tomorrow."

I watched as Dart tossed his can in the trash, attempted

to smooth down his unruly hair, then disappeared.

Leaving Knightly standing alone.

He leaned back against the card table, making it wobble. He probably was oblivious to the card game he was disturbing. He was *definitely* oblivious to the girl five feet away whom he'd managed to insult from head to toe in two minutes flat.

I couldn't stop myself from replaying his words, his harsh, ugly words. The more they ran through my head, the angrier and more irrational I grew. Phony? Snakes? How *dare* he? He's the one who drove a damn Viper.

My lungs started to squeeze, and each breath I pulled in was heavier and faster. My legs really shook now, cutting off circulation to my feet.

Almost out of obligation, I stood.

When he saw me, Henry Knightly's expression barely changed. There was a hint of mild surprise in his eyes, but otherwise, he seemed unfazed.

A more fainthearted person would have walked away and made a beeline for the nearest keg. But I never cowered from a challenge. As I wove around the tables, nearing him, Knightly pulled his hands from his pockets and took a step back, giving me a wide berth.

"Snakes," I said, when I was close enough that I knew he could hear.

He tilted his head like he was listening to a child. "Pardon?"

"Just so you know, referring to someone who loves the planet as a tree-hugger is just about the lamest thing I've ever heard. This isn't nineteen-eighty."

"Loves the planet," he repeated slowly.

"That's correct," I said. "And I'm so sorry you haven't met anyone hot. Especially someone who isn't a phony, right?" When he didn't speak, I shook my head in dismissal and turned away, spotting Mel heading in my direction. "And here's a piece of advice," I threw in as I started backing up, "be careful whose opinion you trust."

"Springer, I *have* to tell you—"

"Shhh," I hissed, looping my arm through Mel's and leading her away from the scene. By the time we reached the bar, I'd told her everything.

"So, to recap," she said, grabbing a Diet Coke from a tub, "the guy thinks your braids are repulsive."

"He called them snakes," I confirmed and took a sip from her can.

"And you care because…?"

"I *don't*." I stroked one of my precious blond ropes between my fingers. "The guy's toxic, just like Lilah. They're a perfect couple. You should've seen him, standing there with his arms crossed, pinned to his body like he was in a straightjacket. Probably afraid to touch anything that wasn't properly sterilized."

I kicked an empty plastic cup that bounced my way.

"He doesn't know the first thing about my life. *Him* calling *me* a phony while he stands in a corner and doesn't speak to anyone. That's rich."

I looked at Mel, who was being uncharacteristically unopinionated.

"Mel?" I said over someone talking into a mic. "Don't you have anything to add—?" I cut myself off as a new thought occurred to me. "Wait, you don't *agree* with him, do you?"

Her gaze darted around, down at her nails, up at a stop sign, everywhere but at me. When she finally settled on me, a sad, empathetic smile curved her mouth. "Okay, fine." She took in a deep inhale. "That *was* quite the transformation last year, Springer. You have to admit that."

I opened my mouth but didn't speak.

"It's like, one day you're hanging out with your friends like any normal chick, wearing a skirt, pink tank top, and strappy sandals, and the *next* day you're off meat, you've got those things in your hair, and you're picketing City Hall to save some endangered mountainous tribe in Costa Rica that no one's ever heard of."

"*I* heard of them," I defended. "And I…I still wear skirts."

"Change is good," she continued. "And obviously college is the place to do it. You know me, I *love* your feminist passion and your *adorable* cynicism…" Her voice went singsong. "And your protests, your sit-ins, the occasional liberal rants—"

"Got it, Mel," I snapped, rubbing my arms.

Mel and I had been best friends since we were ten. She was supposed to be the one person who loved me no matter what crazy things I did. I'd never been able to talk to my mother about my life—she was way too flaky, "emotionally stunted" as our family shrink called it. And my father, he'd never been around for me to rely on.

Mel knew my reasons—she knew I'd been struggling like hell to stand out last year, to really make a difference and get noticed. True, maybe some of my decisions brought the wrong kind of attention, but still, it made me a little nauseous to think that even *Mel* considered me some kind of joke. A phony, to echo Henry Knightly.

Angry tears pressed against my eyes, right there in the middle of the party. I clenched my stomach muscles, chomped down on the inside of my cheeks, and looked away. Right after my father left when I was ten, I used to cry a lot. I never cried anymore—didn't solve anything.

"It's just"—Mel sucked in her lips—"you can come off a little…abrasive." She took a step backward, deliberately, comically, as if she were afraid I would retaliate with a karate chop.

"Hilarious," I mumbled.

"Just remember, not everybody gets you like I do."

"I know."

She put a hand on my shoulder. "You okay, babe?" she asked, sounding genuinely concerned. "You are the coolest person I know, Spring Honeycutt. Do you realize that? And that's saying a hell of a lot, because I myself am *exceptionally* cool." She squeezed my arm. "Never, *ever* allow *anyone* to make you feel badly about your decisions, okay?" Her smile twisted. "Not even a ho-bag like me."

"Ho-bag." I knocked her shoulder. "And I won't," I promised, my voice hitching with emotion.

It was rare for Mel and me to wax sentimental with each other these days. My cynicism had become a barrier, the protective shield I wore, even around my closest friends. Sometimes I regretted that. Few were the times when that shield slipped and I allowed myself to be vulnerable with anybody.

"The dude's a jackwad," Mel said, facing the crowd.

I exhaled a cathartic snicker. "This is true."

"Oh my." There was a smile in her voice. "But he's a

jackwad who is totally checking you out. Jeez, though—he is gorgeous."

I rolled my eyes. "Jackwad."

"Hope you're not talking about me."

I whipped around. "Alex, hey."

"Hey yourself," he said. Somehow, he was even cuter than an hour ago. Or maybe I was comparing his pleasant expression when he talked to me with Knightly's sour looks and ardent distaste of all things Spring Honeycutt related.

"This is a great song," Alex said, pointing disco fingers in the air. "I simply must dance with you." He held a hand out, gallantly. "Please don't make me go out there alone. I have a sinking feeling I'll make a super-ass of myself if you're not with me."

"Okaa—" Before I completed the word, Alex whooped, grabbed me around the waist, and pulled me to the dance floor in a whirlwind.

"Can you ballroom?" he asked after we found space between two gyrating couples.

"I don't think so," I answered, feeling breathless and giggly.

"I'll teach you." He picked up my left hand and rested it on the front of his shoulder. After taking my other hand in his, his free hand moved to my waist, then slid lower to curve around my hip. I gasped in surprise when he pulled me close. "Follow me."

He took a step forward, causing me to step back.

"Excellent," he said. I laughed awkwardly and gripped him tighter, enjoying the feel of his hard shoulder muscle under my hand, the aftershave, the lazy blue eyes as he box-stepped us in a circle. Right after he twirled me under his arm, he pulled me close, his other hand sliding to my hip.

"So," he said, his voice dropping low. We were so close now that I could feel his breath on my neck.

"So?" I replied.

"So…" He turned his head to the side. "How well do you know him?"

I followed his eyes, then blinked in surprise when I realized he was peering at Henry Knightly.

Chapter 5

It was late, and since I couldn't imagine how my evening could possibly improve, thanks to those ten minutes spent in the arms of Alex, I considered going home, getting a jump on the sleep I wouldn't be getting until late December.

Before taking off, I figured I should find Mel or Julia and let one of them know. Last time I'd seen them, they were on the other side of the dance floor. Instead of walking around the outskirts, it would be quicker to cut through the center, so I headed into the mass of mingling people. Someone knocked my shoulder. "Sorry," I muttered, rubbing my arm. Someone else brushed past the other side, knocking my right shoulder. Next thing I knew, an arm looped through mine, much too tightly, and spun me around. Then my other arm was clutched. I was caught in the center of dance traffic—or was it some kind of demented conga line?—and going the wrong way. It looked like the line was headed toward the big sorority house on the corner, the one where Lilah lived. I did not want to end up in there.

But there was no free space or figurative light ahead, so without bothering to look behind me, I disentangled my arm, bent forward, hands on my knees, and started backing up like a reversed torpedo. My body bumped into other bodies, disconnecting them, while other bodies leaped out of my way, cursing as I torpedoed past. I didn't stop moving until I was out of the core of gridlock and along the periphery of the dancers.

Finally free, I splayed my fingers across my chest and took in a deep breath, my heart pounding hard under my hands. I just needed to stand still for a few minutes, undisturbed, then I'd be okay—

"Impressive mode of escape."

I squeaked and whipped around, my heart shooting right back up my throat.

"And pretty effective," Henry Knightly added.

I wasn't sure if I was supposed to reply, even though he'd clearly addressed me. And what was he still doing here? Hadn't he told Dart that he was leaving?

He tilted his head to one side, taking in whatever my expression was. "You look slightly—"

"What?" I stuck out my chin, bracing myself to hear some kind of insult. If he said one word about my braids, I might deck him…just as soon as the feeling came back in my right arm.

"Slightly *anxious*," he completed. "Do you need a…" My hard gaze shifted to the red plastic cup in his outstretched hand. I shook my head. He took a drink, then lowered the cup, fingering it in his hand.

I folded my arms and turned away, attempting to ignore

him. My breathing was still a little too uneven to trust myself to head back into the crowd, even if to get away from this guy.

"So…"

Oh, jeez, please no boring platitudes.

"So, how long have you been here?" he asked.

"Since about nine," I answered, staring forward.

"No." His voice was louder in my direction. "How long at Stanford?"

"Oh." I glanced at him. "This is my third year."

"You're a junior."

"Yep."

Even with the blaring music coming at us from every direction, deafening silence surrounded Knightly and me. I rocked back and forth on my heels, more than ready to take the first step away from him as soon as my body would allow it.

"What did Lilah mean when she asked if you'd saved any more cats?" he suddenly asked.

"Nothing," I replied. "Long story."

He tipped his head, dark eyes regarding me. "I saw you."

"What?"

He shifted his weight, moving closer. "With the cat. I was there."

I stared back at him. "You…"

"There were a bunch of other people, too. When Animal Control showed up, you left."

"I was late for class," I explained, feeling a little stunned. "But I wish I could've stayed to find out which animal hospital the officer was taking it to. I want to check on it later."

"Palo Alto Veterinary Clinic," he said. "That's where the cat went."

"How did you…"

He shrugged. "I asked."

"Oh." More than stunned now, I had no idea what else to say. Was this guy an animal lover, too? More likely, he was practicing at being an ambulance chaser.

The song changed. Couples left the dance floor while others took their empty places. Out of my peripheral vision, I saw Knightly shrink back, but only to throw his cup in a trash can. Then he was right back at my side.

"This is a good song," he said, maybe noticing my unwavering focus on the couples in front of us. "Do you like it?"

"Not particularly. I don't dance to men."

"Excuse me?"

Gah. I shouldn't have said anything in the first place. My self-inflicted music policy had been necessary in order to re-hone my focus, but a pain to explain. It wasn't like I was anti-men—on the contrary! I was a complete sucker for a good love song, often to the point of distraction. I could waste away countless hours listening to the cheesiest Bruno Mars ballad while thinking about some guy. But right along with braiding my hair, changing my major, and painting my first picket sign, I put myself on a chick-only music regimen. Not having that added distraction was kind of empowering. But I wasn't about to explain that to a total stranger in the middle of a street party.

"I don't dance to male singers," I said.

Knightly blinked. "Oh." He looked a little relieved, then his face cracked into what might have been a smile, little lines crinkling the sides of his dark eyes.

"Something funny?" I asked, attempting to block out the fact that his smile brought unexpected warmth to his face.

"Um, absurdly funny. I thought you said you don't dance *with* men."

"Oh." I couldn't help exhaling a laugh at his mistake.

"Maybe when the song changes, we should go out there." His voice was confident yet inquiring, his expression serious in a teasing way. The whole picture was very…I don't know. Sexy? "But only if the song is lacking in masculine presence, of course."

I liked the elevated way he spoke. Dang him. Here at Stanford, my use of common colloquialisms made me ashamed to be among other intellectuals. Damn it all to hell that he used better grammar than I did.

"Why would I want to dance?" I asked.

He seemed amused by my question. "Appears to be the universal and conforming ritual at the moment."

"I'm not a conformist."

"Obviously," he shot back. I noticed that his brown eyes had flecks of gold in them. And were those freckles on his nose? Good gracious.

Fairy lights blinked behind him like stars; the night breeze blew through his curly hair. The guy looked like a freaking Calvin Klein model holding a pose. I could handle ogling at his hotness from a safe distance out Julia's window, but honestly, it was unsettling being face to face. What was more unnerving was the way he was watching me, raptly, like I was the only person in a sea of hundreds.

When he leaned toward me, my shoulders tensed, causing a few braids to tumble free. His gaze shot to my hair.

"Careful," I said. "I wouldn't want you too close to my snakes." I gave him a look. "They bite."

In my not-so-subtle way, I'd broached the subject calmly, opening the door for him to apologize for what he knew I'd overheard. Even though there was no way he could explain away the things he'd said, nonetheless, I was morbidly curious to hear his rationalization.

"I like snakes," he said matter-of-factly.

"Ha." I rolled my eyes. "Sure ya do."

"And I happen to enjoy a good bite."

I blinked, but his gaze remained fixed on me, the intensity of his dark eyes making my stomach flutter. I was not about to fall for this guy's game, even if it was completely original.

He moved closer. "Dance with me."

"I didn't come here to dance."

"You were earlier."

I remembered meeting his eyes briefly when I'd been on the floor with Alex.

"You can do better than him," he said, evidently recalling the same moment. "And I'd steer clear from him if I were you."

My mouth fell open.

"Dance with me," he repeated before I had the chance to tell him off.

I almost laughed. "No."

"Why?" His eyes did not waver.

"Seriously?" Was this guy for real? "You—someone I just met—are warning me to stay away from a friend I've known for two years, like you're my brother or something, and…and I *heard* you." I pointed toward the card tables. "I heard what you said to Dart Charleston about me, about my *hair*. It was an hour ago. Do you think I already forgot?"

He looked over his shoulder toward where I was pointing, then back at me. "What do you think you heard me say about you?" He stepped forward. If he got any closer, he would seriously be invading my personal space.

"Just keep your opinions to yourself until you get to know someone, and—"

"Is that what you do?"

The nerve of him.

Okay, so yeah, whatever, maybe I *had* made some snap judgments before I'd officially met him, but so far, weren't they pretty much true?

"Of course," I said, planting my hands on my hips.

"And that's why you flipped off my car earlier tonight?"

My breath caught, much too audibly. "I…I didn't…flip off your car."

"You did." He slid his hands into his pockets, his posture easing. "You were with two other women on the street, you stopped in front of my driveway and gave my Viper the finger. I watched the whole thing out the window."

Frack.

He'd seen that? Mel, Julia, and I had been on our way to the party. We had to walk past the house across the street, and I couldn't help…well, I mean, what moxie must a college student have to own a car like that? He had it coming.

"Look, if I did do something like that—and I'm not saying I did—all I meant was…well, our generation has to be more responsible and—"

"So you're implying my car isn't responsible or I'm not responsible?"

When I didn't reply, he took another step, practically

right in my face now. Any closer and I'd be forced to dance with him after all.

"Maybe you should take a drive with me." His voice dropped low. "Then you can make up your mind about both." His gaze scanned down my face, pausing briefly on my mouth.

Woo-boy.

If only to break eye contact, I dragged my gaze past his shoulder toward the side of the street.

Lilah stood there, watching us, hands on hips. She was flanked by a pair of her sorority sisters wearing matching tight red cardigans. The glare she was shooting at me could freeze fire. To her, I couldn't imagine what Knightly and I looked like, less than arms-length apart, leaning toward each other, me flushing lustful red like a girl talking to the boy she was crushing on.

Frack. Frack. Frack.

Lilah broke from her group and sauntered our way, death and destruction in her eyes.

I lifted my hands. "I'm out of here," I announced, backing away.

"Spring."

Hearing him call me by name muzzled my anger, tripped me up momentarily. There was something in his tone, something unfinished. But I kept walking, not wanting to give us time to finish.

Chapter 6

"You look very pretty," Julia said.

"Don't sound so disappointed," I replied, looking up at her from my bedroom floor.

"I'm not disappointed."

"Sorry, *disapproving*, I meant."

"I'm not…" Julia broke off when I smiled. "Are you really going out with him?"

"If by *him* you mean Alex, then yes. My shift at the restaurant ran late, he'll be here any minute."

She didn't say anything as she watched me slip on my shoes, but she was humming. In Julia's case, that was worse than outright complaining.

"Do you have something you'd like to share?" I asked.

The humming stopped. "No," she said, but the timbre of her voice was unnaturally high. "Where's he taking you?" She was behind me now, fingering my braids.

"Dinner."

"Hmm."

"Disapproving again," I said as I rolled to my knees then stood, reaching to turn off the radio on my desk and simultaneously shut my closet door.

My room was uber-tiny, but I loved it. It used to be an attic, but the owners decided to squeeze one more rental fee out of the house the year I moved in. The one and only downfall was that the attic stairs were supremely loud and creaky. Last year, I paid an engineering student a hundred bucks to construct a retractable rope ladder outside my window so I could come and go without waking my roommates. To keep out any unwanted visitors, I secured a padlock on the outside of my window when I was out, and when I was in, the ladder was retracted, window locked from the inside.

Before lowering the blinds, I made sure the ladder was down and the window was padlocked, in case Alex and I were out late.

"I wish you were hanging out with us instead," Julia said. There was a slight pout in her voice. "We're watching a movie over at Dart's."

"I told you, there's no way I am hanging around that person."

A few days after the street party, I'd told Julia what had happened between Henry Knightly and me, the things I'd heard him say. By then, I was talking to a brick wall. She'd been hanging out with Dart every day and she just *knew* there had to be some kind of logical explanation. After all, any friend of Dart's couldn't have possibly said such mean things about me.

I grabbed my purse and hooked the strap over my head

and shoulder.

Julia flopped down on my bed, humming again, but lifted her head when we both heard the doorbell two flights down. Following that was the sound of Anabel's high heels rushing to answer. I moved toward my door, half worried that Anabel would find a way to steal my date right from under my nose.

"When will you be home?" Julia asked.

I was halfway through my threshold when I said, "When will *you* be home?"

She exhaled a dainty giggle. "I hope you have a really nice time, Spring," she said sincerely.

I waved good night and hopped down the stairs.

"Hi, Alex."

"Hey, you. Ready to go?" He was wearing that same attractive, carefree swagger from the party. "Looking good."

Personally, I thought Alex was the good-looking one as he stood under the porch lamp. His light brown hair was a little damp and messy, and his face had a glow that looked liked he'd just come from the gym. His hooded blue eyes sparkled as I advanced toward him.

"Are you checking me out?" I asked, arching my eyebrows.

He knocked his shoulder against mine. "It's any man's natural instinct to check you out."

"Try a little subtlety next time," I suggested.

We strolled down the walkway toward his car. It was a modest little gray Accord.

"Sorry," he said as he opened his door, "my, ahem, *Bentley* is being detailed." He pointed across the street to where that odious black Viper was parked crooked in the driveway. Alex lifted his middle finger, making a universally known gesture in that car's direction.

I smiled in agreement and climbed in the passenger seat.

"You two looked pretty cozy the other night," he said after we'd pulled away from the curb. "I saw you talking."

"Who?"

"Henry."

"*He* was talking, not me," I corrected. "Uninvited."

"I wish I'd known that," he said, watching the road. "I would've swept in and whisked you away with me. Far away."

Obviously, Alex was a big flirt. Perhaps that was why we didn't hook up freshman year. By going out with him now, I was breaking my rule about not dating past the second week of the school year. I smiled at him, already at peace with my justifications for accepting the date. Something about him was too charismatic to pass up.

"Don't worry." I patted his shoulder. "Your classes will get busy soon and you'll forget about your obsession with me."

"That's what you think, gorgeous." He downshifted and revved the engine. "I've never let a little thing like school get in the way of a good time. You'll see." He shot me a grin that I felt in my toes. "So, what's the story with you two?"

"What two?"

"You and Henry."

Him again?

"There's no story," I said. "I met him the night of the street party, we're neighbors, that's it."

"Hmm." Alex fingered the patch of hair on his chin. "Bet he's the big cheese already?"

"Doubtful." I rolled my eyes and gazed out the window.

"But *you* know him, right?" I bit my bottom lip, wishing I could suck the words back down my throat. I shouldn't have asked a question like that. By the way the guy had been glaring daggers at Alex the other night, it felt way too personal, and probably something Alex didn't want to talk about.

My date turned to me. "I guess you caught what happened at the party?"

I nodded hesitantly, not wanting to make him feel uncomfortable, especially about something Knightly did. The guy and his Viper nearly ran me over this morning. Okay, so maybe I'd been walking too slowly through the crosswalk, and maybe I didn't really have to tie my lace-less shoe in the middle of the street, but there was no need for him to lay on the horn like that. Was he *trying* to piss me off? Well, *I* was trying to piss *him* off, so I guess we're even.

Alex turned his attention back to the road, staring forward. "The thing is, he and I go way, *way* back. But between you, me, and the bedpost, I'm probably the last person who should talk about him."

That was fine with me — I didn't care about gossip, even Henry Knightly gossip. Right now, I was only interested in Alex. He was a business major, that I did remember. Maybe he might know a thing or two about the economics of sustainability.

Hold on. Oh, buddy. How sweet would it be if the one person who could help me with research for my thesis, the one person whose brain I would have to pick clean, the one person who I was going to have to stick to like a conjoined twin for the next few months…was Alex Parks?

"We practically grew up together," Alex continued. "But

we haven't spoken in years."

I opened my mouth to ask who he was talking about, and then remembered. Knightly was already becoming a tired subject.

"Guy just won't bury the hatchet," Alex said. "Hopefully he's changed, but there are some things a man can't forgive. Live and learn, right? Like I said, I'm the last person who should be talking about him."

Alex *did* talk, however. As we drove downtown, I learned that Knightly and Alex had attended the same prep school in Los Angeles. For two years they were "thick as thieves," as Alex put it. But at the beginning of their senior year something happened.

"I got expelled, thanks to that guy." His voice was harsher than I expected, his long fingers gripped tightly around the steering wheel.

I pictured the way Knightly had looked the other night. Part egotist, part sexy beast. It was easy for me to ignore the sexy part, harder to block out the jerk.

"How?" I couldn't help asking.

"We were both on the soccer team. Same position. Henry was first string, I was bench. Which I didn't mind," he was quick to add. "I didn't need the spotlight like he did, but when I started getting more time off the bench, he got pissed, and the next thing I know I'm being hauled into the dean's office. A laundry list as long as my damn arm of bogus infractions thrown at me. The grapevine said it was Henry. " He scratched his chin. "I was expelled the next day."

"Why didn't you protest?"

Alex didn't speak for a few minutes; he was staring blankly through the windshield, as if remembering something unpleasant. I didn't want to add to that.

"Because of his family and connections," he said at last, "there was nothing I could do. He was the one born with a silver spoon in his mouth, not me. I've had to work like the effing devil for everything I've got."

I understood this. I could also understand the bitterness he was harboring after four years. What I *couldn't* understand was how he'd bent over and taken it, hadn't fought the decision of his expulsion, hadn't disputed it.

"But, ya know, I never owned up to the *crimes*." Alex chuckled, but there was a bite of anger underneath. "Kicked out on my ass, anyway. It was a shame, too, because I actually liked the guy, thought of him as a brother. I know his family, his little sister." He muttered something under his breath that I couldn't hear while he ran a hand through his light hair. "But after a while, you gotta call a spade a spade, right?" After he pulled into a parking space, he turned to me with a sigh. "I guess money can buy you anything. It even bought him admission to Stanford Law. Guy hasn't worked an honest day in his life." He touched a finger to my chin. "Believe me."

"Well, the bigger they are the harder they fall," I offered, caught up in Alex's rainfall of cliché sayings. "I mean, I do. I believe you."

"Thanks," he said. "Ready to eat?"

"I'm starving."

The main drag of downtown Palo Alto was packed. Seemed all of campus was out attempting to savor one last bit of freedom before life as we knew it completely stopped. We had only a few blocks to walk, and once I was able to actually stroll beside him, Alex made it a point to laugh at whatever I said and touch me—my hand, my elbow, my shoulder. It was the usual repartee that goes along with a first date, when you don't know much about the other person. I was an expert at the first-date routine because I seldom allowed myself a second.

"Have you ever heard of a movie called *Annie Hall*?" Alex asked as we stopped at a crosswalk.

"Woody Allen."

"You know The Wood-Man?" He nudged my shoulder. "I might have to marry you."

The light turned green, and we joined the queue of other crossers.

"Do you remember what happened on Alvie's first date with Annie?"

"It's been a long time since I've seen it. Did Alvie forget his wallet? How typical."

"They were bantering in that neurotic Woody Allen way," Alex said, shooting me a sideways glance. "Kind of like we were doing the other night." He took my hand and tucked it into the crock of his elbow. "Alvie said to Annie something like, 'At the end of this date, I'll want to kiss you, but it'll be awkward and embarrassing from all the tension. So, why don't we get it out of the way now while there's no pressure.'"

"Clever," I said.

Alex peered at me with that lazy smile he wore so well. "The thing is," he said, raking a hand through his hair, so charmingly nervous, "I think I'll be feeling some similar pressure at the end of our date."

He stopped walking. So did I. It took two seconds for my mind to catch up to where his already was.

After correctly assessing my grin of agreement, Alex stepped up and placed a hand on my cheek. But then he paused and glanced around, inspecting all the people ambling down the sidewalk around us. The next thing I knew, he grabbed my hand and was pulling me away.

We walked very briskly next to each other for about five seconds, and I followed him around the corner to a parking lot. It was valet only and, aside from the dozen or so parked million-dollar vehicles, it was vacant.

Without a word, he grabbed my free hand and yanked me forward. There was barely time for me to giggle before the kissing began. His arms were strong around me, and his lips were soft on my lips and chin and neck. Just as he had done on the dance floor, his hands were on my hips, swaying me like we were moving to music. His mouth had a minty taste, not exactly toothpaste, something sharper.

Not that I was a prude, but even at the end of a date I would not have completely sucked face with a guy… and here it was the *beginning* of our *first* date. But for whatever reason, I wasn't letting anything slow me down. I felt determined and a bit defiant, like I was trying to prove something to someone.

Plus, it had been a long, dry summer back in Coos Bay, Oregon. My mother spent most of June complaining about how my father had refused again to pay for any of my tuition. Not that I was surprised…I hadn't expected anything from my father in years. My two brothers and I decided ages ago that the sooner we forgot about him, the better. The rest of the summer, Mom delved deeper into her crystals and tarot cards. My brothers came home for only one visit. I was working two full-time jobs, anyway—no time for dating or fun. Maybe that was why I was so into Alex's kisses.

His hands slid to the small of my back, still rocking us to the beat of an unheard rhythm.

Julia had a theory about there being two kinds of kisses. The first kind of kiss is when you want to experience the purely physical pleasure of kissing. There can be heat and excitement and plenty of sparks during this first kind of kiss, but it's mostly just doing whatever will bring personal gratification. These kisses are fun and freeing and preferably non-committal. The first kind of kiss is corporeal, touching only your body and the shallowest of senses, but never deep emotions, and never your soul or your heart.

What I was experiencing in that dimly lit parking lot was the first kind of kiss. Obviously so, since I was cognizant enough to realize that Alex was merely filling a physical desire and nothing more. My emotions, soul, and heart were all fully intact. Perfect.

According to Julia, however, there is a *second* kind of kiss. This kiss comes with a whole list of prerequisite regulations. There is commitment, caring, giving, sacrifice, compromise, relationship, and especially love. Apparently, all of the above-listed rules make the second kind of kiss something more magical and earth-shaking than even the steamiest first kind of kiss.

As Alex's hands moved up and down my spine like I was his bass fiddle, I couldn't imagine a thing like that were possible. But Julia did have her harebrained theories.

First kind or not, Alex was a great kisser. Very creative. I probably could have kept it up for the full fifteen minutes — that was usually my limit before I grew bored — but when a valet attendant tried to push past us to get into the blue

SUV Alex had me pressed against, we pulled apart.

"Well, you're full of surprises," I said, a bit breathless.

He touched my chin with one finger, then ran it down my neck. "Want to go back to my place?"

"What?"

Almost as if he were snapping out of a trance, his intense expression dissolved and his lazy smile was back. "Come on, gorgeous." He took my hand, linking my arm through his, and we walked out of the parking lot. "You pick the restaurant."

"I can't believe you stole your moves like that," I said, thinking what a pervy beast Woody Allen must be in real life.

Alex laughed and shot me a sideways glance. "If that's what gets your engines blazing, I'll be sure to talk about Henry more often." He put his hand over mine and squeezed.

Knightly? I almost tripped over my own feet. *Why on earth would Alex be thinking about him? Or assuming that I would be thinking about him while we were kissing?*

Chapter 7

"I'm sorry. No more empty tables."

I moaned and glanced over the hostess's shoulder at the unusually, overly packed café.

"It's the rain," she explained with a shrug. "No one wants to be outside."

"Yeah," I agreed, perturbed that all of Stanford apparently chose to eat at *Oy Vey Café* that morning.

"You can get your order to go," she suggested, then pointed behind me at the dozen or so people already standing in line. I guessed that was my only option.

"She can join me."

Henry Knightly was sitting at a small, round table by a fogged-up window, gesturing at the empty chair across from him.

"Is that okay?" the hostess asked me.

"Um, well…" I looked over my shoulder to the queue at the To Go counter. Had it doubled in the past five seconds?

"If not," the hostess continued, "I could really use this chair at another—"

"She's joining me." He pushed out the chair with his foot. "Have a seat, Spring."

"Jeez, be a caveman, why don't you?" I muttered under my breath as I walked toward the table, confused, but cold and famished. *Stupid rain.*

I sat across from him, ordered my breakfast, and pulled a paperback from my bag, preparing to ignore our close proximity. Not that we were exactly strangers anymore. Classes had been in session for three weeks—I ran into him practically every day, though we usually didn't speak. All those things Alex told me on our date were hard to forget. I didn't trust this guy…I barely liked him.

"What are you reading?" he asked.

I peered at him from over the book I'd been using as a shield and lowered it an inch. "*Huis Clos, suivi de Les Mouches*," I answered before flipping off the French-to-English switch in my head.

His eyebrows twitched. "Jean-Paul Sartre?"

I put in my bookmark and placed the paperback on the table next to my poppy seed muffin. "Are you taking French?"

"No, no." He took a bite of the bagel in front of him. It had some kind of pink spread on it.

For some reason, I found that extremely odd. Was it strawberry? Henry Knightly ate strawberry cream cheese?

"I'm studying Latin," he continued. "It helps with the law terminology. Plus, it's a dead language." He eyed me, kind of deadpan. "I'm trying to resurrect it."

"Single-handedly?"

He exhaled what could have been a laugh, then took a sip from a tall, silver travel mug. "If that's what it takes."

While he checked something on his phone, I watched him from across the table, wondering why he was in such a talkative mood. We hadn't exchanged this many words since the party. I also wondered where he was off to so early. I knew most post-graduate courses were taught in the afternoons to accommodate students who had jobs. Knightly did not have a job.

He wasn't wearing a *complete* suit today, just dark gray pants, a white shirt with blue pinstripes, and a gray-and-black-striped tie. A dark gray jacket was draped over the back of his chair. Most professors didn't dress up as much. To me, the formalness of his attire went hand-in-hand with the formal attitude that he wore like so many argyle sweaters.

I stirred at the contents of my turquoise over-sized porcelain mug, staring down at the brown liquid swirling around like a whirlpool.

"Some weather," he observed.

"Yeah," I answered.

"What class do you have this morning?"

I hated small talk. Why hadn't I grabbed my food to go? Why was there still a friggin' monsoon outside and why'd I leave home sans umbrella?

"Statistics," I said, nibbling around the edges of my muffin.

"Nothing after that?"

"Why are you asking about my classes?"

"Because you're sitting right in front of me and it's polite."

"Oh, you're polite now?" I couldn't help blurting. "Run

over any pedestrians lately?"

Something in his expression seemed pleased by my outburst.

I took a breath and looked down at my plate. "I guess I don't *thrive* on chitchat like some people."

"You might be out of practice."

I lifted my chin. "And what? You're the grand master of communication?"

"How would you know if I am or not? We don't know each other very well." His eyes were wide with amusement at whatever he was thinking about saying next. "Don't you think it's time we remedy that? I know *I'd* be willing to do something about it."

My teeth stopped moving mid-chew. His eye contact didn't waver, causing the temperature under my collar to heat up a degree or two. In a parallel universe, I might have thought he was flirting with me. But that seemed as probable as discovering spotted owls living in Trump Tower.

I swallowed and quickly picked up my novel, letting the bookmark slide onto the table. I held the book in front of my face, staring blankly at the pages for a few moments, not liking the way my heart was beating so unsteadily. When my focus on the page finally sharpened, I realized that the words were upside down. I casually turned the book right-side-up, hoping my dining companion wouldn't notice.

No such luck.

A weird noise was coming from the other side of the table. I lowered my shield. "What's so funny?" I asked, surprised to see Knightly chuckling into a fist.

"Your buttons," he said.

I looked down at the top I was wearing. It was a black

pullover sweater, no buttons.

"No," he said with another chuckle. "Your *buttons*, Spring." He pointed at me, his fingers like a gun. "They're very easy to push, aren't they?"

"Depends on who's pushing them, and where." I nearly choked on the unintentional innuendo that had spewed out of my mouth. Wow. Now I was flirting back? I reached for my glass of ice water and held it up to my suddenly dry lips. When I snuck a glance at him, his mouth was frozen in a boyish grin, pleased as punch.

"Sorry," he said. "I'm embarrassing you."

"No, you're not."

"You're blushing."

"I don't blush," I stated, setting down my glass with a *thud*, rattling the silverware. "And is this the type of polite conversation you had in mind?"

"I'll take what I can get." He shook his head. "Buttons."

"You know what?" I said, after dabbing my mouth with a napkin. "I think I liked it better when we were ignoring each other."

His eyebrows shot up. "Ignoring?" A moment passed before he leaned back in his chair. "Okay, fine, you're not blushing." He tapped his chin, then his mouth slowly curved into a smile.

It was a nice smile. In fact… Huh, Henry Knightly really should smile like that more often. I was momentarily dazzled by the way his brown eyes went squinty, giving the rest of his face an almost innocent countenance. He was mesmerizing.

"So, Spring Honeycutt, are you going to tell me what classes you have today, or should I look up your schedule online?" He reached for his phone.

"Statistics," I repeated. "Your roommate's got a class right across from me."

"How do you know that?"

I stared at him for a beat. "Because he's dating *my* roommate."

"Oh." A shadow seemed to eclipse his expression for a moment as he took a drink. "That's right. And what do you have after statistics?"

"I've got a four-hour block for research." I rested my elbows on the table. "Is there anything else you'd like to know?"

He opened his mouth, but then paused as though rethinking a question. "If you're a junior, is the research for your independent study thesis?"

"How did you know?"

He lifted his travel mug and took another drink. "Lucky guess. Have you picked a subject?"

The question made my stomach roll and my heart stop at the same time.

"What?" Knightly asked, probably noticing all the color drain from my face.

"Nothing," I replied, toying with my teaspoon. "Yes, I have a subject. I started working on it over the summer, actually, but a few weeks ago, my advisor…"

"Oh," he said. "He's making you change it."

"He says I need a new angle." I paused, not knowing how to explain further to a layman, and not really having the stomach to get into the whole thing. "It's complicated."

"I'm sure it is." He pulled back a tiny smirk. "Knowing you."

"Funny," I said, not laughing.

Knightly pushed his plate to the side. "It might help to talk about it."

"Just making polite conversation?"

Another of those steady smiles appeared on his face. My pupils might have actually dilated. Man, I was going to have to keep on my toes to stay immune to this guy.

"You don't really want to hear about my project," I said.

"What else do I have to do?" He glanced toward the window. "It's raining."

He was right. I had no place to go, either, and who knows, maybe talking through it out loud with someone who had no clue about the subject matter would rattle something loose. I sighed and rested the side of my head against my palm. "Okay, well, basically my main focus is on biological systems remaining diverse and productive over time. Sorry, that was too technical. What I mean is—"

"Sustainability."

I frowned. "You know what that is?"

"I do." When I didn't go on, he gestured for me to continue.

"Anyway, since you know what sustainability is, you're probably also aware that land development is destroying the environment. Yeah, I know, this isn't news, but I'm trying to prove that the continued usage of developed land could be even worse; it should be revitalized back into nature. No new patches of forests or mountainsides or wetlands are suddenly going to appear in the middle of an urban system. We've got all we're ever going to have right now, today. And it's not enough."

"Isn't that an overly simplistic way of looking at it?" he asked.

I stared across the table at him. "No."

"Are you sure?"

"Look, do you want to hear the rest of this or do you want to argue?"

His eyebrows pulled together like he was about to say something else, but then he shut his mouth and sat back.

"Like I was saying." I gave him a look. "At this rate, we're going to be living in a dystopian world in three generations."

"A what?"

"Dystopia. The yang of utopia. Think: opposite of the Garden of Eden. Like *The Hunger Games*. Have you read that?"

He shook his head, bewildered.

"It's a novel, similar to *1984* in the—"

"You're getting your research from novels?"

"Of course not. I was making a comparison." I kneaded a fist into my temple, annoyed with all the derailing. "Anyway, what I mean is, we have to take back industrial land, that's the only way to save it. I've got the environmental research, but Masen, my professor, wants me to learn more about the business end, the economics of it, the legal side."

Frustrated at the thought, I cupped my hands over my face, feeling—not for the first time in three weeks—at a complete loss. If I thought too much about it, I would worry myself sick. Then…I would drown.

"I've got a hard deadline coming up," I mumbled through my fingers, mostly to myself. "I've read some articles and books and sat in on a few urban econ lectures, and I've even talked to a couple econ majors. How can no one at Stanford understand what I'm talking about?"

"Email me your outline."

Knowing I must have misheard, I peeled away my fingers

and looked up. "What?"

"Your facts are wrong."

I dropped my hands. "No, they aren't."

"They are. I can help."

"No, you can't." I pushed back my chair, wondering if he was purposefully insulting me or if this was his personality. "Why would you want to help me, anyway?"

He shrugged. "Maybe I think we got off on the wrong foot," he answered. "Maybe I've been wanting to make up for that."

"Do you *have* another foot?" I asked skeptically.

He stared back. "What?"

My bad joke was lost on him. "Nothing," I said. "Anyway, I'm not letting you read my outline. I don't even know you."

He leaned forward, resting his crossed arms on the table. "Spring, do you know what I'm studying to be?"

"A lawyer," I said. "You're in law school."

"That's correct." He rubbed his chin, reminding me a bit of Professor Masen. "My undergrad was in finance, but I'm studying corporate law with an emphasis in property development."

I stared at him, my brain grinding into gear at what his words implied. A second later, I felt cold fingers slide up my spine, and my heart started pounding under Henry Knightly's heavy gaze, but it was for a different reason this time.

"Does that mean…"

"That means," he said, "if you're an environmentalist, then I'm your worst nightmare." We stared across the table at each other, an invisible wall bricking between us. "But it also means that if you want to learn about the economics of land development"—he steepled the tips of his fingers under his chin—"then I'm the man of your dreams."

Chapter 8

I lingered outside the doorway of the private study room on the third floor of the library, unwilling to step inside just yet.

I still couldn't believe it, couldn't believe my stupid luck. Of all the people who could help me—who were *willing* to help me—with my research project, it was Henry Knightly.

Stupid, fracking karma.

After breakfast at the café, I ran home through the rain and looked him up online. Or his family, rather. They were land barons, all right, had been for generations. When I'd Googled the Knightlys last year, digging up dirt when Knightly Hall was under construction, I had only scratched the surface. They did indeed own land all throughout North America, the biggest chunks around Wyoming, Idaho, and Montana. Prime farm and cattle real estate.

What they must have done to the landscape, I didn't want to imagine. They'd had no issue bulldozing a strip of green to erect their namesake building at Stanford. Why would they treat twenty thousand innocent acres in the northwest any differently?

Halfway through my statistics class, my phone had vibrated with a new email. Again, he'd asked me to send my outline. I put off the inevitable for as long as I could, but as I calculated how many days I had left before Masen would be breathing down my neck, I finally realized I had no choice. I sent him my outline and fifteen minutes later, he emailed back, wanting to meet.

"Are we doing this or not?"

I jumped at his voice coming from inside the study room. How had he known I was there? Had he seen my shadow? Heard me tiptoe toward the room? Jeez, could he *smell* me? Could money buy super senses?

"Spring, I've got my own class in an hour."

I closed my eyes for a second, gripped the strap of my backpack, then entered the room.

Knightly sat at a small table, a stack of books off to the side, and one of those slick black mini-laptops in front of him. He wore the same shirt and tie as this morning, only the top button was undone now, and his tie knot was loose. It was a good look on him. Now if he'd flash one of those smiles, this might be bearable.

"Hey," I said, "sorry I'm late, I— "

"It's fine." He didn't look up as I sat down.

Okay, so we were back to Mr. Charm then.

"I've been going over your outline and the list of resources you cited," he said, clicking the down arrow about twenty times, staring at the screen.

"And?" I asked when he didn't go on. "And you think it's crap, right?"

"Not all of it," he said, highlighting a paragraph on the screen.

"Well, that's a relief," I muttered, leaning on an elbow. "I didn't assume we were going to see eye-to-eye on this, obviously. I know about the land your family owns."

He finally lifted his chin but didn't speak. I'd expected him to jump in, to debate with me like at breakfast, to say something. But he was just sitting there with a blank expression.

His silence made me tense.

"I…I know what they—what *you*—believe in," I added, unable to stop myself from filling the silence. "And you should know, I didn't come here to argue with you, or to hear a lecture, or for either of us to change our minds. I'm here because I have no other choice. Just so we're clear. Okay? Don't think you can trash my whole belief system then walk away."

He leaned back in his chair. "I haven't said anything yet."

I blinked. "Oh. Well… But I know what you're thinking."

A tiny smile twitched the corner of his lips, a hint of that same smile that had halted me at breakfast. "How could you know that?" he asked, smoothing down his tie.

"Because I know your type," I said, choosing to continue the argument instead of focusing on how looking at his smile made me want to lick my lips. "You've got a finance degree, you come from money and drive a sports car. You voted Republican, didn't you?"

His eyebrows lifted slightly. "Is that a crime?"

"I wish," I muttered, turning to a clean page of my notebook.

"Wow," he said, deadpan. "Anything else about me you'd

like to get off your chest?"

Suddenly, everything Alex told me came flooding into my brain. How Knightly had been jealous, judgmental, accusatory, and then Alex was suddenly expelled from high school. The memory of what Knightly had said about me at the party—what I'd *heard* him say—was also front and center in my mind. And how he'd yelled at the movers to not touch his precious car, and how he hadn't spoken one word to Julia.

He may have been helping me out of a pretty huge bind, but I wasn't about to trust him, despite the way he was watching me with that almost-smile, and the way one stray lock of dark hair had fallen across his forehead, begging for my fingers to push it back then continue running through his hair.

I had to ignore that and remember the rest.

He was all I had. I knew I had to play nice, so I smiled as pleasantly as possible and sat back. "Nope, I'm all done." I glanced at his computer with my outline on the screen. "Now it's your turn. What do you really think?"

He angled his laptop so the screen was facing me. Aside from Professor Masen's last assignment, I'd never seen so many red strike-throughs.

This was going to be a very long semester.

Part II

Winter

"I had never loved anyone before…so I naturally thought that it was not in my nature to love. But it has always seemed to me that it *must* be *heavenly* to be loved blindly, passionately, wholly… And I would have allowed myself to be worshipped, and given infinite tenderness in return."
From *The Scarlet Pimpernel*

Chapter 9

As I came down the creaky attic stair from my bedroom, I ran into Anabel leaving Julia's room.

"Oh, hey Springer," she said, trying to display an innocent expression, which made me instantly suspicious.

"What were you doing in there?" I asked.

"Nothing," she said, glancing into Julia's room. "Just having a chat. Girl stuff. Have a nice Thanksgiving!" She waved her fingers and walked away. Little chats with Anabel usually included requests to borrow a pair of shoes you'd never see again, or unsolicited, unorthodox dating advice. When it came to Julia, neither was a good idea.

I rounded the corner and entered her room.

"Ready to go?" Julia asked, smiling brightly.

"Almost," I replied, giving her a quick assessment. I'd have to ask her later what she and Anabel were discussing.

Two suitcases were open on the foot of her bed. The rest of the mattress was covered with separated stacks of clothes laid out in uniformed organization. Julia was singing to herself, methodically folding a white sweater. "You're packed, right?" she asked.

I groaned as an answer, adjusting one ear bud as some very appropriate angry chick rock lulled in my ear.

With midterm exams over, we were now well into the meat of the winter quarter. Papers, research projects, advisory teams. Madness ahead. I'd dropped my three jobs to concentrate on school. Now was the time to focus, the big push to the end.

It was the first time I'd stepped foot in Julia's bedroom in weeks. Despite the various piles of clothing, it was immaculate. Even with her mind intertwined with her heart, she was still as orderly as ever. I did notice that the calendar on her pink wall had not yet been turned from October to November, even though we were more than half-way through the month.

"Planning on staying forever?" I asked, eyeing the enormous pile of clothes in her suitcase.

"I wish." She smiled wistfully.

I scooted over a pair of red jeans so I could sit. "This is going to be the longest seven days in the history of the world," I moaned.

"So dramatic," Julia replied. "You'll be fine."

"With you and Dart making kissing faces to each other over the turkey and cornbread stuffing, not to mention the other inhabitant of that house."

Julia lifted her eyebrows at me. She'd been packing all morning. Anabel was heading out any minute, spending the week with her family. I seldom left for holidays anymore. My brothers were also staying away at school, and last I heard,

Mom was going on a nature retreat, probably not even realizing it was Thanksgiving. I didn't want to spend another holiday in my tiny hometown, didn't need another reminder of what my life might be like if I didn't succeed in college, if I didn't get out and make something of myself in the world. I loved my mother, but I did not want to end up like her.

I should have gone on vacation with Mel, who was driving up to her grandparents' house in Washington. She'd invited me, but I turned her down.

Julia actually *wanted* to stay in town for Thanksgiving. Because Dart was. So the two of us had the whole house to ourselves.

That was, until we learned that one of our landlord's other rentals had termites, so all of his properties were being fumigated over the long break. The exterminator was arriving early tomorrow. Those of us who were remaining in town were forced to stay elsewhere while the toxic spray did its thing.

Julia was singing again, stowing her makeup bag in the small outside pocket of her second suitcase.

"What's that there?" I asked when my eye caught a piece of black lace tucked in a corner.

"Oh." Julia covered it with a sweatshirt. "It's nothing," she said, looking down, moving more clothes around. "Just something from Anabel."

"Is it lingerie?"

"No. Well, sort of." She tucked some hair behind an ear. "It's nothing, really. I probably won't ever wear it."

She seemed so embarrassed, I almost laughed. "Bunny, it's none of my business what you wear for your boyfriend; just be careful about what Anabel gives you, whether it's a push-up bra or relationship advice."

"I will. And what about you?"

"What about me?"

"You really like Alex," she said. "Or should I *ask* that? Because it's tough to tell with you."

I played with the cuff of my sleeve. "What's not to like?"

She twisted her lips but didn't speak for a moment. "Now it's *my* turn to say be careful to *you*," she finally said.

"Your concern is duly noted."

In the purely conventional respect, Alex and I weren't dating, because dating involved actually going out to places, maybe sharing a meal. The moments Alex and I spent together always began the same way our first date had. No more, no less. A controlled release of pheromones and hormones was a nice way to break up a tedious day of studying. Alex was good for that. Sometimes we talked a bit about his past with Henry Knightly, although I wasn't very comfortable with the topic, so I usually cut him off. And I never breathed a word to anyone else about what he'd told me the night of our first date.

"We don't know anything about him," Julia said, hauling suitcase number one toward the door.

"*You* don't," I said, "but I do."

"I asked Dart about it a few weeks ago, because it's obvious Alex and Henry have a history."

I glanced at her. She was fiddling with the zipper on her suitcase.

"He knows they went to high school together and had a falling out. Dart said Henry doesn't like to talk about it."

"Of course he doesn't," I agreed, bending my knees to sit cross-legged.

Julia frowned.

Very easily, I could have put her mind at ease. Alex and I had a good run, but the rush of dopamine and norepinephrine stimulating my senses had rapidly decreased. I was crazy-busy, and I was bored. It took a lot to hold my interest, no matter how good the kissing.

"Do you trust Alex over Henry?" Julia asked hesitantly.

"I do."

"Even after all his help with your thesis?"

"Just because he's been spending a few nights a week lecturing me on how wrong I am doesn't mean he isn't an even bigger ass to other people. In fact, it probably *proves* he is. Who knows how big a jerk he is to his actual friends."

She looked down, running her fingers over her lap. "We've known each other for more than two years," she began, eyes lowered. "You didn't used to be so closed-minded."

"The guy called me hypocritical the other day because I ate an egg." I rolled my eyes. "I'm an Environmental Vegetarian, not Gandhi. And last week, he told me I'm a haughty elitist. How can I be an elitist if I don't have any money?"

"Your attitude, maybe?"

I sat back. "Meaning?"

From her bent expression, I could tell she was sorry she'd said the words in the first place. Her fingers nervously twirled at the ends of her hair, giving me the same worried, detached look Mel had that night at the street party.

"Well…" Julia pressed her lips together. "You can come on a little strong."

"Me?" I asked, trying not to sound shrieky. "It's his fault.

He's so political about everything."

She stared at me for a moment then burst out laughing. "Hello black pot, have you met the black kettle?" She swatted my knee and stood. "All right, Springer, time to go."

"No, bunny, please," I whined. "Let's take out a loan and stay at a hotel."

"Funny," she said. "Before we go, I need you to do me a big favor."

"Anything," I said, kicking my feet off the bed.

"Say two nice things about Henry."

"Anything but that."

"That way, during the week if you happen to feel, umm, *incensed*, you can bring those to mind." She fingered her hair into a ponytail. "Just two things. You can even make them physical. That's easy. Hello, you're not *blind*—"

"Fine," I cut her off. "He's a…a good shaver."

Julia rolled her eyes.

"And his face is very symmetrical."

"Hot," she said sarcastically, but I'd apparently pacified her enough for the moment. "Grab your bags. It's time."

Chapter 10

Dart was all smiles and excitement when he opened the front door, one hand gripping the top as it swung open. "Hi, sweetheart," he said to Julia, resembling a kid about to take a pony ride.

"Hi," she replied, managing to blush. They'd been together for three months and she still acted like every time they saw each other was their first date. Apparently, Dart was a sucker for good girls. And you couldn't get more "good" than Julia.

I wondered if she would have the guts to wear that mystery item of black lace for him. Then I reminded myself to have a serious talk with her about Anabel. Someone like Julia did not need to be guided by the resident Kardashian sister of Stanford. But when Dart moved in to kiss Julia and she tilted her face so he got her cheek, I figured that talk could wait.

My time previously spent inside the Knightly/Charleston

abode was fleeting, and I'd never been over when Knightly was there. I preferred to keep our relationship—such as it was—at a professional distance.

This was not supposed to include sleeping in his house for a week.

The place wasn't your typical college bachelor pad. No flashing neon signs on any of the walls, no beer cooler coffee table, no kitschy lava lamps, and not a single barbell or free weight scattered on the floor, which was what I usually tripped over when entering any other testosterone-filled dwelling on campus.

As we crossed the threshold into the living room, Knightly was sitting on the couch, bent over a stack of opened textbooks, a laptop at his side. He was wearing dark pants, and the top two buttons of his solid blue shirt were undone. A dark blue tie was draped over the back of the couch.

"They're here." Dart beamed, ushering us in.

Knightly looked up from his work, his expression cordial. "Hey, there," he said, closing his book and standing. "Is there anything I can do? All the bags in?"

Julia and Dart were too busy cooing at each other to answer.

"Got everything. I think we're set," I answered, kind of feeling like a idiot.

He nodded and it was quiet again. I should have been used to his patches of silence by now. We'd had five study sessions in the last month; half the time we were debating, the other half, you could hear a pin drop. We were experts at the classic impasse.

"Umm, we really appreciate this," I forced myself to

utter, trying not to sound like I was swallowing medicine. "Thanks for letting us stay."

"Sure," he replied. "Once I learned your circumstances, it didn't make sense any other way. We're neighbors."

"Right," I said. "Neighbors."

He eyed me. "Why do you say it like that?"

I felt like laughing. Last time we'd met to go over my thesis, we'd almost come to blows. Well, I'd almost come to blows while Knightly had sat there, watching in silence as I'd become more and more angry at the way he thought my project should go. But if *he* still considered us just neighbors, then fine.

"Never mind," I said.

Dart's shoulder bumped me as he swept by. He had one of Julia's suitcases in his hand. She followed behind him, towing the other on its wheels.

Knightly glanced at me. "I suppose they know where they're going."

I smiled a little awkwardly.

"May I?" he asked, looking down at my side. I wasn't sure what he meant until he picked up the straps of my bag.

"I can carry it."

"I'm sure you can, but I've already got it," he said, walking deeper inside the house. I followed him around a corner to a narrow hallway.

"Have you been here before?" he asked.

"A few times. Only the living room."

"We'll save the grand tour for later. I'll give you the five cent version now. It's a very logical setup. Purposefully logical. There are five bedrooms and only the two of us." He glanced over his shoulder. "Dart and myself, I meant. Not you and I. How would that look?"

"Frightful," I said, laughing.

He led me up the stairs.

"Each room is painted one dominant color," he explained. "You most likely didn't notice the red room we just passed. It's the only bedroom on the first floor. Lilah will stay in there."

"Can't wait," I muttered.

He paused on the landing, his brown eyes sizing me up. He must've read my sour expression. "Oh, that's right. You two don't get along. Why is that?"

"*I* get along fine. She's the one who wants me dead."

Knightly thought for a moment then nodded sagely. "Got it. No more questions."

"Thank you," I said, and we continued up the stairs.

"This is Dart's room." He gestured to the first room behind a closed door. "Gold. I told him he could repaint, but he likes the color, calls it Zen. Your roommate is across the hall from him. Naturally."

"Naturally," I echoed, walking past her room. I heard muffled voices through the crack in the door.

"Also Dart's," he said, gesturing to a bathroom as he breezed by.

We passed by two more closed doors without any details. I guessed they were being saved for part of the later "grand tour."

The last door of the hallway was wide open, lights on. "I'm assuming green is your favorite color, Ms. Environmentalist."

"How long did it take you to think that one up?"

Knightly stood at the doorway, allowing me to enter first. The room had clean, bright white walls with three-inch green, black and white checkered borders around the ceiling and floor. Behind green striped curtains, one huge window faced east. The cozy boudoir was fancier than any hotel room I'd stayed in.

"Thanks. This is really nice."

"You're our first official guest," he said, leaning against the door frame. "Lilah doesn't count, in my book." He dropped my overstuffed *Adopt a Rainforest* duffel bag in front of him. "Well, you should have everything you need." He turned on his heel and took one step into the hall. "Bathroom's next door. It's mine. We're sharing."

And he disappeared.

I stared at the empty doorway where he'd been standing.

Sharing a bathroom? With Henry Knightly? That won't be awkward at all…

My mind quickly calculated how much I had on my one emergency credit card. I moaned, arms hanging limply at my sides. I hated feeling so helpless, so financially strapped. I wished I could call my mother to bail me out, but that was never a realistic option. After I graduated, hopefully I wouldn't have to stress so much about money.

But for now, like a good little soldier, I hung clothes in the closet, tossed shoes under the bed, gathered together my absolutely necessary toiletries, and headed next door.

The bathroom was immaculate, not a speck of dust, not a single lock of hair. Even the glass shower doors were spotless. The room was the same combination of brown, gray, cream, and black as the living room, and smelled of aftershave, pinecones, and bleach.

The cabinet unit was a warm cinnamon color with black hardware. There were two doors on either side, and three drawers in the center. The middle drawer was empty, and had been pulled out almost all the way and left open. Knowing my host's etiquette, I was sure this was meant for me. My few hair products, toothbrush and toothpaste, soap, and face cleanser all fit nicely inside.

After securely locking the door behind me, I snuck a peek at the shelves behind the mirror. An electric toothbrush, green Speed Stick, a small brown bottle of cologne with an Italian label peeling off, and an urn of MAC hair putty.

On the counter next to the sink sat a blue-and-gray-glazed pottery mug of shaving cream and a lathering brush.

Yep, I thought as I took a quick whiff of the spicy foam, *that's him*.

The linen closet next to the shower was that same warm cinnamon. I creaked open the door and examined the contents. Nothing out of the ordinary there, either. Down on my knees, I stuck my head under the sink. I didn't know what I was expecting to find as I ruthlessly snooped through other drawers and cabinets. Perhaps I was hoping for that one item that would tell me all about him, that elusive clue to confirm everything.

But whatever it was I was searching for, I didn't find it. Henry Knightly had all the earmarks of any other twenty-three-year-old conservative student of jurisprudence.

I headed downstairs to join the others, somewhat disappointed.

Everyone was in the kitchen. The grand meal wasn't for a few days, but Julia was already in full-blown domestic mode, chopping vegetables for nibbling, and a platter of crackers and dip sat on the table. Dart was rinsing something at the sink. When Julia came up behind him, she slid her first two fingers into the back of his jeans at the waist. It was a tiny gesture, to which Dart didn't even react. I don't know why it caught my attention.

As far as I knew, Julia hadn't had sex yet, being a little more old-fashioned than your average twenty-one-year-old. There was only one other virgin in the room that I knew of.

I guess I was just...I never had time for such entanglements. My philandering youth was spent trying to get into Stanford, and then trying to *stay* in Stanford.

Well, that's what I told myself. If I was being brutally honest, the thought of even the tiniest chance of having to stop my life to have a baby scared every ounce of all-the-way libido out of me. My mother had me at seventeen, and never let me forgot how she sacrificed everything to keep me. She struggled, my whole family struggled. I was not going to spend the rest of my life like that.

Catching a glimpse of Julia and Dart in an intimate moment surprised me. The beginning of their relationship was all-consuming. Which wasn't odd for Julia—she never let the physical get very far. She was always more emotionally invested. That was probably where Anabel's gift of black lace came in.

Dart's hand slid to her side, curling low around her hip. Huh. Maybe they *had* already slept together. Julia and I were close, so I was a little surprised she hadn't told me. I couldn't help sneaking more tiny glances their way as they huddled over the sink. Her fingers were out of his jeans, but the way they were standing next to each other, her hair up in a pony tail, his hand on the back of her bare neck. Innocent, yet...not.

I swallowed and looked away. Having that kind of comfortable, complete intimacy was not in the cards for me, not with my parents' disaster of a marriage as my prime example. For as long as I could remember, I wanted no part of that. But suddenly, watching Julia in her bare feet lift up to her tiptoes to kiss Dart on the cheek, I wondered if I might be missing out on something.

Chapter 11

Julia and Dart awoke at the crack of dawn to put the turkey in the oven. After that, they headed out for a drive up the coast, leaving the other remaining, and still sleeping, members of the household to tackle the rest of the Thanksgiving dinner preparations.

One by one, each of us staggered into the kitchen. Lilah baked two pies the night before and was now attempting "homemade" cranberry sauce (out of a jar). I volunteered for rolls, vegetables and other non-meat menu items. Knightly sat in a kitchen chair eating a bowl of cereal. He didn't look up once, focused on his iPad.

"Will you taste my filling?" Lilah asked him. Her mildly disguised double entendre was not lost on me. Clueless to the lewd request, Knightly gestured with his spoon that his mouth was full.

I smiled down at the bread dough I was kneading.

Undaunted, Lilah continued variations upon her request

until she was summoned to her phone, leaving the kitchen. She hadn't said one word to me.

With empty cereal bowl in hand, Knightly stood up from the table and walked to the sink. He rinsed his bowl and put it in the dishwasher. He wore long black shorts and a green T-shirt with some faded and unintelligible navy blue wording across the front. Italian, probably. I think he was about to go for a run.

"Well," he said, wiping his hands on a bar towel, "it looks like you've got everything under control here. So" — he backed up toward the door — "I'll let you — "

"Um, nooo." I lifted my hands to show that I was up to my elbows in flour. "You're not planning on leaving everything to the womenfolk, are you?"

He tossed his iPad on a chair by the door then came to my side. "What is that?"

"Bread dough. There's nothing to it."

"Do you want…help?"

"Are your hands clean?"

He looked down at his hands and nodded.

With one finger, I scooted the dough in front of him. "Show me your skills."

His gaze held on me, assessing my challenge. After a moment, he took the dough and sat down, while I walked to the sink to scrub my hands. He was elbow-deep by the time I returned.

"You don't bake, do you?" I guessed.

"Not unless I have to. This is a workout. Could you grab me something from the fridge?"

"A little early for a beer, don't you think?" I said as I pulled the refrigerator open, about to reach behind the half-empty takeout cartons from last night, expecting to find rows and rows of dark bottles. I was surprised to find absolutely no alcoholic beverages whatsoever. How very *un*-collegiate.

"No beer," Henry said. "My paternal grandfather died of cirrhosis of the liver when he was forty-five." His chin was tucked, kneading away. "I've never had a drink in my life."

I stared at him for a moment. What a thing to admit. And he seemed almost proud of it. Well, not that being a teetotaler was something shameful. In fact, I couldn't help wishing my own father had followed that particular practice when he was in his twenties, instead of boozing it up and leaving my mother home with three kids. Five years sober or no five years sober, I still hadn't forgiven him for choosing alcohol over his family all those years ago.

"You weren't drinking at the party?" I asked, remembering perfectly that he'd been holding a red Solo cup.

"No," he said. "I knew I had to keep my wits about me that night. I heard there were snakes."

I snorted under my breath. "You're killing me."

"I'll take a water, though," he said, "if you can manage."

"I can manage." I slid a bottle from the door shelf.

"Yeah, thanks," he said, preoccupied, as I set it in front of him. With no luck, he was trying to scratch his cheek with his shoulder. I was familiar with Murphy's Law in the kitchen: the moment your hands are incapacitated, every inch of your face—and other various body parts—inevitability begins to itch.

"Could I get a little help here?" he requested, his voice pinched.

I sat down across the table from him and rocked my

chair back on two legs.

He let loose a rough exhale of frustration then rubbed his cheek with the back of his hand, leaving behind a flour smudge.

"Sweetie, you got a little something"—I pointed at my own cheek—"right there."

Henry stopped kneading to return my smile, only his was much more menacing than mine. I examined my nails. A moment later, something small and sticky hit my face.

I blinked, glanced up and dabbed at my cheek. "*Et tu, Brute*?"

His sinister smile grew as he flicked his fingers like a whip toward me, sending more chunks of dough in my direction. Most of them landed short.

"Aww, you missed," I said as my chair legs dropped down on all fours. I leaned forward, elbows bracing my weight. Henry followed suit, his floury palms flat on the table, angling toward me. His gaze flicked to something to the side of him then back at me. His smile widened.

That's when I noticed the open bag of flour on the table, closer to him than to me. Without needing to turn around, I knew that behind me on the counter sat sugar, salt, pepper, oatmeal, baking soda, bread crumbs, and other substances of the grating, powdery, confectionary persuasion.

Two seconds later, our respective chairs flew out from behind us. Five seconds later, like an explosion of snowy dynamite, flour was everywhere.

He stepped right, I stepped left. And so we danced…

After a particularly dastardly pitch of cornstarch on my part, Henry blinked and coughed, shaking his head, white dust falling from his dark hair, catching in the curls.

He went on the offense.

I staggered back, temporarily blinded, clutching the edge of the counter so my feet wouldn't slide out from under me. It was hard to breathe with cocoa powder up my nose, and I sputtered a laugh, making myself choke. When I regained focus, Henry was at the sink, filling a tall glass under the faucet.

"Whah-ha-ha-ha," he taunted over his shoulder.

"Dry ingredients only. *Dry*."

"I don't remember hearing rules." He shut off the tap when the water reached the top rim.

I backed away, hanging onto the counter. Henry was blocking the only suitable exit out to the backyard. I was trapped. The hair on my arms stood on end when he took a single step forward, full glass in hand, aimed right at me.

"You wouldn't *dare*!" I rasped, slipping and sliding in retreat.

He dipped his fingers in the glass and flicked. Large drops of water soaked into the front of my T-shirt.

I was desperate for a weapon, any weapon. That's when I spied Lilah's bowl of bright red cranberry sauce sitting on the corner of the table, just begging to be tagged into the ring. Henry's eyes went wide as I slid it off the smooth surface and into the palm of my hand, my arm cocked like a baseball pitcher.

"Put that down," he ordered.

I pointed my chin at him. "You first."

"Not a chance." His grin made my arms prickle again.

Additional verbal and nonverbal threats were issued. Promises of everlasting revenge were pledged, but neither of us lowered our weapons.

"One inch closer," I cautioned, eyeing his shirt, "and it's bye-bye to that Armani Exchange you're wearing."

"I have another." He was about to flick more water at me, when suddenly, while stepping on an exceptionally puffy mound of flour mixture, he lost his footing. Thanks to this brief distraction, I made my move, lunging forward, sword unsheathed.

With me two seconds ahead, he whipped around, pitching the water in my direction. It only tagged my shoulder. I ducked and bobbed behind him with just enough time to dump the entire bowl of slimy cranberries over his head.

And then, with my arm still in the air, I froze. Surprised, maybe, at my easy triumph.

That was my mistake.

With a yelp, I whirled around, making a beeline toward the patio door. But I was a breath too late.

Henry yanked the back of my shirt, then caught my wrist. "Not so fast, Honeycutt."

By one arm, I was pulled back and spun around, my feet sliding across the slippery floor. I could see the whites of his eyes and teeth beneath the red jelly oozing down his face. I wriggled and squirmed against his clutches while he smiled fiendishly, dragging me toward the sink.

Flour and water coupled with the white V-neck and blue-striped bra I was sporting was *not* the impression I wanted to leave on Thanksgiving morning.

"Stop!" I squeaked, struggling to break his grip.

"Nope." He stopped dragging me long enough to seize my other wrist, holding me securely by both hands.

"Let's call it a draw," I offered. "We're even, okay?"

"I'm about to *make* it even," he said, his voice low. When

I tried to squirm away, he let go of my wrists long enough to slide his hands up my arms and take hold of my shoulders. I couldn't help thinking that in a parallel universe, it might look like we were about to embrace.

This thought slowed me down, though I did try once more to pull free, pretty halfheartedly. I felt strange, a little lightheaded, as I looked at his face through my flour-caked lashes. His hands were strong and warm around my skin. Capable.

The next thing I knew, my feet were sliding again. This time, however, Henry wasn't pulling me to the sink, he was pulling me to him.

He wasn't smiling anymore. Neither was I. His intense gaze slid to my mouth, and just as my eyes were drifting down his face in a similar manner, I noticed a tiny drop of cranberry sauce trickling down his nose. Like a thick, crimson tear, it dripped off the end.

I tipped my chin and laughed. "Armistice?" I asked, panting to catch my breath.

When I leveled my chin, Henry was examining me skeptically. "Only if you declare defeat." Because of his stern expression under all that red goo, another laugh bubbled up my throat. His fingers pressed into my skin, his eyes flashing to the sink.

"You win, you win! No water!" I begged. "Now, unhand me, sir."

Instead of letting go, he gripped my shoulders, leading me a few steps until my back hit the wall. "Not until you say it," he whispered. He was close again, closer than before, making me hyperaware of his strong hands, the warmth of his skin, his long fingers curling around my arms.

"Say what?" I asked after a hard swallow.

"Repeat after me: Henry Edward Knightly, the third, is the king of the kitchen."

"The *third*?" I couldn't help cackling.

"Say it," he demanded, his fingers gripping my shoulders, pressing me against the wall. "I don't know why you're fighting so hard against it, Spring." His voice turned eerily calm. "You know what's coming if you don't completely obey me. I *will* dunk you, and believe me" — he glanced down at the front of my shirt — "I'll enjoy every second of it."

"Okay, okay!" I closed my eyes and took a deep breath. "Henry Knightly is the king — "

"No," he cut me off, moving his hands to either side of my neck. "Henry *Edward* Knightly, *the third*."

I opened my eyes just so I could roll them and mutter something mocking. But his face was nearer than I expected, his hands gentle on my neck, holding me in place. He stared into my eyes, not blinking. We were so close, almost chest to chest, and for a moment, I forgot I was supposed to breathe.

Without another word, he bent his flour-covered face to mine, and I stopped breathing altogether.

When he kissed me, there was an explosion of stars behind my eyes. His body shifted, pressing me hard against the wall, leaving me no choice but to grab on to the curves of his elbows. His hands still held my neck, fingers moving over my skin, his thumbs brushing across my cheeks. I could taste the sugar on his lips, the flour and the sweet tang of cranberries, a delicious combination that made my mouth water. Without realizing it, I parted my lips, needing a deeper taste.

Before I got the chance, it was over.

But I couldn't move away, didn't want to open my eyes, needing to remain in the moment when I'd caught a glimpse of what Henry might be. Not the arrogant tutor or the mute Greek statue, but the man who made me laugh, pushed my buttons, had a food fight in his spotless kitchen, and managed to blow my mind in ten seconds flat.

His strong hands were still holding me; I could smell his skin, hear him breathing, still near enough to kiss. My throat ached at the thought, and I felt his heart racing, going faster than mine.

"*Now* we're even," he said in a low voice. Then I was released. He stepped back and wiped the back of his wrist across his sauce-covered nose.

"This…this isn't over," I managed to say, choosing to totally ignore what had just happened—if he could do it, so could I. I ran my fingers down my braids, attempting to strip away the pasty goop. Somehow, the bright red cranberry sauce covering the top half of his body had transferred to my hair and all down the front of my shirt. My mind went wonky, imagining how that had happened.

"I will have my revenge," I forced myself to add.

"I'm counting on it."

When he pulled back a slow grin, the pit of my stomach flooded with heat and I caught myself staring at his cranberry-stained mouth. I needed to get out of there, now, before I did something I would regret.

Henry picked up a hand towel off the counter, wound it, and snapped the end in my direction. "Now step out back," he said, "so I can hose you off."

Chapter 12

"What is your answer, *dear*? Everyone's waiting."

I shook my head, not at Lilah's impatience, but at myself. This whole dreadful game had been *my* idea.

"And she can't skip her turn," Lilah continued. "That's not fair to the rest of us." She sat on the floor across the living room from me, her head propped against the side of the recliner Henry was in. She glared at me blatantly. The miserable cow was out for blood. She would probably never forgive me for ruining her cranberries.

Cranberries...

My eyes automatically drifted to Henry. He was laughing and saying something to Dart.

"She can skip one turn if she wants," Julia said, re-explaining the rules of the game. Dart's arm was draped across her shoulders as they sat in the middle of the couch, their feet entangled around each other's on the coffee table. "We each get one pass if we choose to use it," she further clarified. "Are you passing, Springer?"

"No," I said. "I'll answer. Give me a second."

Lilah sighed loudly enough so that everyone looked at her, then rolled her eyes and pulled out her cell. Why didn't she leave if she was so bored?

Two hours ago, this "game" of ours started out as a combo Truth or Dare, Twenty Questions, and True Colors. In our turn, each of the five of us asked a question—a probing question, a question meant to confront ethical dilemmas, expose insights of the answerer, or challenge particular values. Some were more superficial than others, but they were all meant to be answered analytically.

That was the *idea* anyway. Why hadn't I suggested Monopoly instead? Or maybe a nice game of Russian Roulette?

Julia's and Dart's answers usually had something to do with each other, while Lilah's were mostly about money or foreign travel. I didn't mind any of this, because I was interested in only one participant's answers. Although when a straight-faced Henry claimed that cocoa-covered cranberries were his favorite food, I had the unique experience of choking on my Diet Coke and having to answer, again, Lilah's question of why her special side dish had disappeared.

"Come on," Lilah growled, rolling onto her stomach. "It's not brain surgery."

"Okay, *60 Minutes*," I finally offered after way too much thought for such a benign question.

Julia cleared her throat and eyed me.

I exhaled, wishing she didn't know me so well. "Fine. *True Blood*," I muttered into my soda can. "I like vampires and *True Blood* is my favorite TV show, okay? I loved it till I hated it."

"That's it?" Lilah sneered. "That's what took you so long?"

"Interesting dichotomies," Henry said to me. "I loved it till I hated it," he quoted. "Elaborate."

I liked the way he was leaning forward, almost on the edge of his seat. He certainly had a way of making it feel like he and I were the only ones in the room, just like that night at the party when we'd talked for the first time. I hadn't forgotten how that made me feel…caught off guard, but in a pleasant, curious way. He was making me feel a lot of new things lately.

But we weren't the only ones in the room now.

"I wasn't dichotomizing," I said. "Merely speaking facts."

"What's your answer, Henry?" Julia asked.

"*Seinfeld*," he said, propping his feet on the coffee table. The gray, taupe, and blue diamonds on his argyle socks matched the navy blue V-neck sweater he was wearing. We all looked at him, surprised by his answer. "It's the thinking man's sitcom. Timeless. Even in syndication heaven."

Huh. Who knew?

I also learned that Dart used to row crew at Duke until he tore his shoulder. In addition, his likes were: walks on the beach, tennis whites, and John Mayer. Coincidentally, so were Julia's. Or maybe that was no coincidence. Maybe they were one of those gaggy perfect couples. The only thing they seemed to not have in common was PDA. While Dart was willing to show his affection at any time, Julia was the sweet and bashful type. Though if I had to bet, I was sure she let loose when they were alone.

"Favorite song to sing in the shower?" was the next question on the table.

"I don't sing," I stated.

"Neither do I."

This answer from Henry brought loud hoots from Dart. "You lie, man!"

Henry's stern expression held fast as he glowered at his housemate.

"I've actually been getting a little more sleep these past few mornings," Dart went on, "without you making your normal morning racket."

Henry actually flushed. "I said I *don't*—"

"You do! Personally, I enjoy your rendition of 'Put A Ring On It.'"

"Dude," Henry muttered, dropping his chin, massaging the back of his neck.

"But I believe you're most impressive when you hit the high notes of 'Livin' on a Prayer.'"

"I think…" Henry said. "I think we should move on."

Dart stretched his arm toward Henry, hand in a fist. Henry only regarded it impassively. "Dude…" Dart coaxed. Henry leered at the extended olive branch, laughed under his breath, then bumped fists with his best friend.

"Favorite piece of classical music?" This was my question. I found it interesting when asked in the right company and when answered honestly. Actually, I'd run out of questions. Henry was up to answer first, but he didn't right away, so I answered for him. "*Clair de Lune*. Right?"

"How can you possibly guess something like that?"

"Elementary." I took a swig of Diet Coke. "Put ten men in a room and play ten different pieces of classical music, six will say *Clair de Lune* is their favorite. There was an actual study." I gave Henry a look. "At *Duke*, maybe."

He folded his arms. "Rudimentary research," he accused, but I could tell he was trying not to smile.

"I don't disagree." I pulled up my feet to sit cross-legged. "It's the same theory if you were to ask those same ten men what their favorite flower is. Seven will say iris, but only if you show them a picture."

Dart seemed confused at first, but nodded in agreement after thinking it through, probably picturing an iris. "Yeah," he said. "She's right about that one, too" He pulled Julia close. "I *love* irises, sweetie." He kissed her temple. "How do you know that, Spring? Another research project?"

"Sort of," I said. "Men can't help it, they're naturally attracted to the iris flower because it looks exactly like the inside of a woman's—"

"Spring," Julia cut me off. A moment later, however, she pressed her lips together and laughed under her breath. Dart was watching her, looking confused but amused. The subtle subconscious connection evidently hadn't occurred to him yet. Henry, though, was chuckling heartily into both hands.

"Three guilty pleasures?" Julia asked, then she and Dart gave their answers and cuddled. Lilah sneered out something about Amsterdam.

While pondering on the subject, I ran my index finger along the top of my can. *Three guilty pleasures?* If I was going to be honest, this would take some thought.

"Sports/Talk radio," I began, counting off the answers on my fingers. "Strawberry frosted Pop Tarts, and novels."

"French novels?" Henry asked.

"Gross—no." I cringed at the insinuation.

"Not *those* kinds. I meant like the one you were reading when we ate breakfast together at the café."

This caught Lilah's attention. She dropped her cell, sat up and glared at me. Her acrylic fingernails were like claws as they dug into the knees of her designer jeans.

"British," I explained. "Nineteenth century."

"What's your favorite?" Henry asked.

"Why?"

"I'd like to know."

"More of your polite conversation?" I asked, tilting my head. "Nothing else to do because it's raining?"

Henry laughed and leaned forward. "You remember me saying that?"

"Kind of hard to forget."

Lilah had risen onto her knees, glancing from Henry to me then back at Henry like she was watching a tennis match.

"So?" Henry prompted. "What's your favorite book?"

"*The Scarlet Pimpernel*," I answered, trying to ignore Lilah's icy glares, which was difficult, as I could actually feel them. "What's yours?"

"*To Kill a Mockingbird*. Why *The Scarlet Pimpernel*?"

We needed to move on before Lilah really did stab me, but I didn't think Henry would let us until I gave an answer. "Well, for one reason, I like how it mocks the evil of the bourgeoisie."

"You have a problem with the wealthy social class?" he asked. "Maybe it was the French revolutionists who needed to be mocked."

"Ha! Talk about oversimplification." I folded my arms. "It was the aristocrats who caused the war. Those people were excessively concerned with respectability and success and money." I looked directly at Henry. "Sound familiar?"

He shrugged. "That's no crime. It was how ten generations were taught to live."

"And that's an excuse? Wait, let me guess, that was how *you* were taught to live."

He took a beat. "I learned a lot from my father."

Even from across the room, I could see he was trying not to smile. Deliberately pushing my buttons, and enjoying it. "Ya know what, never mind." I threw my hands in the air.

"Are you declaring defeat?" Henry asked. "Again?"

I felt a flush creep across my cheeks. "There are other people in the room," I said after clearing my throat. "I'm sure they're not interested in this dysfunctional conversation."

"I am," Dart said.

"Me, too," echoed Julia. "You guys are more entertaining than *The Real Housewives.*"

I sighed. "Have you even read the book?" I asked Henry, more calmly.

"He doesn't read novels anymore," said Dart. "French or otherwise."

"Anymore?" I asked, picking up on that word. "But you said *To Kill a Mockingbird.* Why is that your favorite? Or was?"

Henry didn't answer right away. His elbows were on the arms of his chair, his fingers under his chin. After a few long moments, I thought that maybe he didn't want to share his answer. Maybe it was something personal. But how could that be? It was just a story.

"I think enough top secret information has been divulged tonight," I said, breaking the silence. "I'm done playing."

"About time," Lilah muttered. "Henry, want to watch a

movie?"

"My mother read it when she was a teenager," Henry said, picking a piece of lint off his lap. "*To Kill a Mockingbird.* The day she accepted my father's proposal, she gave him a copy and told him that Atticus Finch is the kind of father she wants her husband to be."

Oh. Well…frack.

My insides went all weak and spongy as Henry Edward Knightly, III, and I gazed at each other. I felt weird, the same flutter in my chest that I'd experienced the first night I met him, coupled with what felt like a hot air balloon inflating inside my chest, pushing against my heart.

"Atticus Finch," I said, "is arguably the most memorable father in western literature."

Henry tilted his chin, appreciation in his eyes. I swear I could taste cranberries on the back of my tongue.

"But you do realize," I added quickly, "that he was such a remarkable father because he was a widower."

Henry blinked, his gaze moving to the empty space next to me, then dropping to the floor. For a frantic moment, I wondered if he was angry, or worse, hurt. I had no knowledge of his parents. Maybe his mother had died and he really was being raised by a widower. And there I went making an insensitive crack. I wanted to staple my mouth shut.

"Touché." When I glanced at Henry, he was grinning. "Please remind me to call home later and tell my parents what you said." He closed his eyes and laughed as if replaying my words in his head. "That might be the funniest piece of literary insight I have ever heard. A *widower*." He rocked with laughter. "Classic."

"Are we done with this?" Lilah groaned.

"I'm not nearly done," Henry said, tilting his head just enough so I could see him looking down at her. Then he tilted his chin to me and winked.

I'd been winked at plenty of times before, but never had the attention felt like actual intention. That flutter was back in my chest, my palms were tingling, and I couldn't look away from the man in argyle.

"We're almost finished, Li," Dart assured his sister. "We still have to get Henry's answers first. Three guilty pleasures."

"Oh, yeah, umm." Henry pulled himself forward, fingering his chin. "Let's see. Harley-Davidsons, comic books, and…" He raised a lightning-quick smile at no one in particular. "And a certain woman who's not afraid to tell it like it is. *Definitely* my guilty pleasure number one at the moment." He slowly moved his eyes toward me and winked again. "Oh, and cranberries."

The chair beneath me, the floor, the whole world seemed to melt away and I was hovering, floating, suspended in mid-air, secured in the atmosphere by Henry's eyes.

The room went silent, and I became very aware of how hard my heart was beating. I could hear it behind my ears. Could everyone see it through my shirt? I dragged my gaze to the front window, studying the leaves moving under the porch light, willing my neck and cheeks to not turn red, willing myself not to spring from my chair and—

"I would have thought clearcutting is one of your guilty pleasures, Henry." Lilah had addressed him but was staring at me.

"Clearcutting?" I repeated.

"I *thought* that might piss you off, Spring," Lilah said, looking and sounding terribly pleased with herself.

"Don't tell me you're *for* that," I said to Henry. "Even after all we know?"

He folded his arms. "There's no evidence that—"

"Yes, there is. And you know that. It's in my research. We've talked about it. A lot."

"That study from the University of Oregon is riddled with holes and fictions. And didn't you once compare the situation to *The Hunger Games*?"

"You're seriously bringing that up?"

"I'm bringing it up because your facts are wrong."

I sprang from my seat. "Stop saying that."

Henry was on his feet, too, meeting me in the middle of the room like we were two boxers. "This is what we call a debate, Spring," he said. "We're exchanging ideas, improving each other's knowledge base. Or didn't they teach you that at Occupy Wall Street?"

"Oh, good one," I said, getting right up in his face. "Real mature."

He took in a deep breath then let it out, placing his hands on his hips. "We were talking about this the other day. Nature has its worthy place, but there is no evidence that cultivated and harvested timberlands are any less healthy than forests left to themselves. Our former president worked with legislators for eight years to resolve this very issue."

"This isn't a debate," I pointed out. "You're lecturing me. Again."

He kept talking, practically right over me. "More than fifty percent of wild fires burn down old-growth trees."

"Exactly!" I exclaimed. "The trees burn down because people like *you*"—I poked his chest—"keep screwing with the environment. And for the record, that *former president* of yours is a *moron*…if you'll pardon the expression."

His face drained of color. After a moment, he parted his lips, shifting his jaw back and forth. "Spare me your liberal opinions," he said, reaching one hand up to massage the back of his neck. "And the word *moron* is not an expression. So who's the moron here?"

I knew my face was red, if not purple. Knightly turned around and mumbled something under his breath that I couldn't hear.

"What did you say?" I asked, staring at his back.

"He called you pigheaded," Lilah answered with a sneery smile.

"Lilah," Dart said in a warning voice. "Stay out of this."

She shrugged and examined her nails. "That's what he said. I heard it."

"Really." I glared at Knightly when he finally turned around. "That's what you called me?"

He looked me dead in the eyes. "The shoe fits, doesn't it?"

"Okay, okay." Dart cut in, stepping between us like a referee. "You're both badasses and overly opinionated, and we're all impressed."

I was so ready to go upstairs and put this night out of its misery. Julia and I were going home tomorrow. It couldn't happen soon enough.

"You called her something else once," Lilah said. "What was it, Henry? Oh yeah, a dirty hippie."

"Lilah!" Dart snapped. "I think you'd better shut up."

I stared at Knightly, waiting for him to say that he'd never call me something so offensive…waiting for him to say anything in my defense. But he didn't speak. After a long moment, he wasn't even looking at me.

As reality set in, the room around me turned bright white, then it tilted to the side. My eyes felt dry and stingy. I slammed them shut, pressing a hand along my brows.

How had this happened? How had I allowed myself to let down my guard? Sure, I needed his help with my research, but I shouldn't have begun to think of him as a friend, someone who understood me like no one else.

"Spring, are you okay?" Julia asked.

"Fine," I muttered. "Good night."

"Don't go. Not like this."

"Let her go if she wants," Lilah said. Her eyes narrowed as they held on mine. "Henry, I need to talk to you about something important, anyway," she added, still staring me down as I headed toward the stairs.

Chapter 13

Behind the locked door, I turned the faucet on full blast, and dipped one hand under the tap, focusing on the way the track lighting over the mirror distorted the shape of my fingers beneath the stream of water.

Distracted for the time being, my breathing grew more stable. I grabbed a towel and ran a corner under the water. My eye makeup smeared down my cheeks as I rubbed it over my face. I dropped it into the sink and stared at myself in the mirror.

It had been ten years since I looked like *this*: the flushing cheeks, the flaring nostrils, the overall scrunchiness of my face. Yep, I was about to cry.

But I wouldn't.

Getting into a stupid argument with Knightly did not warrant tears. I'd known from the beginning what I was getting into, and just because he could be charming and warm and human was no excuse to have gotten close, close enough to allow him to hurt my feelings so deeply that I felt actual pain in my chest. If I got burned by backfire, I had no one to blame but myself.

After shutting off the water, I climbed onto the counter and sat with my feet in the sink. Time ticked on, but I wasn't ready to leave the bathroom. It was the only room with a lock. So I memorized every ingredient listed on the back of the bottle of mouthwash behind the mirror. *He should really use a kind with no alcohol*, I found myself considering. *I can always recommend my brand—*

But no, I couldn't. In fact, barring any accidental run-ins with him in the kitchen, I could probably get away with not speaking to him for the duration of my sentence under his roof, and if not for one or two more research sessions, perhaps for the rest of my life.

A knot twisted in my stomach. When my eyes caught their reflection in the mirror, I winced at who stared back. If I'd seen some other girl looking as shattered as me, I would've sworn she was severely depressed.

I slid off the counter and onto the rug. My teeth were brushed and flossed with more time and care than necessary before I switched off the bathroom light and quietly creaked open the door.

Usually lit by an overhead light, the hallway was pitch-black. With my first step out into the dark abyss, I crashed into a large object right outside the door and lost my footing, momentum spilling me forward. Someone caught me right before I was about to face plant on the carpet, and together we rolled to the floor.

"Are you okay?" Knightly whispered. His arms were all the way around me, holding me in a tight grip as we lay in the middle of the hallway.

"*What* are you *doing*?" I hissed, sitting up and scooting away, untying our tangled limbs.

"Waiting for you. I've been out here for an hour." His voice was still low, and I wondered if everyone was asleep.

"You could've knocked if you needed in," I said, copying his quiet tone.

"I don't need in. I need to talk to you."

As my eyes adjusted to the dark, I noticed that he was bare footed. He wasn't wearing his sweater anymore, either, just the light blue collared shirt that was underneath it. It was un-tucked now, unbuttoned a quarter of the way down, and rolled up to his elbows.

I bit my lip, annoyed with myself for taking the time to notice what he was wearing and how many buttons were undone.

"It was wrong of me," he said, "what I said to you earlier."

"Which part?" My vision was becoming more accustomed to the dark, and I could see his eyebrows were knit together.

"All of it," he said after a moment. "Probably."

I nodded, not knowing how to respond, or if I had to respond at all.

"This is my home," he continued, "and you are my guest, and…"

And?

"And I shouldn't have said what I said."

I wasn't sure if he was attempting to apologize, or merely pointing out that he had perhaps made a slight error in judgment by first insulting my beliefs, and then by calling me a moron, pigheaded, and a dirty hippie.

"Any reply?" he whispered.

I had nothing to say.

"Are you angry?" he asked.

I lifted my chin, looking directly at his shadowy face. Apparently my expression answered his question.

"Right." He nodded a few times. "You should be angry with me." His mouth twisted into an uncomfortable smile. "We all have our hot issues, and it just so happens that you and I have one in common…in *opposing common*."

He put a hand on my arm. I flinched and banged my elbow against the wall behind me.

"Why is this so difficult?" I grumbled, rubbing my sore funny bone. "Why do you enjoy tormenting me and making my life miserable? Why is that?"

When he chuckled, I pushed his hand off my arm.

"Oh. I thought you were being…" He examined me more closely, his head cocked to the side. "I don't enjoy *tormenting* you, and I'm certainly not trying to make you miserable. That's the last thing I want."

A dull pain of loathing for both him and myself made my brain achy and exhausted.

"But clearly," he added, "you think I am, so I must be guilty on both counts."

"Why do you always talk like a bottom-dwelling lawyer?" I growled softly.

"Practice makes perfect?" He was trying to joke, but I was having none of it.

"*Fils de salope. Tu es tellement arrogant*," I muttered, as I stared at the dark wall over his shoulder. I didn't mind my French being extra vulgar, since I knew he didn't understand. "*Quelle connerie.*"

"*Je suis impressionné.*"

My eyes shot to him. "*Excuses-moi*?" I replied automatically. "*Tu m'as compris*?"

"*Oui*." His expression was poker-faced while he lifted a small, apologetic shrug. "*Je parlais très bien français depuis de nombreuses années, parce que j'aime voyager et...comme tu sais, le français est la langue d'amour.*"

Stunned into silence, I could only gape at him.

"*Tu es sans voix, le Printemps. Quel est le problème*?" His accent was perfect, elegant, incredibly sexy...which really ticked me off.

"I *don't* have a problem," I murmured, purposefully answering his question in English.

"Don't be embarrassed. Your French is very good, especially the curse words."

"I asked you once outright if you were studying French, and you said no. You lied?"

"I'm not studying French now. I've been fluent for years."

"Splitting hairs," I grumbled. "I'm sure you'll be a great lawyer."

"Listen, there's something you should know about me." He took a beat, waiting until I was looking at him. "I never lie." It almost sounded like a promise.

This man sitting across from me, I had no idea who he really was. Was he the amoral hypocrite Alex made him out to be? Or was he the devoted brother who I'd heard Skyping with his younger sister for an hour on Thanksgiving, and two hours the next morning? Was he the forbearing comrade who allowed himself to be openly roasted by his best friend? Or was he the habitually arrogant pain in the ass who had nothing but condescending things to say?

Or…perhaps he was that magnetic, congenial guy who took time out of his demanding law school schedule to help me. The guy who could turn my logic to mush with just one kiss.

The truth was, I didn't know. He'd made me smile once tonight—then kicked me in the teeth.

I was tired of the roller coaster, tired of the war.

"Why can't you just apologize for making me look like an idiot?" I finally said. "And then we'll be done with each other forever."

"You weren't the one who looked like an idiot. *I* was. And…" His voice dropped lower. "I don't want to be done with you forever." He placed a hand on my arm again. I didn't mind this time. "I am sorry. Will you please forgive me?" He squeezed my arm, reminding me that he was near. But that was impossible to forget.

"I don't want to fight anymore," I whispered. It was the only thing I could think of to say. And it was the only thing I knew I really meant.

"Neither do I," he replied with another squeeze.

"Then we won't, okay?" I said. "Because I need you."

Henry's eyes went wide, and the pressure of his hand on my arm grew heavier. "Spring."

"For research," I quickly added. "I need your…help."

"Oh," he said. "Of course. Whatever you need, for as long as you need. I'm here for you."

He stared down at his hand on my arm. When his thumb swept across the inside of my elbow, it felt like my skin lit up. His gaze moved back to my eyes, and on his face was an expression I'd seen a few other times. It wasn't his charming smirk or his annoying lecturer's leer. Henry was looking at me like a man looks at a woman.

For a change, I didn't force myself to turn and retreat. In fact, I was caught in a gravitational pull, curious about what the next moment would bring…

"Heeeenryyyy?"

Unfortunately, the next moment brought Lilah, her abrasive voice calling from downstairs. "Are you awake?"

He withdrew his hand from my arm and pressed a finger to his lips. "Shhhh."

I nodded slowly, in complete agreement.

But Lilah was unyielding. "I heard something. Is that you?"

Henry sighed and craned his neck to look toward the stairs. His thick voice answered her in the affirmative, but that he was on his way to bed. Even at two in the morning, I could smell his aftershave, his soap, his hair gel. His scents were like a cloud around my head, making me woozy. Being this close to him, in the dark, was like hearing Bruno Mars. I needed to get out of there.

My stirring caught his attention. "Are you leaving?"

"It's really late," I said, though I didn't move away.

"I guess it is. Thank you for"—he ran a hand through his curly hair—"well, thanks."

"You're welcome." I still didn't move, not ready to leave. But I couldn't just sit there, wondering if that moment we'd shared would ever return. So finally, I padded down the carpet around me, making sure I hadn't dropped anything during our earlier tumble. I found my phone down by our feet.

"Any men in there?" Henry asked, eyeing the device in my hand. "Singers, I mean."

"None."

"Never?"

"Not *currently*," I emphasized.

"Why is that?"

"Do you really want to get into it right now?"

He laughed quietly under his breath. "Probably not." He eyed the phone again. "No Linkin Park?" I shook my head. "Tim McGraw?" I made a face. "Justin Bieber?" I dropped my chin, gazing at him through my lashes. "How about Long Kiss Goodnight?"

My heart gave one hard, painful thud then seemed to stop cold. "*Now*?" I gasped, choking on the single syllable. "We probably shouldn't, I mean…we —"

"Oh, uh no," he said. "That's the name of a band. Long Kiss Goodnight."

"Oh. Yeah. I know." *Good grief. Pull it together, woman.*

Henry was quiet for a moment, then snagged my phone. "Give me this thing," he said, standing up. "You'll get it back in the morning with a new playlist. Allow me to educate you."

Without another word, he walked to my bedroom, returned a few seconds later with my laptop under an arm, stepped over me, and disappeared into his room.

Chapter 14

"Ms. Honeycutt?"

The back of my head whacked against the wall when I jumped. I opened my eyes and blinked a few times, dragging my mind to the present, focusing on Masen's face sticking out his office door.

"Come in," he said.

I tore out my ear buds—the sweet sounds of a new-to-me Maroon 5 song still running through my head. Was it any wonder my mind had drifted?

After a deep inhale and swallow, I eased myself to my feet, prepared to focus on the most important meeting of my college career.

This was our first appointment since he'd rejected my outline rewrite back in October. Since then, I'd worked like crazy. After a while, I could see what he was getting at when he'd broached the subject of the new angle. Now, my theory had a depth and richness that had been missing before.

Potential.

I hated to admit it, but Henry's help and insight had kind of made all the difference. In fact, I wouldn't be where I was without him. After Thanksgiving, it wasn't as though we were miraculously eye-to-eye—we still didn't agree on key issues—but it was like the distrust and tension were gone. Another kind of tension had taken its place, however. And I could never really look at him without tasting the tang of cran—

"Take a seat."

I jumped again, then lowered myself into an old leather chair across from my professor's messy desk. He had a hard copy of my new outline in one hand and was rubbing his chin with the other. We were apparently skipping conventional pleasantries, because Masen dropped my paper on his desk and jabbed a finger right in the middle.

I gripped the arms of the chair, bracing myself for bad news.

"Better," he said.

I breathed and unclenched my balled-up toes. "Thanks."

"I'm impressed that you took my advice. I wasn't sure you would about something like this."

"No," I said, "you were right. I needed a new perspective."

"It needs work but I definitely think you're on the right track." He passed my paper across the desk. "I made a few notes."

A few? The thing looks like a rainbow threw up on it.

"But I really like this part." He drew a circle around section three.

"You do?" I said with a smile, still feeling so relieved that I wanted to stretch across the desk and kiss him. Kiss anyone! Who can I kiss?

"Tell me." He leaned back in his chair. "Who have you been working with on this?"

My throat went dry, thinking of exactly who I wanted to kiss.

I tried very hard to stay in the present, to concentrate on Masen's words for the next half hour, but even when we were done and I was back at the library, my mind kept hopelessly drifting, drifting, drifting…

"Hey."

I jerked my gaze from my notebook to find Mel staring down at me.

"What are you doodling?" She walked around the table to take a better look. "Is that argyle?"

I stared at my paper. It was indeed a cluster of argyle diamonds. "No, it's, uhh." I quickly scribbled over the sketch. "Pizza."

"Pizza?" She examined the doddle again. "Wow. You really suck at drawing."

"Right?" I laughed, closing my notebook. "I guess I'm hungry."

"Well, then, let's chow."

"I can't," I said, dragging over my laptop. "I've got a paper due and two tests to cram for. I'll be here all night."

Mel pulled at the back of my chair. "You have to eat, babe. Come on. We'll hop over to your place and I'll cook for you. How does that sound?"

She didn't have to threaten bodily harm to convince me to get out for a while, to eat something solid before I pulled an all-night study session. She wasn't the best chef in the world, but the thought of someone cooking for me did sound incredibly comforting.

After not much of a fight, I allowed her to lead me home.

• • •

"And it's also a maturing experience," I said. "I'm learning a lot about myself and the world around me."

"Watch out for the car!" Mel yelled.

I froze in place, one foot hanging off the curb as a pickup made a tight turn around the corner. After it passed, Mel grabbed me by the arm and yanked me back. "Pay attention to where you're walking," she said. "You're in La-La Land."

"I'm not in La-La Land," I defended. "I was just—"

"You were *just* talking about Henry Knightly."

Was I? I thought I was talking about school.

"So?" I said defensively, zipping up my coat, suddenly regretting being dragged from the library.

"So, I haven't seen you for two weeks." She dug through her book bag, her hand resurfacing with a tube of pink lip gloss. "I want to hear about you." She applied the shiny tint to her lips.

"I *am* telling you about me."

"Oh?" she blinked and dropped the gloss in her bag. "Oh," she repeated with an accompanying nod. "Okay. Continue. But without stepping into traffic, please. You were saying it's a maturing experience to hang out with Henry."

"Yeah," I said, trying hard to remember where my earlier train of thought had been headed. "That's how I'm looking at it," I added, dipping one foot off the curb. Mel narrowed her eyes at my daredevilness.

"Last I heard, you were about to jump off the Golden

Gate because he was the only person willing to help with your thesis." She linked her arm through mine and pulled me to the middle of the sidewalk as we walked toward my house.

"That's still true."

"But you're spending all this time with him."

"It's called research."

Mel's expression bent in confusion in the gathering twilight. "I thought you hated the guy."

"I never said that."

She thought for a moment, biting her lip. "Are you still fighting?"

"We disagree but we don't *fight*." I paused, considering if this was wholly truthful. "Not anymore. We kind of made an agreement about that. We're more productive now."

A blue BMW drove toward us. It slowed, and Julia waved from the passenger side, Dart behind the wheel. All shiny teeth and shiny hair, they were a commercial for Old Navy. He honked the horn; Mel and I waved back.

"Disagreeing with Henry is natural. We're so different," I continued, then laughed at just how understated that was. "You know me, and you know how Henry is."

"Not really," she said. "I don't know him. Not as well as *you* do."

I rolled my eyes, ignoring her vocal inflection.

Mel stopped walking to dig through her bag again, swearing impatiently under her breath. "I know I have a Kit Kat in here somewhere."

"Chocolate before dinner? How unlike you."

"Better than a cigarette," she grumbled. "I quit smoking last week. Ah-ha!" She pulled out a candy bar and held it up like the Olympic torch.

"You *quit* smoking? When exactly did you start?"

Mel tore open the candy bar wrapper with her teeth. "The week before that."

I laughed. "Anything to get you off the dreaded cocoa bean."

"It's a vicious cycle," she said, taking a big bite, eyes closed, sugar being absorbed into her blood stream, endorphins all abuzz. The candy bar was gone in approximately three bites. She wadded up the empty wrapper then grabbed her phone. "Tyler's calling again."

"Ah." I smiled. "The elusive summer boyfriend in Washington. When will I get to meet him?"

"I'm going to pretend I didn't hear that." She shot me a withering glance. "I've been inviting you up to my grandparents' house for ten years. Just say the word and we'll go." She smiled down at her phone and texted something. "What I wouldn't do for seven minutes in heaven with Tyler right now."

"Classy, Mel."

"Speaking of," she said as we neared my house, "how does Alex fit into the steaming and beefy pot of testosterone stew you've got simmering in your Crock-Pot?" She eyed me up and down.

"I haven't seen Alex in a few weeks," I said. "Not since—"

"Thanksgiving. I know." Mel's words had an I-told-you-so behind them.

When I huffed, I could see my breath. "To answer your question, Melanie, Henry and I don't discuss Alex Parks, okay?" I actually felt my chin sticking out, like I was appalled at having to explain myself.

We crossed the street, passing by a frat house. A group of guys were outside playing Frisbee wearing only shorts. It was dark and freezing. Mel stopped to gawk.

"I don't particularly care about whatever happened between Henry and Alex," I added, "and I'm sure Henry doesn't either." I broke off, worried that I might have said too much. As far as I knew, Mel had no knowledge of their turbulent history, and it wasn't my place to share.

"Very diplomatic," Mel said. "You should run for office."

We stopped in front of my house. No lights were on. Across the street, the black Viper was in the driveway, parked crooked like always.

"So, if you're not allowed to argue," she said, "that means there's no political discussions between you two, no money talk, no women's lib, no Alex. What do you guys *do* in that tiny study room? There's not even space enough to... Ohhh." She grinned and hooked her arm through mine. "Does he brush his teeth first? And use mouthwash? He looks like he has a very clean mouth." She moaned and stared off into space. "Mmm, I bet it's like kissing a tunnel of minty freshness, right?"

"What?" I exclaimed. "I haven't been kissing Henry Knightly!"

The front door across the street slammed. Mel and I jumped about a mile. I whirled around to see Henry standing under the porch light, wearing a black leather jacket. No doubt, there was some form of argyle attached to his body.

"It's a little early for you to be home, isn't it, Spring?" he called out, pointing at his watch. I felt Mel tighten her grip on my arm. "Don't tell me all campus libraries burned to the ground."

Without bothering to look at her, I knew Mel's curious eyes were glued on me, studying my every move. I could practically hear her panting as she waited for my answer. Henry was halfway across his lawn now.

"I have a study group in an hour," I called back.

"Stopping home for some tofu first?" he asked as he changed direction and started walking toward his car.

"Funny," I muttered. I heard him laughing.

The Viper's car alarm chirped twice and its lights winked. Henry ran a hand through his hair. It was extra curly tonight, like he'd let it air dry after a shower.

"Holy-mother-of-sexy," Mel whispered. "Seriously, Springer, he's hotter than the friggin' Sahara. Look at that body and that face…those lips. How can you not jump his—"

"Shut *up*," I hissed.

"Are we still on for tomorrow night?" Henry called, pulling open the door of the Viper.

I snuck a quick glance at Mel. She was gawking at me now, waiting for my answer. "Um, yeah," I said as he climbed in his car.

"Bye, Henry," Mel sang, her voice high-pitched and childlike.

He regarded Mel blankly. "Right. Take care, now."

After he closed the door, Mel broke from me and doubled over laughing.

The Viper's engine roared to life, and Henry revved it a few times, the tailpipe emitting gray exhaust. It wafted up, blending in with the night fog. He backed out of the driveway then straightened out. I couldn't see him through the dark tinted windows, and after he drove past, I let out an exhale. Mel was still wiggling her fingers after him.

"Stop that," I snapped, slapping her hand. "He's going to think—"

"What?" she asked eagerly.

"Nothing." I laughed, bumping her shoulder. "You're such a ho-bag." I was relieved Mel hadn't circled back to the kissing thing. I didn't know how I'd explain Thanksgiving morning. Me covered in cocoa powder and Henry with cranberry sauce running down his face…our mouths—

"So you're going out with him tomorrow night?"

"It's not a *date*."

"Aren't you going to the lecture on campus? The keynote is the lady who chained herself to the redwood tree. I thought that was right up your alley."

"I *am* going."

Mel took a beat. "Henry Knightly is going with you to the tree lady?"

I rubbed my nose. "He said he was interested."

Mel tossed her head back, erupting in cackles. "Oh, babe. *That* is the funniest thing I've heard all day." Cold breath billowed from her open mouth like smoke from a chimney. "So if the two of you aren't talking about all his money or his sweet butt, and you refuse—for some insane reason—to tear off those designer suits and have your way…what do you do?"

"His sweet butt?" I repeated.

"Yes, and don't dodge the subject. This is fascinating. So? What do you do?"

"Well, when we're not studying, we talk music sometimes. He was appalled when he learned I'm listening to strictly female singers." This seemed like a good subject, because Mel perked up.

"You're still on that all-chick musical kick?" she asked.

"I was until he confiscated my phone on Thanksgiving and added a new playlist. All men." I made a face.

"Anything good?"

My left hand was in my coat pocket, my thumb absentmindedly running over the face of my phone. I felt a jolt, almost as if my fingers knew what was in there.

"Um, yeah, there're a couple tolerable songs," I admitted. "I was going to delete the whole playlist right away but thought it would be rude, since he took the time to load it."

"Aww, how polite of you. Especially since none of his songs interest you."

"Yeah," I mumbled, wishing I hadn't brought up the subject.

"I don't know, Spring. I've seen guys flit in and out of your life. To most of them you don't give the time of day, and the others, like Alex, you treat like your personal scratching post."

"Ew."

"I've never known you to be your *real* self with a guy. Not lately." She paused. "Not ever, actually. You and Henry have an interesting relationship."

"We're not in a relationship," I countered. Mel was starting to bug me. I walked to the mailbox and wrenched the face open.

"I'll put on some water for the noodles," she said, walking up the porch steps.

I nodded as I sifted through letters. A few seconds later, almost naturally, my attention tiptoed across the street. On the second floor, the window of the second bedroom was glowing yellow. *Henry left his light on again. I swear he does that on purpose, just to make me march over there and give him another lecture about wasting energy.* I sighed and walked inside my house.

When I peeled off my coat and entered the kitchen, Mel was perched on a stool with one elbow on the breakfast bar, her hand cupping the side of her head. I didn't appreciate her inquisitive eye.

"I'm starving," I said. "Where's the food you promised?"

"Pasta water's on the stove." She swiveled around on her bar stool. "But first things first, babe." She lifted her open hand. "Where's your phone?"

Chapter 15

Stalling wouldn't be any use, not with the way Mel was staring at me, an impatient gleam in her eyes. Reluctantly, I reached for my coat, wishing I hadn't shared so much with her on our walk home. I searched from pocket to pocket, though I knew exactly where my phone was located.

"I told you," I said over my shoulder, hedging, "I think I might have deleted his playlist already."

By the eager smile Mel was wearing, I knew she wasn't buying it.

As I pulled out my phone, she hopped from her stool and was at my side in a flash, her palm level before me.

"Fine," I said. "You can *see* it."

She grinned with excitement, grabbed my phone, and ran a thumb across the face. A second later, the lights illuminated.

"Huh," she said, her finger working the menu. "His playlist appears to be the last set of tracks you were listening to. Crazy, no?" She lifted her twinkling eyes. "Unless you have another playlist entitled *Spring's Education of the Male Voice.*"

"Oh, right." I rubbed my ear. "I *was* listening to it a while ago…while I was…waiting to see a professor and…and it distracts my thoughts, which, you know, I need sometimes."

Mel ran a finger down the list of ten songs, just as a sizzling sound across the kitchen caught my attention. I left her and went to the stove to turn down the burner. Water was bubbling and splashing from the pan of boiling noodles. I stirred the contents then checked under the lid of the smaller pot of red sauce. Mel continued to examine the playlist, while I chewed impatiently on the inside of my cheek.

"Interesting array of artists," she finally offered. "But I don't recognize any of these titles."

I stabbed a fork into the middle of the noodles, twisting it around until a hardy serving broke away. "I think he made them up," I said, folding the noodles in with the sauce, although suddenly I had no appetite. "I mean, track one is the guy from Fleetwood Mac but it's obviously not called *Meet Me in the Tall Grass.* And track two—"

I shut my mouth when Mel Cheshire-Cat-grinned. A second later, she spun around to exit the kitchen, jamming in an ear bud.

• • •

I sat alone at the bar for as long as I could stand it, my dinner untouched on the counter.

"Oh, my holy mother of crap."

At least Mel was talking now, if only rhetorically. It was the ten minutes of preceding silence that was really getting to me.

"Are you *joking*?"

Her outbursts from the living room were similarly irritating. Finally, after her third eruption, I took my bowl of vegetarian spaghetti and walked into the living room. All the lights were out. Mel was curled at one end of the couch, knees pulled in. She didn't notice me, too busy concentrating on whatever song was playing, a confused expression wrinkling her face. I could tell by the way she moved her finger across the face of the phone that she'd started that particular track over. A smile pulled at a corner of her mouth.

I lowered myself into the arm chair across from her, taking a bite of noodles, chewing slowly, watching her advance to the next song. It played for about five seconds before her jaw dropped. Tearing one ear bud from her head, she called toward the kitchen. "Springer! Get your butt in here, pronto!"

"I'm sitting right here."

Mel shrieked and jumped.

She stared at me as I calmly took another bite of noodles, chewed, swallowed, then dabbed the corners of my mouth on a napkin.

"So you…you *do* realize what this is," she said at last.

I thought for a moment then shrugged, slurping in a single noodle.

"Have you asked Henry about these songs?"

"I thanked him when he gave me back my phone the next morning, but he hasn't brought up the subject since."

"Spring." She rolled her eyes. "For someone with all your brains, you can be exceptionally dense."

She'd lost me.

"Babe." She held up the phone. "These are make-out songs."

Now was my turn to wear the stunned expression. "No, they're not."

"Babe." Her voice was unbelieving as she pointed down at the thin, silver rectangle in her hand, as if its mere existence were evidence.

"Henry Knightly did *not* make me a playlist of make-out songs," I maintained.

"Yes, he did."

I snagged the cell out of her hand. "No." I stared down at it. "There's no Marvin Gaye or Prince or…or Barry White."

"Is that your idea of kissing music?" she asked. "Not very original. Not like Henry's list. Shhh, new song." She pressed a hand over the one remaining ear bud. "Daaamn."

She had it all wrong. I knew this, because I knew Henry. At least I thought—

"He's a *genius*," Mel blurted. "These are way more subtle than Marvin Gaye. Trust me." She skipped to the next track. "Ohh, double damn. Come here." She grabbed my arm and yanked me down beside her. "Put this on." She jammed an ear bud into my head then started a song. "Listen to this while picturing Henry, then I dare you to look me in the eyes and tell me you don't feel like straddling him."

I did as she asked, if only to ease my own mind. When I felt the first uncomfortable sputter of my heart, I glanced at her. Her eyes were closed, head back, fanning her face. "Minty freshness," she murmured.

More like cranberry sweetness, I almost corrected.

"I'm deleting these," I snapped, pulling out my ear bud. I went to grab my phone, but Mel held it over her head, out of reach. "Melanie Gibson," I said through gritted teeth. "Give it to me."

She stood up and shook her head, her brown ringlets bouncing as she took a step back. "I'm probably totally wrong about it," she insisted. "I'm sure your nice, respectable, Republican neighbor didn't mean *anything* by it." She smiled like an idiot.

Choosing not to continue the debate, I walked my half-eaten dinner into the kitchen and dumped it down the sink.

Later, after Mel left for home, I sat in the dark living room, tucked in two ear buds, and played track one, with Mel's theory on my mind. Before the end of the first chorus, my throat had gone dry and I stared down at my phone, amazed at how completely dense I'd been all this time. I skipped to track two, then three. By the time I'd listened to the entire playlist, my palms were sweaty and a funny, impatient feeling spun inside my stomach and chest. It might have been lust, it might have been panic.

Either way, I did not feel in control of my emotions. And I needed to be in control—that was the whole point of my making all the big changes last year. I was taking control, steering my life. And if Henry's choice of a simple Rob Thomas song from ten years ago made me feel so severely *out* of control that I really *did* want to straddle him instead of study, then it needed to go.

Right before I left for campus, I plugged my phone into my computer and deleted all ten tracks.

Chapter 16

The muffled curse from outside my window made me laugh.

"You okay down there?" I called.

"Fine." The hammering started up again.

I snickered and packed a pair of jeans and two sweaters into my duffel bag. No Doubt was quietly streaming from my laptop on the floor.

With only the moon and a small flashlight to guide him, Henry was outside, having volunteered to fix the loose rung on the rope ladder that hung outside my window. Then he went on to MacGyver some hooks to keep it secure against the house. Every once in a while the hammering would abruptly stop, and I'd hear murmurs of swearing.

After about twenty minutes, Henry's fingers curled around the edge of the sill, and he was halfway through my window, hammer between his teeth, like Rapunzel's prince. Once inside, he slid the glass closed.

"You're sure it's done?" I asked skeptically, hefting

my bag toward my open bedroom door. "If you've booby trapped it to unravel under my weight, I'll sue."

"You'd never win," he said matter-of-factly. "I'd bury you in technicalities." He set the hammer on the ledge of the window, glanced around the room, and rubbed the back of his neck. He seemed distracted, which was odd for Knightly, though this glimpse into his awkwardness was not entirely unappealing.

"The burden of proof is on the state," I defended, wondering if a little more lawyer talk would make him more comfortable.

"Precisely my point, I'm good friends with the D.A.'s office."

"Aren't you the legal eagle," I said, crossing the room, pushing in drawers as I passed.

"All packed?" he asked, finally stepping away from the corner by the window. He'd been in my bedroom once before, so I figured his preoccupation had nothing to do with his surroundings.

"All packed, you?" Henry nodded. "Do you want a soda or something? There's plenty downstairs."

He shook his head. "Do *you*?" he asked abruptly, like he'd suddenly remembered his manners. "Or would you like to go out? Get something to eat?"

"It's almost midnight, Knightly." I pointed at the neon red numbers on the alarm clock. "We've both got to leave at the crack of dawn."

"True," he said, finally smiling, though he still seemed preoccupied. "I'll go." A bit hesitantly, he turned toward the window.

"You *can* use the front door, everyone's awake downstairs.

I think they're going out later. Or you can stay up here for a while. Hang out, if you want. Unless you're tired." I fanned my face. "I'm wide awake. Leftover adrenaline from my last final."

"Same here," he said. We turned in unison toward my window, hearing sounds of night-before-vacation *soirées* down the street.

Henry smiled again, more genuinely this time. "Definitely staying." He shrugged out of his jacket. Underneath was a black sweater with gray, blue and green argyle diamonds on the front.

Argyle is something of a lost art, I thought as I watched him drape his jacket across the back of my desk chair. *But dammit all if Knightly doesn't pull it off.*

"Mind if I change the music?" he asked, pointing at my laptop, though he didn't wait for an answer. Lowering to the floor, he ran a finger over the touch pad. "Where is my playlist?"

"Corrupted," I said. "The tracks suddenly wouldn't play, so I had to delete them." I really hated to lie, but honestly, after what Mel had insinuated, Henry's songs kind of freaked me out.

"That's strange."

I picked at my thumbnail. "Uh-huh."

"Well then, I guess these will have to do." He sat back on his heels and continued scrolling through my iTunes library. "Janis Joplin," he said, wincing. "Seriously?"

"Sometimes it makes me happy to be furious." I sank onto the floor beside him. "Now, if you'll allow me." I reached over and took control of my laptop. "I will educate *you*."

Two hours later, my sweater was off. So was Henry's.

And his shoes. My glowing laptop screen and the street lamp outside my window were the only sources of light in the room.

"I quite like your coffee house girls," he said. "Your Sara and Ingrid."

"Better than Fiona Apple?"

Shoulder to shoulder, we lounged on my imitation sheepskin rug in front of my laptop. As I reached to adjust the volume, Henry grabbed my wrist. His hands were more calloused than I would've thought, yet his grip was gentle. A surprisingly nice combination. I didn't mind it anymore when he happened to touch me. It didn't mean anything. We were friends, study partners...who happened to have shared one kiss about a million years ago. Since Masen had approved the second draft, my research sessions with Henry were probably over. I wasn't sure how I felt about that.

"Much better than Fiona Apple." He grimaced, hadn't cared much for Fiona or Hole or early Alanis. Too much blatant feminist angst for him. "Your people can do better."

"*My* people?" I said, sliding my hand out from his hold around my wrist. "That's an incredibly chauvinistic thing to say."

He groaned. "You know that's not what I meant."

I screwed up my eyes, fighting back a teasing smile.

"Another of my idiosyncrasies requiring improvement?" he asked. I nodded. "Duly noted." He winked and rolled onto his stomach, reaching to scan to another song.

Since that incident in his dark hallway, Henry and I hadn't shared another romantic moment. Not even close. I considered that a blessing—after all, I couldn't be expected to take studious notes while he talked if I was constantly wondering if he tasted like cranberries. Things were better this way. Like I'd told Mel: a maturing experience.

Most of the time, Henry was pretty entertaining to hang out with. His constant oozing of self-confidence had been annoying at first, but the more time we spent together, the more natural that feature was. He wore his convictions well. Relaxed and confident was not an altogether disgusting combination.

He was reading off the track list of an album, making critical yet pretty hilarious comments under his breath while I silently gazed down at the back of him stretched across my white rug. I couldn't help it. He was right there, making me stare.

He wore jeans tonight. A rarity for him. And a pleasure for me. Earlier in the evening, he'd pulled off his sweater, and what remained was one of his million-dollar plain white T-shirts. It was V-neck. Fitted. Very nicely fitted. His hair was as tousled as I'd ever seen it. He had a cowlick in the back that was always smoothed down with gel. Tonight, dark curls poked up in some places while falling carelessly in others.

He turned a bit, and the profile of his jaw and cheek caught the light.

Zowie.

Weeks had passed since I'd allowed my thoughts to remember him as that stunningly beautiful guy outside Julia's window. To me, he'd become like a faceless and bodiless Unix. Tonight, however, any blockhead could see that Henry Knightly was chiseled from the very stones of Mount Olympus. Bedeck him in chain mail and fleece and he was Adonis, Hector, Odysseus…with just a touch of Fifth Avenue.

"Knightly?" I whispered to his back, though I had no idea what I wanted to say.

"Honeycutt?" he answered.

Nope, not a clue.

"Yeees?" he replied a second time.

Still watching his profile, I sighed again and finally responded with, "You're clueless."

He craned his neck to leer at me over his shoulder. "And yet you're here with me in the middle of the night. What does that say about you?"

"That cluelessness isn't necessarily indicative of intellect?" I rattled off, having a difficult time thinking straight or seeing anything but his twinkling brown eyes. His tousled hair. His mouth.

Henry chuckled. "Appalling habits we share, don't you think?" he said as he rolled onto his knees.

"What habits?"

"Presuming too much," he began. "Wrongfully judging. Doubting our own eyes." He rubbed his jaw. "That's the worst of the bunch, isn't it?" He pressed play, and music filled the space between us. He'd just downloaded a new song. Bruno Mars.

"I…" My mouth was suddenly dry. "I just remembered something."

Henry blinked up at me when I stumbled to my feet. "What?"

"Um…Coos Bay is getting a lot of moisture this winter," I said, backing up toward my door. "I'm just going to run downstairs and get my raincoat so I don't forget to take it home."

"Okay," he said, maybe wondering why I suddenly had

to be out of the room.

The moment I was down my creaky stairs, I pressed both hands over my heart and exhaled. After a few more breaths, I felt better, calmer. My head was clearer, too. Maybe I'd been breathing in his cologne or something. That should be my next rule: no hanging around guys who smell like heaven. Or play me Bruno Mars. I really needed to make a list.

I grabbed my coat and was back in my bedroom a few minutes later, but Henry wasn't down on the rug where I'd left him. He was in the corner by the window, his phone at his ear.

"Yeah." He paused to laugh then noticed me. "Okay, okay, but look, I gotta go. See you later."

I glanced at my alarm clock. "Who was that?" I couldn't help asking.

"My father."

"It's three in the morning."

"Not where he is."

I folded the coat across my bag. "You're not spending the holidays with your family?"

"I am," he said. "I just remembered something that I wanted to run by him."

I sat down on the rug. "But you didn't spend Thanksgiving with them," I suddenly remembered. *I* hadn't gone home because home was depressing, but why hadn't Henry left?

"It wasn't worth traveling overseas," he explained, taking his same spot at my side on the floor. "During the shorter breaks, I sometimes go to my extended family in LA and Washington, cousins, aunts, grandfather." He shrugged. "Or sometimes I'll go with Dart to New York. So, anything happening downstairs?" he asked, turning on a new song.

Why did I get the feeling he was trying to change the subject?

"Dead quiet," I reported, leaning back against the bed frame. "Anabel is out for the night, and I'm guessing Julia is with Dart at his place or they're in her room."

"Really?"

"You sound surprised."

"No, I…" He scratched his chin. "She was over earlier today and I caught part of their conversation. I didn't think they were hanging out tonight."

I almost laughed. Julia had been looking forward to tonight all week. She'd even had another "chat" with Anabel, though who knows what came of that. I couldn't help feeling excited for Julia.

"Why are you smiling?" Henry asked.

"Oh." I cleared my throat. "Nothing, nothing. What song is this? Turn it up."

• • •

Sounds from the street had ceased hours ago. Henry laid stomach-down on my bed with his head hanging over the edge, while I lolled comfortably on the floor. I could hear his even pattern of breathing above and thought he was asleep.

Which was why his question startled me. "What do you want out of life?" he asked.

"Pass." I cracked one eye open to find him frowning down at me. "Topics like that are outlawed for us, remember? No more arguing."

He bent his elbows and placed them flat on my bed, chin on top of his hands. "I'd really like to know, though. Tell me."

He chuckled and rubbed his eyes, adding, "Please?"

From his tone, I knew it wasn't wittiness he was after, it was information. I could give him that. "Well, if you must know, I want to change the world."

Even though it was dark, I could see he was smiling. "That's a pretty tall order. Do you have a plan? Besides spreading the joys of sustainability, I mean."

I couldn't help laughing. "That's definitely step one. And since step one could take the next twenty years, I might stick with it for a while."

Henry laughed quietly and ran a hand over his face. "I like your answer very much," he said, his eyes following me as I sat up. "And I use the word *like* because I can't think of another verb to do the sentiment justice."

I smiled in the dark, amused at how I'd grown so used to his verbal formality.

"I'm all for you changing the world," he added.

I couldn't help feeling a little glow, and was grateful for the dimness of the room in case I was blushing. "Speaking of change, it's getting late." I handed him his crumpled scarf that I'd been using as a pillow. "Or *early*, I mean." I flexed my bare feet out in front of me. "We're both leaving in, like, two hours."

"Right," Henry said, running his index finger and thumb over his eyelids. "I guess I should go now." I didn't think he'd actually been asleep, but he did seem distracted again, like there was something he wanted to say but hadn't. He'd behaved the same way when he'd climbed through my window six hours ago.

He slid off the bed and onto the floor beside me. After a yawn and stretch, he bent forward, leaning across my legs.

I wasn't sure what he was doing, until I realized he was reaching for his shoes.

His left shoulder pressed against my right. Even in the half-dark, the definition in his reaching arm caught my attention. Tight tendons stood out on the inside of his elbow and forearm as ropes of muscles flexed and contracted every time he moved. His T-shirt stretched against the hard ball of his bicep. I didn't see Henry in short sleeves often due to chilly Bay Area weather. I was enjoying the view.

He grabbed his shoes and straightened, his shoulder still touching mine. I bent my knees and scooted a few inches back, giving us both a little space. Henry eyed me as I moved away.

"Before I leave," he said, fumbling with the laces on one shoe, "I'd like to tell you something—two things, actually, if you don't mind."

His voice sounded thick, hesitant, and his cadence was more formal than usual. I excused this, blaming it on how we'd just stayed up all night even after a week's worth of stressful finals.

When he lifted his brown eyes to me, there was a softness in them that I recognized. The next thing I knew, it was like we were back in his hallway, legs entangled on the floor, Henry's hand on my arm. But this time, my music was playing in the background, we were on a sheepskin rug, totally alone, no roommates to disturb us, no Lilah to interrupt.

"What," I whispered, "do you want to tell me?"

I thought I knew. I hoped I knew. I was petrified that I knew.

Henry scooted forward, and I automatically leaned in

to meet him. Part of my brain thought it was strange how I wasn't trying to stop, while another part was relieved beyond belief.

He blinked his long lashes and pulled back an inch. "What was that?" he whispered.

"What was what?"

Henry's eyes flashed to the window, both of us hearing the same rustling from the other side. "Wait," he cautioned as I rose to investigate. I felt him hold the back of my shirt for just a second, maybe cautioning me, but I didn't heed the warning.

The first thing I noticed was that I'd forgotten to haul in the ladder after Henry had been working on it earlier tonight. I hadn't locked the window on the inside, either. I stood before the glass and peered outside. It was pitch black at almost five in the morning, no hint of sunrise. Only my reflection showed as I slid open the glass and leaned over the ledge.

A wet pair of lips crashed against mine.

I gasped and hit the back of my head on the frame, staggering away from the window.

"How's the sexiest girl on campus?" Alex was halfway through the window before I could do anything.

"Stop," I hissed. "What are you doing here?"

"On my way back to the Frat house. Saw your shades open." Effortlessly, in swung his legs, followed by his lanky body. "Thought I'd drop on in, ya know? Like old times." Grinning ear to ear, he bowed, his long arms going to my waist. I could smell a fraternity party on his breath and clothes.

"Alex, *don't*," I growled, pushing my elbows against his

chest. I had not forgotten who was behind me, witnessing from a front row seat. Freeing myself as much as I could, I turned around, hoping, actually, for a little help.

But Henry just stood there, his jacket draped over one shoulder, staring at me.

In his altered state, it took Alex a few seconds longer to notice Henry. When he did, he chortled softly and swayed back on his heels. "On your way out, Knightly?" he slurred, his voice a mixture of laughter, smugness, and nerve as he threw one arm around me. "I'll take it from here. Buh-bye."

A muscle jerked in Henry's jaw, but he was no longer looking at me. "Leave," he said. His voice sounded threatening, and the look in his eyes was more than hostile.

But Alex didn't move. He was actually...smiling.

Henry's eyes shifted to mine. "Tell him to leave your house and never come back."

"Why?" I couldn't help asking, a little alarmed by his sudden aggression. I mean, I knew they had a history, bad blood and all that. And Alex waltzing through my window was certainly unwanted and a little creepy, but that was my problem, not his.

Henry didn't answer me for a moment; maybe attempting to control his anger. "Spring," he finally said, echoes of his stern, lecturing voice that drove me insane, "tell him to go. You do not want to be alone with him."

I was about to ask him why again, but the fury on his face made me stop. When he released a sharp exhale and glared at Alex, I knew my words weren't needed. So I stood still, not knowing what to expect. A fight? Would some punches be thrown? Maybe I'd hear some impressive swearing out of Henry.

But without a word, he turned and was gone out the door. Temporarily paralyzed, I could only stare after him, expecting him to reappear, *hoping* he would reappear. But then I heard the front door slam and my stomach hit the floor.

"Good riddance, douchebag."

"Hey," I growled, swinging around, torn between running after Henry and dealing with Alex. When Alex grinned, folded his arms, and leaned against my desk, the priority was clear.

"How dare you just show up here?"

"Come on, Spring," he slurred.

"No, listen to me. This is totally inappropriate. He's right, you need to leave."

Alex snorted. "Why?"

I was too exhausted to get into anything heavy with him and too bewildered by Henry's behavior. He said I shouldn't be alone with Alex, and yet hadn't he just taken off and left us alone? I would think about that later. Right now, I needed this presumptuous frat boy out of my bedroom.

"Alex, you're drunk. Go home and sleep it off." I just wanted him gone, the smell of him, the sight of him…all of him, just *gone*. I was almost willing to drive him back to the frat house myself, but after a moment, he shrugged and began crawling out the window.

Not trusting him to actually go, I kept my eyes on him the whole way down the ladder, never losing track until he stumbled around the corner. Then my gaze automatically shifted to the house across the street. Henry's bedroom light was on and it looked as though the blinds had just moved back into place. My impulse was to slide down the ladder and try to explain myself, explain that I didn't make it a habit to let Alex Parks—or any guy—in my bedroom at five in the morning. But before I could get one leg through the window, his light went out.

Chapter 17

"Was your whole family home for New Years?" I asked, reaching to take the plate Julia was holding. "All six kids?"

"Yep," she answered, then clicked her tongue. "Yes-sir-ree bob." She kicked the empty dishwasher closed. It wasn't a violent action, and yet it was. Julia was seldom moody. It was probably jetlag—she'd landed pretty late last night. Or maybe it was the stress of the upcoming semester. Classes were starting again in two days.

"How was your vacation?" she asked as she walked around the kitchen, mindlessly opening and closing drawers. "Did you have a nice time at home?" The lilt in her voice was forced. She grabbed a sponge and began scrubbing the already clean sink.

I sighed at her question. My family—not exactly my favorite subject. But Julia didn't seem to want to talk about her Christmas vacation, so I pulled up a bar stool and sat, drumming my fingers on the island. "My mother apologized the entire time, thinking there weren't enough gifts under the tree. Like any of us cared."

Julia nodded, scrubbing away at nothing. She hadn't bothered pushing up her sleeves, so they hung over her hands, soaking wet. It was then that I noticed she was wearing the baggy pants to a tracksuit and a faded black T-shirt with a gray long-sleeved shirt underneath. Her hair was tied in a loose ponytail. No socks, no shoes, no makeup.

"Robby and Curtis were completely obsessed with the high school playoffs," I continued for the sake of conversation. "I love my brothers, but they really do drive me mad."

Julia didn't answer, didn't seem to be listening. I watched as she cleaned both sides of the sink, ran the disposal with nothing in it, held the sponge under hot water, rang it out, then tossed it in the dish drainer.

"Oh, and get this." I slid off the stool and leaned against the counter. "They went to visit my dad, my brothers did." I paused and stared at Julia, waiting for a reaction. After a moment, she lifted her eyebrows. "I know, right? So random." I straightened a row of mugs. "I guess he wants to make amends or whatever. He's getting remarried this summer. I don't know. They wanted me to go to visit him too, but no way. Not after all this time."

It still stung when I thought about it. Robby, Curtis and I were supposed to be in it together, a team against getting hurt by Dad again. If they wanted to reconcile, I guess it was just me now.

"Anyway," I added, not wanting the bitterness to spoil my mood, "we didn't kill each other, and there was hardly any blood." I smiled. "So all in all, it was a successful

Honeycutt holiday."

Julia lifted a smile at the conclusion of my familial anecdotes. It was forced and insincere, but at least she was no longer scrubbing her fingers raw. She bent over the sink, eyes closed. Some of her hair spilled forward, falling loose from the sloppy ponytail. Her shoulders were lifting and falling, very measured breathing, and I wondered if she was contemplating being sick.

Okay, this was no jetlag. She'd seemed okay when I was talking, so I reached for a new subject. "Where's Anabel?" I asked. Our social butterfly roommate's calendar was probably already full, even on the day she returned from vacation. Evidently my question was rhetorical, because Julia broached her own.

"Have you heard from Alex?" she asked, picking up that over-used sponge.

I yanked it from her hand.

She turned to me, puzzled. "Well?"

"Well, what?" I tossed the annihilated sponge in the trash.

"Alex?" she prompted.

"Oh. Uh, no. But actually, I'm inviting him over tonight." My stomach made a roll, as I wasn't too jazzed about seeing him. The winter break was only two weeks long, but in those two weeks, I'd made a couple of decisions, decisions that still surprised me. Alex would need to know about one of them, since it involved him, and someone else we both knew.

"Tonight?" Julia asked.

"I'm giving you a heads up because I know you and Dart don't feel comfortable around him. You might want to hang out across the street."

Julia's face went all scrunchy, and I saw the first tear.

"What's wrong?"

Her hands flew to her face, covering her eyes, sobs breaking from her throat. "And I thought it was weird," she began, already in the middle of a story, "to not hear anything all that time." She backed into a corner of the kitchen and slumped to the floor. I joined her, sitting on my knees.

"It didn't work," she muttered tearily. "It just didn't work."

I hadn't noticed before, but her eyes were bloodshot with dark circles rimming the bottom lids. Looking at her made me wince. "What didn't work?" I asked.

"She told me to play hard to get, but...but..."

"Who told you?" I asked, touching her shoulder.

"But I think it made him mad. I don't know what...what happened." The last word barely squeaked out before the weeping took over.

"Bunny, it's okay."

"No, it's not. Because he didn't call me, not for a week."

"Who?" I wasn't following her at all now.

"I mean, we've been together every day for four months. Every day, Spring. And then he doesn't call for a week? Not even on Christmas." She sobbed through a sarcastic snort of laughter. "Who does that?"

"Oh." Dread rolled in my stomach. "Dart?"

She sniffed and nodded. "So I finally called him. I mean, I can, right? I'm *allowed*. This isn't nineteen fifty."

"Sure," I said, trying my best to follow.

Julia yanked down a dishtowel from the sink. "At first he didn't say much of anything," she said, wiping her cheeks. "But I know him, Spring. I *know* him." She shot a fierce look at me. "He's in my blood! I gave him everything, every part of me. Do you understand?"

I nodded, even though I had no idea what she meant.

What I did know was this: In the four months they were together, I'd never seen two people happier or more compatible than Julia and Dart. To anyone who was fortunate enough to be caught in their love wake, it was obvious these two people were made for each other. Dart may have been more animated about it, but I knew Julia's heart—its tenderness, its complete devotion—and I knew it belonged to Dart.

"He said…he said he thought we should take some time apart," she continued, her lower lip wobbling. "I was shocked; I didn't know what to say." Misery and fear blazed behind her eyes. "I don't need *time*. I need Dart." Her lips sealed in a broken frown. "We *shared* things, Spring, *new* things." She lowered her head, voice dropping. "Something I can never get back."

Oh. So they had slept together. No wonder she was so shattered. First love, first sex. My heart broke for her all over again as my mind raced, searching for answers. It didn't make sense, though. First of all, why would Dart not call for a week and then breakup over the phone? Not at all his M.O.

"*Je ne sais pas…Je ne sais pas,*" Julia murmured as she crumpled into a ball, hugging her body.

I did my best to calm her, floundering words of comfort and encouragement about men snapping back like rubber bands, but honestly, I was just as confused.

"I want him back," she cried. "I want him back *here*. Once he's here we'll work everything out."

Classes were starting soon, which meant Dart would return to town any minute. I stroked her tangled hair, silently joining in her confidence. If there was some mistake, surely it would be cleared up two seconds after Dart was in the presence of Julia, falling in love with her all over again.

"Let's get you upstairs," I suggested.

Julia's body was weak and tense, but she nodded. Just as I was about to gather her up, the front door opened and slammed shut.

"Spring? Have you heard?"

Good gracious, woman.

A few seconds later, Mel rounded the corner into the kitchen, nearly tripping over our huddled mass. "Oh." She frowned down at Julia. "Looks like you just found out."

Being my best friend notwithstanding, sometimes Mel lacked tact. I gave the still-weeping Julia a tight squeeze before I stood. "This isn't a good time," I hissed at Mel. "Something's wrong."

"Damn straight," Mel said, gawking down at Julia. "Why didn't she know before now?" She turned to me. "Why didn't *you* know?"

"What are you talking about?"

"Dart." She bit her lip. "Gone. I swear, I thought you knew, I thought—"

"Gone?" Julia blurted. "What do you mean, *gone*?" Her porcelain face was blotchy and tear-stained as she stared at Mel. "Where's Dart?"

Mel opened her mouth but didn't speak for a moment. "Moved out," she finally said, sounding a little guilty. "I heard it just a few minutes ago f-from"—she bit her lip—"from Lilah."

My heart stopped cold when Julia gasped. It was a primal sound, like a wounded animal. I never wanted to hear it again.

Mel leaned toward me. "Why didn't Julia kn—"

"Zip it," I hissed. "Give me two seconds to think." I pressed my fingertips over my eyelids. "Okay, okay, I need to call Henry. He'll know what's going on. He'll—"

"Springer." I felt Mel's hand on my shoulder. "They're both gone." It took a moment for her words to register. "*Both* of them."

I didn't bother taking the time to rearrange my expression of shock before I lowered my hands.

"He didn't say anything to you?" Mel whispered.

I opened my mouth but only shook my head.

"Apparently," she said, "Dart is spending this semester operating a YMCA-type place somewhere overseas. Lilah didn't tell me where Henry went, but she kept talking about some castle and Switzerland. That sounds like a place he would go." She shrugged. "All I know is the house across the street has new tenants this semester. They're gone."

I tried to remain calm, tried to *not* show that it felt like I'd just been slapped. What I was going to tell Alex tonight, and what I'd hoped to tell Henry five minutes after that… It was all for nothing now. I took a deep breath, needing to collect myself. There would be a later time and place to process what that meant to me. Right now, there was a greater problem at hand.

"Jules?" I said, slowly approaching her.

She lifted her head and stared up with blank eyes, strands of red hair tangling in her tears.

"I'm sorry," I whispered.

Her eyes searched my face for answers. But I had none.

"I'm so sorry." I lowered myself beside her and slid an arm around her trembling shoulders. She leaned her head against me and quietly sobbed, while I stared at the wall, trying to remember what it had been like before my feelings changed, wondering why my chest felt like it had been hollowed out with a spoon.

Part III

Spring

"They're certainly entitled to think that, and they're entitled to full respect for their opinions…but before I can live with other folks I've got to live with myself. The one thing that doesn't abide by majority rule is a person's conscience."
From *To Kill a Mockingbird*

Chapter 18

"Spring. A word?"

I stood in place, my backpack hanging off one shoulder. "Shh"—I choked on my own tongue—"Sure, Professor Masen." I smiled as brightly as possible while walking with dread toward the front of the emptying classroom.

He sat at his desk, doing the chin rub. "We're three months into the new semester. You've canceled our last two appointments and missed a deadline."

"Oh, uh, I know. I'm…" I was about to say I was going through a personal crisis, but how lame was that? And I couldn't very well tell him the truth—that I'd lost interest in writing my thesis. Not something you should admit to your advisor.

Despite the skipped appointments and deadlines, I was hoping Masen hadn't noticed. But evidently, I wasn't that lucky.

For the past few months, I'd been having trouble concentrating. Things weren't coming as easily as they should, and every single one of my professors had it in for me—I could tell. I didn't know how I'd managed to get so far behind, which subsequently added to the stress. One minute I was in full-blown panic mode, and the next, I couldn't be more indifferent. Either way, I was not being productive.

Masen cleared his throat. "You've been...what?" he asked, attempting to finish my unfinished sentence.

"I've been...really busy in my other classes," I fudged. "Anthropology is kicking my ass."

He read something on his computer screen that I couldn't see. "You're taking a really full load again this semester, but it isn't too late to drop a class."

"Drop a..."

"You only need fifteen units to keep your scholarships."

"I can't drop a class," I blurted, indignant at the very suggestion.

My professor gazed up at me and leaned back, his ancient chair squeaking. "Then I suggest you fix whatever is broken," he said. "Time is running out."

"I know, and I will," I promised, even though I had no idea how to repair what was wrong with me. I couldn't even name it. I was afraid if I fed my symptoms into WebMD, it would spit out that I had a broken heart.

• • •

I usually didn't get car sick, but this particular stretch of highway on the way up to Washington was twisty and turny like a roller coaster. I half expected to look over and see Mel with her hands off the steering wheel like we were taking a corkscrew at Six Flags.

"Mel," I said, my right hand holding onto the grip above the door while my left pressed against my churning stomach, "I swear to you, if we hit an on-coming truck and actually live to tell about it, I'll run you over."

She took a hand off the wheel to tilt her white sunglasses, but she didn't slow down.

"Why are you in such a hurry? Spring break is a full seven days."

"Thought you were in a rush to get out of dodge," she said, her glasses perched on the tip of her nose. "If I may quote you." She cleared her throat. "'I will go anywhere, to the world's end, with you, Mel.' That was two days ago. Changed your mine already? How fickle."

She let her foot off the gas and we slowed way down. The car behind us honked.

I glanced through the rear window. "I'd just like to arrive in one piece." The car was now tailing us. It honked again as we continued to decelerate. "Mel, have you ever heard of road rage? It'll be bad enough if we splat into a tree, but to get shot, too?"

"Overkill?"

"Ya think?"

Mel laughed and floored it, the tires of her Jetta squealing against the concrete.

She'd been inviting me up to her grandparents' house for years. I'd always turned her down, due to papers and projects and protests. But this time, I was more than happy to take her up on it, even though picking up and leaving for a week when I should've been catching up on homework was not the most industrious of decisions. But I'd done it anyway.

I closed my eyes and rubbed my temples. When I opened them again, a mile-marker sign whizzed by. We were somewhere in the middle of our journey. Three hundred more miles to Vancouver, Washington.

Yes, this little vacation was just what the doctor ordered, if that doctor was of the philosophy of running away from your problems. I needed space, I needed to clear my head, and I needed to get back on track. Somehow, somewhere, I'd fallen off course. When I'd made the big change the last time, I'd switched majors, braided my hair, and figuratively burned my bra. I had no idea how to deal now.

I swallowed down the pukey mass bubbling up my throat. "Are we there yet?" I whined.

"We're stopping in a sec. I'm in desperate need of sustenance—more specifically, a candy bar."

"What happened to the one you brought with you?"

Mel's brow furrowed. She reached back to the floor behind her seat, pulled a plastic shopping bag forward, and sat it on her lap. She sifted through it, keeping one hand on the wheel.

"Huh, I could've sworn…" She lifted her sunglasses so she could see into the bag more clearly. "I had *two*, actually," she mumbled, bemused. "There're only wrappers now. Didn't… Wasn't… Ohhh." She let out her breath, smiled in extreme relief then went back to looking glum.

I stared at her for a moment, absolutely befuddled, until I realized how Mel's train of thought was just plain impossible to follow sometimes. "Uh, yeah, what's going on over there?" I asked, tracing circles in the air around her face.

"I just realized I had one of my daze-outs."

"Daze-outs?" I echoed, wondering if I should make her pull over so I could drive.

"Yes, I've recently raised a new theory about me and junk food."

"Ahhh. I'm all ears."

"It's quite simple, really. Someone offers me chocolate cake or donuts or something, I kind of black out, then come to and I'm covered in crumbs and feel like I want to barf, and yet I have no recollection of eating anything. It's the strangest thing. We've been on the road for four hours and I've already scarfed two candy bars, Spring. I don't even know what kind they were, but they were good, I think. Like I said, I don't remember."

"You should write this up for *The New England Journal of Medicine*, get that publication you've been after."

"Don't make fun of me; I'm dead serious. Have you seen how much weight I've gained? Six pounds since summer."

"No!" I gasped mockingly. Mel had a fabulous body. "Don't feel too badly. I've gained four."

"Really? You don't show it."

"I have my own theory about that."

"Listening," she said, accelerating to pass an RV.

"Well, you know that I'm a huge fan of the invention of the light bulb, yes? And no one loves the second gen iPad more than me."

"Keep talking."

"But I am *convinced* that the greatest invention of our time is the lowrise, dark denim, bootcut jean. Hides absolutely everything."

"Oh, babe, you are so right. Cheers to that." She held up

a can of Diet Coke, toasting herself.

"Look, there's a 7-11. I have an overwhelming craving for a Milky Way."

In lieu of pulling over to a restaurant and getting a healthy meal like two normal people, we stocked up on junky snacks. My driver opted for three chocolate bars and a Big Gulp of Diet Coke with two shots of lime, while I limited myself to a six-pack of mini powdered donuts and a frosty glass bottle of cream soda.

"How's Julia these days?" Mel asked. There was a glob of chocolate on the tip of her nose. "I haven't seen her in weeks. Does she really wear Dart's underwear around the house?"

"That's disgusting. Where did you hear that?"

"People talk."

"They shouldn't."

"Stupid minds will believe anything," she said.

I took a long drink of soda, bubbles clogging up my throat. "To answer your question… Oops, ha-ha, that wasn't me"—my words came slurring out between two carbonated belches—"I am not going to gossip about my roommate."

Mel snickered through her chocolate-covered teeth.

"I mean, I *love* Julia, but sometimes…" I hiccupped, feeling slightly intoxicated from sugar. "Well, I *will* say it's been a tough three months for all of us, and just leave it at that."

"Oh, Spring, honey, that's so *sweet*," she cooed in sarcastic pity.

"What's sweet?"

"You"—she pushed out her bottom lip—"thinking I'll just 'leave it at that.'"

I hiccupped.

"You're in my car, babe," she added. "You must pay the piper, and you know the toll. So Julia's finally stopped crying all the time, true?" she asked, questioning me like I was her hostile witness.

I nodded, taking another swig from my long-neck bottle.

"She's going to her classes and not flunking out yet?"

"*Yet*"—I held up one finger—"being the operative word here." I tossed the last donut in my mouth and took my time chewing. "I'm sure the worst is over."

Truth be told, life with Julia these days was no picnic. That once sparkling and cheerful liveliness had completely vanished from her countenance. The Julia we loved was crushed and hidden somewhere beneath the frail, dejected creature who spent most of her free time moping around the house, though *not* wearing some guy's boxers.

At the beginning, and in some minute way, I shared in Julia's grieving, but the more time that passed, the more I was convinced that everything had happened for the best.

After a few more innocuous tidbits were shared, I said, "I feel pukey."

Mel grimaced. "So do I. But I have one more question." She looked down at her lap covered in crumbs and wrappers. "Where am I? And what happened to all the candy bars I just bought?"

"That's two questions."

An hour or so later, I was pecking at my phone. Three e-mails from Julia, one short note from my lab partner, and an ad wanting to fix my erectile dysfunction. Okay…?

No other messages.

My heart sank like a rock, but the next second I was absolutely livid with myself. I hated when an aftershock snuck up on me like that. After three months, I'd hoped they had stopped.

Henry was gone, hadn't said good-bye, and never contacted me again. I bit the inside of my cheek and stared out the window at the layers of green hills and pine trees. Even in my most cynical moments, it was impossible to deny how much that hurt. We'd been going somewhere. At least I *thought* we had been. And then it was like a rug was yanked from under me. Bits of my life went flying into the air and even after three months, I hadn't been able to gather them up. Some, like school, I was slow to confront.

One night on campus, I could've sworn I'd seen him by the quad. By the time I'd done a double-take, he was gone. Or at least, the tall, dark-haired back that I'd seen was gone.

After that embarrassing display, I'd resigned myself that his moving was the best thing that could've happened. My reasoning was pragmatic: First, I was better off without him. Hadn't his arrogance driven me insane? His mega-conservative opinions exasperated me beyond the pale? Yes.

Second, he'd taken up too much of my time, been too distracting at the end of the semester when I should have been studying for finals and not cooking up stupid questions to ask him just so we could meet to "research." Okay, so maybe that wasn't his fault. I gnawed my thumbnail.

And that car, those stupid suits. He wasn't a lawyer yet, after all.

Yes, it was a good thing, a very good thing. I blinked, realizing that I'd been staring at my empty inbox.

I had another problem now. An almost daily reminder of Henry's absence was Alex's presence. We had a class in the same building at the same time, and there was no escaping him. I didn't end up inviting him over the day we found out Dart and Henry had moved, but we did have that little chat later. My reasons why we couldn't hang out like we used to sounded flimsy and vague, but he'd shrugged me off, protecting his pride, and said we'd always be friends.

Whatever.

After that, he was distant with me and pretty testy. I didn't care, so long as he stayed away. Even though I still didn't know what happened between him and Henry all those year ago, my gut told me who to trust.

As far as I knew, I was the only person Alex told about being expelled from Elliott Academy. But that changed in January. It was like, the second he knew Henry was gone, he couldn't stop talking about how unfairly he'd been treated in high school. And by Presidents' Day, there wasn't a Cardinal within a five-mile radius who didn't know the whole sordid account.

Alex's story also began to include his foe's younger sister, and what a ghastly character *she* apparently was. "A carbon copy of her brother, all right!" Alex told anyone who would listen.

Needless to say, Alex and I drifted apart. Well, *he* drifted while *I* swam madly in the other direction.

"So," I said to Mel as I switched off my cell and set it on my backpack, "I finally get to meet Tyler."

Mel turned to me from the oncoming freeway, face alight. "Ahh, Ty baby." Her mouth split apart in an open smile, then she licked her lips. "He's absolutely delicious."

Here's what I also knew: Tyler was her on-again/off-again boyfriend from years of summer vacationing at Grandma's. He was attending college in Seattle but would also be in Vancouver for spring break. Mel warned me that she intended to spend a lot of time with him. I was fine with that. I'd brought stacks of homework and had grand intentions of hunkering down in one of the spare bedrooms of the Gibsons' home that surveyed the lake. I had a lot of catching up to do.

"He'll curl even *your* toes, Springer," Mel added. "I swear to all that is holy and chocolate that you will faint dead away."

Doubtful. She and I didn't share the same taste in men, and her idea of toe-curling meant nothing more than a good body and straight teeth. Perhaps I'd grown discerning.

"The best thing about him," Mel beamed, "is he's dumb as a sack of hammers. Seriously, the boy gets his current events from Conan."

"That's the *best* thing about him?"

"It's refreshing. After spending months surrounded by eggheads and bookworms—"

"Present company excluded?"

Mel held up her cell. "He's texted twice since lunch. Oh, you haven't forgotten about tomorrow night?"

I groaned aloud, wishing *Mel* had forgotten.

"We'll have a good time, you'll see."

"Fabulous. Just what I don't need this week, a freaking blind date."

"It's not exactly *blind*. Tyler knows him. It's more of a…a…"

"Set up?"

"No, no." She shook her head, probably not wanting to give me further reason to bow out. "Not a set up, I swear! In fact, Ty didn't even know his cousin was in town this week.

Not till last night. Well, actually." She snickered affectionately. "Knowing Tyler, he's probably known about it for weeks and forgot to tell me."

That didn't help. "This *cousin* person? You're expecting me to converse with him for how many hours? Why do we have to go all the way to Portland for a basketball game? Can't we just do a quick dinner? Didn't you and Tyler already have plans for tomorrow night?"

After my fourth sentence, I realized how many questions in a row I'd just asked, so I shut up.

"These new plans are better," Mel said. "I thought the Trail Blazers were your NBA team."

I shrugged.

"It's not even an hour in traffic down to The Rose Garden from Gram's house. Ty's cousin got us floor seat tickets, babe. *On the floor.*"

That was kind of cool, and Mel was right, I was a sucker for the Blazers. The *one thing* my father passed on to me. And I'd never been even close to the floor.

"They're playing the Lakers," Mel added. "You're telling me you're willing to skip that?" She gasped. "Oh, Spring, what if Leonardo Dicaprio is sitting courtside?"

I couldn't help laughing. "If that's the case, I promise I'll give Tyler's cousin a big, wet kiss."

Chapter 19

The blue sky shone bright through the skylight above my head. I was on my back in the middle of the four-poster bed, gazing up, my laptop and three textbooks face-open at my side. This morning had been surprisingly productive. While Mel visited with her extended family, I studied, focusing on social science though *not* rewriting my thesis…which was what I *should* have been doing, but whatever, at least I wasn't trolling Facebook.

"Spring, the guys'll be here any minute," Mel called as she whipped past my door.

I'd been ready for an hour and was now comfortably letting all my reading from earlier sink in. *Machiavelli. Susan B. Anthony. The Cotton Gin…* White puffy clouds rolled by, obscuring my view of blue as evening approached.

My eyes popped open when I heard knocking at the front door downstairs.

"They're here," Mel hollered from the bathroom. "Will

you run down and let them in? Otherwise Grandpa will talk their ears off. He's *mucho* embarrassing."

Some conventional girls would never answer the door for a date, let alone a blind date. I reminded myself that I didn't care about conventions, so I rolled off the bed and grabbed my jacket.

Knock knock knock.

"Coming!" I called to our impatient dates as I headed down the stairs. More knocking. "Jeepers, hold your horses, Dicaprio."

I paused before the closed door, taking an extra second to prepare before I reached for the knob.

A bouquet of bright wild flowers was thrust under my nose. "If you don't kiss me in three seconds, I'll die of death," the presenter declared from behind the garland. When I said nothing, he lowered the flowers, stepped forward, and came within an inch of my mouth.

"Oh." He opened his eyes in the nick of time. "I…I thought you were Mel."

Tyler. Still crowding my comfort zone, he stared at me vacantly, then stepped back and hid the flowers behind his back. "Uhh, she around?"

"Sure." I opened the door wider, a bit stunned. "Come on in."

He was alone.

We walked together to the couch. His little mistake must have unnerved him, because he wouldn't look at me; he kept moving his eyes from the floor to the bunch of flowers on his lap.

"So, you must be Tyler?"

"Yeah," he said after a soft snort of laughter. "We have

a date tonight—me and Mel, I mean, not you and..." He broke off.

When he wasn't talking, I could see how Mel would consider him delicious. The boy definitely had the makings of a Leo, pre-*Titanic*. He had one of those cherubic baby faces that you couldn't help staring at. Huge, round blue eyes, silky blond hair that looked like it was washed with baby shampoo, and full pink lips that I'm sure Mel couldn't wait to sink her teeth into. Heck, I'd almost had the chance.

If this was Mel's date, I was mildly interested in seeing mine.

"I feel so stupid," Tyler mumbled. "Mel will never let me live this down."

"She never forgets the embarrassing moments of a friend," I agreed. "But don't worry, it's our little secret."

Tyler laughed, finally relaxing, then he focused on me. "Have we met?"

"Not before..." I nodded toward the front door. "I know Mel from school. And *home*."

Tyler took a beat, his big blue eyes filling with comical mortification. "Now I *really* feel stupid." He slapped his forehead. "You're Spring."

"Correct."

"I'm so out of it. Jet lag, I guess." Tyler hadn't flown home from Seattle, he'd driven. And there was no time change. Mel was spot-on about him being a cutie pie, and also about that sack of hammers.

"I totally forgot you were coming. Oh, yeah. We're doubling or whatever, right?"

Whatever? I sensed a dark cloud hovering over me.

"With your cousin," I said, hopefully jogging his memory.

"Right." He stared at where his wrist watch would be, but he wasn't wearing one. "He should be here by now." Then he actually looked around the living room, maybe thinking his cousin was playing hide-and-seek. "He's usually punctual."

"Hi, guy."

Tyler swiveled around then sprang to his feet, presenting the flowers to Mel. I pretended to read a magazine while the two love birds reunited, rather boisterously. A few minutes later, Mel dashed upstairs to freshen up and grab a sweater. Tyler plopped down next to me, more at ease.

"So," he said, flicking the magazine in my hand, "I've heard a lot about you." *Lovely.* "Mel's told me a million stories."

"None are true," I sing-songed. "I've heard some things about you, too."

"Those are all true."

The mahogany grandfather clock in the corner struck six. "We'd better get going soon," I said. "You sure your cousin's coming?"

Tyler walked to the fireplace mantel and took down a framed portrait of the Gibson family from about ten years ago. "I haven't talked to him since yesterday, but yeah." He set the frame down then disappeared into the kitchen, returning with a bag of potato chips and a soda.

My stomach rolled, warning me of incoming awkwardness. Mel *had* told me stories about Tyler, many of which ended with him being quite…flaky. The last thing I wanted was to be the third wheel. I could just as easily watch the basketball game on TV. Or better yet, work on my thesis.

"Like I said." Tyler crunched on some chips. "He's always on time. He has the address, but I doubt he's got GPS on the Harley."

"He's riding a motorcycle?" I asked. "In March? In Washington?"

"I know, right?" He didn't seem worried, but that did nothing to ease *my* anxiety. He put down the chips and leaned forward. "Your hair is wicked awesome. How do you get it to do that?"

"They're braids," I said, displaying a single rope. "I pay someone every two months."

"Wicked."

"Thanks." I looked away but could feel his eyes still lingering on me, so I grabbed another magazine.

"Don't you want to know anything else about Trip?"

"Trip? That's your cousin?"

He nodded, still chewing.

"Uh, sure," I answered, letting the magazine drop to my lap. "So?" But Tyler only kept on with the chewing and grinning. "He has a motorcycle?" I prompted.

"Only when he's in town, or at home, I think. Not all the time." He scratched his head. "He keeps his one here in a storage unit. Ha-ha. I guess he doesn't trust me enough to leave it in our garage."

"Is he in school?"

"Back east for a while." He crammed four chips into his mouth. Mildly repulsed at his manners, I was only half listening. Unlike Mel, Tyler was *not* a fountain of information. "He's west coast now—well obviously, right? Since he's coming tonight." He held up one finger. "Wait, I think my mom said something about him being overseas again after Duke. He's always traveling. I can't keep up."

Sounded like cousin Trip might be just as flaky as Tyler.

Flake or no flake, he'd better show up soon. He had the tickets.

"Anyway," Tyler continued, more sureness in his voice, "he was back east, but now he's in California."

"Where in California?" I asked politely, as I flipped to the middle of the magazine.

"Stanford."

I glanced up from the magazine. "Huh. That's where we go." I lowered my eyes and flipped another page. "Small world." After reading exactly two lines of the article about the new renovations in old town Vancouver, my mind grabbed onto something he'd said. A moment later, the magazine began sliding from of my hands, and I couldn't feel my legs.

No.

"Did"—I coughed, my voice strangled—"did you say Duke?"

Tyler nodded.

"And Stanford?"

He kept nodding and popped open the can of soda.

"No way." I swallowed hard and stared up at Tyler's baby face.

My mind grabbed onto something else. Hadn't Henry once mentioned he sometimes spent time with his extended family in Washington? And isn't "Trip" a common nickname for "the third?" I shut my eyes, the rest of my body joining my legs in numbness.

"He's in law school," I muttered, mostly to myself.

"Hey!" He sounded shocked. "How'd you know?"

I waited for his brain to connect the dots. It was slow coming.

"Oh, duh." He slapped his forehead, as if that would help. "I'm such an idiot."

This was confirmation enough and I sprang from the couch. "Mel!" I called from the foot of the stairs, not bothering to hide the panic in my voice. "Melanie Deborah Gibson! Get down here!"

"Five more," she called back.

"No!" I yelled in alarm. "Get down here instantly! You won't *believe*—"

I jumped and spun around at the sound of fist on wood.

Chapter 20

I stared at the front door.

Another knock.

I turned to Tyler, who wore a semi-confused expression, then I went back to staring at that big, brown wooden door, wondering if it was too late for me to run upstairs and crawl out the skylight.

Knocking.

"One of you get that!" called Mel.

I was able to unthaw myself just enough for my legs to retreat the rest of my body to the couch. I sat down, ramrod-straight, and folded my hands on my lap.

"I'll get it," Tyler said, then hollered, "come in!"

The front door creaked opened.

I crossed my legs, uncrossed them, then snagged whatever magazine was closest to me.

"Hey, man," Tyler said as he greeted the new guest. I glanced up quickly, but they were behind the open door. My eyes didn't need confirmation, though. I knew it. I felt it.

"Hey. Good to see you," the visitor replied and I heard him slap Tyler on the shoulder as he entered the house. I stared blankly at the upside-down magazine in my hands.

The cousins chatted briefly by the door then Tyler kind of snorted. "Oh, I believe you two know each other."

I peeked over the magazine just in time to see Tyler step to the side.

Upon seeing me, Henry Edward Knightly, III, turned from white to green to red faster than a strobe light. I thanked my lucky stars that I'd had twenty seconds of preparation. He took less than five to return to his normal color. "Spring," he said after a few rapid blinks, his expression already more composed than mine. "Hey there."

"Hi," I replied, feeling the hair at the nape of my neck stiffen. *Should I stand? Should I stay seated? What's the precedent?*

"This is a surprise." He strolled toward me, hands in his pockets, armed with that illustrious confidence.

"Yeah, for me, too," I said, leveling my chin, my fingers crinkling the edges of the magazine.

I wasn't sure if I was supposed to hug him in greeting, bump his fist or what. Our relationship was never defined. And we hadn't exactly left each other in the best of circumstances. And yet, after three months, it felt as if no time had passed.

For a frightening moment, all those things I'd planned on saying to him the first day we were back after Christmas came rushing forward. The feelings came back, too, or the memory of them, at least. The excitement I'd felt, and the nervousness of stepping into the great unknown. And then the startling disappointment.

"How've you been?" he asked.

"Fine," I said, bouncing my knee. "*Great*, in fact. You?" *Dang, was I always this flustered around him? I don't remember that.*

Henry didn't answer right away, but I could see a smile tugging the side of his mouth. I had no idea what that was about. "Fine, thank you," he finally said.

The guys sat on the couch. Henry was looking at me, and my neck felt hot, so I focused on my nails. Why had I let Mel paint them the color of an eggplant?

For the next sixty seconds, there was nothing but the clearing of throats and muted fake coughs. I stared over his shoulder toward the stairs, mentally begging Mel to join us and break the tension.

"Your date tonight," Henry said to his cousin. "Is she—"

"It's Mel," I answered for Tyler. Henry's face was blank. Of course he didn't remember her. "My friend who looks like a young Sandra Bullock. You know her."

"Sure." He nodded, but his face showed no recollection of the name or description.

"Speaking of Mel," Tyler said. "We should get going." He stepped over Henry's long legs and headed for the stairs.

"So," Knightly said after a few moments of silence, "you're here for the whole Spring Break week?"

"Yes." I re-crossed my legs and set down the magazine. "Must be nice for you."

"What do you mean?"

"You and Dart left school. Every week is spring break for you."

He cocked his head to the side. "Oh?"

"And you're living in some castle now," I added.

"Who told you that?"

"Who do you *think* told me?"

He leaned back and draped one arm along the back of the couch. "Ahh, Lilah." He lifted a crooked smile. "You must've hated that." His grin expanded, quite unapologetically.

It suddenly dawned on me that he was wearing glasses. Black horn-rimmed specs, probably Armani or something similarly Italian. That wasn't the only change I noticed. His hair was longer, curlier, a little messy. And did he look more toned, too? Svelte and chiseled. Probably from playing cricket or riding horses, or whatever people do who live in castles. He obviously hadn't been living off a steady diet of college crap like I had.

"Must be nice," I repeated. "Not taking classes this semester."

His brows knitted together. "Dart's not," he said. "I am."

I returned his puzzled expression. "What does that mean?"

"It means I'm very much in school."

"Where?"

"Most of my classes are in the Neukom," he replied. "It's on the other side of campus by—"

"At *Stanford*?"

"Why would you think... Oh. I guess you heard what Lilah's been saying about that, too?" He rubbed his chin. "I don't know where she gets her information."

I shrugged, still a bit stupefied.

"So, all this time, you thought I...?" He pressed his lips together and straightened his glasses.

When he didn't finish his thought, I pointed at his new eyewear. "What's the deal with those?"

"I've been busy," he explained. "They're easier. I got out of the habit of wearing contacts."

"And where's all that stuff you put in your hair?"

He raked his fingers through the top of his uncharacteristically tousled curls. "Fell out of that habit, too. What was it you once called it? My *Ronald Reagan Complex*. Republican narcissism run amuck?"

I laughed. "I can't believe you remembered that verbatim."

"A portrayal like that isn't easily forgettable. I'm so glad I chose not to wear a three-piece suit tonight." He dusted off the lapel of his camelhair, cashmere/wool jacket. "I would never live it down. And *you*..." He broke off, his gaze sliding to the braids hanging over my shoulder.

"What?"

"Nothing," he replied. "It's just...it's been a while."

Done talking, he leaned back and steepled his fingers.

He was doing it again. In a matter of five minutes, Henry Knightly was pushing my buttons, making comments that were deliberately confusing. Barring the glasses and curlier hair, he hadn't changed one iota.

A coffee table book was on his lap now. He was flipping through it, keenly studying the glossy photos of Canadian wildlife, but it was obvious he wasn't reading. I could see a smile twitching the corner of his mouth. Finally he let loose the chuckle he'd been holding back.

"What's so funny?"

He closed the book and leaned forward. "Spring Honeycutt. We've gone to the same school for seven months, and I just drove seven hundred miles—"

"For a date with me."

He ran his fist over his smiling mouth. "That's not *exactly* what I was thinking," he said. "But it is nice to see you."

Nice to see me. Was it nice to see *him*? Was *nice* causing my mouth to go dry and making me wonder what might have happened back in my bedroom the night before vacation if Alex hadn't shown up?

Henry stood and strolled to the bay window, staring out the hill covered with pines. "So, how are we going to handle this?"

"Handle what?"

"Tonight. It's our first date." He turned to me, making my pulse skip.

"It's a basketball game, Knightly," I said after a swallow. "That's all."

Henry blinked at me and slid his hands in his pockets. "Right, Honeycutt." He nodded, curtly. "That's all this is."

Neither of us spoke for a few minutes until, thankfully, Mel and Tyler came downstairs. Mel stared at Henry like she was seeing a mirage. "Ty just said it was you, but I…"

"Hey," Henry said to her. "Good to see you again."

She blinked. "Yeah." She blinked once more then glanced at me. "Weird, huh?"

Again, Mel and her classic lacking of tact.

"Why don't you two drive together?" Tyler suggested, his arm around Mel. "We have a lot more catching up to do."

Mel shot me a questioning look as we grabbed our purses from the banister while Henry acquiesced to the proposed travel arrangements. Our foursome headed out the front door.

"Didn't you come on a motorcycle?" I asked.

A little notch sliced into the skin between Henry's eyebrows and he pointed to a black, ragtop Jeep parked at the far end of the driveway.

"Yours?" Though I didn't really have to ask; it was parked crooked.

He nodded, spinning a silver ring of keys around his index finger, catching them in his hand.

"Was the Lamborghini store closed?" I teased. "Poor you."

"Have you missed making fun of me?"

"You're just hard to recognize without a Viper wrapped around you."

He lifted a distant smile. "Yeah, I really miss that car."

"Where is it?" I asked, climbing in the passenger side. Henry was right behind me, closing my door once I was in. "Aren't you two connected like twins?"

He slid in the driver's seat, twisted the key in the ignition and revved the engine. "The Viper was a loaner," he said, adjusting the mirror. "You didn't know that?"

"No," I replied, surprised. "I assumed it was yours."

"Only for six months." He shifted into reverse and backed out of the driveway. "One of my father's companies has a vested interest in sponsoring a racer." We were tailing Mel's Jetta out of the subdivision. "The Viper was a sort of lend/trade-out constituent as part of the negotiations, but only for the first two quarters of their fiscal year."

"I hope what you just said made sense to you."

He chuckled. "The forecast shows no rain tonight, but would you like the top up?" I shook my head, wrangling with my braids as they danced around my face. Henry reached into the backseat and grabbed a blue baseball cap with three gold letters scripted across the front. He handed it to me.

"*Cal?*" I screeched, making the word sound like

swearing. "Stanford's sworn enemy? I'm not wearing that." I tossed the hat at his chest like it was a live grenade. "Do you want us to get struck by lightning?"

"There's another back there. The Giants. Very benign."

"My hair is fine, Knightly."

He flipped up the visor and slid that offensive blue cap on his head, turning to me with a grin. I rolled my eyes, trying not to laugh at his childlike expression. Pushing my buttons...

"Cardinals killed the Bears last fall," I said, flicking the bill over his eyes.

"I know, I was at the game. And, yes, Spring, I was sitting on the Stanford side."

"Then why do you have a *Berkeley* hat?"

"My sister is looking at it as a possibility for next year. She's much more open-minded than I am."

Henry's sister. I remembered hearing about her from Alex. "Is she here too, on vacation?"

He turned on the blinker as we idled at a red light. "No, it's just me. We've got family in Scappoose, about thirty miles away. I spend vacations with them when I can."

The inside of Henry's Jeep was a little untidier than I would've expected, especially after sharing a bathroom with him for a week back in November. As he drove us at a very conservative sixty-five miles per hour south to Portland, I took the liberty of rummaging around. Assorted road maps, empty water bottles, that Giants cap, two Duke sweatshirts, a polo mallet (I think), and wedged in the small door pocket on the passenger's side was a paperback.

"*What* are you doing with *this*?" I fanned the pages of the worn book under his nose.

He glanced at me but said nothing.

"I thought you only read odes to the sixth amendment, or the memoirs of Lee Iacocca and Rush Limbaugh."

"I like stories," he said. "*That* particular book is for emergencies only, in case I break down on the freeway and have nothing to do till Triple A comes. But, tell me." His face warped serious. "What *is* a pimpernel, exactly?"

I stared down at the book on my lap. My favorite book in the world. "It's a flower," I explained, running my fingers over the cover, "and a metaphor."

"After the way you talked about it that night, I wondered what I would think. If I would see what you see." He cut me a glance. "French bourgeois and all."

I flipped to my favorite chapter — *Richmond* — remembering the first time I'd read it, smiling a little dreamily. "What do you think so far?"

"Interesting," he offered, then concentrated on the road.

"That's it?" I said over the noise of traffic.

He lowerd his visor and squinted at me, puzzled.

"You can't possibly create a respectable judgment about a story until you've finished." I sandwiched the book between my hands protectively. "When did you start reading it?"

"January."

"You've been reading it for *three months*?" I accused, flabbergasted. "How far have you gotten?"

Henry tapped his chin. "Let's see, I just finished *Richmond*, so I am approximately two-thirds of the way." He glanced to me. "My third time through."

Chapter 21

Mel's arm was linked through mine as our foursome, now temporarily divided, strolled toward Platinum Level parking. The overall mood was somber leaving the Rose Quarter, interrupted by thwarted Trail Blazers fans yelling obscene commentary about specific Lakers players.

"Why does he have to be such a sore winner?" I said, hoping Knightly heard me, even though he and Tyler were still a ways behind us.

"I thought it was kind of cute the way that one player gave him a high five at the end of the game."

"That was Kobe Bryant, Mel."

"How does Henry know him?"

I shook my head. "I have no idea."

"So, I was thinking," Mel said, "do you want to go up to Beacon Rock tomorrow?" We turned down a row. I could see Henry's Jeep parked next to Mel's car under the yellow florescent lights. "A little impromptu overnight campout?"

"I'm seriously so behind in my classes. I've got about five hundred pages to read."

"You can bring your books," she said, quick to anticipate my excuse. "Just imagine reading *Walden* with the leafy forest as your backdrop and the murmuring river your soundtrack."

She knew I was a sucker for ambiance. "Sounds heavenly," I admitted. "I haven't been up there since we were kids." I smiled, further imagining the peace and quiet I'd been in search of. The perfect place to chill and reboot. "Okay," I said. "I'm in, although I doubt your Jetta will make it without four-wheel drive. Does your grandpa—"

"Ty!" Mel tipped her chin up. "We're taking your Durango tomorrow, right?"

"Hell, yeah," Tyler called in reply from behind us.

"Umm, what?"

"We're all going," she said, patting my arm. "Did I forget to mention that?"

"Melanie." I lowered my voice. "If I didn't know better, I'd think you knew Henry was going to be here all along."

"I didn't, I swear," Mel defended. "But man, I so wish I could've seen your face when he showed up. Beyond epic."

"Yeah, it was a real scream."

"I'm surprised at the sarcasm," she said as we passed by a group of guys watching replays of the game on an iPad. "I thought you'd be happy to see him."

Happy? Was I? "He pretty much disappeared on me in December," I whispered, a little elbow of resentment poking my ribs.

"But you weren't dating or"—she cleared her throat dramatically—"anything. Right?"

"No," I admitted, though I felt another jab of resentment

for some reason.

"Okay, then, so, camping? It'll be fun."

"It does sound fun," I admitted. "But I don't know. It might not be a good idea."

"It wasn't *my* idea," she said, casually jerking her head behind us.

I glanced over my shoulder. The guys were a few yards back. Tyler had his hand on Henry's shoulder, saying something I couldn't hear. Henry looked a little stunned, and I wondered if those two were having the exact same conversation Mel and I were.

• • •

"How are your classes?"

Small talk. Le sigh. The last thing I wanted to discuss with anyone was school.

I tipped my chin toward Henry, two spaces over in the backseat of Tyler's SUV. His left elbow was propped on the arm rest of his door. Before answering, I allowed myself a few seconds of thought, deciding how detailed I wanted to be with a guy who might not even care.

"Fine," I answered. Yes, limited details were best. My murky academic life at present was not my favorite subject, anyway. I stared out the window at the soft morning scenery flying by as Tyler drove us to the campground.

"How's our thesis?" Henry smiled, teasing me by using the pronoun "our."

But instead of being amused, more of that repressed bitterness that had resurfaced the night before flicked the back of my neck. How *could* Henry have just left me high and dry like that? For all he knew, my professor hated the whole thing and I was flunking out.

"Fine," I repeated.

"What did Masen say about the new theory in part five?"

I gazed out my window. "He hasn't seen it yet."

"Why?"

"I haven't turned it in."

I heard him shift in his seat, rotating toward me. "Why not?"

"Because I don't think it's ready. In fact, I might want to scrap it and start over." This wasn't at all true, but I felt like lashing out.

"That's irrational." His expression was stern, and I could suddenly see the future Henry arguing a case in a courtroom, throwing out objection after objection. How annoying. Today he was dressed in dark jeans, a white crewneck T-shirt, and a dark gray wool sweater that both zipped and buttoned up the front. Kind of overkill.

He leaned on the cooler separating us. "You do realize that's going to put you a year behind? Don't you think you should…"

The act of folding my arms silenced him, my non-verbal communication screaming at him to butt out.

"Sorry," he said, raising one hand to shield his face. "I'll spare you all unwarranted guidance."

"Thank you, Counselor for the Prosecution."

"I just don't want you to waste your time," he said, choosing *not* to let the subject drop.

"Waste my time?" I echoed. "Is that what you think I'm doing?" I sat back, reeling in my frustration. It probably wasn't fair to erupt like that. After all, he had no idea how badly I was stressing about school.

"Sorry, that was rude," I said and leaned my head against the seat. "I'm turning it in to Masen soon. Though it still needs a lot of work." I exhaled a wistful sigh. "I wish I could take a semester off to get it done. That would be pretty amazing, actually."

Henry nodded and turned to the window. "Interesting."

"What about you?" I asked. "Are you going to clue me in about why you moved?"

He seemed confused, as if my question caught him off guard. Did he think I hadn't noticed that he was suddenly gone?

"It was short notice," he said while running a finger along the rubber at the base of the window. "The opportunity had always been there, but it didn't present itself until the end of the year."

I was aware that he was speaking English words, but the cryptic-ness of their meaning was lost on me. "You never told me there was a possibility of you moving."

"No." He dropped his hand and turned to me. "I didn't."

I glanced at the front seat. Mel and Tyler were arguing over control of the stereo. "You took Dart, too," I said, my voice dropping a notch. "And to *Switzerland*?" I could hear the accusatory tone in my voice.

"I didn't *take* him," he argued. "An opportunity presented itself for him, as well."

I folded my arms. "That's quite a coincidence."

"And not to Switzerland," he muttered like it was the most ridiculous thing in the world.

"Then why is that what Lilah's telling everybody?"

"I have no idea," he said. "I haven't spoken to her in

months. I *was* there for a few days over the break, but—"

"In Switzerland," I confirmed, giving him flat eyes.

He nodded but did not elaborate. "I'm living across the Bay now. Oakland."

"In a castle?" I asked, again with the flat eyes.

"No, it's a HUD apartment." He adjusted his glasses. "Furthest thing from a castle." Before I could ask what the devil he was doing living in the projects, he explained. "We bought a complex that was about to foreclose. Dart and me. Two hundred families would be displaced if we didn't take care of some major renovation. It was easier just to move in for a while."

"*You*"—I couldn't help saying, deadpan—"are living in public housing and doing construction."

"Well, Dart did most of it, since he has more time on his hands and needed a project."

My mind couldn't frame the picture, so I rewound, snagging on something he'd said. "Dart's been at school all this time, too?"

"No," Henry said, looking out the window. "He left California a few weeks ago."

"Why?"

"Another project," he said vaguely.

"Where?"

Henry flicked a piece of fuzz off his jeans, then his gaze rolled back out the window. "Uninteresting topic," he said.

I groaned loudly, wanting him to hear it. It felt like pre-Thanksgiving all over again. One step forward, two steps back. Still, I couldn't keep my eyes from drifting over to his side of the car. His face was emotionless. Giving nothing away. Typical Knightly.

"So," he said a moment later, "are you seeing anyone?"

"Ha!" My eyebrows were probably somewhere up in my hairline.

"What?"

"*You* can ask personal questions but *I* can't?"

He raised a tiny smile.

"No," I said. "Nothing new or exciting to report there. And yourself?"

"Much too busy."

And that was that.

Not even my loyalty to Julia or my own morbid curiosity could compel me to keep chipping away at the proverbial man of marble. In front of us, Mel and Tyler were discussing, rather loudly, whether to listen to talk radio or music. I leaned back and shut my eyes. *Their* conversation was more entertaining than ours.

We arrived around ten in the morning. Our overnight spot was beautiful. To the east lay foothills, the gateway to the Cascades, with the Columbia River cutting a pass through the mountains like a blue-green snake. Beacon Rock, the core of an ancient volcano, was quite a sight, parked on the banks of the river, sporadic pines peppering its otherwise bald head.

Once outside the car, I took a deep breath and spun in a slow circle. Surrounding us on all sides were green and fragrant Douglas firs, pines, and maples. Spongy ferns filled in the lower landscape, dotted with blood red rhododendrons and a rainbow of spring wild flowers. The wind blew through the tops of the trees, and its accompanying harmony was the chatter of geese, the flutter of hummingbirds and a woodpecker hammering away on a tree above. Somewhere out there, I could hear the rippling of the Columbia ribboning its way between the trees.

Closing my eyes for a moment, I allowed a tranquil smile to spread across my face. When I stopped my spin and opened my eyes, Henry was watching me, a tent pole in one hand.

"What are you doing?" he asked.

"Reminds me of home," I explained. "I'm from Oregon."

"I know that." He gave me a sideways look and walked off. Jeesh, what was *his* problem?

I turned back toward the eastern horizon. Last year, I'd read an article about this very spot of forest. Pictures from several decades earlier depicted an enormous bare patch from clearcutting. I'd been furious at the time, but as I stood there, gazing up at that same spot in person, I would've never known any logging had taken place all those years ago. The forest was completely grown in with tall, healthy trees as far as the eye could see. Sure, Henry had preached to me about new growth afforesting, but I'd never *seen* its results.

To my personal vexation, it was surprisingly impressive.

I left the dusty white Durango and wandered toward the campground. The guys were setting up the tent. Henry was down on his knees, jacket off, pounding tent pegs in the ground with a mallet. No directions were used, and in a matter of minutes, the tall orange structure was assembled.

Staring up at the finished product, something occurred to me. "Uh, Mel?" I muttered, as I handed her a sleeping bag from the back of the Durango. "I realize it's very roomy, but there's only *one tent*."

When she grinned, I cringed. Of course this was part of her plan.

Sensing my alarm, she relaxed her devilish smile. "Don't worry," she said in a sotta voce whisper, as we dragged a heavy cooler toward the center of camp. "There will be no hanky panky inside the tent." She nodded toward the guys. "Tyler knows that."

"Good, thanks," I said, letting go of my held breath.

"What goes on *outside* the tent…" She lifted one eyebrow. "Just don't try to find us if we wander off the trail for a while."

Henry walked toward us, his arms full of large rocks. After shooting me another intense look, he knelt down and began arranging the rocks in a circle for our fire.

"Thanks for the warning," I whispered to Mel, watching him. "Something's pissed him off. I think he wants to murder me in my sleeping bag."

"That's not what he wants to do to you in your sleeping bag," Mel murmured.

I glared at her. "Pardon?"

"Nothing." She snickered.

Our troop tooled around the thick woods all day, romping halfway up the trail toward Beacon Rock, then turning back a different way when the sun arched to the west. At around five, we were forced to end our hike early after I slipped on a mossy rock by the river, tweaking my ankle.

"Think of your happy place," Henry prescribed, his left arm around me, acting as my crutch. "We're almost back to camp."

I winced, regarding the trail ahead of us. Mel and Tyler had disappeared into the bushes, leaving us alone. "Really," I insisted, trying to squirm free, "it doesn't hurt that much." I attempted to limp away from him. "See, I can walk on my own." It was a pitiful attempt.

"You're favoring your right side," he observed, wrapping his arm around me again. His hold was iron-tight this time. Even though he had a five o'clock shadow going, he still smelled like that ceramic bowl of shaving cream in his bathroom back in Palo Alto. Something about that smell was making me feel dizzy, or maybe my foot hurt more than I thought.

"Hold onto me till we get to the car and I can check it out," he said. "I feel responsible. It was my long pass of the Frisbee that sent you flying." He tightened his grip, hoisting me closer so that even my healthy foot was barely touching the ground as we walked.

Maybe thinking he was taking my mind off the pain in my ankle, Henry described a little Tahitian town he'd visited a few times. White sand, clear blue water, friendly and accommodating neighbors. It sounded like a little piece of heaven.

"Perfect place to finish your thesis," he added. "Under a banyan tree, laptop shaded by an umbrella. Endless Diet Cokes."

"Don't tempt me," I said, trying not to wince.

The sun was low and the fire looked warm and inviting by the time Henry and I returned to camp. But my escort made us stop at the Durango first.

"Get in." He opened the rear door at the back of the car. "Or do you need me to lift you?"

I snorted a laugh, but he made a move toward me, so I quickly hopped onto the edge of the tailgate before he got any macho ideas.

Kneeling down, he took ahold of my ankle between

his two hands, then lifted my leg, resting it on the tailgate. Gently, he pushed up the bottom of my jeans to my knee. I gasped quietly the moment chilly air hit bare skin, but then instantly calmed as his warm hands encircled my calf muscle, gently pressing in as they ran down my skin, a tender massage. When his examination paused and his lingering hands felt way more exploratory than medical, my breathing suddenly picked up speed. I stared at the top of his bent head, my fingers curling around the edge of the door. One of his hands slid to the sensitive backside of my knee while the other wrapped around my ankle, gingerly manipulating my foot this way and that way.

"Am I hurting you?" he asked. I could feel him breathing on my skin as I held my own breath.

Before answering, I swallowed then shook my head.

"No sprain," he said, his eyes lifting to mine. "A mild bruising." His skin was so warm that it surprised me when I felt a chill shoot through my body. His hand behind my knee slid down to my ankle so both hands were around it. For a second, I had a flash of him holding the sides of my neck… right before we—

"Ready?" he asked, leaning an inch closer.

I nodded automatically.

"Good." He stepped back and drew my jeans down to cover my leg. "Come on." He turned toward the fire. "Let's eat."

• • •

The woods around us were dark, and two owls on either side of the fire hooted back and forth. I grabbed my copy of *Walden* and peeled myself off the stump I'd occupied for the past few hours. A combination of that morning's early wakeup call, the long drive, the sun, the hike, and the potential of bodily injury had officially worn me out.

"I'm going to bed," I announced, heading toward the tent. "You staying up, Mel?" When I turned around, both Mel and Tyler were looking at Henry, who was sitting on the ground on a blanket, staring vacantly into the fire.

"It's ten thirty," Mel replied. "I'm not tired."

I covered my yawning mouth with one hand. "I'll see you in the morning." The early spring wind had picked up once the sun set, and it was chilly. I hurried into the tent.

No formal sleeping spots had been designated, so I unrolled my sleeping bag and situated it in the far right corner, farthest from the flap. I was hoping I would be fast asleep by the time the others came in. Mel promised no hanky panky. Still, I did not want to know what was going on once the butane lantern was turned off.

Feeling strangely modest, I crawled into my sleeping bag to change out of my jeans and sweatshirt and into my soft and snuggly flannel pajama pants and long-sleeve T-shirt. I fluffed and punched my pillow before lying back, prepared for exhaustion to overtake.

I pinched my eyes closed, then opened them. I rolled onto my side. It was probably an hour of tossing and turning later when I threw back the tent flap and wandered toward the campfire, huddled in my pajamas and coat.

Henry sat before the yellow fire, toasting a very well done marshmallow off the end of a wire hanger. He was alone.

Chapter 22

"*Comment maintenant vache brune*?" Henry asked. His voice was quiet, he eyes red and sleepy.

"Did you just say, 'How now brown cow?'" I asked as I ambled toward the fire.

He smiled, keeping his eyes down.

I stood across from him, warming the front of my body. "Where are the others?"

"Night hike." He pointed the end of the hanger toward the dark woods. "I wouldn't expect them for a while."

I rotated, warming my back now, remembering Mel's warning about not trying to find them if they split away from the group. Mel and I were best friends, but there were some sides of her I didn't need to see.

"Probably not," I agreed.

"Can't sleep?"

I turned my head in time to see the crispy marshmallow slide off the hanger and disappear into the licking flames. "I guess I'm restless," I said as I walked past him to the stump I'd been sitting on earlier. "Ever had one of those nights when your mind is racing but you can't figure out what you're trying to think?"

"More often than I'd like," he replied. "Especially lately."

I rubbed my eyes with the heels of my hands. "Probably too much caffeine."

After staring into the fire for a moment longer, Henry tossed the hanger to the side and shifted his weight toward me. "Spring—" He cut short, his head snapping to the side.

A shiver ran up my spine when I realized he'd heard a sound coming from the woods. My eyes shot in the direction of where he was looking, but I saw nothing and heard nothing...until Mel and Tyler stumbled out of the darkness. I glanced at Henry, who had already relaxed his stance.

Mel was hanging onto Tyler's hand and swinging it between them. "Still holding out?" she said to Henry, then she noticed me sitting on the other side of the fire. "Oh, hey Springer. Thought you were asleep."

"She tried," Henry said. "Now that you two are back"— he rolled to his knees and stood up—"Spring and I are going for a drive." He walked over and stopped in front of me. "Ready?" He extended his hand to help me up.

When I didn't react, his eyes went tight and his jaw clenched. The expression screamed impatience, like I wasn't going along with some secret plan we'd earlier devised. After a moment, he sighed and grabbed the end of my coat sleeve, pulling me to my feet.

"Toss me your keys, man," he said to Tyler. The silver ring flew through the air.

Without a second thought, I followed. "It would appear,"

I announced to Mel over my shoulder, "that we will be going for a drive." I didn't look back to take note of her expression.

The engine hummed softly as we wound along the dark road away from the campground. I didn't take the time to dissect what Henry's motivation might have been. A drive sounded nice and the car was warmer than the tent, with less bugs.

I slouched down in my seat, kicked off my shoes and propped my feet on the dashboard. When we first got in the car the radio was on, but Henry turned it off at once, so it was quiet for the first few minutes. After fishing around the inside pocket of his leather jacket, he pulled out his phone and plugged it into the jack. He held the silver device in one hand, working his thumb along the face. I could tell he was scanning through music tracks.

A song came on. I recognized it immediately, but he skipped past it as well as the next few, which I also recognized as part of a familiar, and now deleted, playlist.

"Track six, please."

Henry turned to me, lifting an eyebrow. A few seconds later, my request came spilling through the speakers. "You like this one?"

"Very much," I admitted. "Dave Matthews Band. Classic nineties."

"I always suspected there was more to you than Alanis Morissette."

I exhaled tranquilly and closed my eyes, taking in the much needed serenity. The darkness, the bluesy ballad, the rhythm of the moving car, that aftershave...

"Are you hungry?" he asked in a low voice. I liked the way it sounded coupled against the music. "We're close to a town."

"No, thanks," I said. Just as it had been back in the tent during my tumultuous hour of tossing and turning, my mind was racing again. Murky thoughts jumped, abstract and disconnected images flashed behind my closed eyes. Motorcycles, a black Viper, an argyle sweater hanging over the bend of a palm tree.

Suddenly, the car was stifling, and it felt like a pile of hot bricks was stacked on my chest. I snuck a quick glance at my driver. He seemed pensive, too. His lips were pressed together in a line and I could see his strong jaw muscles working. Although I'm sure his Rhodes Scholar brain was focused on something more substantial than mine was.

Don't be an idiot, Spring.

"Feeling any better?" Henry asked after the song ended.

"Yes, thanks," I replied, allowing my eyes to linger on his face, but that only made my hands break out in a cold sweat. Sudden hot flashes coupled with chills? I was probably coming down with the flu. "Where are we going?"

"Don't know." His brooding eyes smoothed out. "I haven't been this way in years."

A new song came on, prompting a question that I'd tucked away months ago. "This playlist." I pointed at his cell balanced in the cup holder between us. "What was your motive?"

"You don't like it?"

"No, I do," I blurted. "I was just"—I rubbed my nose—"a little surprised by some of your choices." Of course I was remembering the theory Mel had insinuated, how those ten songs were all tied together with a similar "theme."

"As far as there being a common thread, there isn't."

I exhaled, choosing to believe him over my sex-on-the-brain best friend.

"You got me thinking," he continued, "that night at the party when you said you don't dance to male singers. I was creating a sample. Show you what you've been missing." He smiled at me briefly then moved his focus back to the road. "I guess I jumped at the chance when you allowed me to load a playlist."

"I didn't allow. You confiscated my phone in the middle of the night." I chewed my thumbnail for a minute. "Tell me about the last song."

Henry lifted a surprisingly big grin then chuckled under his breath. "To tell the truth, I pulled in a ringer for that one." He adjusted the seat belt across his chest. "I called my sister Cami that night, told her what I was doing, and for whom." He gazed out the side window. The headlights of an oncoming car flashed across his glasses. "She's a few years younger than you, but I credit her with impeccable taste in most everything. I ran off the list of songs I already had in mind, she went on to approve and delete. The last was her suggestion."

"Your sister?"

He turned to me, our eyes meeting. "Yes."

My stomach made a little spin, and that pile of hot bricks on my chest felt heavier. And hotter.

"Does she, um…does she live…" I stopped short, realizing that I had no idea where Henry came from. His family had homes all over the world, but other than Elliott Academy in LA, Washington, Duke, and Stanford, I didn't have a clue about his past life.

"Cami lives in Zürich right now," he said, answering my

unfinished question.

I nodded.

"I'm sure *you* find the idea of attending a private, all-girls boarding school in Switzerland passé, if not offensive, but with my parents away from home so much…" He trailed off, pressing his lips together. "It's an exceptional school. She'll go Ivy League if she chooses."

I thought of Henry calling his sister in the middle of the night to discuss music. If it had been one a.m. in California, what time was it in western Europe? My attention was pulled by Henry tapping his knuckle on his side window. "I wish it were warmer," he mused, changing the subject. "I know a great spot by the river. Are you still cold?"

I nodded mechanically, although I wasn't cold. Quite the opposite.

He cranked the heater. "Would you like to wear this?" he asked, unzipping his leather jacket. I politely declined but was stirred by the chivalrous act. Then I remembered I was *supposed* to be a self-sufficient woman, an independent feminist. I dug my middle knuckle into my temple, massaging a tiny circle. Nothing in my brain was working correctly tonight.

"I read a case once about a man who killed his wife because she always kept their house set at eighty-five degrees." Henry turned the car onto what looked like nothing more than a dirt road. "One day he snapped; shot her in the heart." He turned to me, grinning. "His attorney got him off. Justifiable homicide."

"Is that the kind of law you want to practice?"

He crinkled his nose with an air of repugnance. "The case was required reading. I enjoy studying about trial lawyers, but I lack the particular…subtleties."

There was a time when I thought Henry would have fit the role of sleazy ambulance chaser perfectly. I didn't know what I thought now.

"Once upon a time, I planned on working for the D. A.," he continued. "But that won't work, either."

"Why not?"

"From what I know about myself and the kind of life I want to live, I'm better suited for private practice."

"More money in that?" I zinged without thinking.

Henry glanced at me, not bothering to hide his frown. He actually looked hurt. "The money will be sufficient," he replied coolly, setting his gaze back on the road, "but if I work for the D. A., I can't do pro bono as much as I'd like. *That's* why I want my own practice."

"Pro bono?" My feet slipped off the dashboard, jerking my body forward, straight toward the windshield.

He swore in alarm as his right arm jetted straight out to his side, catching me across the chest. Driving one handed, he swerved back and forth across the center line.

"Pro bono?" I repeated after he'd pulled his arm back.

"What's the matter with you?" He stared at me, his eyes blazing with shock.

"Doesn't that mean for free?"

He exhaled gruffly and ran a hand through his hair. "Is that so hard to believe?"

"I just never thought that you...someone like you—"

"Not all lawyers are sharks, Spring," he cut in. "And not all of them are out to kill trees and pollute the water. I plan on doing a lot of good."

"No, I...*yeah*." I swallowed. "I'm sure you do." I turned to face him full on, trying to make my face convey what I was feeling, to let him know he'd won this battle. "I'm sorry, Henry. I didn't know."

"That's the trouble with you," he muttered, tight-lipped. "You thought you had me pegged from the beginning. That first night. Didn't you?"

I felt my eyes going wide, trying to display my innocence. But he was right. People seldom surprised me, and Henry had managed to do just that. Time after time. Just admitting that to myself made me feel miserable. The pile of bricks on my chest was replaced by a lump in my throat.

His next movement startled me when he reached forward, jerking his cell free from the jack. My music abruptly stopped. Only the sound of tires on the road.

"There's a store coming up," he said. "I'm stopping for a drink. Would you like something?"

"*J'ai très soif*," I mumbled. "I mean, I'm thirsty, too."

He laughed softly, sounding more like himself again. "I understood you the first time."

I echoed his laugh, only mine sounded nervous.

Henry pulled the car to a stop, keeping the heater on. "Diet Coke?" he asked as he opened his door.

"I probably shouldn't if I plan on getting any kind of sleep tonight. But…"

"I'll be right back," he said, zipping up his jacket then raking his fingers though his hair.

I watched as he entered the store, surveyed the fountain drinks and chatted with the clerk, finally placing two bottles of water on the counter and one sixty-ounce Diet Coke.

Chapter 23

Our return drive to Beacon Rock was a quiet one. The glowing green numbers on the dashboard read one o'clock. When we arrived at our spot, Tyler was off somewhere brushing his teeth and Mel was heading into the tent.

"I'm crashing," she said after a big yawn. "You guys coming in?" She shivered and wrapped a blanket around her body.

I wandered to the fire, staring into its dying orange flames. "I'm still wound up. I don't think I could sleep if I tried." I scowled at the tent behind Mel like it was an awaiting prison, then slumped onto one of the stumps in front of the fire, plunging my hands in my pockets.

Mel looked at Henry. "What about you?" He shook his head. She yawned again and waved us good night, disappearing behind the tent flap.

Henry poked at the fire with a long stick then threw a log on top. Red sparks shot out and swirled into the black sky.

"I'm fine out here alone," I said.

He lifted his chin. Yellow and orange reflected off the corners of his glasses.

"You don't have to stay if you don't want to."

"I do want to." He dusted off his hands on his jeans and lowered himself to the ground across the fire from me.

Tyler showed up a few minutes later. He wore a bright yellow sweatshirt with the hood up, and a hand towel was draped over his shoulder, a toothbrush poking out of his mouth. "All we need now is your ukulele, Trip. Sing us a few lines of 'Pearly Shells.'" He cackled much louder than necessary. I could guess why he was in such a good mood. "Where'd you two go?"

"Down the road," Henry said.

"Use up all my gas?"

"Probably." Henry pointed an elbow at me. "The heater was on full blast."

"I was cold," I apologized.

"Better find something to keep you warm," Tyler said, and pointed a foot at the blanket spread on the ground in front of me. He snickered then disappeared into the tent. I heard Mel giggle.

The fire sparked and crackled, and the woods were making strange sounds. As the wind blew through the trees, I turned up the collar of my coat; it was unbuttoned so I could wrap it around me and my flannel pajamas like a double-breasted suit, extra protection.

"Cold again?"

"First I can't sleep," I complained, "and now I can't stay warm. I don't know what's wrong with me."

Henry was on his feet, striding toward me like a man on a mission. I couldn't begin to guess his intentions. At an arm's length away, he stopped and bent to one knee. He pulled off the blue scarf that hung loose on his neck, hooked it around the back of my neck, then tied the two ends under my chin.

I stared at his face, but not once did he look me in the eyes. And just like that, before I could speak, he retreated to where he'd been sitting on the other side of the fire.

"Thank you," I said, my heart beating hard from surprise. His scarf was wool and cashmere, softer than the silkiest blanket. I nuzzled my chin into its fabric. It was still warm, and smelled spicy and clean.

"You're welcome," he said, dropping a pinecone into the fire. It crackled, shooting red sparks into the blackness. "Can I ask you something?"

"Sure."

"What do you like most about *The Scarlet Pimpernel*?"

I took one last inhale of the warm scarf before answering. "The friendship between Sir Percy and his men, for one," I said over the songs of crickets and owls. "It's a profound study in male bonding, and when you consider their ethics in history—" I cut myself off, knowing I was being way too analytical. I decided to go for embarrassing honesty. "Actually, the love story kills me every single time. And I adore Marguerite. She's an enviable heroine. Vulnerable but a free spirit at the same time. I admire her loyalty and her passion."

"She reminds me of my sister," he said. "She's as French as a hayseed raised in the country can get." He unwrapped a Hershey's bar from the cooler and took a bite. "When she was younger, I mean. She had to grow up quickly." He threw his wrapper into the yellow flames.

I wanted to ask more about his sister but didn't get the chance.

"Naturally," Henry said, leaning back, "I see myself as the hero in the story, Sir Percy, that rugged idol among men, untouchable, incorruptible, saving his fellow noblemen without so much as a spot on his white pantaloons." He dipped his chin and smiled at something private, poking a stick at the fire. "But honestly, I related more with the cop in the story."

"You related to Chauvelin?" I asked, taken aback. "The wicked villain who chases our hero across England and France, destroying everything in his wake?"

"No, Spring. I felt for the guy who was misunderstood." Our eyes locked. "Don't take things so literally. You misread me, remember?" He lowered his gaze to the fire. "But don't worry, I saw through it." Still staring into the flames, he took a beat. "I saw through you."

My hands were sweaty-cold again as my fists clenched in my pockets. "I think you *are* like Sir Percy," I said.

He looked up. "In what way?"

"How about by wearing a mask half the time?" I suggested. "Playing a deliberate and studied part?" I could hear my voice becoming accusatory, remembering the past…how he'd disappeared from my life without a word, and exactly how much that hurt me. "Never, *ever* showing your true character until the final chapter."

"I'm not playing any part," he stated, a bit indignantly. "When will you see that?"

"When you *show* me, Henry." My words came out too

loud, and we both turned toward the dark tent. "Sometimes," I continued in a whisper, when no one stirred inside, "I feel like I don't know you at all, and other times...I feel..." I trailed off and pressed my fingers to my forehead. "I don't know what to believe anymore."

I'd meant this to put an end to our circular non-discussion, because really? What did it matter what I thought of him? Or how he made me feel? Did it matter that I'd bought new lip gloss in December? Or how my heart sped up when I knew I was about to see him?

"What are you feeling right now?"

My head snapped up at his words, and I stared across the fire at him, wondering if he was some kind of mind reader.

"About *me*, Spring," he said. "What are you feeling *right now about me*?"

That was easy. He was Knightly. I was supposed to hate him. Right?

Only...it wasn't hate that was making my skin break out in prickles, and the back of my mouth flood with the taste of cranberries, and my heart pound every time our eyes met.

"Whatever you're feeling about me right this second," he continued, "believe that. Please."

The wind shifted, smoke concealing Henry's face, and for a frantic moment he completely disappeared from view. When the wind shifted again and I could see his face, my panic instantly dissolved, but a different frantic sensation was right on its heels. All at once, I was dying of thirst, and there was only one oasis. He was my quenching, delicious water, and I was prepared to crawl through a burning desert for just one taste.

Henry was on his feet, his glasses off. "I'm coming over

to you," I heard him say. But had his lips even moved?

I don't know if he'd strolled over to me like a mere mortal, or hurled his body fearlessly through the flames like a Homer-esque mythical beast. He was suddenly on the stump to my right, but he wasn't facing the fire like I was, he was facing me. I felt myself being swiveled around and scooted to the edge of the stump, my knees sliding between his. I clenched my fists inside my coat pockets, feeling tiny pin pricks at the tips of my fingers, my heart hammering with nervous anticipation.

He reached out and took my face between his hands, holding me like I was a piece of precious china. His thumbs moved across my cheeks, his fingers on the back of my neck. And then…my screaming thirst was doused.

His nose felt icy cold, but his cheeks were warm from the flames. His skin smelled of campfire and aftershave, and I wasn't tasting the tangy-sweetness of cranberries this time, but delectable, irresistible cinnamon and chocolate.

S'mores…

He kissed me once then drew away a few inches, still holding my face. I took in a sharp breath, extremely disappointed that he'd stopped. But my longing lasted for only a moment, because he leaned in.

Just like in his kitchen on Thanksgiving morning, I beheld an eruption of lights and sparks behind my eyes, my insides reacting to a natural instinct I couldn't name, had never felt before. As the kiss deepened, those sparks exploded, pounding and glowing in my chest.

I leaned into him, running my hands over his scruffy chin and cheeks, his neck, any skin I could find, up into his hair. My fingers gripped and tangled around the soft curls, my head filling with more stars.

Again, he pulled his face back an inch. Not ready for another break in our kiss, I followed him forward. He moved back a little more. Was he teasing me?

Confused, I forced my eyes to focus on his.

Henry's fervent, sexy gaze was right on me, parching my throat dry in an instant. The side of his mouth pulled into a grin. He was unbearably beautiful.

"Hold on," he whispered. "Close your eyes."

I untangled my fingers from his hair, moved my hands to the tops of his shoulders and obeyed his request. My breath hitched as I felt a rush of cold air when Henry peeled apart the front of my coat and slid his arms around me. I was pulled forward. Warmth again. With my face at his neck, I breathed in, feeling giddy.

We adjusted into each other, so we fit just right. His nose was on my cheek, moving in a circle, sending fresh tingles through my body. My spine felt flimsy and flittery, like an uncoiling spool of ribbon. While on its exploratory mission, his hand froze in place when it touched a two inch space on the small of my back between where my T-shirt ended and my pajama bottoms began. The touch of skin on skin made us inhale in unison.

"You *are* cold," he whispered. "Let's do something about that." Quicker than I thought possible, he pulled me forward onto his lap and slid his hands up the back of my shirt. Heat and silky warmth pushed through my bloodstream.

Millions of moments ticked by, but I was conscious only of his hands, his lips, the buzz in my head.

I returned to consciousness again when Henry suddenly drew in a sharp inhale. I opened one eye, then quickly released my grip on his neck, noticing the four red marks from my fingers.

He kept his eyes on mine, his lips curving into a slow, sexy smirk. "Atta tiger," he breathed over my mouth.

"I…clawed you," I whispered. "Why didn't you stop me?"

"I wasn't complaining." He lifted a smile that melted everything in me that wasn't already goo. "I was complimenting."

After another kiss that was far too short, he slid me off his lap and stood up. The front of my body was suddenly freezing, missing his warmth, his arms, his breath in my mouth. The weight of his hands was heavy as he placed them on the tops of my shoulders and looked down at me. His hair was thoroughly mussed up from my fingers, rendering him even sexier than I'd labeled him just moments ago.

"I'm going to stoke the fire now," he said.

A bit out of practice at interpreting suggestive innuendos, I didn't quite understand his meaning, but I was pretty sure I got the gist. So, I smiled, slid my hands around his waist and went to stand. But Henry held me in place.

"No, Spring," he said after a soft laugh. "I mean, stoke the fire, the actual fire." He nodded toward the fading embers behind him. "What did you think I meant?"

"Nothing," I said, exhaling a giggle. "The fire. Right."

He bent down and kissed the tip of my nose. "Don't move."

As I watched him walk away, I pressed my lips together. They were already swollen, probably from the stubble on his neck that I couldn't stay away from. I knew I would have telltale markings on my face tomorrow morning—more obvious evidence of making out than even a hickey. There'd be no way to hide it then, to hide what we'd been doing for the past hour.

But the question was, would I *want* to hide it?

Henry was down on one knee before the diminishing cinders, rebuilding our neglected fire. When he finished, he opened the cooler and took out a bottle of water. He held up another one, pointing it at me, but I shook my head. He unscrewed the lid and took a drink.

"You completely dehydrated me," he said in a low voice. Then he winked.

Holy frack.

I took in a gulp of cold night air, but that only made me more lightheaded, feeling simultaneously dizzy and extremely alert from breathing in the smell of his neck for so long. These were uncharted waters for me, but I wouldn't think about that. Now was not the time to dissect everything or analyze to death in my Spring way.

When he was finished with his water, he didn't return to his spot next to me, but instead sat on the blanket at my feet, facing the roaring fire. He leaned back against my legs, his body warm and solid.

"Do you remember that time in my kitchen?" he asked in the tiniest of whispers.

My heart sped up as I remembered that morning. "Yes," I answered, looking down at the back of his head, his dark hair blowing gently.

"Then there was that night up in my hallway and the morning before vacation…in your bedroom."

"Mm hm." My chest was getting hot again.

"It happened once, then it didn't happen again, twice." His right hand wrapped around my right ankle. Even after the past hour, his touch was still a shock to my system, a very welcomed shock. "I promised myself I would never allow another opportunity to pass." His other hand was around my other ankle now. "I know you know what I mean."

I did, indeed.

His hands slid inside my pajama legs, moving up and down on the lower part of my calves. I closed my eyes and breathed slowly as blood zinged through my veins. "I hate to disappoint you, Knightly, but I wouldn't have kissed you either of those other times." My protest sounded humorously unconvincing, because even as I spoke, I shifted forward, laying a hand on his shoulder.

"Honeycutt." He sighed impatiently. "Yes you would have." He squeezed one of my legs. "And I wasn't talking about just kissing you."

My heart pounded hard and fast, almost painfully, and I glanced to the side, noticing how close the tent was to where we were sitting; too close for anything more to happen between us tonight. Although every time Henry touched me, I knew what I wanted.

Calm yourself, Springer. You're together, and you've got plenty of time.

This was further confirmed when Henry reached back and took my hand, gently tugging me forward until I was seated on the ground beside him. "Hi," he said, wrapping an arm around me and scooting me until there wasn't an inch between us.

"Hi." I tucked my chin to rest against his chest. "What are you thinking?"

"I'm thinking the same thing I always think when I'm around you." He kissed the top of my head. "I've been talking way too much."

"Acknowledging that you're loquacious doesn't answer my question. Tell me what you're *feeling*."

In my entire life, I'd never asked a guy that question. I didn't know what possessed me to inquire now. What kind of answer could he possible give me? I bit my lip and waited.

After a moment, he shifted, his arm around me loosening. "Okay," he said. "This is genuine sentiment, Spring. Are you ready?"

I took in a deep breath. I didn't want the mood to be spoiled by Henry being, well, Henry. "Ready," I said.

Before he spoke, he took my chin in his hand and tilted my face to look me in the eyes. "I feel like tonight is Christmas and my birthday," he whispered. "And I just got everything on my list. *That* is how I'm feeling."

I let this sentiment sink into my soul. A moment later, I pulled back, slid my chin from his hand, and rolled onto my knees. Henry blinked up at me, uncharacteristically vulnerable. His eyes were soft and brown as we gazed at each other. I put both hands on his cheeks then ran them down the sides of his neck, stopping when I got to his shoulders.

"Well then," I said, pushing his body back, my body following him down, "happy birthday, Henry," I whispered. "Again."

The chirps of night crickets turned to croaking frogs, and before we knew it, the orange sun was a dim line on the eastern horizon. It was still plenty dark and I was not ready for morning.

"Are you sleeping?" I whispered. Henry lay on his back, and I was on my side, both my arms linking through one of his, my forehead against his shoulder.

My question seemed like a logical one; it had been

about five minutes since either of us had spoken or moved, and that was the longest we'd gone without kissing all night.

"Thinking, not sleeping," he whispered, pressing his lips to my hairline.

"About?" I asked, resting my chin on top of his shoulder so I could look him in the eyes. Henry in the dim white light of pre-dawn. Swoon City.

He took a deep breath, twisting his back in a little stretch. "Timing," he answered. "And irony."

"Timing and irony occupies your mind at five in the morning? Is that the effect I have on you?"

"The effect you have on me…" he repeated. He was looking past me, up at the murky sky. "Actually, I was thinking about being back at Stanford, in the house across the street, and being here now. *Timing*."

I gave his arm a squeeze. "And irony?"

"The irony is, back in December, I felt like I was spending all my energy trying to *not* be overtly obvious about my feelings." He turned to me. "And you never knew?"

I lifted my eyebrows.

"Should I have said something then? I tried to, you know."

"Timing," I whispered, rubbing my cheek against his shoulder. The soft wool blend of his sweater felt itchy compared to his skin. Even though we'd been together all night, I couldn't get over the feel of him, his taste, that potent, delicious smell of his neck. I was higher than a fan at a Bob Marley concert.

"But still, I'm torn on this subject," Henry continued. "I realize that arrogance is *supposed* to be a turn off." There was a smile in his voice. "I guess my being sucked in by your wily ways was all part of your plan."

"Oh, yes," I said after a laugh. "My plan. You fell right into that. It only took seven months."

He laughed softly and stared at the sky again. "Really, what would your reaction have been the night before vacation if I'd kissed you?"

"You mean *tried* to kiss me?" I corrected, letting go of his arm to run my finger over his chin.

He scoffed—that charming arrogance. "There would've been no *trying*, Spring," he said. "What would you have done?"

"Most likely I would've punched you in the stomach," I answered, running my finger back and forth across his bottom lip.

Henry was quiet for a moment. "And *then* what would you have done?" he asked. "After I kissed you a *third* time, I mean." The man was nothing if not persistent.

"Probably kicked you in the ribs." I propped up onto my hands, my face hovering over his, only to lower myself down, settling halfway on his chest, my nose at his neck.

Henry slid his hands inside the back of my shirt. It seemed to be his favorite place to linger, like his neck was to me. We both needed to feel skin. It was a little surprising how I never once felt nervous or uncomfortable, scared about what might happen next. More importantly—unlike with every other guy—I was never once bored.

"And after a fourth time?" he asked, sounding relaxed.

"Haven't you had enough rejection?" I whispered, planting kisses down his neck and taking deep inhales.

He didn't reply. His hands slid out from inside my shirt and ran down my back from my head to my waist, long strokes, like he was painting me. I tilted my chin so I could see him, but his gaze was turned away, as if purposefully ignoring me. His eyes seemed to be intently focused on something else now, something he was holding in his hand on the other side of me, but I couldn't see what it was.

His free hand cupped the back of my head, his fingers kneading tenderly. He turned his other hand toward the light, and I could finally see what it was that he was fingering so gently. It was one of my braids.

Almost reverently, he moved it to his mouth and kissed it.

Chapter 24

"Spring. Spring? *Spring*!"

"What?" I gasped and jolted forward, my seat belt yanking me back. In the process, I banged my elbow against the cooler on the seat next to me. After multiple blinks, I focused on Mel's face between the two front seats.

"What's the difference between a crow and a blackbird?"

Sheesh, is that all?

"Sorry, were you napping or...?" Her gaze slid two spaces over.

I also took a quick glance in that direction. Henry was staring out his window at the passing scenery of pines and telephone poles. Fist at chin, his expression totally blank.

I breathed out quietly and returned to Mel, rubbing my elbow. "Umm, blackbirds are small, waders, they have specific songs, while crows are larger." I forced myself to be thorough. "For example, ravens are commonly referred to under the generic umbrella of *crow*."

"Ew! Ravens are huge and creepy," she complained.

"Right?" I agreed, nodding eagerly.

Satisfied, Mel returned to her seat, relaying my information to Tyler, who was driving us back to Vancouver.

I rounded my lips and released a quiet exhale, sending another sideways glance toward Henry.

A little grin was on his face now, but he was still looking out the window. "You were thinking about last night, weren't you?" he guessed in a voice only I could hear.

I hissed air through my teeth to shush him.

"Yeah." He blinked slowly and gave me a very intense look. "So was I."

"And what about those little blackbird things? The tiny ones?" Mel asked, turning to me again. Before I could answer, her expression bent. "Are you okay, babe? Your face is totally flushed."

I was about to lift my hand to check the temperature on my forehead, but Dr. Melanie beat me to it.

"No, you don't *feel* hot." She grabbed my wrist. "But your pulse is going like a hummingbird and your hands are freezing. Here." She tossed a blanket over the seat to me. "It's probably making you too cold sitting between the window and the cooler. Ty, why didn't you dump out the ice? Tyler? Henry, help me move it. No, *this* way."

Mel deftly leaned over the seat, unlatched my seat belt and pulled me forward by the arm so Henry could push the cooler over, leaving me in the middle seat next to him.

"There," Mel said, examining my new position. "Much better." She nodded and returned to her seat. "We've still got four days to go. Mustn't get you sick." She started barking at Tyler to watch the road.

I sat stock-still, Henry right beside me. I didn't have the guts to look at him just yet, but I could feel his shoulder shaking in a suppressed laugh. I tried to casually lean away. He leaned away as well, propping an elbow on the armrest.

A moment later, the blanket over my lap moved slightly, and I felt Henry's hand on my arm, then it slid between my back and the seat. My eyes popped open and I stared forward as his fingers tiptoed up. I couldn't help arching my back, my breaths becoming shallow.

"What are you doing?" I whispered, trying to regain control of my faculties. He laughed quietly, his fingers manipulating the very sensitive nape of my neck. My back arched again. "S-s-stop…" I almost whimpered.

"Why?"

"Because." I bit my lip. "Because if you don't stop, I'll start purring. Do you want to explain that to them?"

His smile grew but he did remove his hand and set it on his knee. "Spring," he whispered, "do you honestly believe they think we were up all night *discussing old times*? That was a brilliant explanation, by the way, as to why my sleeping bag was still rolled up in the corner of the tent."

"They *know*?" I gasped under my breath, my eyes moving to the front seat where Mel and Tyler were in the middle of a lively debate over the GPS.

Henry shrugged. "I didn't say anything. After you jumped a foot away from me when Mel came out of the tent this morning, I figured you wanted to keep it between us for now." He tilted his head. "Is this weird for you? Us?"

"A little," I admitted in a whisper. "I'll tell her later tonight. She's going to make such huge deal about it. I just… I don't…"

"It's okay, I don't mind," Henry said. "In fact" — the blanket over my lap moved again — "I like making you purr." His hand slid up the inside of my shirt, his fingers tracing the line of my spine.

"I…" I actually did whimper this time. "I think I'm gonna have a stroke."

"Kiss me," Henry whispered. "You'll feel better."

The suggestion made me bite my lip, but I managed to pull it together and lean back on the seat, squishing his hand, forcing him to pull it away.

"No?" he mouthed when I shot him a look. He groaned in frustration then unbuckled his seat belt and lean forward between the two front seats so he could check out something on the dashboard. He peered out the windshield at something else. After a moment, he sat back and buckled in.

"Less than a quarter tank of gas left," he reported out of the corner of his mouth. "I happen to know there's a gas station ten minutes away. I'm sure we'll be stopping to fill up, and *they* will be busy pumping gas and bickering. Won't even notice." He lifted a mischievous half smile, still staring straight ahead. "I suppose I can wait until then."

"Wait to what?"

He turned to me, his expression all business. "Well, Spring, since you obviously won't let me ravish you now, I'll have to wait till we stop." Without moving his gaze from me, he nodded out the window. "Once there, I will peel you from this car, drag you behind the building, and properly devour you in private for five minutes. Deal?"

My stomach made a weird kind of synchronized flex-and-flip, then melted like butter on hot toast. Still eyeing me, Henry began drumming his fingers on his knee impatiently.

When his gaze slid to my mouth, that flipping in my stomach went into overdrive.

Butterflies, I realized. Henry Knightly was giving me butterflies.

"Deal!" I blurted.

"What?" Mel asked, looking back at me.

"Oh, ummpp." I puffed out my cheeks and gave a huge, dramatic shrug, pointing out the window. "I don't— Nothing."

After she returned to Tyler, I released the air from my cheeks.

"You should be an actress," Henry said. "Complete natural."

I pressed my lips together, suppressing a laugh. His fingers were still tapping his knee. I stared at it, wishing above everything I could touch him. Well, maybe not above *everything*. Maybe—

"Do you mind if I change the subject?"

I ran a hand across my clammy forehead. "Please."

"That night before the end of semester, when I asked what you wanted out of life, you told me you want to change the world."

"Yes?" I said, tugging my lip, irritated that Tyler was driving so freaking slow.

"What did that mean, exactly?"

"I may have been overshooting that night," I admitted. "Making sure to outdo you."

"Diabolical." Henry grinned.

"But right now, for example, my Local Communities class is setting up a comprehensive recycling program using Palo Alto as a prototype." Appreciating this distraction, I crossed my legs and fingered one long braid. "We're hoping to branch out to San Francisco, maybe get some national exposure."

"Recycling?" he repeated skeptically.

"Baby steps."

"You know, there's no definitive proof that recycled goods—paper specifically—is using less finite resources. Your trees are still in danger." He tapped his chin with his index finger. "I only bring it up to help you know your facts. That, and on a personal note, there's always the rise I'll get out of you."

I rolled my eyes. "You love that, don't you?"

"Not to mention the topic of land development in the Great Basin." He grinned. "Did you add that to part nine of your thesis?"

"Oh, um, no." My butterflies were temporarily netted. "I've actually been having a little problem with that section."

Henry looked at me, all teasing gone from his countenance. "Why didn't you tell me?"

"When?" I lifted my brows. "You were gone."

His eyes didn't move from mine. I could see a flicker of confusion in them at first, then comprehension. And then regret. I felt regret, too. Or at least a tiny hint of it. Last semester, hadn't I decided that I'd relied on him too much? Trusted him when I should have been independent? Because, when he was gone, I felt worse off than before.

"Spring." He leaned over, pressing his shoulder against mine, holding it there. "We'll work on it together." He lifted a hand and pinched the bridge of his nose. "I'm sorry, I...I don't know your schedule this semester. Can we meet at the library on the first Thursday we're back?"

"I think I have that evening free."

"Hand me your phone." But he didn't wait, he just grabbed it from the outside pocket of my purse and tapped in a few words. "It's on your calendar now. Don't be late."

"I won't, and thank you," I said, a little amazed by how easily I accepted his help again.

For a few seconds, I felt a void between us, a wall, as if we'd reverted back to platonic student/teacher mode, like last night never happened.

Just as a new kind of regret was about to seize me, he took my hand under the blanket, then moved it onto my lap. His eyes were smiling, and I wondered if he could sense the utter relief I felt the moment he touched me. He flipped my hand over and skimmed his fingers across my palm, between my fingers, up my wrist, tracing a circle.

"We'll meet on the top floor of the Meyer," he said, sandwiching our palms together, trapping heat. When our eyes met, he gave my hand a squeeze. "There's a study room behind the stacks. It's the only one that has a lock." He cocked an eyebrow. "Think about it."

"It's a date," I said.

"Wear that T-shirt from our food fight." His eyes gave me a quick up-down. "Dead sexy."

When I inhaled, every molecule of incoming oxygen was tied to that clean, spicy, manly smell, his scent that I'd been breathing in for the past twelve hours.

"T-ten minutes to that gas station, you say?"

"More like two now," he corrected after a glance out the window.

"We're stopping to fill up," Tyler announced.

I shot a glance at Henry. He smirked charmingly.

The car slowed, and we idled, waiting to turn left into a

small Chevron station. There were no other cars pumping gas. Tyler was instructing Mel on what exact snacks he wanted from the mini-mart, then he turned his head to us, asking what we wanted. Henry and I declined, almost in unison. Tyler also announced that both he and Mel would be using the "facilities" first, and we'd have to wait our turn. He added that we might want to wander around because he was going to fill the tires, too.

The plan was flawless. I pulled on my lip and stared out the window, my mouth a combination of cotton-dry and salivating. I wondered if I would be able to wait until we were behind the gas station like Henry planned.

After approximately one million years, the car finally pulled up next to the gas pump. Tyler grabbed his wallet from the visor and climbed out of the car. He opened Henry's door, expecting that we would be getting out. Tyler headed toward the store.

Mel was fussing with her seat belt. Taking way too long.

My heart pounded behind my ears.

"You guys staying here?" she asked without turning around.

Henry's fingers wrapped around my hand as he answered Mel that we were staying. Mel climbed out and was about to close her door when Henry called out, "Would you mind picking up two bottles of water?"

Mel was wearing sunglasses, so I couldn't see her eyes. Without missing a beat, she nodded and shut the door.

"Preemptive measures," he explained. "I plan on dehydrating *you* this time. Even things up."

"You think of everything."

He leaned toward me, a pouncing mountain lion look

in his eyes. It was all I could do to hold up one finger to stop him. Over his shoulder, my eyes followed her. I could count the seconds in my head, the number of steps it would take until both Mel and Tyler were inside the store. My calculations gave us six seconds more.

Henry was on me in three.

What took him so long?

Chapter 25

"Mel said she'd be downstairs any second."

"Yeah, right." Tyler chuckled. We both knew it would be more like hours.

After returning from the kitchen, he sat on the couch and grabbed a *Sports Illustrated*, while I was cross-legged on the floor at the coffee table, attempting to skim a chapter in my *Women of the Twentieth Century* textbook.

Grueling.

I'd planned on napping on our two-hour drive back to Vancouver, but Henry's little pit stop made that entirely impossible...

"I missed you," he'd said the second Mel and Tyler were inside the mini-mart. A bit too preoccupied with his neck to notice, not until my feet hit the ground did I realize that Henry had actually picked me up in his arms, carried me out of the car and around to the back of the gas station.

We'd used every second of those five minutes: Henry

backing me up and pinning my hands against the stucco building. Henry holding me still then running his mouth up and down my neck until my knees gave way. Henry intertwining his fingers with mine. Despite all the kissing that had gone on the night before, the simple, certain gesture of repositioning his grip so he could weave his fingers between mine felt hugely intimate.

"Time's up," he'd said into my hair, releasing me. But I'd made the scandalous decision to give us an extra ten seconds, by first pressing my palms against his chest, feeling his strong, pounding heart, then slowly sliding my arms around him. I lifted up on my toes, hooked my chin over his shoulder, then clasped my hands behind his back, sealing us together.

No lips, no tongues. We were hugging.

"Ahh, this is…very…" He exhaled a little moan when I'd squeezed tighter, making our bodies a single line. "Springer." His breath hitched. "Now you're making *me* purr—"

"Are we a tad sleepy this evening?"

My eyes popped open, suddenly realizing where my mind had been. Tyler was still across from me on the couch. I could practically hear the smirk in his voice.

"Maybe you and old Henry shouldn't have stayed up all night, hmmm?"

"This is a boring subject," I offered, tapping a yellow highlighter to my open textbook.

None of us would be getting much rest tonight either, because once Mel hauled her fashionable behind downstairs and Henry showed up, the four of us were heading to Portland to see a concert.

After reading the same sentence three times, I allowed

my head to drop down on my book, resting on one cheek. If I had thirty seconds of quiet, I knew I would be out like a light.

"*Sooo…*" Tyler broke the silence again. I was amazed by how that single word was laced with so much insinuation. It was a strain to lift my head, but I managed. His big blue eyes twinkled, regarding me just as Henry had this morning. I wondered when it was that I'd become completely transparent.

"You and Henry, eh?"

My spine elongated indignantly. It was a natural reflex. "Me and Henry, what?"

"Hey now, I'm just shooting the breeze while we wait," he defended. "I don't like silence. But…you know what I meant." He made slobbery kissing sounds.

I rolled my eyes. "Nothing happened between us." But it was a ridiculous, useless attempt. If he was anything like his cousin, Tyler would see right through me.

I stared at the front door, fingers thumping impatiently under the table. I couldn't wait to see him, couldn't wait to hear the Jeep roaring up the driveway. If not for the overly interested eyes of Mel and Tyler, I imagined myself busting out the door the second I heard the grinding of gravel, maybe running and jumping into his arms like I'd seen in a chick flick.

Huh. I smiled to myself. *And just like that, I've become a romantic. I blame Bruno Mars.*

It felt much longer than five hours since Henry had left us at Mel's to drive back to wherever he was staying this week. Had he mentioned a grandfather? And now, per his latest text, he was currently en route to the house. En route to me.

Butterflies.

I stared vacantly down at my textbook, trying to keep any kind of smile off my face, trying to not let every giddy, girly emotion show. When I looked up at Tyler, making sure my blank expression was firmly in place first, his smarmy grin had disappeared.

"Oh, I thought for sure." He ran his fingers up the back of his baby blond hair. "Mel *did* tell me you guys were just talking last night, but I assumed…"

I had to bite my lip to keep from hooting out loud. Tyler actually bought that load?

"Just catching up. Like I said." I confirmed my earlier fib. "Henry and I lived across the street from each other at Stanford, remember? And we worked on a paper together."

Tyler nodded, fully convinced. "That's cool," he said. "For *you*, at least."

"What do you mean?"

"You seem like a nice girl, and you're Mel's best friend."

"So?"

He took a long swig of soda, like he was preparing to tell a lengthy story. "I didn't think Henry hooked up with chicks, all casual like that." He wiped his mouth with the back of a hand. "Well, he usually doesn't."

"Usually?"

He set down the soda can and linked his fingers between his knees. "Okay, so there was this one time, the beginning of last summer, right? Just after he graduated from Duke, Henry was about to go off to Sweden or wherever with his family." He looked over his shoulder then back at me. "He called it *filling his canteen.* Ha-ha! I guess he figured he'd be away from American women for a while. So, anyway"—he leaned forward, his elbows on his knees—"right before he left, he hooked up for the weekend, just because he knew he wouldn't be getting any all summer." Tyler sat back and crossed his legs.

"Hooked up," I repeated, not quite certain what he meant. I knew the term, of course, but I also knew its ambiguous definition. I waited for further explanation, also wondering if Tyler's face was about to break into that stupid grin and he'd say he was yanking my chain.

But he went on. No stupid grin.

"Yeah," he said, smiling approvingly. "Ya know, *tapped* that thing."

"Oh," I said, perfectly understanding him now. I leaned an elbow on the coffee table, feeling envious and a little jealous of some unknown girl, just because she had been with Henry first. I looked down and couldn't help smiling, confident in the knowledge that our time would come soon enough. And I could wait.

"I think she was the sister of one of his buddies at Duke," Tyler continued, pulling me from my daydream. "Oh, yeah!" He smacked his own forehead. "She was his roommate's sister. Guess she was visiting her brother back east, and Henry took the easy in."

Those happy little butterflies in my stomach flew up my throat and out my open mouth.

"It's kind of a mess now for him," Tyler added, lowering his voice like we were sharing a secret. "This chick won't leave him alone. She's at Stanford, too, I guess. You might know her."

The yellow highlighter I'd been gripping slipped from

my hand and rolled under the coffee table. "It's a big school," I deflected, while picturing the girl in my head. Her straight, bleached out hair, her angular features, and that scowl of loathing whenever she looked at me.

I fought the urge to run the back of my hand over my lips, rubbing off Henry's kisses.

"I don't know about you Stanford girls, anyway..." Tyler went on, but I turned away, focusing first at the landscape painting past his shoulder, then down at my open book, the words on the page whirling around. I took in a long breath, held it, blew it out, reeling in my disgust.

Of course it wasn't fair of me to be pissed at Tyler; he was only the messenger. And to be angry with Henry over this wasn't exactly fair and impartial, either. What he did before we met had nothing to do with me.

But the thought of Henry and Lilah together did show an amazingly low—and I'm sorry, *desperate*—lack of taste and judgment on Henry's part. From out of nowhere, I felt on the brink of laughter, considering all the years she must have pined for him. No wonder her hatred for me reached new levels last fall. On top of my beating her out for the internship two years ago, the girl was actually jealous.

Tyler was talking again, still droning on about the women at Stanford. I couldn't help wondering if he and Mel had had a fight earlier, if that was why he was suddenly so bitter toward the female population of Palo Alto.

"Over the holidays," he continued, "I was with Henry for, like, one day. I was kind of asking him advice about Mel." He shot me a look. "He didn't know who I was talking about, though."

I laughed. "I'm sure your secret is safe."

"Mel and I are pretty off-and-on, you know? I was frustrated at the time and not sure what to do. Anyway, Henry told me about this other girl he knows, same kind of thing, I guess. She was dating one of his friends. She…" I was only half-listening, staring down at the table, noticing the subtle marbley veins in the wood, different levels of brown and black, reminding me of Henry's hair. "She started blowing hot and cold, like, mind games, hard to get and whatever," he went on. "Henry told his friend flat-out to break up with her."

A sudden coldness wrapped around my core. "What do you mean, he *told* him to?"

Tyler smiled. Perhaps he and Mel did have something in common: a love of gossip.

"I don't know all the details." His voice was hushed yet excited. "But from what I figure, Henry had to practically convince this guy, this buddy of his, to dump her."

Whatever creature had lurched in my stomach five seconds ago, it was now doing back flips while wearing spiky shoes and a spiky helmet. "When"—I swallowed, trying to feign indifference—"was this?"

Tyler thought for a minute, fingering his chin. "Recently. End of last semester." He scooted over, closer to me. Something in my expression encouraged him to continue without me questioning further. "So, like, he didn't break them up literally, he just *convinced* his buddy to dump her. Hilarious, right? I mean, who has the rocks to do that? Only Trip. Classic."

My gaze slid from his face, my vision once more taken over by images of Henry. But this time, the picture included Julia crying on the floor of our kitchen because the guy she loved had disappeared. My vision expanded to show Knightly standing over her, wearing a haughty smile.

"Seemed pretty proud of himself, too," Tyler added.

"He *said* that?" I blurted. "Henry *actually said* that?"

"Well, like I said, I don't know the whole story, but... Hey, you were his neighbor. Did you know the chick he dumped? I take it she was a hick." He wrinkled his nose. "Small town. No money."

I knew my face was flushing, heat and fury rolling up from my chest. "Your cousin should learn to mind his own damn business."

Tyler threw his head back and burst out laughing. "I would *love* to hear you tell him that. Yeah, that'd be *really* hilarious."

I saw red as I stared at him, and knew I was about to spring from the floor and cause real damage if he kept talking. It was only a matter of time.

"Anyway." Tyler finally stopped hooting. "His buddy's totally free and I'm sure his sweet little ex found herself a new"—he cocked an eyebrow—"stud."

Instead of going all Karate Kid on his ass, I found I had no strength. I dropped my face in my hands, my cheeks and eyelids so hot I was sure my temperature had spiked over a hundred.

"Hey," Tyler said, "you okay?"

"Migraine," I murmured through my hands. "Agony." I stumbled to my feet, pain impeding my vision. I reached for my textbook but only bumped its corner. It fell to the floor and I didn't bother picking it up. "I'm not going tonight." I moved toward the stairs. "I'll tell Mel."

"What about Henry?"

I whipped around, using the last of my strength. "Tell him to go frack himself."

. . .

Not having the presence of mind to remember that Julia was home in Florida for the week, I called our house first. No answer. After the second time I got voice mail on her cell, I left a message.

"Julia?" I spoke after the tone. "Julia, I'm sorry…sorry I haven't returned your calls this week. I've been…busy. I'm sorry." I rubbed the heel of my hand over my throbbing forehead as I paced around the four-poster bed. Even the faint light from the late afternoon's overcast was killing my eyes. "There's so much I need to tell you, bunny. I'm just… so sorry."

Of course she would not understand why I was frantically apologizing, but betrayal to a friend, even unintentionally, wasn't something one could blurt out over the phone. When I didn't know what else to say, I ended the call.

All the while, Mel was banging at the bedroom door. "Spring? Springer? What do you mean you're not coming?"

I tossed my cell on the bed, and mumbled something through the door about not feeling well.

"Will you be okay?"

I would.

"Do you want me to stay home with you?"

I did not.

"Well, all right," she quietly said. "Grams won't be home until tonight. Will you be okay alone?"

I assured her that I would.

From the window, I heard the faint hum of a motorcycle down below, drawing closer to the house. Two tires on the gravel driveway. Thirty seconds later, Mel's voice was in the living room. Then Knightly's. The sound was nails on a chalkboard that I couldn't drown out. I glanced at the doorknob where my backpack had been hanging earlier with my ear buds inside. I sighed, realizing they were both downstairs. So I sat on the edge of the bed and, to block out that excruciating voice from below, I pressed my hands over my ears.

A few minutes later, I felt the vibration of the front door shutting. I waited, lowering my hands just in time to hear the sound of a car driving away.

They were gone.

I picked up my cell, trying Julia again. Still no answer. I held my hands over my chest, feeling hot and tense, my heart pounding too hard. I tried to breathe but couldn't seem to take in more than tiny puffs of air. Everything hurt.

I felt like a traitor—to Julia, to myself, to everything I believed in. Even though I'd *unknowingly* been fraternizing with the enemy, I couldn't stop the guilt. To block out that feeling, I concentrated on the anger, the betrayal. The only solace was that it had only been kissing.

Yes, despite what I'd wanted to happen, I'd only *kissed* him. And it meant nothing. He meant nothing.

Weakness and gravity pushed me onto the pillows, but that made my head throb more fiercely, so I rolled to my side and slid off the bed.

With all the lights off, the living room was murky. Shadows and bits of late afternoon sun broke though the overcast, painting shapes and curves on the eastern wall. At the foot of the stairs I stopped, glancing around the room. My backpack was sitting by the coffee table, the textbook and highlighter I'd dropped lying neatly on top.

Still standing on the last stair, I remembered there was also a bottle of aspirin in my bag, but I couldn't seem to get my feet to move me in that direction. Instead, I stepped forward to the wall by the front door, leaned against it, and slid to the floor, my knees bending in front of my chest.

I shut my eyes, but my brain inside spun so fast I couldn't focus, so I stayed curled in a ball. Less than a minute later, a noise startled me conscious.

I lifted my chin in time to see the front door next to me creak open.

Chapter 26

"Spring?"

I toyed with the idea of saying nothing, hoping he'd give up and back out the way he came.

"Spring? Are you awake?"

"I'm right here." *Dumb ass.*

Knightly jerked around. "Oh." He exhaled a startled laugh, then cleared his throat. "You're all right?"

"What are you doing here?" I pulled myself to my feet, gazed longingly toward the top of the stairs, but didn't think my legs could carry me all the way up there. So, robot-like, I moved toward the couch.

He was right behind me. "I wanted to check on you. Tyler said—"

"I'm fine."

He stepped in front of me, blocking my way. "You don't seem fine."

My temples throbbed, and while the rest of my body was

clammy and cold, it felt like my head was on fire.

The dimness of the room cast a shadow over his frame. I scanned him quickly.

Nothing in his appearance had altered in the last five hours, causing images to flood my mind—images of a certain campfire, a certain gas station, and a face that had been so near to me for so many hours that I could see nothing else every time I closed my eyes.

It was an honest struggle to throw up a mental brick wall before any more memories and feelings could break through. A fresh jolt of anguish struck as I looked into his face now. Longing mingled with antipathy…I didn't have the emotional experience to handle that; my feelings for him were too mixed up, too raw.

"I don't know what to tell you," I said. Stepping around him, I grabbed my backpack and hooked it over one shoulder. The simple gesture of moving made my body twinge in pain. That must've shown on my face.

"What's…?" Henry asked, sounding alarmed.

When I tried to step around him again, he reached for my hand. The touch of his skin made me flinch. He didn't let go.

I almost said something…but didn't.

Midway through last semester, I'd grown a distaste for arguing with him—not our innocuous debates that often ended with a clearer understanding of each other's views, but the *real* fights, the rows that left us both in bad moods, worse off.

As I stood before him now, trying my hardest to not look into those chocolaty eyes with the golden flecks, even as the quarrel was building on my tongue…I made a decision to let it pass. I would rather say nothing of it, *think* nothing of it, than fight. I didn't have the strength. Or the heart.

Once I convinced him that I was fine, he would leave and I would never have to deal with him again.

Yes, it was a cowardly response, but the last thing I wanted to do was feel worse.

"Will you please sit down?" He took my arm and gently persuaded me to the couch. I didn't bother protesting, because it truly felt like my knees were about to buckle. He sat on the next cushion, not too close. Maybe he thought I was carrying something contagious. At least that would keep him at a distance.

"Can I get you something?"

"I told you I'm fine," I said coldly, trying to not breathe. The heady scent of him still registered in the back of my throat, making my mouth water.

"I don't think you are."

I made myself look his way. He was smiling, only slightly. Mostly though, I could tell he was concerned, anxious even, at what he was observing in me. A fist squeezed around my heart, knowing that a very big part of me longed to ease his anxiety. But then my stomach rolled, reminding me why I couldn't.

"Are you tired?" he asked.

"Of *course* I'm…" But I made myself stop, not allowing my mouth to remind me aloud why it was that I was tired, why we'd been up all night. I sat forward, ramrod straight and pinched my eyelids together, concentrating on mentally folding an origami swan, blocking out the reasons for my anger.

Numb. Nothing. Blank.

"Ah, I see," he said, and I felt my backpack leaving my shoulder, sliding off my arm. "Why don't you relax and put your feet up." His hands were on my shoulders, pushing me back against the cushions. I didn't fight this, either.

I was aware that Henry had left the couch only when he returned. When I peeled my eyelids apart, there was a napkin and an open can of ginger ale on the coffee table before me. I closed my eyes again. A few seconds later, I felt the cold can between my hands. Mechanically, I lifted it to my lips and took a sip.

"Feeling better?"

"I said I'm—"

"Fine," he finished for me. "I heard you the first three times." He was studying me, wearing that anxious/concerned expression again, but when he met my eyes, he lifted an encouraging smile. "I was going to bring this up later," he said, "but since you're feeling fine and all…"

"What?" I asked, setting the can on the coffee table.

"I have news. A surprise."

Oh, goodie, the angry side of my brain jabbed. *Are you leaving now? Is that the surprise? Bon voyage, buddy. Don't trip on your way out.* The very next moment, my chest and throat burned with anguish. I didn't want him to go anywhere.

"A surprise for you."

I pinched my dry, burning lids together in a long blink, then glanced across the room, trying to focus on anything else while he continued talking.

"Of course, there are two floors, like I was telling you yesterday," he was saying. "Plenty of space—too much, really, but it's a perfect getaway. Well-deserved, I think." He laughed, but it had a bite of something else to it. "I don't know what my family will say. Camille will be in favor; my parents, though, I don't know. My father will freak out, but I think my mother will understand, maybe…"

I continued to sit still, my head throbbing, my stomach knotting up, not having a clue what he was going on about.

"But I don't care. I haven't for months, obviously. It's a wonder I haven't been thrown out of the program." Another bitter laugh. "Law school, my family…none of it means much right now. I tried to put off any decision, thought moving would help, but nothing did any good, because here we are. At this point, the thought of living any other way is impossible."

When he lifted my hand off my lap, I glanced at him, straining from the pressure writhing behind my eyes.

"We can go tomorrow," he said. "Or tonight. Right now, if you want."

When my eyebrows pulled together, it caused a new pain in my head. "Go?" I said, realizing I hadn't been listening. "Where?"

He pressed his hands together, mine between them. "Tahiti."

Even though I was physically immovable, my brain was working now, catching up to what he'd been saying.

"What?" I pulled my hand free.

He seemed mystified by my reaction, because he only stared at me. A moment later, he sighed and the lines in his forehead smoothed out. "The invitation might seem out of the blue to you, but I've been thinking about it, about you, a lot, and you know how I feel…"

He looked into my eyes and leaned in.

I almost allowed it to happen. Part of me wanted

it, wanted *him*, *needed* him. I could practically taste the delicious water waiting to quench my aching pain and thirst. My hands longed to touch him and feel him one more time, while another part of me knew better, and I followed its command.

"Don't," I said, scooting away and standing up. "Don't do that."

Knightly remained on the edge of the couch, looking a little rattled. "Why are you so upset?"

I put my hands on my hips. "Hmm, where should I begin?"

When he rose to his feet, I stepped back, keeping a distance. Henry stopped and watched me guardedly, like he was waiting to see if my head was about to burst into flames.

"Spring," he said, sounding genuinely concerned and more than a little anxious. "What's really going on? What's wrong?"

"This *plan* of yours," I began. "You expect me to drop out of Stanford, leave my whole life, and fly across the world?"

He moved toward me cautiously, his hands out like a cowboy approaching a wild mustang. "I'm sorry if I was undiplomatic about it. I'm not romantic, but I *am* only thinking of you. You can take a break there, finish your thesis. It's all arranged."

"You're crazy, you know that? You're insane, you're— *Why* are you *laughing*?"

He slid his hands in his pockets, his huge grin about to break. "I so enjoy when you get like this."

"You *enjoy* when I'm *angry*?"

He took a beat, his brows furrowing. "No, not angry," he corrected. It was one of the few times I'd seen him backpedal.

"You know when I'm just pushing your buttons."

"You need to leave," I said, realizing my do-not-argue plan had failed. "Right now."

His smile dropped. "Why?"

I nodded toward the door, but he didn't move. "I *swear*, Henry Knightly"—my voice was getting louder and higher pitched—"if you don't *leave* this *instant*—"

"Spring."

I jabbed a finger at the door, demanding that he go.

"I'm not leaving." He took a step forward. "I'm in love with you."

I blinked, and air whooshed from my lungs in one hard gust. "What did you say?"

He took another step. "I love you."

For a moment, I still couldn't breathe—I was in shock, his simple words derailing my anger completely. But the moment was up as quickly as it had come. He might as well have said his favorite color was blue.

"So?" I said, forcing my voice to regrip the anger.

I could both see and hear him take in a sharp breath.

"So?" He ran a hand through his hair. "I love you and I want you…to come with me, to *be* with me."

"You seriously think I'll run away with you because that's what you happen to want at the moment?"

Words were flying at me, I could actually see them in my mind's eye, forming into sentences. Aiding and abetting these words were memories from the past, bruised feelings that were supposed to be gone, that I *thought* were gone. I only had to open my mouth and they came tumbling out.

"May I remind you that the night we met you treated me like an ingrate? You were rude and judgmental because of what you heard and because of the way I looked, like I was beneath your dignity."

"That's not true."

"Why don't you take *Lilah* to Tahiti? I'm sure she'd be thrilled to pick up where you two left off."

Knightly turned completely white. I thought this would please me, but it didn't. In fact, it felt like the wind had been knocked out of me again. Once more, I wanted to go to him, to take back my words, to wrap my arms around him until the hurt in his eyes went away. In some sick, ironic twist, I knew that comforting him would comfort me. If the past didn't exist, nothing would be in our way.

But the past was rushing back, too quickly for me to block, and it was very real.

"*Lilah*, Henry!" My voice broke. "What were you thinking?"

At that point, I didn't know if I wanted an explanation from him, or an apology, or what. All I knew was suddenly the thought of them together was revolting.

He spread his hands. "Lilah was... Spring, she means nothing to me. It was nothing."

"Nothing?" I repeated. "You have sex with her and that's nothing? Even you can't be that crass."

He dropped his hands but didn't reply.

"Is that what you expect out of me, too? I'm so sorry I disappointed you by not tearing off my clothes in front of the campfire."

"I wasn't going to sleep with you last night. It's been one day, we're not..." He trailed off and thrust another hand through his hair. "Lilah was a mistake that I've regretted every day since. Believe me."

"Yeah, sure," I scoffed, remembering how she was all over him at the street party. Sure, he hadn't looked extremely into it, but I never witnessed him fighting her off.

"Well, I'm certain your family took to her much more than they ever would to me. Now you'll never have to worry about what they'll think." I was so mad my mind went blank, yet the words kept flying out like darts aimed at his heart. "I know all about your family, and your *sister*. *Alex* told me everything."

Knightly's face warped from white to red. "Don't believe anything he says," he muttered, almost like a threat. "I warned you to stay away from him."

"You *warned* me?" I echoed. "For your information, Alex told me about the crap-load of things you did to him in high school."

"Me?" He pointed at his chest, sounding indignant. "To *him*?"

I nodded firmly. "And you obviously haven't changed. You're still duplicitous to anybody who happens to *not* have a million dollars in the bank."

"That's absurd," he muttered, pacing the room like a flea-bag lawyer working a jury. He stopped and took a few breaths, raking both hands through his hair. "So that's the reason you're upset." He dropped his chin and exhaled, calming himself down. "Do you honestly believe what he told you?" When I didn't reply, he spun around. "It's not true," he said, his voice full of entreating. "You know me."

"Do I?"

I'd spoken aloud, but I was asking only myself.

I don't remember him reaching out or holding me by the arms, but there he was. His hands moved up to my shoulders, slight pressure to keep me still, reminding me of last night.

"Yes, you do," he said softly, staring into my eyes. "Think. Please."

So I did. About him, and about me. About what I thought to be the truth, and what I felt was true down to my toes. His kindness toward his friends, his brilliant mind, his patience with me, how strong I felt when we were together, how he challenged me and made me fight for what I believed in. From day one.

The anger was dissolving, and the queasiness settled. Because, yes, I knew.

"I…I guess I'm not sure what really happened between you and Alex," I admitted softly. "And maybe it doesn't matter, because what I feel…" He gripped my shoulders, easing me toward him. "I feel…" I touched his face, my fingers running across his chin, his parted lips, resting on his cheek.

Henry placed his hand over mine and exhaled, long and ragged, his whole face showing exquisite relief. In unison, we shifted our weight.

But suddenly, I was thinking again of those things I knew about him, one being how he treated his friends. Like a flash, I recalled what had brought us to that room in the first place.

I'd only known Tyler for two days. Was it fair of me to trust him over Henry, without even asking?

"Did you do it?" I dropped my hand and stared up at him.

"No. Spring, Alex Parks is a pathological liar. I'll tell you exactly—"

"No." I cut him off. "Did you do what Tyler said?"

He blinked, looking confused. "What?"

"Did you break up Julia and Dart?" I asked point blank, even though my voice was shaking. "Did you have anything to do with that?"

Henry just stared at me. For a moment, I wondered if he didn't understand what I was asking. Did he need me to rephrase the question?

But no. The longer our eyes locked and the longer he didn't respond, the clearer the answer was.

"What the *hell*, Henry." I brushed his hand off my arm and took a step back. "You *did*?"

He stared down at me, bemused, making me want to shake him by the shoulders like a child.

"How could you do that? *Why*?"

"I…" he began, but then stopped. "It was the right thing to do. She didn't love him. You know that."

"What?" I shrieked, balling my hands into tight fists, feeling like I might actually hit something.

"Dart's like a brother to me. I couldn't watch him make the same mistake. I knew it wouldn't work out with her."

"What *same mistake*?" I asked. "And you have no way of knowing it wouldn't work out. She hasn't been the same, Henry. Her heart is broken; her *spirit* is broken." My voice cracked. "And it's your fault."

"Spring, just—"

"I can't do this." I pointed back and forth from him and to me. "What you did to Julia and your so-called best friend is despicable. So whatever little head game you're playing with me, it's over. Do you understand?"

He shifted his weight but didn't speak.

"First Alex, then Lilah, and now Julia. Who knows how many people's lives you've screwed with."

"I haven't screwed with anyone. You don't know what happened. Just listen." He reached out but I dodged him.

"I cannot *be* with someone, *trust* someone who's capable of what you did. I could never love you. Never."

He flinched at my last word.

"We're done, Knightly," I said, speaking more forcefully so my voice wouldn't break again. "Now... This minute... *Pour toujours—*"

"Yeah. I get it, Spring." The harsh vibe in his voice matched his expression. "After all I've said, this is still how you feel?" When I didn't so much as blink, he exhaled sharply. "Then there's nothing more to say."

I folded my arms. Nothing more to say.

He still didn't leave, and I could feel his eyes on me, but I chose not to look at him until he finally moved to the front door and turned the knob. Sometime within the last turbulent hour, the sky had opened and it was pouring down rain.

Have fun on your little motorcycle there, buddy.

He paused under the threshold, staring down, not seeming to notice the rain, almost as if there was one more thing he wanted to say. But he didn't. He never looked back.

Once he was off the porch, I kicked the door shut. Through the rain, I heard his Harley start up, the tires angrily kicking up gravel as it screeched away. The sound faded out in a matter of seconds.

"There," I said aloud, dusting off my hands. "Well done, Springer."

After staring at the closed door until my eyes stung, I tore my gaze away and marched upstairs. I paced around my room in circles, my wits going wild, thinking of all the other things I wished I'd have said to him.

Then I halted in place, remembering all the things I *had* said.

Without warning, my stomach heaved and I bent over, both arms around my middle. Knowing I had seconds to spare, I flung open the door, raced across the hall, and slid to the floor in front of the white toilet bowl, salivating and sweating, awaiting the looming upchucks.

Twenty minutes later, after intervals of returning semi-digested food back to nature and resting my burning face against cold porcelain, I peeled myself off the floor and crossed to my room.

Hail hammered against the skylight over my head. Lightning crashed and thunder rumbled. I put my hands on top of my head and tucked my chin, trying to shield myself as figurative hail pelted me from above.

I had no strength left, nothing but a strange sense of carved-out hollowness.

Defeated, I crumpled onto the bed and cried...cried for the first time in ten years.

Chapter 27

I glanced at Mel, who was watching the freeway, occupied by her own thoughts. It was strange and unsettling. New territory. It was the first time in our life-long relationship that I knew more about something than her.

The remaining few days of spring break had consisted of me in the guest bedroom under the pretext of studying. I'd turned off my cell, unsure of what to tell Julia, but also dreading any other communication.

Nothing was said on the subject of Henry Knightly the rest of the time in Vancouver. The only thing Mel probably suspected was that I'd kissed a guy then refused to talk to him a day later.

You stay classy, Spring.

I didn't want to talk about it, didn't want to *think* about it. My blood pressure was already skyrocketing as we headed back to California, flying south on I-5. I ran my fingers over my forehead and pushed back against the head rest, staring out the window.

It was my own fault. I'd stepped into the mouth of the beast and had to live with the stench till it wore off. Served me right for getting close to a guy like Knightly. When would I learn that men, all men, were the enemy?

This reminded me of the card I'd received from my father a few weeks ago. An invitation to his midsummer wedding, sent in the guise of a birthday card, the first card he'd sent in five years. Ha! There was no way I was going to any wedding, even if my brothers swore Dad had changed, that he was reaching out to me. I wasn't ready to believe that. Especially not now.

Reviewing some history notes from a class blog took up the next hour or so of our journey. My phone vibrated. I'd purposefully not checked messages for days, but it was probably time. I snuck a glance at Mel, who was yammering on her cell. My left temple began to throb as I tapped my Stanford e-mail icon then quickly scanned down the messages. There were plenty from friends, classmates, and even one from Professor Masen. I didn't have the stomach to read that one yet.

I jumped when my phone vibrated again. This time a calendar prompt popped up, alerting me of an event that was to take place in fifteen minutes. I stared at the screen. It wasn't something *I'd* entered into my calendar. Knightly had put it in there, obviously. Though it wasn't the event I'd seen him enter, our date to work on my thesis—that wasn't until next week. This was something else, something…personal.

He must have entered it when I wasn't looking, when we'd been next to each other in the backseat of Tyler's car, me momentarily distracted by someone's hand up my shirt.

Sweat pooled in the palms of my hands, under my hair, across my forehead, as I read the short event again and again, wanting—almost desperately—to be where it said I should be, with whom, and doing what it said we should be doing.

After I'd read it a fourth time, everything in me dropped. Then spun.

"What's so captivating?"

Mel's voice startled me. When I turned to her, she took one look at me and winced.

"Crap, Spring! What's wrong with you?"

I didn't know what she meant. Had all my hair fallen out? Was I bleeding from the ears?

"You look like death."

Funny, because I felt like death.

I lowered the sun visor to look in the mirror. There she was again: the same girl I'd seen when I locked myself in the bathroom at Henry's house, and again just a few days ago, alone in the spare bedroom, pacing around like a lunatic. My eyes were bloodshot with dark, puffy bags, nostrils white and flaring, lips pale, brows heavy and lifeless. My face was completely void of color except for the red splotches marbling my neck like a funky rash. But the expression in my eyes…that was the kicker. It wasn't that I looked shocked or sad, it was worse than that.

My face was exactly like Julia's on that day she discovered Dart was gone.

Oh, sweet, fracking irony.

"Spring?" Mel shrieked, still gaping.

When I opened my mouth to reply, my stomach heaved and I doubled over, a gasp of pain exiting from my throat. I felt the car swerve then slow, the sound of gravel under tires. When we stopped, my window was suddenly rolling down. I sat up and hung my head out the side.

"If you're going to be puking again," Mel said from what sounded like several million miles away, "you should at least have food in you. You haven't eaten in two days. Dry heaving is bad for the esophagus."

My right cheek was pressed against the outside of the car door, and my braids twisted over my eyes as the top half of my body hung upside down, suspended by my seat belt.

"Keep breathing, babe." Mel's hand was on my back, rubbing and patting in comfort. As blood pooled in my brain, I was able to breathe easier, and my stomach settled. When I pulled my head back inside the car, Mel had a Diet Coke in her hand, holding it out to me. I pressed it against my forehead. The coldness of the can felt nice.

"Thanks," I whispered. "I'm fine." I attempted to smile after I took a few sips. "I'm just tired, I guess."

"Tired, right," Mel said, rubbing my arm. "We'll sit here for a sec."

"No, it's okay. I know it's a long drive." With alarm, I searched for my phone, which had fallen to the floor in my jostling. I grabbed it and pressed it against my chest.

"No hurry," Mel said, eyeing me. "There's a restaurant up ahead. We'll stop for a while." She started the car and we pulled into the parking lot.

The restaurant wasn't crowded, and we sat in a corner booth. When I insisted on only a salad that I knew I wouldn't touch, Dr. Melanie took over, ordering an array of vegetable sides, soup and bread.

My cell was on the table, the calendar event still showing.

I picked it up and held it between my hands. Then, I couldn't help glancing one more time at what Henry had secretly scheduled for us to do:

Subject: *My mouth*

Location: *You*

Notes: *Don't move. My mouth is on your fingers, eyelids, your face. My mouth, your neck. Your mouth. My hands, your back, skin. Your mouth. My mouth, your tongue. Your mouth, my mouth. Your stomach, my mouth, my hands. Under your hair. Under your shirt. My mouth on you.*

When the phone pinged another reminder, my heart made a mighty *thwap* and I grabbed for my glass of ice water.

Mel was watching me closely, elbows on the table. "We don't have to talk about it. I mean, I know you think I'm a gossip and everything." She rolled her eyes. "But this is you." She kicked me under the table. "You know you can tell me anything and it goes no further."

I lowered my eyes, reading his words again, need and misery hitting me like a tsunami.

"Take another drink," she ordered, scooting my glass over.

"Mel," I began, staring down, "there's something I have to tell you."

"I'm listening, babe."

"I kissed Henry when we were camping."

Well, it was a six-hour kiss, but who's counting?

"Uh-huh."

"The next day, I found out something...bad. That's why I didn't go with you guys to Portland. Did you know Henry never left? He stayed behind at the house after you and Tyler took off."

"Really?" Her expression was smooth, no scheming grin, eager to hear the latest scandal. She looked like my best friend.

"He came barging in." I swallowed, feeling pukey again. "He told me…" I lowered my eyes. "He told me he loves me."

"Poor Henry."

"Why do you say that?"

"You obviously threw him out," she deduced. "And now you feel guilty."

"Guilty," I echoed. "You don't know what I said to him."

"He probably deserved it."

"Probably." I laughed bitterly. "What I thought I knew about him, then after what Tyler told me — "

"*Tyler* told you something about Henry?" she cut in. "That little gossip."

I had to bite my tongue about the whole pot calling the kettle black.

"Henry did deserve what I said, but…" Suddenly, tears built behind my eyes and a huge lump blocked my throat. "Is it possible to feel so strongly about someone, to be so overwhelmingly attracted and connected that you want to forgive anything? How healthy is that? How stable?"

"I don't know." Mel shook her head. "I've never felt that way about anyone. But you and…"

I lowered my hand that was holding the phone. She stared at it, then at me. "I don't know what to do," I said, my bottom lip quivering. "I'm such an idiot."

"Careful," she warned with a kind smile, taking the phone from my open palm. "That's my best friend you're talking about."

While she read the subject line of the event and then the subsequent, rather detailed, description that Henry had entered, I was busy staring down at the plate before me, my fork scooting the carrots and rice from one side to the other. A few seconds later, my cell was being pushed across the table.

"Steamy," she offered, pointing at the screen. "And is that part even legal? Why aren't you with him right now?" She glanced at the phone. "Doing *that*."

So I told her everything.

Of course she'd heard Alex's story floating around campus, but she knew nothing about Henry breaking up Julia and Dart.

"Who do you trust more?" Mel asked, running her finger along the rim of her glass. "Henry or Alex? Or *Tyler*?"

"Henry didn't deny the Julia thing," I said, feeling miserable.

"Okay, okay." Mel moved her plate and glass out of the way and placed her hands flat on the carved up wooden table. "Let's go over this logically. First, what's this about Lilah?"

"Oh." I shuddered and shook my head. "He just slipped up, so to speak. You know guys…a pretty face throws herself at him, and he loses all ability to think logically. I assumed Henry had a higher threshold, but we're all susceptible at some point."

As proof, I almost added that I'd fallen prey to Alex.

"I don't know if it was a casual thing between them last summer," I continued, "or if he thought there was more to her back then. He's probably known her for almost as long as he's known Dart. So it wasn't like a one night stand."

"They hooked up?"

I nodded. "Pretty sure."

"Ew. She's such a gnarly hag."

"I agree. But think about it. If you only saw her and didn't know the evils of her inner soul, she's, ya know, beautiful."

"Gross." Mel made a gagging face.

"He seemed shocked that I even knew about it."

"That's because he knows how you feel about Lilah, and obviously knows how Lilah feels about you. That was probably why he was so engrossed by you at the party. Make no mistake, Lilah told him crap, so he assumed you'd be some wheels-off psycho demon chick and not a smokin' hot super-class super-babe."

"Whatever," I muttered, trying not to smile. "Regardless, I think I kind of overreacted about the Lilah thing. You're well aware of some of the road kills I've paired with in the past, without so much as an iota of feeling, so I can hardly get bent out of shape about Henry hooking up with Lilah. I actually feel sorrier for her."

"Okay, so the Lilah thing is vile but forgivable," Mel stated. "Let's move on. What about Alex?"

I didn't speak for a moment, taking the time to properly hate myself. "I fell for everything he told me hook, line and sinker. I didn't think twice. And what if everything he told me—told everyone—isn't true? I still don't know what happened between them. Henry didn't tell me." I bit my lip. "Well, I guess I didn't give him a chance to explain. But you know what, Mel? I told him neither of those things mattered: what he did with Lilah"—I shuddered again—"and what I *thought* he'd done to Alex. I told him I didn't care, because...I..." I exhaled slowly, pressing my palms against my burning cheeks. "But what he did to Julia, I just can't…"

"Yeah." Mel groaned. "That's tough to swallow. When you called him on it, he didn't sound remorseful?"

"No. Because he *isn't*. He thinks he did the right thing butting in like that. I have no idea why. What could possibly justify that?" I pounded my fist on the table. "I can't be with someone who treats people that way. He says he loves me, but then he does that to one of my closest friends." My throat felt tight, tears stung my eyes. "I don't know how to forgive him for it," I whispered.

Mel didn't say anything. She probably sensed that I couldn't talk about it anymore. I leaned an elbow on the table and planted my face in my hand. "So much drama," I said. "A year ago, I was free and focused. I was happy."

"Were you?" Mel asked skeptically.

"Well, I was cynical and hardcore and full of crap, too, but at least I had a plan." I twirled a braid around my finger. "Now I don't know *what* I am."

Chapter 28

Masen didn't even wait for the first person to stand up after he'd ended class. "Spring," he said. "Come see me."

Lilah's eyes shot my way but I didn't react, not giving her the satisfaction. Today in class was the first time I'd seen her since I found out—

Well, anyway.

"Where's the rest of it?" my professor asked when I got to his desk. He held out the twelve-page outline of my thesis. The third draft.

I was about to ask him what he meant, but why hedge?

"That's all of it. I believe I've touched on the points we talked about last time," I said, trying to sound like the expert I claimed to be, but my legs were shaking.

"Section nine," he said, flipping to the end page. "You alluded to the point but it's completely vague." He took off his glasses. "This is the crux here, you see?" He pointed at it. "The whole argument of your theory funnels down to this: In the long run, over, say, a decade, *is* land development detrimental or beneficial? And why? You've posed this question along the way, but here you have to answer. Section nine is where your new angle should really come into play."

"I know," I said. "I'm still tweaking that part."

He lifted his bushy brows. "Still? I thought you had most of the body written. Your final deadline is three weeks before the end of semester. In two months."

"I haven't forgotten," I said, my turtleneck feeling hot and strangly. I didn't have the guts to tell him that my research was done. My notes were typed up. What he held in his hand was all I had. Foolishly, I thought I'd get away with it. For the last few months, I hadn't been as into my research as I'd been in the fall, and I'm sure that showed.

"We talked about this before the break," he said. "You promised me you were getting back on track."

"I know." I nodded vigorously. "I was—I *am*."

"I'll give you one more chance to finish a complete outline before I approve the topic with the committee," Masen said. My stomach hit the floor. I thought he'd gotten the thesis committee's stamp of approval months ago. "Otherwise"—he passed me my paper, the top page stained with a coffee ring—"I'm afraid I'll have to give you a fail."

My mouth fell open. Wasn't it only back in September that we'd talked publication? A few months later, he'd said what an excellent job I'd been doing on the new version of my thesis.

And now I was on the brink of the first fail in my life.

I assured Masen with everything in me that I would fix it, truly this time, whatever it took, and that I'd have the new outline—the final draft!—on his desk Monday morning.

That was in five days.

Before I'd exited the classroom, I was visualizing that last section, moving the different parts around in my head. There was a lot of great information there, but there were holes, pretty significant ones that I couldn't fill myself. I knew only one person who could help.

I walked outside and sat on a bench, other students rushing past on their way to class, oblivious to my internal struggle. The bells of Hoover Tower chimed out the noon hour.

I didn't know what to do. On the one hand, I could not get an F on my sustainable living research paper, not while there was a breath left in my body. On the other hand, I couldn't do it, couldn't imagine the scenario of picking up the phone and...

My mind was whirling, thinking up any and every possible solution, but I slowly realized I had no other choice. It was either *that* or fail. Zombie-like, I pulled out my cell and scrolled to the last time he'd called me back in December.

It rang once before rolling to voicemail. Actually, it was one of those half-rings, meaning his phone was off or he was on another call. My mouth went dry when I heard his voice asking me to leave a message. I closed my eyes and began to speak.

He didn't call back or confirm in any way, but I knew he would show, because I knew he was free tonight. I knew this because we'd already made plans to meet. After I rushed up the stairs, I nearly fainted when my phone pinged, reminding me of our originally scheduled meeting on the top floor of the Meyer Library. The room behind the stacks. The one he told me had a lock on the door. I was fifteen minutes early.

Henry was already there.

He sat at the table, head bowed, just finishing writing on a piece of yellow notebook paper. He tore that page off the pad and placed it on top of a stack of other printouts beside his laptop. He must have heard me, because he looked up.

"Hi," I said, not quite able to meet his eyes. "Thank you for coming."

"I figured you must be pretty desperate to call me," he said, speaking down at the table. His tone wasn't completely chilly. "And you're welcome." He pulled out the chair beside him. I walked around the table and sat.

"Looks like you've been here a while," I observed conversationally. "I hope you didn't skip a class."

"I don't really have to sit in on my classes this semester," Henry said. "They're all recorded and archived online. I'd rather be there in person, but it's not necessary. A few weeks ago, I considered doing the rest of the semester remotely."

"From a castle in Switzerland?" I couldn't help saying, hoping to lighten the mood. I was relieved when he smiled.

"Maybe." He turned to face me. "But then I decided to stay around here."

"Why?"

He didn't answer, but he kept his eyes steadily on mine. "Anyway," he finally said, "this is probably what you'll need." He slid the stack of loose papers toward to me. "You can read over those and if you have any questions, we can talk about it."

"Thanks," I said. But I didn't want to sit there and read to myself. I wanted to get into one of our classic debates. I wanted him to push my buttons and challenge my opinions until I got so impassioned that I wrestled him to the floor, pinned his shoulders down and—

"I've got my own reading to do," he said, interrupting my runaway fantasy. "So let me know if you have a question."

I nodded, wiped my palms on my jeans and stared down at the neat stack of papers. I read for a while, trying very hard to concentrate. A group of guys walked past the room and stopped right in front of the open door, having an animated and rather filthy discussion about the busty redhead working the circulation desk.

Henry scraped back his chair and walked to the door, giving the guys a look before pulling the door closed. His hand lingered on the knob and I couldn't help noticing how his thumb brushed along the protruding lock button. When my gaze moved to his face, he was watching me. Slowly, steadily, my temperature started to rise, thinking of what we might be doing at that very moment…if only I hadn't damaged my relationship with the one man I wanted to trust. If only.

"This floor is usually pretty deserted," I observed, trying to keep myself in my chair.

"That's why I chose it." A shadow crossed his face and he dropped his gaze. "And it's got the best vending machines. Hershey bars." As he returned to his seat, I could almost catch a tiny glimmer in his eyes. Maybe he was also thinking about that chocolate bar we'd shared beside the campfire… barely a week ago.

"Henry," I couldn't help saying, though I had no idea how to continue.

He'd been typing something on his laptop, but turned to me. I could see the gold flecks in his eyes and the tiny freckles on his nose, the ones I'd traced with my finger while he'd hummed in my ear. I'd been so relaxed with him, so at peace...yet out-of-control, *free* of control in the most spectacular way.

My sudden need was so surprising, it almost scared me. But was it temporary? Would I forgive him now and resent him later? The thought of doing that to either of us made me physically ill. I wanted to trust him, wholly, so very badly. I wanted him like I'd never wanted anything in my life.

Maybe I wasn't ready to act on that, but didn't I owe it to both of us to say something? Talking...that used to be what we were good at.

"Henry," I repeated, licking my dry lips.

He lowered his hands from the keyboard. "Yes?" He tilted his head, brows bent. "What's—" Before either of us could continue, his eyes flashed to my cell sitting face-up on the table, ringing with an incoming call. My stomach turned to ice when a thumbnail-sized picture of Alex's face appeared on the screen.

I glanced at Henry, who was staring at it. A second later, he closed his laptop and scooted back his chair. "I'll let you answer," he said, not looking at me.

"Wait." I grabbed my phone and silenced the ringer.

"If you have questions about that," he said, glancing down at the papers before me then walking to the door, "you can email."

"Henry." I held up my cell as evidence of...something. "It's not what you think." Right as the words left my mouth, the phone began ringing again. Henry's dark eyes glared at the face pointed directly at him.

"Unbelievable, Spring," he muttered, his tone angry yet detached. I'd never heard him speak like that before.

"What?" I flipped my phone over and looked at its face. It was Alex again.

We stared at each other until finally Henry clenched his jaw, opened the door and left. I watched him stride all the way across the room then round a corner toward the stairs. When I was conscious enough to realize that my phone was still ringing, I cocked my arm and threw it against the wall as hard as I could. It smashed apart, leaving a dent in the wall.

"Frack," I yelled, slumping into my chair.

. . .

With back-to-back exams and a paper due, I couldn't make it to the Apple Store for three days. I chose a white iPhone this time and one of those ultra-protective cases, as insurance for the next time I had the urge to hurl a two hundred dollar device against a concrete wall. I was dying to get home and charge it, feeling a little out of touch with the world.

I plugged it into my laptop then laid face down on my sheepskin rug. After a few minutes, I heard bleeps and chirps. I rolled over and grabbed my phone, watching the numbers of new emails appear on the screen. And one new text.

I sat up.

TONIGHT. MEET ME AT THE LIBRARY. MIDNIGHT. YOU KNOW WHERE. PLEASE COME, SPRING.

The text had been sent an hour after he'd walked out of that study room...three days ago.

A tiny primal scream escaped from my throat as I stumbled to my feet, grabbing a jacket as I dashed from my bedroom. I'd had to run across campus plenty of times, but I think this sprint broke all my records. When I skidded around the corner, my heart tanked, finding the study room in the back corner dark and empty. Of course I didn't expect him to still be there after three days, but I had to check. I leaned against the doorway and pulled out my phone, sliding my fingers down the face, not knowing what I should write back to him, but knowing I must.

SORRY, my fingers raced. PHONE DIED, JUST GOT YOUR MSG. I'M AT THE LBRY NOW. CAN YOU MEET?

Send.

<MESSAGE UNDELIVERABLE>

I stared at the two words until they spun like a Ferris wheel. I needed to sit down before my knees gave out, so I walked into the dark room and slid into the chair Henry had used three days ago. There was no new writing on the whiteboard and the trashcan appeared untouched, pieces of my busted phone still in the carpet. The room probably hadn't been occupied since our meeting.

I rested my elbows on the table and held my head, breathing in the smell of old books, dusty carpet, and the faintest hint of spicy aftershave…although that was probably my imagination.

When I opened my eyes, I caught a glimpse of something on the chair beside me, the one I'd used the last time I was here. I scooted the chair back to find a few sheets of yellow notebook paper neatly folded in half. No name on it, as if it was someone's leftover trash.

But I knew better.

I grabbed the pages, five in all, flipped on the light and began to read.

Chapter 29

Julia lowered the pages of yellow paper and stared at me. "Alex did...*this*?"

I nodded, fingering my pillow case.

"It's almost unbelievable." She glanced over her shoulder, like she feared we might be overheard. But we were alone in my bedroom. Door closed, ladder reeled in. "Do you think it's true?"

"It has to be," I said. "For Henry to divulge *this*, especially about his sister." I gestured at the three pages of his note in her hand, the pages she'd just read about his history with Alex Parks, the ones I'd read a dozen times since finding them the night before.

The other two pages of the note—the ones regarding Julia and Dart—were tucked in the back pocket of my jeans. Julia knew nothing about them, and I wasn't sure when I should tell her or *if* I should tell her. I hadn't told her anything about Dart yet.

Not even a week had passed since I'd returned home from spring break with the knowledge that Henry'd had a hand in their breakup. I'd read his explanation in the letter several times, but it still galled me. It was either a colossal misunderstanding (which I did *not* believe in) or Henry Knightly was a terrible judge of character and a huge buttinsky. Though that was a bit implausible, too, I had to admit.

"You're sure he's talking about Alex?" Julia asked. "He didn't use any name in the letter but yours."

"I'm positive. He left it in a study room where we were supposed to meet. I'm not surprised he was cryptic. He knew that I'd know who he was talking about."

Julia frowned. "So you think Alex is capable of what Henry says?"

It took exactly two seconds for me to consider. "Absolutely. Even when we were hanging out last September, something about him rubbed me the wrong way." I took the pages and held them up. It was like I needed to repeat the details aloud one last time. "The story about Henry he's been shooting around, he twisted the facts. They both admitted they used to be really close friends in high school, but Henry did not nark on Alex for cheating. Alex was about to flunk out and got caught stealing files off Henry's computer. That's why he got expelled."

"And blamed Henry for not lying for him," Julia added.

"I don't know how anyone can be so ballsy, telling flat-out lies. And now, to know he did *that*..." I passed her the three pages in case she needed a refresher.

"Took off with Henry's fifteen-year-old sister and got her pregnant, just to get back at him," she completed for me.

I winced at her words, picturing what I thought Cami Knightly might look like as a fifteen-year-old, three years ago, going through one of the worst things a young woman possibly could, and then giving up a baby she was never meant to have.

Julia took in a shuddery inhale, as if she was thinking the same thing.

"According to Henry's letter, that was the beginning of his pattern," I said. "And he would know, he's known Alex for years *and* his M.O. He takes girls—after he severely impairs them, or finds them severely impaired—to some, I don't know, some honeymoon cabin at the beach. It's date rape but on steroids. Sleeping with girls either too young or too wasted to know what they're doing, then bragging about never using protection. What kind of sicko does that?"

"I heard that around campus," Julia admitted, tugging at her hair. "But I just couldn't believe it." She'd grown thinner the last few months, paler, too.

We sat on my bed and talked for another hour, dissecting the words of the letter that I had practically memorized.

"When I think of what Henry's family's been through…" I said, feeling queasy all over again. "And I'm sure my hanging out with Alex hurt him, too."

"How were you supposed to know?" Julia said. "Did Henry breathe one word of it to you before now?"

"I think he tried," I admitted. "But I wouldn't listen." I fell back on the bed and flung an arm over my eyes. "Read me the bottom of the last page," I requested.

"Are you sure?" I moved my arm long enough to give her a look. She cleared her throat. "'Spring.' He has very nice penmanship, doesn't he?"

I shot her another look.

"'Spring,'" she began again, reading the end of Henry's letter. "'You are the most intelligent, talented and resolute person I have ever known. Your loyalty to your friends and your absolute sense of self overwhelms me. As I've sat in this room, waiting for you to arrive and then realizing you're not going to, I've taken stock of the situation, and this is what I've come away with: I want you to know how much of a pleasure it was to have had you in my life. You changed me, Spring. Know that, if nothing else. Know that you made me smile and trust and see the future like I never have. Wherever you go in life and whatever causes you choose to undertake will be fortunate to have you. I wish you great success with wherever life takes you.'"

I felt tears clinging to the corners of my eyes as I stared up at the ceiling.

"It sounds like a good-bye," Julia said, folding the pages.

"It was." I sniffled. "That last night, he told me he was thinking about doing the rest of the semester online. My text to him bounced back, so either he's somewhere too remote for his cell to get reception, or it's disconnected." I rolled over. "He talked about Switzerland and Tahiti and he has all the money in the world, so who knows where he is."

"I'm sorry," Julia whispered, stroking my arm.

I looked at her, at her sad smile. "How are you doing, bunny?"

"Better, I think." She didn't sound all that convincing. "Really." She slid back against the wall, pulled her long legs into her arms and rested her chin on her knees. "I'm over Dart. I've moved on."

"That's good," I said, not knowing what else to say. I

still wasn't sure if I should tell her everything I knew. If she claimed she was over Dart, would that help now? I felt a twinge of guilt, knowing that I was lying to one of my best friends.

I rolled onto my knees and sat cross-legged in the middle of the bed. "Things were pretty intense there for a while," I said. "Between you and Dart, I mean."

"Yeah." She ran her fingers down the side stitching of her pink sweatpants. "It was intense."

"I didn't know how to help you," I admitted, trying to express the proper sentiment but knowing I was falling short. "I mean, I didn't know what to say. Girls handle losing their virginity in different ways. I was really worried that with Dart being your first, you would flip out when he left."

"I did flip out," she said, her lips tipping into a tiny smile.

"Yeah, you did," I agreed. "Maybe I expected you to flip out even more."

"Well, there's always tomorrow," she added with another smile. A moment later, though, it dropped and she exhaled. "I still don't know what happened. Something must've went wrong, right? We were so close, so perfect and then..." She broke off and bit her thumbnail. "Not even Anabel's advice helped me keep him."

I sat up. "What did Anabel tell you to do?"

"At first she told me to be all sexy with him. You saw what she gave me for Thanksgiving."

"Yeah," I said, remembering that black lacy whatever in the corner of her suitcase.

"It was too embarrassing. I didn't want to *pretend* to be someone like that, even to get close to Dart."

"Someone like Anabel, you mean?"

She nodded. "A few days before we all left for Christmas, I talked to her again."

I couldn't help groaning. Julia must've been truly desperate to keep going back to our promiscuous roommate for romance advice. I wished I could've helped her back then, but I was even more clueless.

"She told me to reel back," Julia continued. "That to really hook a man, body and soul, I should be cold and distant. Give it to him then take it away. Brigitte Bardot, she kept telling me to Brigitte Bardot."

"That French model from the fifties?"

"She showed me pictures of her all pouty and frowny. She looked like a snob to me, but, I don't know, that's what Anabel said to do, so…"

"So that's what you did," I said weakly, feeling for those other two pages of Henry's letter hidden in my back pocket. It was as if the printed words were burning into my skin, yelling at me to listen as I replayed them in my mind:

"Last year, my roommate was engaged, but his fiancée cheated on him. When it all came out, she told him she'd never loved him, that it was some kind of bet. I don't know the whole story, but I witnessed firsthand the devastation it caused. You know my friend as a pretty cheerful guy, but that person was gone for a long time. As his best friend, it was hard to watch. When he started dating your roommate so soon after, I admit, I wasn't behind it 100 percent. But it was his life to live. She was over at our house a lot, which I didn't mind; I thought she was a sweet girl, and she made him happy. Maybe a week before the winter break, I couldn't help noticing that she seemed like a different person, less talkative, more withdrawn, even a little rude to him. At first

I wrote it off as final exams stress, but one night she was over and I heard her talking on the phone. Someone was coaching her, telling her how to act. Maybe I'd become too protective, but it infuriated me to hear what she was planning on doing. It wasn't fair that someone was messing with my friend again. A few days later we were leaving for winter break. He and I drove together to the airport and I told him what I'd overheard. I told him his girlfriend was playing him. What he did after that, I don't know exactly, but I do know he wasn't ready to go back to Stanford and live across the street from her. I'd do anything for someone I care about, so I chose to move away from campus, too."

I heard a ringing in my ears, and my hand was shaking when I held it to my forehead. I almost couldn't breathe, knowing what I knew now. It made sense. Henry was right, he was only thinking of his friend, trying to help. And I'd yelled at him, wouldn't listen, didn't believe him when he'd tried to explain.

My mind was going numb. I stared at Julia's lowered eyes, wondering if I should come clean about everything. But would it do any good at this point? Dart was still gone. It might make everything worse.

Julia slid off the bed and stood, peering at herself in the mirror. "A few weeks ago, I was really lonely. I missed Dart so much and…" She tucked her hands under her arms, turning away from her reflection. "I…I got so angry at him. He was my first, ya know? It was supposed to be special for *both* of us, right?"

"Um, right," I offered, trying to follow along. I felt so sorry for Julia. Heartbroken for her. But a corner of my heart stung for Henry now, too. He thought he'd done the right thing, even if that meant hurting his best friend. As I gazed at Julia, I understood exactly how he must have felt.

"But then I was thinking," Julia continued, "if Dart could just up and leave like that, I guess it wasn't so special after all." She kicked the metal bed frame, her voice sounding more cynical than I'd ever heard, and bitter, too. "I was wondering, seriously, what's the big deal? It's just sex, right? But I'd built it up to be this huge monumental event, when it was basically like I was getting it over with. If it's not special, I should walk to campus and bring some random guy home."

My spine stiffened. This did not sound like Julia. Frankly, it sounded like Anabel. "But you won't, right?"

She scoffed, that cynical tone still hanging on. "I'd never have the guts. Maybe I should call Alex." She laughed darkly. "He's got the experience and I know he'll—"

"Julia!" I cut her off. "Don't even joke about that."

She blinked, as if coming out of a trance. "Sorry. I didn't mean that. Of course not…not Alex."

"Good," I said. "Because I can't have two reckless roommates. Anabel got kicked out of a bar last week." I reached for her hand, pulling her to sit beside me. "I need you to be my sensible one."

Julia smiled, a real one this time. "I will," she said, but then her posture sagged. "I still get sad sometimes," she admitted. "Very sad."

"What can I do?" I asked, feeling an ache in my throat.

"Nothing. Just…thank you for being here, for being such a good friend to me through all of this."

Now was my turn to move my eyes away. I knew I'd been too wrapped up in my own drama the past few weeks to give her any real comfort. I still didn't feel like I should tell her what I knew about Dart. Not now. I didn't want her to flip out all over again, especially if she considered a good remedy for her blues to be picking up casual sex as a hobby.

"You have," Julia insisted when she saw me turn away. She reached out and lifted my chin like a mother would. "And now, I want to be a friend to *you*." She stared straight at me, as if she knew I was withholding information. "There's something you're not telling me, isn't there?"

I nodded, feeling a tingle creep up the back of my neck.

She leaned back, bracing her arms behind her. "Why don't you go ahead and say it."

I rubbed my neck, trying to dig up the right words, reaching for the pages in my pocket.

"Just tell me, Springer," she said. "Tell me how Henry feels about you."

She tilted her head and smiled at my totally stunned reaction. It wasn't very often that she caught me off guard. I didn't want to discuss what she was asking about, but my other choice was to share with her the rest of the letter. I couldn't do that either.

"Henry," I began. Just saying his name in this context made my heart flip. "Loves me."

Julia exhaled like she was relieved about something. "Yeah." She swept her scarlet hair over one shoulder. "Henry has always loved you. I could see it all over his face. *You*"—she pointed an accusing finger at me—"would just never look." She laughed like a tinkling bell, the first I'd heard of it since December. I didn't mind in the least that her good mood was at my expense.

I bit my lip, not quite as happy as I thought a girl should be while having a conversation about love. Then again, I had zero experience. "He wanted to take me to Tahiti."

She turned somber. "How romantic."

"I told him no. In fact, I told him to go frack himself."
I sucked in my lower lip so it wouldn't wobble. "And then,
I was so pissed that I kicked him out the door." Dullness
pressed against my chest and I sank onto the bed. "In the
middle of a rain storm."

Julia's eyes brimmed with tears. She reached out for my
hand and smiled in beautiful, commiserative silence.

This wasn't like me. I wasn't the kind of girl to fall
apart then slump into exile over a personal crisis, especially
over something as pitiful as the obliteration of an *almost*-
relationship. Yet, here I was. The girl I mocked. Wretched
and depressed. Even more broken-hearted than before.

"I feel blue." I sighed. "What do I do?"

"You can borrow my Prozac," she offered with a smile.
"If there's time later, we might throw in a little endless
pontificating. Maybe play a little Adele?"

"Now you're just reading my mind."

"Or, we can always turn existential, like one of those
Swedish apocalyptic films from the fifties. That should
brighten our moods."

"Okay." I sat up, happy for the distraction. "You be the
cloaked and hooded Angel of Death standing on the stormy
beach, and I'll be the vicar's wife, banished to a life inside an
isolated seaside cottage."

Julia giggled and stood, a bottle of energy water cradled
in both hands. Her expression went theatrically solemn as her
eyes glazed over. "I...am the Plague of Death," she began,
monotone. "I shall hold this brim'd beverage in my memory
between my hands of fate. The silence, the loooooathing,

the high fructose corn syrup." Her arms stretched out to her sides. "Never spilling," she went on, staring straight ahead, "never waking, the prisoner of my life preposterous." She bowed her head and fell forward onto the bed, not spilling a drop.

"And the Oscar goes to…" I said, clapping.

"All right, I gotta study," she said as she stood and walked to the door. Halfway there, she turned back. "Can I ask you something? And don't be afraid to tell me to butt out."

I rolled my eyes. "What is it, bunny?"

She tucked some hair behind an ear. "When was it? I mean, when did you start *changing* toward Henry?" I'm sure she caught the sting that crossed my face, but for once, she didn't back down. "Was it before Washington? Before they moved away?"

I took in a few breaths, like I was psyching myself up to cannonball off the high dive. "Yes, it was before," I answered. "Henry and I…we could…talk. I miss it."

"Talking's nice."

"It's all we did for months. Of course we debated, too." I exhaled a soft laugh, remembering fondly. "But the arguing wasn't genuine, it was more like—"

"Foreplay." She winked and left the room.

Part IV

Summer

"YOU ARE TOO GENEROUS TO TRIFLE WITH ME. IF YOUR
FEELINGS ARE STILL WHAT THEY WERE LAST APRIL, TELL ME
SO AT ONCE. MY AFFECTIONS AND WISHES ARE UNCHANGED;
BUT ONE WORD FROM YOU WILL SILENCE ME ON THIS SUBJECT
FOREVER."
From *Pride & Prejudice*

Chapter 30

"Time to hit the road," Mel said, her head sticking out the passenger-side window of my Subaru.

I stared down at the large envelope in my hands, hovering outside the outgoing mailbox slot. The address of the house across the street from me at Stanford was written on the front.

"You've been carrying that thing around with you for a week," she said. "It's a good plan. He lived there once, so the post office will have a forwarding address."

"I just...I want him to read it."

"You want him to see you scored an A." Mel's white sunglasses sat on the tip of her nose, shading the bright Montana sun.

"We worked hard. He deserves to see how it turned out."

But it was more than that. When I'd started on the final draft of my thesis, it was do or die. And I was *not* going to die. I'd busted my ass for two years to get the opportunity I'd been given. Braiding my hair and angry chick rock were only symbols of what I wanted to be. I knew what I wanted to be now. I didn't need symbols.

All I had left were those final research notes Henry had given to me that last evening in the study room. The more I delved into that, while veering off with additional research of my own, the more I felt the fire return. I'd lost it for a while, but it came back. I wanted the world to know I was passionate again. Was it selfish that a part of me wanted Henry to know that, too?

"So mail it already and let's get going," Mel said. "I'm about to faint from starvation."

I rolled my eyes. We'd stopped for food less than an hour ago. Something about road trips made Mel in need of constant nourishment.

This was the end of our third week on the road, two more to go. My partner in crime was not enjoying herself on the same level as I was. Perhaps I'd been just a teensy misleading in my description of how exciting our summer excursion would be: Two single gals, freewheeling through Idaho, Wyoming and Montana while I did research for a new paper, picking up where my thesis ended, living off the tiny research grant I'd received from the Earth Science department.

Last night, as we'd huddled together on one twin bed, dodging flying cockroaches at a seedy roadside motel outside Great Falls, Mel had very politely informed me that if we visited another effing cow pasture or toured one more sustainable-living-effing-farm, she would feed me to a buffalo.

I believed her.

"Do it, babe," Mel coaxed. "Drop it down the slot and

walk away. It's called closure."

She was right. Mailing Henry my thesis was a good way to put a lid on that chapter of my life. And it was time; I really needed to get started on moving on, even if I didn't feel ready. So I opened the gaping metal mouth, bit my lip, and let go.

"I'm proud of you," Mel said as I slid behind the steering wheel. "Now let's get out of here. You promised me a *normal* hotel tonight. I need a decent shower and a mani-pedi like no one's biz." She dusted her arms like she was wiping off loose dirt. "I feel juicy and disgusting."

"Today's stop is an extra important one," I said, starting the engine.

"I don't give a rat's—" She growled down into her open purse. "I know I have an emergency Kit Kat in here somewhere. Oh man, I'd kill for a cigarette."

"You don't smoke anymore," I reminded her.

"Then I'd kill for some chocolate."

"You're off sugar, too."

"Shut up, Spring. You're ticking me off." She stared out the window wistfully. "I'd strangle my own sweet granny for a chocolate cigarette."

I laughed and ran my fingers through my hair, starting at the scalp and proceeding all the way to the tips.

The braids had come out a week before our trip. Since then, every time I caught my reflection, it was like I was seeing me again, someone who believed in herself and fought for those beliefs, someone whose hair blew all devil-may-care-like in the breeze again. Once that was established, my life made sense again.

Julia and Anabel nearly fainted with joy when they saw

my hair. I laughed at the memory and played with the ends, as if it was a validation of another New Spring.

"It's only about a two hour drive from here," I said to Mel, pulling away from the post office. Mel stuck her fist in her mouth and nodded, still jonesing over chocolate. I was grateful she'd stopped asking where we were going. It would be hard to explain our next stop.

The subject had come up between Henry and me a few times, but he was always vague about it. I knew his family had property all over the west. In fact, we'd been crisscrossing Knightly territory the past week. But it was the homestead just past Ft. Benton that I was interested in. According to my hasty research, it sat on approximately 50,000 acres. We're talking hills, trees, a river and both farmland and some kind of livestock.

On a purely intellectual basis, I was curious about how this land was maintained…if at all. Henry and I had long-standing debates about the pros and cons of land development. Now was my chance to see how his family treated their bit of earth.

"Are we there yet?" Mel asked, cleaning out her purse for the fourth time in a week. She glanced up right as we passed the Welcome to Kingston sign. "Where the hell are we? Spring, it's the Fourth of July."

"I'm aware," I said, slowing down, checking my GPS then making a right on Main Street.

"You promised me fun and adventure. Am I going to have to kill you?"

"There's a museum," I said brightly. "Maybe it has more Lewis and Clark memorabilia. You like them, remember? I believe you used the term *ruggedly sexy*. We can take a tour."

"Oh, goodie-goodie," she zinged. "More pictures of dead dudes no one under eighty's ever heard of."

I bit my lip. The dusty town of four thousand seemed pretty slow-paced, and despite the charming, old-timey wooden buildings and patches of green, it probably would turn out to be a snooze fest. A sign on the side of a tall green building caught my eye: RESTORATION BY THE KNIGHTLY FAMILY.

Huh. So the lineage doesn't just own the land, but it looks like they have a bit of vested interest in the town. That's pretty cool.

We pulled up to the museum and got out. Mel groaned all the way up the walk but wouldn't look at me. I really did owe her a good time after this. The room was bright and cold, rows of framed portraits and other *objects d'art* lined the walls.

A short, roundish woman appeared. She was probably about sixty and sported a bird's nest of gray and brown hair. After welcoming us, she jumped right in, explaining that General Kingston's great-great-somebody rebuilt the homestead in nineteen twenty-five after the storm of twenty-four. Gripping…

As Mel trailed behind us, the bird's nest woman moved to a group of black and white framed pictures, showing the actual renovating. "If you'll notice, all the lumber for the reconstruction was harvested locally. Family's very particular about that."

"And the Kingstons own all the timber, too?" Mel asked, probably trying to stay engaged so she wouldn't fall asleep on her feet.

"The Kingstons?" our guide repeated. "Oh, dear, no. That branch of the family moved from the homestead two generations ago. It's the old General's *daughter's* family. The Knightlys."

"Knightly?"

I closed my eyes, practically feeling Mel's outburst against my back like a gust of wind.

"Are we talking *Knightly* Knightly?" she asked, sliding to my side.

"Shhh." I eyed Bird's Nest.

"Wait. Did you *know* Henry lives here?" Mel added.

"He doesn't *live* here," I said under my breath, not wanting to cause a bigger scene. "His family owns the land and some buildings in town, I guess. I'm sure the Henry we knew has never stepped foot in this place."

When I glanced at Bird's Nest, she was smiling like a wise old auntie. "I take it you young ladies know Henry."

My heart seemed to freeze mid-beat.

"*She* does," Mel clarified, digging an elbow into my ribs.

"That's wonderful! Do you know him from Stanford?"

As I nodded, my frozen heart gave three hard beats. "Wait. *You* know Henry"—I swallowed—"Knightly?"

"He grew up here, dear. They spend most of their time back east now or in Europe, but the two children come home a few times a year."

I held up a hand. "You're telling me Henry lived here?"

"I believe she just confirmed that, Springer," Mel said with a grin.

"*Shhh*," I hissed, knocking her away with my shoulder.

"The children come home every summer and the occasional weekend," Bird's Nest said. "Trip is usually here in June and July."

"Trip," Mel repeated, glancing at me.

"That's what everyone's always calls young Henry." She leaned forward. "He's *the third*."

"Yeah." I cleared my throat. "I know."

Mel snickered beside me, hanging onto my arm. "This is too delicious."

I looked at Bird's Nest. "Do you know if... Is Henry—"

"Trip," Mel corrected.

"Shut *up*," I hissed. Then, "Trip." I coughed, stumbling over the name. "Is he home now?" I held my breath, not knowing which way I wanted Bird's Nest to answer.

"No." She frowned. "But they're expected next week for the festival and ribbon-cutting. You probably already know this, since you know Trip, but the family takes great care of our town. Saved most of us from welfare *or worse* when the beef recession hit." She ran a cloth over a gold frame. "A decade ago, they revamped all the schools. Eighty percent of the graduates go on to college, most of them on the Knightly scholarship. They bought and donated all the historical sites that help keep tourists coming through."

"So they're *do-gooders*," Mel asked Bird's Nest while grinning at me.

"Absolutely," she replied. "They employ only locals to work the dude ranch during the summer season."

"Dude ranch?" I nearly choked again.

"The Diamond W," our guide clarified, "is one of the most successful working ranches for a hundred miles, and our town's biggest commodity. Folks come to experience the *Old West*." She rolled her eyes, but I didn't miss the proud look she carried. "A team of retired ranchers takes groups on horseback up into the foothills. Rodeo every Saturday. Barbeque and cobbler. Folks sure love it."

"I don't know what to say," I muttered.

"About what, dear?" Bird's Nest asked, tilting her head.

Mel was literally doubled over, snorting and cackling. I gave her a shove and she staggered back. "Don't mind her," she said, popping up at my side, one arm tight around my shoulders. "She's just in the middle of a nervous breakdown."

"O-oh, yes, well, should we press on? Or would you rather visit the Diamond W? Next bus leaves in ten minutes."

Chapter 31

"I don't think this is a good idea," I said as the bus rocked and bounced us up the hill. My fingernails dug into the torn vinyl seat in front of me.

"This is epic!" Mel exclaimed. "Aren't you curious?" She peered out the dusty window. "I know *I* am. I can't believe you didn't tell me where we were going today."

"I didn't know he *lived here* lived here," I defended. "I feel like we're trespassing."

"No one will know you're here." She patted my arm. "We'll just tool around for a while, check out the back of some Wrangler jeans, then split. It'll be fun."

I exhaled, still mildly freaked, but at least Mel was excited about something and not complaining about the weird smell coming from the back of the bus.

Along with the dozen other passengers, we were dumped off in the middle of what felt like an outdoor madhouse. People and animals bustled wildly, some loners rushed about, while large groups moseyed. Mel and I stood close together holding hands. Two city slickers.

I spied the house farther up the hill. Of all places to see, *that* was first on my list.

"Where should we go?" Mel asked.

"I'm feeling overwhelmed," I admitted.

"Down by the gate"—Mel gestured—"there're more maps and pamphlets. I'll run down and grab some." That seemed like a smart idea. "Hey." She shook my arm. "You'll be okay here?"

"Sure," I replied, nodding manically. "I'm good."

She eyed me skeptically. "Okay. I'll be back in a flash."

All alone, I felt like a refugee fresh off Ellis Island dropped on an intersection of Times Square. The throng was a mixture of tourists, ranch hands, and what might've been local kids from the town below. Perhaps the Diamond W Dude Ranch was a popular hangout for teenagers.

I tried to stay out of everyone's way, settling on standing in place like a stuffed dummy, my arms pinned at my sides. After a few minutes, passersby started walking around me like I was a flag pole in the middle of the opening.

During our fifteen minute bus ride, I'd thumbed through a slim guidebook that I'd snagged when first arriving at the museum. Seemed "Diamond Dub" (as it was affectionately known) was quite the happening place.

For the adventurous camper, there was horseback riding, cattle drives, catch and release fishing at the trout stream, 4x4 racing, hiking, round-ups, and skeet shooting. City folks could enjoy the hot springs, stroll through wildflower strewn meadows, and visit a souvenir shop. At sunset, the ranch featured hayrides, firesides of cowboy poetry, and a square dance on Friday nights.

On a more economical note, I also read that Diamond Dub raised, broke and bred quarter horses. Its 1,500 head of cattle and other livestock produced beef, pork, milk and cream, many of which were shipped across the country, and all of which provided hundreds of jobs to local families.

"Cowboy up!" someone whooped over the crowd. People whooped back and yee-hawed in reply. I didn't understand why.

Still trying to keep my limbs intact, I pulled the guidebook from my bag and flipped through it again, in search of any information about the proprietors. There was nothing. I was about to toss it in my backpack, but what I spotted on the back cover made my heart stop.

It was a picture of a sunset on the prairie, and silhouetted in the center of the orange and gold glowing ball was a man in a cowboy hat, down on one knee, petting a dog. Even though it was ensconced in shadows, the profile of the cowboy was easily recognizable to me.

It was Henry.

I stared at the picture for what felt like hours, until someone bashed my shoulder.

"'Scuse me, ma'am," a dude said over his shoulder as he walked past.

Ma'am? What the snot? Seeing Henry's picture rattled me. My body felt hot and sticky as I stood beneath the mid-morning sun, and I was suddenly parched. Maybe someone could direct me to a drinking fountain.

I approached a guy who looked like he worked at the ranch. "Pardon me," I said after clearing my throat. But the cowboy rushed past like a gust of smelly farm wind, probably not even hearing me. "That went well."

I tried again with a teenage girl wearing a bright western shirt and a frayed jean miniskirt. "I beg your pardon." She shaded her eyes from the sun. "Can you tell me who I can speak to at the house?"

She smiled, showing a chipped front tooth. "Dunno," she said, then walked away with her friends.

What was with this place? I thought the country was supposed to be helpful and friendly.

Resolute this time, I zeroed in on the man coming straight at me. He was carrying a saddle on one shoulder. A battered black cowboy hat sat low on his sweaty head. He was wearing a dark T-shirt, jeans and brown leather chaps covered with what I *hoped* was *only* mud. By the way he was walking with long, powerful strides, I knew he was in a hurry.

"Excuse me?" I said and tapped his arm that was suspending the saddle.

He stopped walking and stood in place, staring straight ahead.

"Hellooo?" I continued, annoyed when he didn't reply. "Speak English?"

When the grimy rancher finally lowered the saddle and turned to me, every corpuscle of blood gushed to my stomach. He lifted his index finger, nudging the front brim of his cowboy hat up, brown eyes wide like the centers of two sunflowers.

"What...are you doing here?" I managed to mutter, once I remembered how to use my mouth.

Henry unthawed and balanced the saddle against the side of his body. "What am *I* doing here?" he said, removing his hat. "I live here."

"But she told us you didn't...I mean, she *told* us... We thought you weren't here."

"I wasn't." He shifted his weight. "Who's we?"

"Mel," I replied. "She's down the uh…" I pointed toward the bus drop off like a mime. "I had no idea you were here."

Henry's eyes left me and focused past my shoulder. "I flew in late last night." He shifted the saddle to his other side. "The guys"—he dipped his head toward the stables— "were shorthanded this morning, so…"

I offered some kind of acknowledgment to that, then we both stared down, kicking the dusty ground.

"How long are you here?" he asked as he slapped dust off his chaps with his hat.

"Just this morning—it's for research."

His face was smudged with dirt, his hair dark from sweat. And those eyes, just looking into them for the briefest of moments made me feel breathless.

"I swear," I said in a lower voice, "I wouldn't have come here if I knew… I hope you don't think—"

"I don't think anything."

I nodded, my neck sweating.

"Well," Henry said, pointing to the side, "I'd better get this back." He smiled faintly, hoisted the saddle to his shoulder and rushed away.

Deep inside my stomach, a hamster on its wheel was running record time, while my body remained planted in place as firmly as a redwood. After a while, that hamster transformed itself into volcanic lava, creeping like The Blob from the pit of my stomach up the walls of my esophagus.

"That did *not* just happen," I whispered. Panting aloud, I staggered out from the center of traffic and supported myself against the side of a split-rail fence, clutching a post. "Tell me," I gazed toward heaven, "tell me that did *not* just happen." I jammed the heels of my hands into my eyes, cringing and agonizing, remembering a distant past that I couldn't block out: Henry covered in cranberries... In my bedroom... By campfire light. Henry looking stunned when he thought I didn't love him back.

Henry...in a cowboy hat?

"Mel," I whispered. "Melanie Gibson!" I called out as I stepped away from the fence and spun around, scanning the area for my missing cohort. A boy leading a pony by a rope gave me the strangest look. "Mel!" I yelled, ignoring the stares. "Where are you?"

"Spring?"

I spun around.

Her worried eyes inspected me, then she rolled them. "Cause a scene, why don't you."

"C'mon." I pulled her arm. "We have to leave."

"No." She yanked me back. "Have you seen all the cute guys here? They're so rugged and dirty. Melly's idea of heaven. I suddenly have an overwhelming urge to"—she adjusted her bra—"ride a horse."

I covered my mouth with both hands, letting out a little shriek.

Mel's smirk fell. "What's your problem?"

"What was I *thinking*?" I said through my fingers. "What *possessed* me?"

She grabbed my arm. "Babe?"

"He was here. He was standing right here."

"Who?"

"And he was all sweaty and filthy and carrying this thing on his shoulder. In a cowboy hat, Mel. A *cowboy* hat."

"Springer." She squared herself in front of me. "Who are

you talking about?"

"Henry," I whispered. "He was here. *Is* here."

Mel released me and raised a crooked smile. "You don't say."

"It's unforgivable for me to be here. He thinks I'm a creeper." I covered another shriek with my hands. "I didn't want to see him again like this. We have to go," I begged through clenched teeth. "Now. Please."

"All right, all right. But the shuttle down isn't for another two hours."

I pounded my fists against my head.

"Spring." Mel laughed. "It's not the end of the world."

I stopped pounding long enough to glare at her.

"Oh." She tittered. "Maybe it is. Come on, babe." She took my hand. "Let's get out of here."

I nodded, exhausted from exerted emotion, and smoothed the hair out of my face.

"We'll walk back to the car," she said. "You could use some more air, yeah?"

With her arm around me, we set off. We hadn't taken thirty steps before I heard my name being called. Pretending I didn't hear it, I kept walking, faster, pulling Mel along. She stopped abruptly and yanked my arm, causing me to spin a very inelegant about-face.

"Spring," Henry said, trotting toward us. "Hey, Mel."

Mel stared at him, looking a little stunned. Then she giggled under her breath. "Hi, Henry."

"Where are you headed?"

When I didn't answer immediately, Mel jabbed a finger into my ribs. I jumped and squeaked. "We're uh, we're just…" I aimed my gaze down the hill.

"You're leaving?"

He was much tidier now. In the ten minutes since he'd left me, he'd lost the hat, chaps and saddle, and changed into a dark green T-shirt and faded jeans. His face was clean and his usually immaculate curly hair appeared as if it had been hastily combed through with wet fingers. Much to my dismay, he looked sexier than even my imagination thought possible.

"You just got here," he pointed out. "Have you seen the horses or any of the shows?"

"No, umm…"

"You need to see the horses. Do you ride?" His brown eyes were moving back and forth between Mel and me. I think I nodded at his question, but who knows. "I've been dying to take a ride. We should all go."

Out of the corner of my eye, I could see Mel's smile widen. "We'd love that!" she exclaimed. I jerked her arm. She poked me back. "I just *love* horses."

I forced one side of my mouth into some kind of smile. "Sounds like fun."

"Great." His hands were on his hips and, like me, he was breathing a little hard, maybe from his run down the hill. "Why don't you two stay over at the house tonight? There's plenty of room."

I mumbled some kind of refusal that apparently no one heard.

"Fab!" Mel beamed.

"We're having fireworks over the lake for The Fourth," he said. "My parents are due in tomorrow night, but Dart and Lilah are coming in later today." His gaze held on me for an extra second.

"I just *love* Lilah," Mel said with exaggerated enthusiasm.

"It's settled, then. Where's your car?"

"Where the bus picked us up," I answered.

"Keys?" he prompted, holding out his open hand. I dug in my pocket and handed them over. "I'll meet you up at the house. Twenty minutes." He shot off like a cannon.

Still pretty stunned, I kept my eyes locked on him until he disappeared down the hill.

"If the boy keeps up that speed," Mel noted, "he'll make Canada by nightfall."

"Thanks a *lot*, Mel," I snapped, wheeling around. "What did you do that for?"

"Don't worry your pretty little head about a thing." She grinned.

"We can't stay here. It's too weird. I…can't…" My voice petered out helplessly.

"It's cool. He invited us. If he never wanted to see you again, he wouldn't have bothered. He's not *that* polite. So, this is good, right?"

I tried to nod, but a tiny, high-pitched whimper seeped out of my mouth as she took my arm and led me up the hill.

"Spring Honeycutt, the way he was looking at you. *Woo*." She fanned her face. "I really do need a cigarette now."

"He didn't recognize me at first."

Mel ran her hand down the back of my hair, then grabbed a fist-full. "Can you blame him?" She put an arm around my shoulders. "Look, we don't want to be rude, so we're stuck here. Just think about it that way. Okay?"

"Okay," I agreed as we made our way toward the house. "I shudder to imagine what he's thinking right now."

"Oh, babe," she said, giving me a little squeeze. "I know *exactly* what he's thinking."

Chapter 32

"The one by the fence is a solid seven," Mel said. "I could do without the mullet, but...when in Rome."

Mel and I waited in front of the three-level-stacked house with the wrap-around porch. Flanked by tall pines and quaking aspens, it backed up to a skyline of pointy, tree-covered ridges. The whole scene was very picturesque in front of the wide blue Montana sky.

A lop-eared chocolate lab padded over. Mel knelt down, taking its face between her hands. Dangling off its collar, the dog had a red and silver tag. "Its name is *Spring*," she said, reading the tag.

My hand flew to my throat. "Are you serious?"

She laughed, petting the dog behind the ears. "I'm just messing with you. Calm down. You look like you're about to stroke out."

"I might need you to check my vitals in a minute." I was only half kidding.

Mel knew I wasn't in the mood for a talk, so she'd been occupying herself by checking out then rating the ranch hands as they paraded by.

"And this one's a ten-plus," she murmured, ogling over a blond cowboy in tight jeans.

I laughed, grateful for the distraction, until I heard the familiar sputter of my car. Knowing Henry would reappear in a matter of seconds, my heart went banging like a bass drum. Just as he and my Subaru came roaring up the driveway, another car arrived, pulling up behind it. Henry was walking, already halfway to me, when the passenger side of the blue BMW flew open.

"You," Lilah said, staring across the driveway at me. "What are—" She cut herself off, turned her chin to glance at Henry, then back at me. Slowly, her puckered lips stretched, revealing a very toothy smile. "How *amazing*. You're here, too." She rushed to me, overtaking Henry. That was weird. "Henry didn't tell us you'd be here." She cast her glance over her shoulder at him. "Naughty boy."

Henry stood in place, watching me, gauging my reaction. Was he afraid I was going to pummel her? Well, maybe the thought did cross my mind, but after I gave him a tiny nod, he walked back to the cars.

"Spring, hey!" Dart waved from the driveway. "Hi, Mel. Still rockin' that Cardinal crimson?" He pointed at her Stanford T-shirt.

"Yeah, boy!" Mel extended her arms like a cheerleader.

"Lilah." Dart sounded frustrated. "Get your own bags. I'm not your slave."

Lilah's painted-on smile tightened for an instant before turning to her brother. "Coming," she replied sweetly. "We must catch up later, *dear*." The old sneer was back, which made me more at ease than her smile had.

Henry was behind my car, his expression puzzled, staring at my keys in his hand.

"Maybe you should give him a hand," Mel suggested.

I moved toward the Subaru. "It's the silver one," I said, coming up beside him, "with the square head."

"Thanks," he said, his eyes on the keys. He popped open the hatchback door.

Mel was hanging back by the porch steps, knowing that, left to my own devices, I would not be aggressive enough in my present state to arrange being alone with Henry. And I'm sure she knew that was what I needed most in the world.

Lilah was a different story. Even with no one answering her, she was prattling away as she dragged two huge suitcases from the trunk.

My mouth was ajar, ready to speak as I watched Henry fishing around through my cluttered trunk area. Even if I did manage to get my mouth to work, I didn't know what to say. "I'm sorry" didn't seem sufficient, but I had to start somewhere.

"Yours?" he asked from halfway inside my car. He was holding up my Green Peace tote bag. Under other circumstances, I might've been embarrassed by all the empty cans, bottles, and Mel's "emergency" candy wrappers that were strewn about the seats and floor.

"Yes," I replied. The rest of his body was already on the way out, Mel's knock-off Gucci suitcase in his other hand. He stood, facing me, a bag in each hand. "Thank you," I said, tucking the front of my hair behind an ear.

Henry's head tilted as he regarded me. "This is surreal,"

he offered, though it seemed like he wished for a different word. "Listen, can we —"

That was all he got out before Lilah came from behind, dominating the conversation. He shot me a quick glance before he followed Lilah and Mel up the porch and through the front door. I closed the hatchback, shut the driver's door with my hip and jiggled my car keys, not sure what to do next.

"Hey, Spring," Dart said, enfolding me in a quick and friendly hug.

"It's so good to see you," I said, hugging him back. His T-shirt was warm from the sun.

"Long day?"

"It's barely noon," I replied. "Too early to be long."

He laughed at my non-joke and, for maybe two seconds, stared at me. I could almost see what I thought he might be envisioning: Julia standing at my side. His eyes refocused a moment later.

"How have you been?" he asked.

"Fine, fine. You?"

He smiled, running his hand through his stylishly unkempt light hair. "Fine, fine," he echoed. We both turned toward the house at the sound of Lilah's laugh.

The Knightly home was huge from the outside, like the grand fortress atop a hill that it was. On the inside, however, it was much more subtle. There were no ornate Persian rugs, crystal chandeliers, or silk draperies. Instead, the rustic, western décor was warm and welcoming.

When Dart and I entered, Lilah was acting as hostess, pointing out interesting items as we passed. Henry was nowhere to be found, leaving only Mel to pay attention to Lilah. She was such a trooper. She winked at me then quickly turned back to Lilah, nodding and tapping her chin, enthralled.

I lingered in the vestibule, taking in the many focal points of the room.

Past the gray stone-tiled entryway, the floors were light hardwood, covered with thick rugs in various primary colors. Our stack of suitcases was piled at the foot of an open, switch-back staircase. Brown and white-marbled hides and miscellaneous buckskins were draped over the banisters of the second and third floor landings that opened up to overlook the living room. Directly over the brick fireplace was a pair of antlers.

Maybe five minutes later, Henry's voice came from behind me, whispering my name. When I turned around, half his body was around a corner. He motioned with his finger for me to follow.

From the familiar scent of clean mixed with spice, I knew he'd just showered and shaved. He'd also changed clothes again and was now in a white T-shirt and dark jeans. I had a hard time remembering the days when all he wore were Armani suits and argyle sweaters. Both extremes seemed fitting on him.

"Do you have a second?" he asked once we were alone in the hallway.

"Sure," I said, more relieved than I'd felt in months. I wanted nothing more than to be alone with him, to talk to him, to explain, if I possibly could.

"My sister wants to meet you."

"Oh." I blinked, not exactly disappointed. I'd been curious about Cami for a long time.

Henry took a step back and leaned his elbow against the wall in a very relaxed manner. "Just to warn you, she's a little shy, enormously socially awkward, but she's also your biggest groupie."

"Shut up," a soft yet irritated voice came from the crack in the door behind him.

"My groupie?" I whispered. "How does she know about me?"

"I've mentioned you once or twice," he explained. "Spring"—he pushed open the door—"this is my sister, Cami."

Camille Knightly stepped into the hall. Her big brown eyes regarded me through a row of thick black lashes. Naturally blushing, she wasn't wearing a stitch of makeup; she didn't need it. She had the same dark brown hair as her brother, waving past her shoulders, and she stood about five-three, no more than a hundred pounds. The girl was as cute as a button, the prettiest little thing outside the pages of a *Seventeen* magazine.

The way Alex had portrayed her, I'd half expected Cami to be some uppity and pampered, social climbing brat, more like Lilah Charleston and her sorority clones. But that was nothing like this delicate eighteen-year-old in faded jean capris and a pale yellow peasant top.

"Hi, Cami. It's nice to meet you."

"It's nice to meet you too," she said, a little stiffly. She didn't need to be embarrassed, but her brother, who was playfully jabbing her in the back to move forward, probably wasn't making it easier.

"Henry," I said, "would you grab my backpack from the front seat?" I dangled my car keys in front of him. "You can leave it in the living room and I'll meet you later?"

His lips pressed together, forcing upon me his *oh-so-scary* icy expression. But his eyes were grinning approvingly. He took my keys and gave Cami one last poke before leaving.

"I have two brothers," I said. "I know they can be a pain."

"He's always trying to embarrass me," she said in the direction he'd just bolted. "Especially around his friends. He still thinks I'm nine."

"He's just teasing. I think my brothers were put on earth to torture me." I lifted a smile, doing my best to help her feel comfortable. "I've been teased plenty of times by *your* brother, too. Doesn't seem fair, does it?"

She rolled her eyes. "No, it doesn't."

Voices from the living room were drawing nearer. Lilah's little tour must be heading our way. I wasn't willing to move yet, not until Cami was.

"So, I hear you're thinking of going to Cal Berkeley next year. You sure about that?" I made a face. "You know they're just a bunch of communists down there," I joked, presenting to her the bitter rivalry between Cal and Stanford.

Cami laughed harder that I thought applicable. "That's so funny. That's exactly what Trip said."

"You call him Trip, too?"

She shrugged her slight shoulders. "When he's around other people, he likes to think he's some big thing, but up here, he's just loser Trip."

"I love it!" I laughed.

"What kind of car do you drive?"

"It's a Subaru Outback," I said, surprised at the question. Cami seemed a little disappointed at my answer. "Why?"

"I don't know. The way Trip talked, I thought maybe you

had a hybrid or an electric car."

"I hope to someday."

"I get my first new car next month," she said. "Anything I want."

"Have you decided?" Knowing her brother, I wondered if she would go the insanely expensive route like the Viper, the sporty route like his Jeep, or something more conventional…like a nice, medium-sized spaceship.

"My first choice is the Smart Car." This floored me, though I tried not to let it show. "Dad and I made a test drive a few weeks ago, but he says it's too impractical, because I can only fit in one passenger. So I'm getting a Prius. Red, I think. Or blue. What do you think?"

"Well, if you're going for economical, why not a full on electric or natural gas?"

"Dad said anything but *that*." A quiet scoff shook her chest. "So I'm saving up to buy my own. I'll have enough in a few years. He just doesn't grip that this country's in the middle of an environmental crisis. Trip doesn't get it, either," she whispered. "You saw what he was driving around in."

I nodded, placing the appropriate air of horror on my face.

"I think maybe his being at Stanford with more conscientious citizens altered him a little—for the good. Did you notice the white and blue receptacles around the ranch? We're recycling now. Started this summer. It was Trip's idea. Pretty cool, don't you think?"

"Very cool," I replied. "Impressive, actually, and a little… surprising?" I didn't mean my last word to come out like a question, but I couldn't help it. Henry initiating a recycling program?

Cami's brown eyes fluttered. She gave me the impression she was a very old soul, wise beyond her years. "I know my brother can act like a big, stupid gorilla sometimes," she said, "what with his caveman NRA talk, and have you seen his impersonation of Eleanor Roosevelt?"

I shook my head with a groan.

"Spot on," she reported. "It's an important election year, and he still mocks the system. He's incorrigible!"

Behind all her eye rolling and irritation, I could clearly see that Cami adored her brother. I knew for a fact that the feeling was mutual. I couldn't help myself from thinking Cami's tone sounded a lot like mine used to when Henry and I met to study. She was aggravated, yet forgiving. Oodles of love on all sides.

"The Indian blanket hanging on that wall was hand-woven by sweet little Navajo children." Lilah's voice came from around the corner.

I noticed Cami's posture stiffen. "My friend Mel is here with me," I said. "She's a blast. You'll like her."

"Cool." She exhaled. "Trip's probably out back at the grill by now. After lunch, can I show you something? I wrote this paper-thing. It's being published." She waved a hand in the air like it was no big deal. "But I'd like your opinion."

"Sure," I said. We both turned at Lilah's voice growing nearer. "Henry's out back, you say?" I pointed in the other direction. "Can we get to it this way?"

Cami grabbed my arm and we made our escape.

Ten minutes later, we all gathered at the veranda. Henry was adjusting the flame on the gas grill, while Dart and Mel sat on either ends of a long porch swing. Lilah had besieged Cami and they were swinging together in an oversized hammock. Lilah was stroking Cami's dark hair with her spider-leg fingers.

I wasn't relaxed enough to actually sit and attempt a normal conversation with anybody, so I wandered over to the food. There was a spread of typical backyard patio picnic cuisine set up under a blue awning. In addition to that, I also noticed three extra bowls off to the side in dishes that didn't match the rest of the setting, as if they'd been added last minute. Fruit salad, chilled pasta alfredo, and what I knew to be a brick of hard tofu.

When I looked over at Henry, it seemed as though he'd turned his head away from me just a split second before. He was now staring down at the grill, wearing a familiar smirk.

The others joined me under the awning. I loaded up my plate with the three bonus items, knowing full well they were only there because I was. I couldn't help feeling warm and a little glowy inside, enjoying Henry's attempt at hospitable teasing. I sat on a rocking chair, carefully balancing my plate on my lap.

"Still no meat?" Dart asked me as he sat at my side, a dripping hamburger in one hand.

"Eighteen months and counting," Henry answered as he joined us from behind, grilling tongs in hand.

"Nineteen," I corrected.

Dart set his plate off to the side. "You know, Spring, there's something I've always wanted to talk to you about."

"What's that?" I asked, loading up a fork-full of spiral noodles.

"The vitamins and proteins in meat are impossible to replicate, and can't be found in any other foods."

I stopped chewing.

Dart was observing me with caring eyes. "A balanced diet is the healthiest way to live. That includes a little meat sometimes, and a little milk. The idea is moderation."

My eyes flicked to Henry, whose expression was frantic as he stared at Dart like he was about to muzzle him.

"Too much of anything isn't beneficial," Dart went on, "and not enough can be just as harmful."

A few months back, if anyone had the nerve to say that to me, I would have flown off the handle, quoting plenty of other statistics about how a clean and kind, animal-free lifestyle can add years to your life and better the planet. But I hadn't become vegetarian for the health benefits. It was political, a statement…like so many other things in my life had become. That was not the point Dart was making now.

"I know," I said. "I've been reading about that, actually."

After I spoke, Henry exhaled and relaxed the tension in his shoulders.

"Would you like half of mine?" Dart offered hopefully, displaying his plate of meat.

"Not yet." I laughed. "But I'll let you know."

Henry leaned against the back of my chair. "In the meantime, there are two portobello burgers on the grill."

"Thank you," I said, feeling touched again. "And anyway"—I turned back to Dart—"*someone* around here swore he would call me out on Facebook if ever I fall off the wagon." I gave Henry a look.

"Me?" He tapped the silver tongs against his shoulder, smiling innocently. "Honeycutt, I think you know how well I can keep a secret."

Chapter 33

"Come in," Cami sang.

Her bedroom door swung open and Henry walked in

Cami and I were stomach down on her bed, sharing one pair of ear buds plugged into her computer.

"We're leaving for fireworks in ten," he said.

Cami sat up. "Are we going up to the hill? Did you grab the blankets from the shed?" she asked as she slid to a mirror, fingering her hair into a ponytail.

"Everything's downstairs. Spring, it cools off at night here. You might need this." He was trying not to grin as he handed me a purple Los Angeles Lakers sweatshirt.

I was about to tie it around my waist but Cami grabbed it. "You're being a Neanderthal again," she said, then took my arm. "Don't worry about his gorilla-ness. You'll sit with me."

"Okay," I replied cheerfully, even though sitting next to Cami, sweet as she was, was not the way I envisioned the evening.

The rest of the gang was congregated in front of the house. Fourth of July celebrations were in full swing—kids were running around swirling sparklers, and there were designated areas where groups were setting off pinwheels and fountains. Our troop set out to claim a spot to watch the main show.

Dart and Lilah led the pack as we cut through a field. Cami and I trudged behind them, her arm linked through mine. Henry and Mel brought up the rear.

"Dart?" Henry called, suddenly right behind us.

"Yup?"

"Will you give Cami a hand?" Henry gave her a brotherly wink. "This is a steep hill, and look at your shoes. I can't take you anywhere."

"Bite me," she snapped, but then examined her flimsy flip-flops covered in dust.

Henry said something quietly to her in what sounded like German. She immediately dropped my arm and latched onto Dart. That's also when I noticed that Mel had passed us and was walking beside Lilah. Henry and I were behind the rest, alone, for the first time since seeing each other that morning.

The flood of emotions that hit me was almost paralyzing. The first thing I honed in on was the last time I'd seen him, storming out of that study room after Alex called my cell.

My footing stumbled.

"You okay? Slow down," Henry said, catching my arm then letting go. "We have plenty of time." His steps immediately slowed, setting the pace. After a few minutes, the other four were well ahead of us. No one stopped to wait or even turn around. Mel must have had Lilah handcuffed.

"I'm sorry that we didn't get a chance to ride this afternoon," Henry said as he strolled beside me, hands in his pockets. "We've got some nice horses and…" He trailed off and stopped walking.

The sun hadn't totally set yet and when I turned to him, he was silhouetted in orange and gold, just like on the back of that brochure. My heart ached.

"Want to check out the stables?" he asked.

I gazed up the hill at our friends who were almost out of sight.

"We'll catch up with them later." He was already walking back the way we'd just come.

Henry pleasantly greeted several people as we passed them. They all knew him as Trip. I wondered if they worked at the ranch or if they were folks from town he'd known his whole life.

"Cami's very sweet," I said as we cut through a different field, nearing a big red barn.

"She likes you. When I ran up to the house to change this morning, I told her you were here." He kicked a rock. "I've never seen her so excited."

"She's different than what I expected." Henry glanced at me with a puzzled expression. "But *good* different, and… your house is really beautiful," I quickly added, observing the soft yellow glow coming from its porch light.

Small talk, Spring? You coward.

"It's not really *my* house," he said, "but thank you." He unlatched and opened the gate of a wooden fence, allowing me to walk through first. "My great-grandfather would be happy to hear it. He did the renovation—"

"After the storm of twenty-four. I know all about that."

He pulled back a slow smile. "I heard you took a tour this morning. Susanne likes to think of her museum as the nucleus of town. Whatever happens there directly affects the rest of the world. She's a little protective."

We stood under the branch of a tree. Henry was methodically fingering a low hanging branch over his head while I wrapped my hands around a fence post.

A soft evening breeze was blowing, fluttering the leaves. I took the time to breathe in and out, noticing that the unpleasant odors from earlier in the day were gone. Instead, the thin mountain air smelled of earth and grass and life. I took in another breath, letting it hang in my lungs like I was sampling the bouquet of a fine wine.

"You love it here, don't you?" I said. "So peaceful."

"It's my favorite place in all the world, and I'm so glad…"

"What?" I asked when he didn't finish.

He ran a hand through his hair. "I just can't believe you're here."

My heart was pounding again, whooshing waves of blood behind my ears. I gripped tighter at the post. Henry was leaning against the fence, his unreadable gaze moving back and forth from the ground to the dark mountains.

I knew very well by what happened in his floury kitchen and beside that campfire at Beacon Rock campground that Henry was a man of action and didn't ask permission first. Which made me wonder why he hadn't grabbed me for a kiss yet. Was it because we hadn't been alone? Or was that no longer what he wanted?

That's when I realized if anything important was going to be said or done, *I* would be the one who had to bring it up, and stick to it until the matter was settled to my satisfaction. The very notion set loose a different swarm of butterflies in my stomach.

"So, what's this about showing me your horses?" I asked.

He was still gazing at the mountains. "That was my red herring." His mouth moved to smile, but the rest of his face stayed smooth. "I didn't want to take the chance of not being alone with you, at least for a few minutes." He took a step back and nudged a fence post with his foot. "I honestly thought after everything that happened, I would never see you again."

"I got your letter," I blurted before I chickened out. "And I want you to know…" I lowered my eyes, concocting the most magnificent and sincere apology the world had ever beheld. Unfortunately, knowing me, my words were also bound to be ensconced in embarrassing, nervous humor, just to break the tension. Typical cynical Spring.

After one more breath, I forced time and my own heart to slow down, then I opened my mouth and simply said, "Henry, I'm so sorry."

I suppose I should've kept going, but the words were stuck in my throat, shame and guilt choking me mute. Then tears welled—I didn't expect that. Every bone in my body longed for him to forgive me for being blind and judgmental, as well as for being a complete imbecile about my own feelings.

In my heart, I'd forgiven him a million times over.

"No, you were right." He pressed his lips together, his expression growing gloomy. "I still cringe when I remember how I behaved that last day in Vancouver. All those things I said and assumed." He forced his mouth into a smile. "I did actually believe you would come with me, no questions asked. I was horrible, and I apologize."

I laughed softly. "You already did, and I was wrong too."

He held the back of his neck, an air of frustration about him. "I should've asked you about Julia before I did anything," he said. "And I should've told you everything about Parks at the very beginning." He kicked the fence post. "But I didn't want it to come out if it didn't have to."

When he looked up at the sky, I noticed how the bottoms of his eyes were a little shiny. I knew his thoughts had flown to his sister. With that simple realization, the feelings in my heart morphed from guilt and shame into compassion and complete adoration for this weekend cowboy bathed in moonlight.

It was not temporary lust or emotions-run-wild that I was feeling as the booms and sparks of the Twenty-Second Annual Kingston Fireworks Spectacular shot off above our heads. It was calming and grounding and safe, yet I couldn't keep still a second longer.

I inhaled, blocking out everything around me but him, and took a step forward. "Knightly," I whispered. "Every time I think I know what I'm doing, I get knocked sideways."

"Ditto," he said without even the hint of a smile. His forehead was striped with lines of worry and much more gloom than I'd expected. Seeing this, and knowing his stress was my doing, made my heart ache anew. I was prepared to do anything to take that away from him.

So I reached out and took his face. The touch made a wave of uncontrollable longing crash over my head, which normally would have made me want to run away. But not this time. There were no words I could offer. Words seemed to get me in trouble anyway. Actions were called for now, so I held onto him with everything I had and pushed myself forward, finally ready to face the unknown.

"Yes?" he whispered, looking surprised.

I grinned. "Yeah."

The most magnificent feeling in the world was Henry's sweet mouth crashing over mine until neither of us could breathe. His arms wound around me, then slid to the small of my back, pulling me closer. I heard nothing but his breathing—as erratic as mine—and my own heart pounding behind my ears.

"Spring," he whispered, looking into my eyes, making my knees shake. "You're all I've thought about for months."

I slid my fingers into his hair. "This is all *I've* thought about…" As I crushed my body against his, he exhaled a little groan of shock. I was about to back him up when he spun us around. The next thing I knew, I was atop the split-log railing, looking down at his angel face. After my own quiet gasp, I wrapped my legs around his waist, feeling his strong arms encircle me. The spicy, heady scent coming from the top of his head made me dizzy, and I was thankful his grip was tight enough that I could simply let go.

Letting myself go with Henry was surprisingly effortless.

He only had to tilt his chin up for me to kiss him. I tasted the tangy, phantom hint of cranberries on his tongue, and chocolate and sweetness and love. When I gasped for air, he pressed his mouth to my neck, causing my legs around him to tighten. Spaceships and sky rockets and nuclear explosions shot off inside my head. Henry pulled me off the fence, suspending me against him with his own strength, and I had the sensation of floating on air.

As we kissed and touched and breathed, I was partially aware that my soul had left my body and was hovering somewhere above our heads. Sometime afterward, I realized I'd been in the throes of what Julia described as that very elusive second kind of kiss.

"What is that lip gloss, if I may be so bold?"

By then, the moon was high in the midnight sky as we sat on a small bench behind the stables. The barn blocked our view of the fireworks, but we were shooting off sparks of our own.

"Was it the same you were wearing…before?" He pulled his face back an inch from mine, leaving my lips vibrating.

"I don't remember," I replied, draping my legs across his lap.

"I do," he whispered, butting his forehead against mine. "Pineapple. I haven't been able to eat one since March. Maybe that's what made me want to take you to Tahiti." He chomped his teeth together before coming back to me, one finger tracing over my face, down my neck, then gathering up my hair. "I was partial to the braids. Why the change?"

"That's what girls do. We can't grow a goatee, so we cut our hair."

"No, really." He knew my answer was flippant and, even by the light of the moon, I could see he wanted the truth.

I squirmed a bit before answering. "I'm done pretending," I stated, needing to be honest with him. He seemed content, understanding the meaning of this simple answer, and he kissed the tip of my nose, making me feel as if I were glowing on the inside. "I tried to text you," I said.

"When?"

"After I got yours about meeting at the library. I sort of

destroyed my phone so I didn't get the message for three days."

Henry lifted his eyes as if realizing something for the first time. "Oh."

"My text bounced back."

He nodded. "I've been unplugged for a while," he explained. "Shut everything off. I have an old emergency cell that my parents and sister use when they need to reach me and I'm not around a landline."

"Why did you unplug?" I asked.

"I was checking my damn phone every two seconds, hoping to hear from you. After a few days of nothing, I figured I had my answer, and I couldn't stand it."

"I'm sorry," I whispered, touching his face. "I wanted to call you. I guess we're pretty pathetic at the whole communication thing."

"Not anymore," he said. "First thing tomorrow, I'll give you a list of every number and address I have."

"Your first gift to me," I said with a smile. "I'll cherish it always."

Henry laughed softly then gazed off toward the mountains. "Did you know this is the first?" He paused, as if he didn't like the way that sounded. "What I mean is, I've never had a woman here with me, not since I moved away to college. You're my first."

"I'm honored," I said, nuzzling the side of his neck. He pulled me onto his lap so my legs were straddling him. He stared into my eyes and kissed me deeply, causing heat to build in my stomach then spread up my body, honing my focus. Instinctively, I tugged at his shirt, needing it out of my way.

"Spring," he whispered, pulling back an inch. "We're outside." He glanced over his shoulder then back at me. "It's not…ideal for us tonight."

"I know," I agreed, trying to slow the blood flow racing through my veins.

Henry sighed and ran a hand through my hair, resting it on the side of my neck, probably feeling my jumping pulse. "Just kiss me," he requested, so softly. I did. "Again." As I did, his hands slid up the back of my shirt. I shuddered with joy and dissolved…

"Did *you* know," I said, pressing my mouth to his neck, "instead of coming *here*, Mel wanted to take me on vacation this summer?"

His hands stopped moving, then his arms wrapped all the way around me, holding me extra tightly against him. I knew exactly what he was thinking. Yes, we'd come dangerously close to messing everything up forever.

Timing…

"Why did she invite you?" he asked.

I hooked my chin over his shoulder and ran a hand through the back of his hair. "I wasn't doing very well without you," I admitted. It was easier to say this while not looking at him. "She knew I needed to get away."

"Where"—he was back to sounding glum again—"was she taking you?"

"Mexico." When I felt him shudder, I sat back. "You don't like Mexico?"

He was displaying his clenched teeth in a parted-lip grimace. I slid off his lap so I could sit next to him. "My concern isn't so much with the country as it is with the lawless order and behavior in government," he explained. "I fear being kidnapped in a foreign place and ending up in a Mexican prison. The amount of testosterone is not conducive with my polished manners and rugged good looks."

I smiled at his formal cadence. Even in mid-embrace, Henry couldn't help talking like a bourgeois. "It's so tough being you." I ran my fingers down his face. "Have you been there?"

He nodded stiffly.

"Bad experience?"

He thought for a moment then laughed. "The last time I was there, my father and I went hiking in a rainstorm and got lost. Cami called the local *Federales* to pull us out. Humiliating."

"You're close to your family," I observed. This wasn't a question, because I already knew the answer. When his smile broadened, I sighed, missing my brothers, my mother, even my father a little—which was strange. Maybe I missed the idea of family more than anything. Maybe it was time I did something about that.

"You're not?" Henry asked, sensing my mood shift.

We were alone under the stars, wrapped around each other, and I was feeling things I never knew were possible for someone like me. We should be enjoying the reunion, making up for lost time, confessing our feelings, and *not* talking about my family.

But Henry was watching me with that expression I knew so well. He pulled me onto his lap again, making me feel safe and warm, part of something important.

"My parents," I began, rubbing a hand over my forehead. "They never really meshed, even through six years of marriage. I haven't spoken to my father in person for a long time. He had issues; *we* had issues."

"How long?" Henry asked, taking my hand and pressing it to his chest.

"Years." *Too long*, I almost added.

Henry nodded, then pulled me forward, hugging me, his hand moving up and down my hair, then burrowing in to hold the nape of my neck. Revealing this part of my personal history was new to me—I wasn't used to opening up. But being with Henry, his arms like a blanket, his body my pillow, made me want to share.

"My mom," I continued, my face still buried in his chest, "she never cooked for us, but she did manage to put together a sack lunch for me when I was a kid. Each of the sandwiches she made..." I trailed off, heavy emotions coming out of nowhere. "She always took a tiny bite out of the corner before wrapping it." I smiled to myself. "That was her way of telling me she loved me, I guess."

He didn't say anything at first, then he dipped his chin to touch his nose to my cheek. "I hope you realize," he whispered, his soft breath brushing my skin.

"Realize what?"

He gathered me to him, even tighter. "I hope you realize"—he kissed me lightly—"that's one powerful love story."

His words gave me that lighter-than-air sensation again, drowsy and dreamy and safe.

Loved.

"Thank you," I whispered, holding his cheek.

"Will you tell me more?"

Chapter 34

I tucked my hair behind my ears and stared into the glass. Then I untucked it, laying it over my shoulders. I leaned in closer to the mirror then backed away. After a sigh, I turned from side to side.

Strange. Nothing *appeared* to have altered. Yet something had definitely changed, because I felt different inside. Happy, trusting, new.

Still, my unchanged reflection puzzled me, or maybe I was simply reacting to the way I was being seen through Henry's eyes, someone who loved me. I bit my lip, remembering…

"Spring?" Mel's voice startled me as she called through my bedroom door. "Coming down to breakfast?"

I was forced to pull myself away from the mirror and the memories as I answered in the affirmative.

She was grinning ear to ear when I opened the door. "I think I'm your good luck charm."

I was endeavoring, quite unsuccessfully, to hide my huge

smile.

"You're utterly buzzing, babe."

"I am not," I claimed, knowing I most certainly was.

As we walked down the stairs, I could hear Henry's voice coming from the kitchen. It made me want to slide down the banister and tumble into his arms, Lilah's glares notwithstanding.

"Oh," Mel said as she drew my cell phone from her pocket. "You left this here while you and Henry were, umm…" She was smiling again. "Someone called twice for you last night, but I didn't pick up."

I checked the missed calls. "Anabel." I frowned. "Wonder what she wants."

"Did she stay back at school in the house with Julia?" she asked. "Those two have nothing in common. She's probably just bored." Mel's brown curls bounced as she trotted down the stairs ahead of me, leaving me to return the call.

I ducked into the dark library for privacy. Its walls were lined with shelves of leather-bound volumes. Half of one wall was adorned with an oil painting of a gray-haired man in a Navel officer's uniform.

Must be one of the Knightlys, I mused as I gazed at the noble figure, feeling an almost reverent affection. *So different from my family.* I dialed the number, remembering my father's upcoming nuptials and feeling surprisingly happy for him.

Anabel answered after the first ring. "Spring?"

"Hey stranger," I said. "Holding down the fort?"

"I know you're on the road, but I didn't know what else to do. But, I mean, I thought I should tell someone, right?" Drama queen Anabel rambled on for a minute but I wasn't following. At one point, I actually held the phone away from my ear. "I didn't think she was, like, *that* unhappy, did you? But why else would she say that?"

"Anabel." I rolled my eyes. "Tell me again, slowly, what's going on."

When she spoke this time, her words were still muddled and confusing, but the picture they painted in my mind was all too clear. And suddenly, I was stone-cold sober.

"Are you sure?" I asked, feeling simultaneously sick and numb. "Julia actually…did…" I couldn't finish, but swallowed hard and sank into an over-stuffed leather chair. When I'd heard enough, my mind snapped into gear, making the decision. "Okay, okay. Don't do anything else for now. I'm coming home." I was speed-dialing Julia's cell a split-second later. Voicemail. Like I feared.

Just as I ended the call, the library door flew open.

"There you are." Henry's voice boomed brightly across the room. He looked like heaven, pure heaven. All I wanted to do was run to him, but I couldn't move. I couldn't bear to tell him the truth.

"I've been looking all—" His smile dropped and he stopping in place. "Are you…?"

I squeezed my stinging eyes shut but heard him rush forward, felt him take my hands.

"What's wrong?" His voice was almost panicky. When I opened my eyes, he was kneeling in front of me.

"I need to go home," I managed to say. "Right now."

Henry's eyes were large like black Frisbees.

"I need to go home right now," I repeated. When I attempted to stand, he held me down.

"No." His voice was gruff and his grip tightened. "You're

not leaving me now. What happened?"

I tried again to stand, but every limb in my body was weak. The next second, his arms were around me, pulling me to the floor beside him.

"Tell me," he said in a low voice. "Let me help if I can. Please."

"I just talked to Anabel," I said, breathing hard.

"Anabel," Henry repeated, staring into my eyes. "Your roommate?"

I nodded, trying to hold it together. "She told me, she… she flipped out and took off. She's been depressed, I knew that. Maybe I shouldn't have left her. And now she's gone."

"Anabel?"

"Not Anabel." I sniffed, dropping my eyes, not able to look at him as I continued. "Julia," I whispered. "She ran away…with Alex."

All was silent; neither of us so much as breathed. Henry's face was gray and still. His inscrutable eyes drifted from mine to the empty space beside me.

"Julia," he said. "Are you sure?"

I nodded, briefly recapping the phone call.

"They left together last night, so it's been hours," I said. "She's unstable; she hasn't been herself for months. I thought she was getting better, but she actually mentioned something about Alex a while ago. I…" I put a hand over my mouth. "I thought she was kidding."

Henry's grip on me slackened. He stood up, leaving me on the floor, alone.

"You know Alex, what he's done to other…" I couldn't complete the sentence. "I have no idea where they went, but I have to try and find her, or at least be home when she comes back."

Henry was standing in front of a large window, staring out at nothing. The morning sun was streaming through a slit in the drapes, shining on him like a spotlight piercing the dark room. It should've been a beautiful sight, but there was nothing beautiful about his face when he turned around. He wouldn't even look at me.

"You understand why I have to go," I said.

He fingered his chin. "Today?"

"As soon as possible." Gripping the chair behind me, I pulled myself to my feet.

"Driving?" he asked.

I nodded then attempted to call for Mel, but the tall room seemed to swallow my voice.

"It's twelve hundred miles," he pointed out.

I shot him a glance, and his expression showed that he wished he hadn't said anything. I made my way to the door with no other thought than getting on my way, no time to spare.

"Wait," Henry said from behind. "You don't need to drive. We have a plane."

"No, I couldn't—"

A phone was already at his ear.

Nothing specific was given as a reason for our hasty removal and there was no time for *bon adieus*. Only Cami and Henry were with us as we rode in silence to the airfield behind their house. Henry handled our bags from his car to the private plane, all while still instructing and directing unintelligibly on a tiny black flip phone over the deafening jet engines.

Just as I was about to start up the metal stairs, Henry

caught my wrist. "Yes, right, but just hold on a sec." He was looking directly at me but I could tell he was talking on his phone, then he held it away from his ear. "Spring," he said in a rush, "I don't know when I'll see you again." He held my gaze for just a moment before he let go of my wrist and went back to his phone call. I didn't even have time to reply before Mel was pushing me up the stairs to board the plane.

"What's our plan?" she asked as we taxied down the runway.

Still a bit shaken and still feeling where Henry had been holding my wrist, I shut my eyes, my mind whirling too fast. "I don't have one," I admitted.

"Remind me," Mel added. "What exactly did Henry's letter say about where Alex took Cami. Maybe there's something that can help."

I opened my eyes to peer out the window. I could see Henry leaning against the Jeep, arms folded, talking to Cami as he stared toward the plane. Whatever he'd just told her sent both hands flying over her gaping mouth. Then she reached out and grabbed her brother's arm, shaking him.

Chapter 35

Melanie and I didn't speak much during our flight home. Henry arranged for a rental car to be waiting for us at the airport in San Francisco to keep for as long as required. I was grateful for this, because I wasn't in the presence of mind to consider that detail. He also assured that my car would be returned to me as soon as possible.

"I'm going to your house," Mel said as I was about to make the turn onto her street.

"You don't have to," I said wearily. "There's nothing you can do."

"I can sit there with you until she comes back," she insisted. "So shut up."

"Thanks," I said, and hung a U-turn toward home.

Anabel was perched on a barstool in the kitchen when we walked in. She looked worried and tired, like I felt. My first impulse was to grab her by the shoulders and scold, knowing that—with her recent track record—this must somehow be her fault. But now wasn't the time for blame.

"Tell us what we don't know," I requested as I sat beside her, Mel on her other side.

"I saw them leave together," she answered, diving right in. "Alex was over here and—"

"Why was Alex in this house?" I interrupted.

Anabel stared down at her nails. "We've kind of been hanging out this summer."

I glared at my roommate. "I told you to stay away from him."

"I know." She toyed with the ends of her hair. "But campus is a total ghost town and he's cute—"

"Whatever. Why did Julia take off with him if he's been hanging out with you?"

"Like I said, he was over here. It was weird. Julia was flirting with him, like, hardcore. When I left the room for a minute and came back, they were talking, he was *touching* her, telling her about some secret cabin at the beach."

My blood turned ice-cold and I glanced at Mel. Her face was white.

"I'm pretty sure he'd been drinking a little." Anabel bit her lip. "Well, maybe more than a little. And I know she'd been drinking a lot."

"And?"

"Around midnight, he made a phone call. As soon as he left the room, Julia started bawling. She was hysterical, going on and on about needing to, ya know, get some. Have you ever heard her talk like that?"

I shook my head, but then felt chilled again, remembering word for word the conversation we'd had about how, even though she and Dart had slept together, he still left her, and how resentful she'd felt about that…how it hadn't been special after all.

"She wasn't making sense," Anabel continued. "So I told her to—"

"What did you tell her to do this time, Anabel?" Hot dread filled my veins.

"Nothing!" Her eyes grew wide. "I mean, I told her to chill out. She was drunk. I'm not an idiot. Next thing I knew, she wiped her face and got this look in her eyes, staring at Alex when he finished his call. She walked right up to him and said she wanted to see the cabin."

"You didn't stop her?" Mel asked.

"What was I supposed to do?"

"Kick Alex in his family jewels, for one," I suggested.

"I couldn't! She grabbed her purse and they took off before I could do anything. They just left me and…it was just really weird."

"What do you mean?" I asked, feeling another cold shiver down my spine.

"Well, why did he take her and not me?"

"Anabel!" I snapped.

"Sorry." She blinked and dropped her chin, like she was attempting to appear guilty. But I knew better. She was in shock that someone managed to steal a guy from under her nose.

"Were you waiting up all night?" I asked. She nodded solemnly. "You can go to bed. Thanks for calling me last night. I know it must've sucked."

"Yeah," she said, then added right before leaving the room, "and I really am sorry."

I said nothing in reply, I just walked with Mel to the

living room. "It's barely been twelve hours," I said, slumping onto the couch. "What should we do?"

"There's nothing we can do," Mel said. "We can't even call the cops yet. She's not missing and in no imminent danger."

"Imminent," I muttered, coldly.

"Try her cell again."

I did, but I'd been getting nothing but voicemail all day. I left another message, begging her to call.

"We don't know for sure they went to that beach cabin," Mel said, sitting beside me. "The same one he took Cami to."

"That's what he *does*, Mel," I countered, running a fist across my forehead. "You read Henry's letter."

"Yeah," she replied, somberly. "I'm just hoping we're wrong."

We weren't wrong, and I knew it. "He got rough with Cami," I said after a minute. "And she was fifteen. She wasn't the only one; he's been doing this for years, always keeping his exploits on this side of a felony. What does he do if they try to fight back?" I shut my eyes in a long blink. "He's disgusting and deserves to be castrated!"

"Do you know where he takes them?"

"Not the exact location. All Henry alluded to was somewhere down by Monterey, but that's a big place."

Mel and I sat for hours, sharing our worries, while going over possible scenarios and hoping Julia's ex–Navy Seal father didn't call the house. I tried Alex over and over too, but he never answered his phone. Shadows crept across the floor of our living room, slowly morphing the scene from afternoon to evening. Tomorrow, we decided, we would call the police.

Eventually, Melanie's head sank to my shoulder and we

both fell asleep.

My dreams were sporadic, because I slept without rest. The only one I remembered was right before I awoke. The picture in my head was mostly fuzzy, but there were definite fireworks, and a cowboy hat, and a face. The face was the only part of the dream that was crystal clear. When I lifted my arms out to him, there was a sudden stabbing pain in my side, but that didn't keep me from reaching out, even though I felt the knife stabbing me again and again. Over and over.

"Spring, wake up."

I peeled my eyelids apart, feeling Mel's sharp fingernail poking my ribs. Through the dim early morning shadows, she was staring at me.

"Julia," she whispered then pointed at the front door.

I threw my legs off the couch and sat up.

She was standing by the door under the only illuminated light in the room. She wasn't looking at us, but at whoever was lingering under the threshold, unseen behind the open door. She whispered something then an arm reached out, the front half of Dart's body coming into view. Silently, he touched her cheek in the gentlest of ways. She tilted her face so he could cup her cheek, whispered something to him, then he left.

After she closed the door, she stared at it, touching the wood with her fingertips. I knew she knew we were there, but she didn't acknowledge us.

"Are you okay?" I asked, easing to stand. My body ached from having napped in a vertical position.

A few moments passed before Julia turned our way. She appeared unharmed, but she didn't *look* fine.

I walked to her, trying not to wince when I noticed the

marks on her upper arms. Rage and sorrow spun like a tornado in my stomach. Julia must've caught my examination because when I met her eyes, they were brimming with tears, and her lips trembled.

"Jules?" I opened my arms just as she broke into loud sobs. "Shhh." I rubbed her back as she cried on my shoulder. "It's over. You're home."

She couldn't talk for a while. I didn't blame her; it wasn't a story I was eager to hear. As I waited, I silently surmised that the reason Dart had been with her was because Henry must have told him why Mel and I had suddenly left his house that morning. Then Dart must have taken over and tracked them down.

Whether Dart got there in time, I didn't know yet. But considering how long Julia and Alex had been alone, as well as the angry red marks ringing her wrists, it did not look good. When the deeper sobbing started, I had my answer, and felt sick.

Julia wept while I held her and listened. "I'm so sorry," was all I was able to offer. Because I was sorry. It was me who had brought Alex into our lives and I couldn't help feeling tremendous guilt about that.

We went through three pots of tea but didn't move from the couch, me on one side of Julia, Mel on the other. After a while, Julia seemed to want to tell us everything, maybe needing to get it out at least once. Terribly unhappy, more than buzzed on peppermint schnapps, she'd left with Alex. She admitted that everything got pretty fuzzy after that, but they did arrive at a cabin a couple of hours later. She'd been drunk but consensual. I said a silent prayer of thanks that nothing more than rough sex had taken place.

Knowing Alex's tendencies, it could have been worse. She did remember that a condom was used, which seemed pretty miraculous. But that was probably just Alex wanting to cover his tracks in case Julia pressed charges. Still, nothing is 100 percent foolproof. Julia would have to be tested. Mel and I promised to be with her when she took the first one.

Julia remembered still being slick with Alex's sweat when Dart had shown up. He'd rushed straight to her, wrapped her in the bed sheets and carried her to the car. Julia sobbed as she recalled how he'd placed her in the backseat, laid his head on her lap and begged for forgiveness. Mel and I were sobbing, too.

"Dart's a real hero," I said, rubbing Julia's shoulder.

"Yeah," she said, trying to smile through her wobbly bottom lip.

"How did he know where to find you?" Mel asked, passing Julia a fresh cup of chamomile tea. "And so fast?"

"Henry," she whispered, her hand trembling as she took the cup.

"Henry, what?" I asked.

She didn't answer.

"He probably told Dart where the cabin was," Mel explained logically. "He knew the location because of Cami, right?"

Julia stared down at her cup then took a slow sip.

"Is that what happened?" I asked. "Is that how Dart found you?"

"That's what I thought at first," she confirmed. "All I saw was Dart at the cabin. He's the one who broke through the door and got me out. When he took me to the car, we sat there for a while in the backseat. Maybe twenty minutes later, I realized the car was moving."

"Who was driving?"

Julia finally looked at me. "Henry."

"Henry," I repeated, my mind fuzzy. "He was there, too?"

Julia bit her lip and nodded. "I honestly didn't realize it was him at first. I was still a little out of it. Dart never left me for a second, and I guess I hadn't noticed that Henry went inside the cabin after Dart got me out. Alex was still in there. When we stopped for gas an hour later, my purse and clothes were in the front seat. I noticed it then, Spring."

"Noticed what?"

"Henry's knuckles," she whispered. "They were red and —" She broke off. "I have brothers, I know what it looks like after someone has a fight."

My stomach hit the floor. "They fought?"

Julia shrugged helplessly. "I think so."

"Is Henry hurt? Do you know what happened?"

Mel reached over the back of the couch behind Julia and touched my shoulder. "I'm sure Henry beat the living hell out of him, babe."

"Besides his knuckles," Julia said, "he looked fine. Not a mark on him, I swear, Spring. After he dropped us off, he was heading straight to the airport."

"What?" I blinked, rising to my feet. "Henry dropped you off here?" I spun around to the front door, thinking that he might materialize from thin air. "Why didn't he come in?"

When Julia didn't answer, Mel said, "He probably thought you were asleep."

"So? He could've woke me up."

"I don't think he wanted you to know he was with us," Julia whispered, her voice watery with new tears.

"Why?" I stared at her, then at Mel, then at the wall behind them. No one had an answer.

"Maybe he had to get right back to the ranch," Mel offered. "I mean, Cami was still there and, ya know…the horses?"

"What?" I gaped at her.

Mel spread her hands. "I don't know. I'm just *talking*."

I couldn't help exhaling a laugh at Mel's attempted explanation. "Well, thanks for comparing my needs to that of a horse."

Mel batted her eyelashes. "It was too easy, babe."

"Springer, I'm sorry," Julia said, touching my arm.

"Yeah," I replied, feeling sullen again. Honestly, I didn't know what she was apologizing for. For running off and making us worry? For cutting my road trip short? Or was she proxy-apologizing for Henry not coming in to see me? I met her eyes, she looked exhausted and had probably been awake for longer than back-to-back study sessions. And of course, she'd just been through an unspeakable ordeal. "You should go on to bed," I said.

Julia nodded, gave me a hug that I barely felt, then disappeared up the stairs.

"You can leave, too," I said to Mel, pressing my fingertips over my eyelids.

"Yeah, not a chance. I'm making blueberry pancakes then we're getting pedicures. My treat."

"No, thanks," I said, trying to smile, but the fatigue of the past day's events was weighing down my entire body. "Maybe tomorrow. I think I'll just crash."

"You sure?"

I nodded. For a few minutes, Mel argued against leaving,

but I was resolute, and finally, I was alone.

Too weary to climb two flights, I curled myself into a ball on the couch, trying very hard to fight back the thing creeping its way into my thoughts. Even if he'd assumed I was asleep, why would that stop him from coming in? From seeing me? I scowled at my phone, which was just sitting there, all void of new messages or calls. I closed my eyes and wrapped my arms around my legs, thinking of him, missing him.

That glorious Fourth of July, as Henry and I curled around each other, no official words were declared, no tender confessions divulged. I'd chosen instead to let my actions speak. I thought he felt, *knew* what I didn't know how to say.

But he hadn't come inside my house. Why?

He'd done this wonderful, magnanimous service to my little college family, and then disappeared. Not calling attention to himself, simply providing a service that only he could.

Spring, I don't know when I'll see you again. Those had been his last words to me. But what did they mean?

As I sat in the dark living room, watching shadows on the walls, it was almost too easy, too *obvious* to realize I was in love with him, and probably had been for a very long time. Being in love felt different than I thought it would. I wasn't giving up a part of me or sacrificing what I thought I was in order to love him. I'd gained, I'd unfolded…evolved.

This made me smile; in fact, I almost laughed, but my smile broke when I realized there would be no more study sessions at the library, no more vacation trips to Washington, and no more surprise run-ins at his family's house.

Was there anything left?

Chapter 36

"Dart said Henry went back home," Julia relayed. She had most of her color back. Two solid days spent reuniting with the man she loved could do that. We were in her bedroom, she was on the floor inside her closet, reorganizing shoes.

"Oakland?" I asked, lifting my head off her pillow.

"First there, I think, then Montana," she answered.

Well, at least she hadn't said Tahiti. But still, the fact that he could've been in Oakland, so close, and still no phone call, made my heart feel like it was being crushed like a Styrofoam cup.

"So...do you know if he's coming back to school? Classes start in two months."

"I don't know," Julia admitted. "Dart moved back into the house across the street this morning, but I don't know about Henry. I'm not sure Dart does, either."

I was well acquainted with Henry's guarded form of communicating. I wasn't surprised that he hadn't told Julia his plans while they were driving back from Monterey. In all those hours he and I were together at the ranch, I hadn't once asked him if he was returning to Stanford. I hadn't broached the subject of where he'd disappeared to after that last night at the library. For whatever reason, those didn't seem important at the time. They seemed very important now.

"Huh," I replied breezily, trying to blow off this information. But Julia was watching me, and I was positive she could read my eyes. I laid back and covered my face with an arm.

I don't know when I'll see you again. His words rang in my ears.

"Have you called him?" she asked.

I nodded, my throat feeling tight. "I haven't been able to get ahold of him since last spring. He was supposed to give me his new number, but I left the ranch in such a hurry…" I forced my shoulders up into a shrug then let them drop. "So whatever. If he calls, he calls."

"Uh-huh." Skepticism wrapped around Julia's tone.

I sat up and pushed my hair back. "I've been thinking about it, and I decided the whole thing was too sappy. Love and boyfriends and everything. *So* not me, right?" I forced myself to laugh in the sarcastic manner that used to get me through uncomfortable moments. This time, though, it sounded unnatural, and felt even worse.

"I don't care what you say, Spring. Every girl wants someone to be sweet to her." She sat on the bed next to me. "Even cynics like you."

I knew she was trying to help, but her comment made my chest feel hollow and achy. A short time ago, I didn't know how to love, but now I didn't know how to do without love.

"You're fighting against your feelings, honey," she added. "I know how exhausting that can be. So stop fighting and let it flow."

"Flow?" I echoed, giving her my famous flat eyes.

She lifted a smile and walked toward the door. "Yes. Go with the flow." Just as she was about to leave, she turned back. "Do you want to hang out with us tonight?"

"Thanks, but I don't think so." Honestly, the thought of being around a happy couple was enough to make me cry.

Julia nodded and opened the door.

"Bunny," I called, stopping her. "If I haven't told you, I'm really happy Dart's back and that you're, you know, okay."

"Me too." She folded her arms and leaned against the doorframe. "I made mistakes, but I understand everything that happened now."

I swallowed. "You do?"

She nodded slowly.

"Jules, I didn't know how to tell you what I knew. I'm so—"

"It wasn't Henry's fault," she cut in. "Not really." She looked to the side and exhaled. "Mistakes," she murmured to herself. "I made some, so did Dart. We all do. But now, it's almost like we're better than before because of it." She gazed off for a moment. "Every second we're together, I appreciate him more and more. All that time apart, all that wasted time. I'll never be shy about my feelings again. Life's too short, too precious not to love whenever we can." She bit her lip, blinking back tears. "I learned that the hard way."

"Yeah," I managed to choke out, and then watched her leave the room.

Later that evening, I sat alone on my bed. The sun had set hours ago, but I hadn't moved from my room since Julia left. Downstairs, Anabel was hosting an intimate party for twenty. I bowed out with the excuse about needing to write my congressman.

My room was dim and cool, the only light coming from the streetlamp outside my open window as sounds from the sidewalks below drifted up. The moon was high and Stanford's summer populace was alive and ripe.

My fingers clasped behind my head and I stared up at the ceiling. Thinking. Trying *not* to think. The night grew darker as evening progressed. When I rolled over, my gaze moved naturally to the open window. Just knowing his house, his empty bedroom, was across the street crushed my Styrofoam heart anew. I quadruple-checked the ringer on my phone. Never before had I experienced such a lack of control over my thoughts.

Spring, I don't know when I'll see you again.

The intellectual part of me had no desire to keep mulling over the possible meaning of Henry's last statement, so I forced it out. But with no other occupation, my thoughts did wander around the memory of the sound of his laugh…how we'd laughed together, how I admired his mind, loved his music, how he'd kissed my braid—one of the sweet ways he showed his acceptance and respect. The way he pushed my buttons just to make me laugh at my own reaction. How he dealt with me and handled me and let me go it alone, yet never took my crap.

The way he truly was so very good.

With my eyes closed, I imagined us in some future setting…whispering in the dark, sharing a pillow, asking how the other slept.

I drifted to the window and knelt down, resting my elbows and chin on the sill. The cool night air felt nice. "He'll be back," I whispered. "I know he'll be back." Just saying the words aloud made me feel slightly better, as if my faith in us was enough. He'd had faith in us for all those months, and now it was my turn.

I listened to the happy hums of the world below. As the breeze picked up and knocked the blinds against the side of the window, I opened my eyes, their gaze idly drifting across the street.

What they landed on made my blood stop cold. I blinked, sharpening my focus.

Parked crooked in his driveway was…

My Subaru.

I sprung out the third-story window, sliding down the ladder as fast as I could.

Twelve more steps, I counted, my fingers gripping around the rope handle. *Eight more.* My heart pounded behind my ears. In my haste, I did notice that no lights were on in his house, not even the bedroom on the second floor where he might be. *I'll be there three seconds sooner if I jump…*

"Don't!"

From directly below, I heard the warning shout, but it was abruptly cut short as I plummeted toward the ground. We collided mid-air, tumbling onto the lawn in a heap. Mine would've been a perfect ten-point landing had the intruder's body not been blocking my way. Instead, I lay on my side, dazed and spitting out grass.

"Whoever you are," I wheezed once my body regained its equilibrium, "I don't have time to explain the theory of private property or breaking and entering."

The prowler was behind me on hands and knees, quietly gasping in the shadows. I knew I'd probably knocked the wind out of him, and deservedly so! I didn't have time to worry about him, my only thought was to make it through that door across the street and up those stairs.

"I won't call the cops this time," I added, rolling onto my knees. "But you should know I sleep with a wrench under my pillow."

"Feels like you used it on me."

I wheeled around to find Henry rubbing his forehead.

"Are your shoes made of cement, woman?"

"Knightly?" My eyes strained, pulling in every bit of light from the streetlamp.

"I saw you at the window." He crawled over, a hand still at his forehead.

"Did I hurt you?" I asked, only half feeling the pain shooting from my own right shoulder.

"It's nothing." One side of his face was matted with grass and dirt. "Where are you off to in such a hurry?"

"I saw my car and…"

He angled his chin to the light. To say the sight was soul-shaking might be a dramatic stretch, but that's how I felt as our eyes met in the dark.

"How long have you been back?" I asked, silently praying he wouldn't inform me that he'd been around for days and was just now finding the time to pop in and say hello.

"Exactly"—he squinted at his watch—"one minute and twenty seconds." His face was tired and a little weathered, his clothes and hair uncharacteristically disheveled. He noticed my wondering stare. "I left home seventeen hours ago," he explained, smoothing out his collar.

"Oakland?"

"No," he replied, looking a little confused at my assumption. "The ranch. I flew back right after dropping off Julia and Dart, then drove back here in your car." He was brushing grass from the knees of his pants. "You need to have your tires rotated. I would've done that along the way, but I know how you are about accepting unrequested favors."

I think I was nodding, but only half listening to his small talk. There were a few things I needed to say, because, like my sweet roommate had said, life was too short to wait.

"Henry." I jumped in before his voice had time to fade out. "Julia told me what you did for her."

His brow furrowed, playing confused.

"Thank you. I know it must've been…unpleasant." I exhaled a dark laugh. Obviously *unpleasant* was an understatement.

"You don't have to—"

"Please. I need to say this."

The lines in his forehead disappeared as he nodded and sat back.

"There've been mistakes…screw-ups, and I wish there was some kind of magical phrase I could turn to explain, to tell you…" I trailed off and groaned. "Yes?"

I'd stopped speaking when Henry's mouth popped open, dying to butt in. He was holding up one finger now.

"You just can't help yourself, can you?"

"Sorry," he said. "But I have to interrupt here." He scooted around so we were sitting across from each other on the cool grass. The light from the streetlamp was shining in my favor now, illuminating Henry's face. I could see a little welt — approximately the size of my Doc Martin heel — swelling on his forehead. I could also see that he'd just lifted a tiny smile.

"I have no intention of turning this into one of those lectures you find so irritating, but I do want to let you in on a few things."

"Okay?"

"Number one, I really blow at reading between the lines, so don't bother trying to drum up some idiom that isn't one hundred percent clear. Two, I've known you long enough to know there's not a person on this earth who can argue you into something you don't already believe." He lifted another half smile. "A lawyer's worse nightmare. Third and lastly…"

From his expression, I knew he was considering, formulating the sentences in his head before speaking. Some things never changed.

"Lastly, as much as I enjoyed being with you that night at the ranch, and when we were camping, and…in my kitchen." He took a decisive pause, looking me in the eyes. I felt that pile of hot bricks on my chest from all those nights ago. "Well," he continued, "that wasn't exactly the way I wanted it then, and it's definitely not the way I want it now."

His last declaration threw me. Just like that, hot bricks dissolved into cold liquid.

"You don't…" I could barely speak. "You don't want me now."

He stared at me for a long moment, his gaze unwavering. "Don't *want* you?" he repeated slowly. "Springer." He reached across the darkness and took my hand. "I have never wanted anything in my life more than you."

I felt like the weight of the world had flown from my shoulders as I gazed at him, his lips pulling back into a smile. I reached out to touch his face, but he caught my wrist.

"This goes no further," he said, lowering my extended arm down to my side, "until I hear it from you." He removed his other hand from mine, sat back on his heels and folded his arms. "I need this, Spring. I need to hear it."

A set of battling creatures descended upon my insides. One was attempting to calm me, while the other filled me with a totally different kind of nervousness. Because I knew what Henry was after.

Never in my life had I said *those words*. I'd tried to show him before, but that wasn't enough. Henry was braver than me, he'd already said it months ago, fearlessly. I was not feeling as brave.

He sighed impatiently. "Are you going to say it?" he asked. "You know you want to." There he was again, that confident, self-assured, sexy Greek hero who was completely certain of everything he did. His delicious lips pressed together, hiding a smile as he inched closer. "Because I don't know how much longer I can hold out. I traveled for three days straight. The last day was in *your* car, listening to the only CDs you had in there. Alanis Morissette on repeat. She's stuck in my head." His angel face twisted with exaggerated pain. "Any idea what that's doing to me right now?"

"You listened to Alanis?"

"And Fiona." He shrugged good-naturedly, charmingly. "Though I think I prefer—"

"Henry," I cut him off, scooted forward on my grass-stained knees and took his hands. "Henry Edward Knightly... the third," I added in a whisper, giving him a knowing grin. I ran my hands up his arms. "You drive me absolutely crazy." He chuckled softly and looked down. "You amaze me." I lifted his chin. "And I love you."

Before my voice had faded out, Henry's arms were around me. It must change something in your chemistry when you kiss someone for the first time after saying I love you. I would never mock Julia or her theories again. Never.

The next thing I knew, we were down on the ground, adding new patches of green to our previously grass-stained clothing. Henry was already a mess, and personally, the more tangled and twisted he became, the more insanely attractive he grew. I lovingly extracted blades of grass from his hair, while he wiped whatever foliage it was that was stuck to the side of my face.

"Won't it be interesting," he whispered, pressing my hand against his chest, "to actually be with each other in broad daylight without feeling the need to hide behind a gas station?"

"What a kissing tramp you turned me into on our campout."

That spicy, virile, distinctive quality that exuded from his pores was now seeping into my bloodstream. I welcomed it in with every breath.

"Hardly," he said with a laugh, tugging my arm. I obliged by wrapping my top leg around his to further intertwine us. "I don't believe it's considered trampy if you're dating."

I rolled closer so I could burrow into his neck. That smell. "We weren't dating then."

He swept the hair from the nape of my neck, his finger tracing a swirling pattern over my skin. "Details," he said. "But I would like to do this right, just the same."

"Do what?"

Henry lifted his head off the grass, propping it on an

elbow. "May I take you out?" he asked. "A proper date. The first of millions."

"Only if you tell me something," I said, feeling a thrill in the security of a million dates to come with the man I did not plan on living without. "Three things, actually."

He smiled inquisitively. "You have them numbered?"

"They're important."

He tucked some hair behind my ears. "Fire away."

"First. Why didn't you call me?"

"When?" he asked, running a hand up and down my arm.

"Well, *ever*, generally speaking, but yesterday or *today* to be specific."

"I was driving. It's dangerous to—"

"I didn't know where you were," I couldn't help interrupting, squeezing his shoulder. "I didn't know what was happening."

He seemed puzzled by my statement. "Wait. Didn't you know?"

"Apparently not."

"Before you boarded the plane, I told you I would meet you back here."

I peered at him. "No, you didn't."

"Yes." He nodded. "I said—"

"Your exact words were: 'I don't know when I'll see you again.'"

"Right. Well…and you didn't understand what I meant?"

"You assumed with *that* sentence that I would know you were going to take off to Monterey, find Julia, bring her back to Palo Alto, leave again to Montana, drive back, and then come scaling up my wall like a knight in shining Armani?"

"Basically," he said. "It was only three days."

"Exactly." I tapped his chest to add emphasis: "Three. Whole. Days." I sighed at his baffled expression, but then pulled myself onto his chest and kissed him, because I couldn't imagine doing anything else. "Henry, your communication leaves much to be desired."

"I'll work on it," he promised. "And I'll never make you wait three days again."

I dipped my chin to kiss his neck, my hair spilling across his face. "Where did you go after that night you left the note?"

"I stayed with Dart in New York for a while," he said, rolling us so we were on our sides, nose to nose. "He was completely pissed off at me when I told him I might have made a mistake about Julia."

"You told him that?"

"Right after you and Mel left the ranch," he said after a deep sigh. "Even before then...that last day in Washington, you made me think. I realized pretty soon afterward that I'd made a lot of mistakes. Moving to the house in Oakland was meant to be a distraction for Dart until the fall. I was an ass for not telling you we were moving. It was very wrong of me, but at that point, I was trying to convince myself that you were the last woman in the world I should be in love with." He ran a finger from my forehead to the tip of my nose. "Even though I already was madly in love with the most incredible woman in the world." His finger moved to my lips. "And she loves me back." He blinked slowly. "Incredible."

I never had daydreams about what a lover would say to me. But the words he spoke under the streetlights as we lazed on the grass were surpassing any fantasy I could have conjured.

"You said you had three questions for me," Henry whispered, kissing around my chin. "Number two, please."

"Did you beat up Alex?"

He stopped kissing and rolled onto his back. "I may have thrown a few punches, but nothing that will leave any permanent damage."

"I'm sorry about…him." I shuddered. "Back in the fall."

"I know." He was quiet for a moment before adding, "Do you forgive me for Lilah?"

"Of course." I placed my hands on the ground on either side of his shoulders, balancing myself over him. "Especially since you were obviously suffering from the early onset of psychosis at the time."

He laughed. "It truly was a nightmare with her. If she hadn't been Dart's sister, I would've told her off a lot sooner."

"Mmm, I'd love to see that, tough guy."

"In a way, I have her to thank."

I cocked my head.

Henry smiled, fingering the ends of my hair. "If she hadn't already talked you down so much with cautionary horror stories, I might not have paid much attention at first. But seeing you at the street party, I was instantly confused." He grinned. "And simultaneously intrigued. I'm sure I seemed rude that night, staring at you like a creeper, but I was trying to work you out. After I discovered on my own that you're this…this wonderful, brilliant life force, I devoted every spare moment of my time trying to make you forget about the ogre you met that night."

"You have my official permission to cease atoning for the past," I granted after a quick kiss. "Or we might be here all night."

Henry grinned wickedly, and suddenly, I felt myself being lifted and dragged forward, my entire body on top of him. His arms tightened around me, keeping me pinned to him. "Saturday night, then. It's a date?"

I started to nod, but halted. "I can't. There's somewhere important I need to be this Saturday. My father's wedding."

"That's...great?" he offered, clearly confused by my somber tone.

A tiny swarm of nerves fluttered in my stomach, but I welcomed these ones, too. "I haven't seen him in ten years," I explained. "I'm petrified about it, but it's a first step. I know I need to be there. I *want* to be there." I gazed at the good man wrapped around me, the man who I was convinced could help me with anything I needed, and even those things I didn't realize I needed. "Will you come with me?"

Henry brushed the hair from my face with both hands. "Love to."

Someone in my house opened a window, and music spilled out onto the street. Bruno Mars.

"I have a confession to make," I whispered.

"Hmm?"

"That playlist you made for me, it wasn't corrupted like I said. I deleted it on purpose."

He frowned in confusion. "Were you mad at me for—"

"No." I held his face between my hands. "Those songs. I don't know if you meant to do it or not, but listening to them made me want to..." I ducked my chin, hiding my face in his chest, irrationally embarrassed.

His body shook under me with a quiet laugh. "Made you want to what?"

I waited a moment then lifted my chin. "Make out with

you."

"Really?" He cocked an eyebrow, gazing off to the side. "Huh."

"It was kind of torture, because I couldn't back then."

"Ah, Spring. Yes, you could have." He took my face and kissed me until my toes curled. "Any time you wanted." He pulled back, cocking his eyebrow again. "You better believe I'm reloading those songs."

"And ten more," I requested, hovering over his mouth. "Bring it on."

The lawn sprinklers were set to a one a.m. timer. When they came on, Henry grabbed my hand and together we hustled to the sidewalk. Henry with damp hair and his wet shirt unbuttoned halfway down was like staring at a dazzling sunset. I drank in the vista.

"My place or yours?" he asked, little droplets of water clinging to his lashes.

I glanced at my house, the windows glowing yellow, sounds of music and laughter and way too many people.

"Yours, please."

He took me by the hand and we crossed the street.

When I stepped out of the second-floor bathroom, having changed into one of his dry shirts and a pair of drawstring shorts, Henry was just leaving his room, bare-chested, pulling on a dry shirt over his head. Another staring-at-a-perfect-sunset moment. After his head and arms made their way through their respective holes, he blinked at me, looking stunned.

"First those braids, then flour, and now…" He tugged at the shirt I was wearing, the too-big neck hole hanging off one shoulder. "Is there anything you can't don like a goddess?"

"I thought you loved me for my brain."

"I love you for a lot of reasons," he said as he stepped toward me. "I guess you standing at my open bedroom door in the middle of the night looking like *this* is just my lucky bonus."

Damn.

His arms slid around me, backing me against the wall. "If we stay up here much longer," he whispered the next time his lips were free, "I might not let you leave."

In reply, I slid my hands around his waist then inside the back of his shirt, like he'd done to me so many times.

"Spring…" he murmured a little raggedly as I ran my hands up the smooth, hard skin of his back, enjoying it as much as he was.

"I love you," I whispered into his neck. "Never leaving."

He leaned against me, pressing my back against the wall, our bodies a solid line.

"I believe you have one last question," he said as he kissed a trail down my throat. When his last kiss touched my collar bone, he pulled away and looked me in the eyes. I stared back, breathing hard.

"Come, Honeycutt," he said, taking my hand, intertwining our fingers. "You've parched me dry." He led us downstairs and sat me on the couch. "Your last question," he prompted, passing me a water bottle to share.

I scooched back and draped my legs across his lap. "There's a preamble first," I said.

"How unlike you."

"Did you get my thesis in the mail?"

Henry smiled and ran a hand over my legs. "Yesterday. I would've arrived back here two hours sooner, but I couldn't leave until I'd read it. Twice. I'll admit, I was surprisingly impressed, though I shouldn't have been." He reached out and ran a finger along my hairline, stopping on the indent of my temple. "This beautiful brain," he murmured reverently. "But you didn't see my side of the issue in the end." There was a twinkle in his eyes.

I leaned over and kissed him. "Your side is wrong," I whispered, lingering on the corner of his mouth.

"No, *your* side is wrong," he countered, then gently bit my bottom lip. "Publication?"

I touched my forehead to his. "Oxford University Press."

He grinned. "Shut up."

"And a grant that paid for my summer research trip." I twirled a finger around his curls then traced down to the tip of his nose. "Which brings me to my last question. What were you thinking when you first saw me at the ranch?"

Henry sat back and held a fist to his grinning mouth. "Several things," he admitted. "You'd somehow found your way to my home. I knew that meant something. After that, I wasn't too worried. Either you loved me or you didn't. I felt you did, so I let the chips fall."

I smiled, knowing I would never tire of his logic, ever awed by his faith in us. "You thought all of that when you first saw me?"

"Not right then. My very first thought was fear you would think I was stalking you."

"*You* stalking *me*?" I laughed. "*I* was the one who showed up at your house out of the blue."

His arms circled me, tightly, remembering this fact with approval.

"*And* I was the one who busted in on your family reunion

with Tyler."

"That's right," he said, narrowing his eyes. "What is the punishment for illegal pursuit in the state of California?" He touched his forehead to mind, his eyes gleaming. "I believe the penalty is harsh and extensive. Ready to pay up?"

"Neither incidence occurred in California," I stated. "Ergo, the law clearly states—"

I didn't see it coming, but suddenly he had me in a bear hug, whispering Latin jurisprudential terms into my ear as he rolled us off the couch.

"If this is your way of showing approval of my intelligence," I said, pinning his shoulders to the floor, "then maybe I'll demonstrate my knowledge of human anatomy later."

"Now you're really speaking my language." He shifted his shoulders, but I held him in place.

"I have great hope for us," I said, gazing down at him. "Despite our opposing views on—"

He covered my mouth with his and then slowly rolled us so he was on top. This took me by surprise, startled a bit by the feeling of the full weight of a man pinning me flat. Then Henry smiled above me, propped up by his elbows. I had an overwhelming desire to extend my neck and finish that kiss until we both exploded.

"Opposition makes for good debates, Spring," he whispered, leaning down to nuzzle into the side of my neck. "And I plan on having very good debates with you for at least the next ten presidential elections."

"Despite the rallies and protests"—I rubbed the back of his neck—"and lectures and fracking?"

He growled into my hair. "Especially the fracking."

"In that case," I said, breathing in the smell of his skin,

"I am even more optimistic about our future compromises."

When Henry kissed me, I was hyper aware of his body, the way it shifted and changed, and the way mine responded almost too naturally. Everything I felt with him was just plain natural, meant to be.

"There's a 5K charity run benefitting clean-up of San Francisco Bay next month," he said a moment later. "Why don't I sign us up for that?"

"Only if we help clean up the beach afterwards. *I'll* sign us up for that."

Henry laughed into my hair. To sweeten the deal, I tugged up the back of his shirt so I could run my hands from the small of his back all the way up to his strong shoulders. I noticed the way it made him tremble against me, and wondered if my body had reacted the same way every time he touched me like that. "What do you think?" I whispered.

"I'll do anything you say," he replied, kissing the side of my neck. "By the way, there's something I have to confess."

"What's that?" I asked, though I was barely able to hear anything besides blood whooshing behind my ears and his sweet breathing.

"I've been a vegetarian for three months."

"Nooo!" I laughed, hugging him even tighter. "I have a confession for you, then."

He pulled back, balancing on his elbows, gazing down in a way that made my body temperature shoot through the roof. "Yes?" he asked.

"I... Sorry, wow, this is hard to say."

His expression turned somber. "Spring, baby, you can tell me anything. I promise."

"Okay." I took in a deep breath. "I ate a hamburger last

month. Two, actually."

Henry rolled off me and covered his eyes, crumpling in laughter.

I couldn't help giggling as I watched his eyes water.

"See, Honeycutt," he said at last, gathering me to him. "We're more compatible than we thought."

I kissed his cheek, his nose, his eyelids, his cranberry mouth. "And so it begins."

Acknowledgments

This story has been around for a while, and every person who has touched it has made it better, shinier, and smexier.

Stacy Honeycutt Shakespeare-Abrams: thank you for taking a chance on a story that wasn't quite ready, for trusting me and for asking me the right questions to make it ready. As always, your insight is invaluable. I love that you know when Spring is in a good mood and when Henry's clothes aren't *that* important. You deserve a pair of argyle "stockings" with your name on them.

Erica Chapman: thank you for stepping into this project, for your enthusiasm and excitement and for messaging me in the middle of the day when we both should've been working. And for loving sexy Henry as much as I do.

Karen Grove: I'm beyond thrilled to be writing for Embrace. The new adult genre is such a fun age to write. Thank you for giving me the okay and for making me think all deep and hard and stuff. Dang you!

Sue Winegardner: thank you for always being around to talk me through when I've written myself into a corner and for telling me when my characters need to be just a little bit more likable. Oh, and thanks a ton for getting me hooked on British fruity malt loaf.

Nancy Carr: Remember that night we were driving back from the opera (and we'd worn jeans...*faux pas*!) and you helped me finally come up with a way to fix that huge plot point? Yeah, that was pretty awesome. Thank you, bunny, for meeting me for custard after VM and VB and for being the best beta reader ever to walk the face of the earth.

Susan Smith: Remember when this used to be a stage musical and you wanted so badly for Henry to bust out a little Sister Hazel? To this day, every time I hear that song I think of you...and Henry...and a bunch of Bingleys dancing across the stage to Gershwin. Frack, that would've been cool.

Jen Long: *merci beaucoup* for your lightning-fast French proof, and for helping me with those tricky swear words. And sorry you accidentally sent that one email to your boss...

Thank you to my publicity team at Entangled, to Jessica Cantor for creating a cover that causes my heart to pound, and to all the other Entangled authors who make writing for EP such a freaking joy.

Thank you to my family and friends who are always so patient and understanding with me when I'm tucked away in my writer's cave. And to my mother who gave me the gift of Colin Firth in a wet shirt. I haven't been the same since.

Most of all, thank you to Jane Austen. Girl, two hundred years later, your words and characters still rock our world.

26451453R00210

Made in the USA
Charleston, SC
08 February 2014